DARWIN'S SECRET

*

DARWIN'S SECRET

A Novel of the Amazon

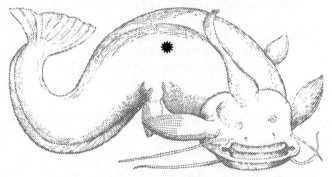

Richard Hoyt

DOUBLEDAY

New York · London · Toronto · Sydney · Auckland

All of the characters in this book are fictitious,
and any resemblance to actual persons, living or
dead, is purely coincidental.

PUBLISHED BY DOUBLEDAY

a division of Bantam Doubleday Dell
Publishing Group, Inc.
666 Fifth Avenue, New York, New York 10103

DOUBLEDAY and the portrayal of an anchor with
a dolphin are trademarks of Doubleday,
a division of Bantam Doubleday Dell
Publishing Group, Inc.

Library of Congress Cataloging-in-Publication Data

Hoyt, Richard, 1941–
  Darwin's secret: a novel of the Amazon /
Richard Hoyt. — 1st ed.
    p.   cm.
  ISBN 0-385-24382-0
  I. Title.
PS3558.0975D3   1989
813'.54—dc19   89-31154
                                                    CIP

BOOK DESIGN BY CHRIS WELCH

July 1989
FIRST EDITION

For Laura Hoyt

So that the reader won't be intimi-
dated or tongue-tied by the confusing *X*'s and so miss the music of
Portuguese words and Brazilian
place names in this story, he or she
might remember that an *X* at the
beginning of a word has an *sh*
sound, as in *sugar*. The community
of XuXu is pronounced *Shoo-Shoo*;
XuXuians (residents) are *Shoo-Shooians*. Again: XuXu is *Shoo-Shoo*; Xu-
Xuians are *Shoo-Shooians*. The letter *H* is silent in Portuguese:
Loucofilho becomes *Loucofilo*,
Igaranha becomes *Igarana*, piranha
is *pirana*, and *senhor* sounds similar
to *señor* in Spanish. The city of
Belém is pronounced *Belain*.
Santarém, likewise, is *Santarain*.
                              R.H.
                              Portland, Oregon

CONTENTS

CONTENTS

Contents

DARWIN'S SECRET

*

1

WHAT HIPÓLITO BALDO HEARD

❋

The great white catfish of Amazonia was first reported by the reflective Spanish explorer Don Hipólito Baldo in 1684, although for almost three hundred years just which of the many tributaries of the Amazon actually harbored the leviathan remained a mystery.

In October of 1684, Baldo and his small party set out from the coast of Peru in search of the fabled gold of El Dorado—the gilded man. They crossed the Andes near the border of modern-day Peru and Ecuador to the headwaters of the Amazon and set off by raft down the Marañón River to the Solimões River. By February 4 they had reached a point on the Solimões more than a thousand miles from the Atlantic and about a hundred miles west of its intersection with the Rio Negro near the present city of Manaus—this joining of waters forming the Amazon River.

The party encamped at an Indian settlement later to become the town of Manacapuru; there Baldo entered into his journal his thoughts on catfish and the adventures that lay ahead:

We have fallen in with Emilio Gonzalvo, a Portuguese who has spent the last twenty years of his life mapping the interior of Amazonia. Senhor Gonzalvo is returning downstream to the village of Manaus, which he uses as a base and as a contact with the outside world.

During an awesome thunderstorm tonight, an old man told us of a monster catfish that lives somewhere in these waters. Upstream, I had seen a catfish that was nearly three

3

meters long. I had never imagined a freshwater fish that huge. He told me those fish grow as large as five meters and can pull a canoe under the water, a fact which Gonzalvo confirmed. But he told me there exists an even larger catfish that is pure white and grows as long as seven to eight meters. I asked him where this fish lived and he said, "Out there." "Where out there?" I asked. "Out there," he said gravely, gesturing toward the lightning and thunder.

"Pure white catfish as large as sharks. I've heard those stories too," Gonzalvo said.

I have learned to treat these stories with respect. I was first skeptical of stories of a catfish that makes a sound like an untuned stringed instrument. Only when I heard a chorus of these strange fish one night—for they could only be fish, there being no birds or other animals in sight—did I believe. Just how they make their vibrating noise is entirely unclear. As to the stories of catfish walking from one pond to the next on their fins, only when I was taken out at night by torch and saw them for myself did I see and believe. This land is filled with strange and wonderful flora and fauna and people of such unusual beliefs that I have come to expect almost anything on the next stretch of river.

Our Indian guide tells us that we will be shortly visiting the tQuati, people who worship vines that hang from the tall trees of this remarkable forest. Our guide says the tQuati believe vines are a physical connection between earth and heaven, which is a charming conceit. After that we will call upon the Ch, people who flatten their lips and worship leeches.

It's clear that the Jesuits have preceded me to this part of the river. The priests make their work easier by assigning Christian identities to pagan idols; the old man who told me about the white catfish also told me in all sincerity that a certain lizard, believed by his people to have beneficent powers, was in fact Jesus. As he told me this we watched a tethered lizard, which must have been a full half meter long, plod slowly around a stick.

4

The old man told me the Christ/lizard had walked on the Amazon and parted the Solimões to allow an old woman and her grandchildren to cross to the other side. This same lizard had once risen from the dead, which was a sign from the spirit world. When he finished telling us about the lizard's abilities, he cut its heart out with a knife and gave us each a small piece to eat so that we might share Christ's miraculous powers.

One is obliged not to scorn these people, for we are their guests and at their mercy. I swallowed my piece of lizard's heart very quickly and without a blink to get it over with; Emilio Gonzalvo chewed his extremely slowly and thoughtfully, holding it in his mouth as if analyzing the taste.

As I finish this entry by the flickering light of a candle, the power of a lizard coursing through my veins, I wonder what the priests will teach the worshippers of vines?

When Hipólito Baldo's sober account reached Europe, his leviathan catfish were duly entered into a colorful New World zoo of the public imagination, this menagerie containing real beasts as well as the inventions of opportunists and con men. Europeans were at first willing, if not eager, to believe the most fanciful tale from faraway Amazonia, and an account such as Baldo's was eagerly received. But as the great basin was explored and mapped out over the years that followed—and the fanciful separated from the factual—Baldo's great white catfish was written off as mythic, the invention of a primitive mind.

However, Baldo's report of curious finned beasts and giant catfish was not all hyperbole. Biologists eventually recorded more than 1,300 species of fish in Amazonia, more than in any other river basin in the world. An Amazonian catfish, *Brachyplatystoma,* competed with two other claimants to being the largest freshwater fish in the planet: the huso, a sturgeon of the Amur River in Russia, and the white sturgeon of the Columbia and Frazier river systems in North America. Specimens of all three species have been caught that were thirteen feet long and weighed more than a ton. Other catfish contenders for the title include the goonch, called the freshwater shark of the Jumna River in India; *Silurus glanis,* a native of the Danube; and *Pangasius* of Thailand. The goonch runs to eight feet and both *Silurus glanis* and *Pangasius* to ten feet.

Baldo made no mention of these giant white catfish having any sort of untoward appetite beyond what would ordinarily account for their size—those claims would come later. What the leviathans ate remained a mystery, as did exactly where they did their eating. Did they feed in the Xingu or the Tapajós or one of the other clear waters flowing north from the Mato Grosso? Or were they to be found somewhere in the vast forest basins drained by the Madeira or the Solimões, the great yellow-brown rivers flowing east down from the Andes? Or did they lie in a forgotten stretch of one of the old black rivers flowing south from Colombia and Venezuela?

It was not until almost a hundred years after the rubber boom of the 1890s made Manaus an island city in a sea of forest that reports of the unusual catfish began to center on the Purus River in the southwest interior of Amazonia—at a place called the great depths. Indian fishermen avoided the depths, believing them to be inhabited by bad spirits and so taboo.

2

AN INCIDENT IN AMAZONIA

WIDELY HELD TO BE TRUE

✳

The caravan of somber Mercedes-Benz sedans spent most of the morning in a canopied forest where monkeys and colorful birds—invisible in their high green home—screeched and jabbered at the wavering bursts of the Japanese chain saws at point. The trees on this ghost of a road were all two years old or less and cutting them required only a couple of *mmmmmaaaaaaaaa-mmmmmmmaaaaaaa* chain-saw runs, but the jarring racket of gasoline engines was a shocker in the stillness of Amazonia.

This was one of those cases where optimistic men with machetes and axes, eager to get at the mountain of gold at Loucofilho, had passed through this way shortly after the mother lode was discovered; at Santarém there was a road south that intersected with the trans-Amazonia highway. This was not a road designated by the maps, only a temporary passage through the impenetrable forest, a scar only partly reclaimed by brushy regrowth.

At Loucofilho, where the average daily temperature ran from 92 to 93 degrees Fahrenheit with a relative humidity of 98 to 99 percent, thousands of men from all over South America competed for the gold in a tangle of nearly naked bodies covered from head to toe with mud, urine, excrement, and unidentifiable grayish-brown, sour-smelling slime. There were those who had flown in to Loucofilho who claimed that, as they approached, the mountain looked like a living skin that writhed with bodies, and as they drew nearer on the road from the airstrip, the mountain took on the appearance of an incredible anthill of human beings. This was elemental, primal competition. Men had been killed for infringing one inch onto a neighbor's yard-wide claim.

The miners at Loucofilho had spent all their lives repressed by generals and priests, living off superstition and hope, eating beans and rice in a lethargic zone of brutal heat where the soil was worthless and nothing worked and everything ran late. And as they dug and scrapped and fought and did without, the rock-hard, determined diggers of Loucofilho dreamed of one day owning a Mercedes-Benz.

There were other automobiles that were nearly as expensive and perhaps mechanically almost as good as a Mercedes. The miners didn't want a damned Volvo; Volvos were for gringo potato eaters. They didn't want some curious French car with a stupid lion or whatever that was on the grille. The four circles of the Audi meant nothing to them. A BMW was good, but not *the car.* In the end what made them eat their hearts out for a Mercedes was that splendid, elegant hood ornament sticking up there announcing to the world they had made the big strike.

Although it was hyperbole that a Mercedes was literally worth its weight in gold to the bedazzled miners of Loucofilho, it was the machine of dreams; cocaine was cheap, a South American export, and a fabulous brothel had been assembled, the women willing to do almost anything if the price was right. A miner who had truly hit life's big seam would pay anything for an automobile of such exquisite grace and beauty and engineering skill as a Mercedes-Benz.

The caravan of Mercedes-Benzes was preceded by eight men, two with M-16s, in case of bandits, and six laborers with either machetes or chain saws at their disposal, whichever was needed for making the road passable again. Mostly, however, the brush was simply mashed flat by the four-wheel-drive tow truck that drove at point. The tow truck had wide, knobby tires, as did the two four-wheel-drive trucks that followed, one with supplies, the second with gasoline.

When there was no need of machete or saw, the men in front and the two guards rode on the two trucks as they idled forward, *crunch, smunch, crunch, smunch* over the road that could barely be discerned in front of them.

The thirty new Mercedes-Benzes followed the trucks.

The sedans were all luxury models, some silver, some jet black, others an austere, executive gray, very responsible— all covered with a layer of fine dust. Neither the dust nor the heat nor the humidity bothered the drivers, who eased their sedans carefully over the flattened underbrush in air-conditioned comfort.

The lead Mercedes was driven by a North American wearing slacks and a shirt currently popular in Rio de Janeiro. He wore aviator's sunglasses, a diamond-studded wristwatch, and alligator shoes. He drove with his left hand, his right hand between the legs of his girlfriend, a naked young blonde with cornflower-blue eyes and very pale pink nipples on wonderful white breasts—there being considerable privacy in the Amazon basin.

"Play with those things," the driver said. "Play with those things for me. You like doing that, don't you? Play with them for me. Tell me you like playing with them."

"Ohhh. I love it. You know I do."

"Don't you dare stop now."

"Like this? Do you like this?"

"That's very, very sexy. Does your bare butt feel good on that leather seat? Isn't this leather great?"

"Mmmmm. It's wonderful."

He removed his hand from between her leg and held it under his nose, inhaling deeply, his face all satisfaction. "I like all that wiggle, wiggle action down there."

"I can't help it."

He lit a neatly rolled joint and inhaled deeply. "I like the way you roll a joint," he said, holding his breath. "I never could roll a decent joint; I'm all thumbs. Would you like my hand back there?"

"Oh yes."

He gave her the joint and returned his hand. She jerked involuntarily at the first touch of his hand and returned eagerly to the rhythm of her squirming.

"After a while I'll stop the caravan and fuck the living shit out of you," he said.

"Promise?"

The caravan had come to another halt. The North American turned off his Mercedes to turn his full attention to the girl while they waited for the men with the chain saws to clear whatever obstacles were growing in their path.

The girl, grinning, turned on the leather seat to make his attentions easier. "If they have to chop a whole bunch of trees, maybe we could knock off a quickie. You could tell everybody to stay in their cars so we won't have people wandering around."

"I don't hear the chain saws." He removed his hand from between her legs.

"They're having to clear some brush first, remember that stuff they had to clear out yesterday afternoon."

The North American and his girlfriend suddenly saw dozens of tiny men standing in the brush, most of whom had wee little blowpipes and tiny bows and arrows aimed in their direction. Those not armed with blowpipe or bow and arrow wore heavy leather gloves and struggled with heavy spools of brand-new barbed wire. There were two bearers for each spool, the weight pulling at their shoulders.

The guards with the assault rifles had not been heard from.

"Maybe you better put your pants back on." The North American slipped an automatic pistol and two extra clips from the glove compartment.

Wide-eyed, the girl slipped into a blouse and skintight jeans without taking her eyes off the little Indians. "Are these the tQuati? You said we'd be crossing through the territory of the tQuati."

"They probably are the tQuati."

"But they're harmless, you said. There'd be no problem coming this way. They worship vines hanging from the trees."

"That's what I said."

"They don't look very friendly to me."

The North American said nothing. He took a deep breath.

"What are they doing with barbed wire way out here?"

"Beats the hell out of me." The man weighed the extra

clips in his left hand. He thumbed the safety off the pistol. He started to open the door.

He closed it quickly when a tQuati dart glanced off the window inches from his ear.

3

AN ARK OF LEARNING

✸

It was not without reason that Nicholas Bodan filled up the remaining space on his credit cards to buy an airplane ticket to Belém and passage on a riverboat to Loucofilho. Simply put: letters from the lawyers were like the fins of patrolling sharks, threatening to consume Bodan with legalese, and there came a point when he no longer gave a flying fuck what the government or his ex-wives wanted.

Bodan was a veteran author; he had been through versions of this crunch before, although not as severe. A person could not create and read that crap at the same time, so he simply didn't open the letters, a tactic which his former wives were aware of and which infuriated them. As each new fin arrived at his mailbox, he merely sailed it into a pile of unopened letters that were like scouts prefacing legal sorties on his nonexistent bank account. Each arriving demand twisted his insides.

Without exception, he knew, they all said the same damned thing: I-don't-give-a-squat-about-you-bub, where's mine?

Mine. Mine. Mine. Mine.

A cheerful monologue it was, neither the government nor his former wives having the time or inclination to listen to his side of the story.

Bodan didn't imagine himself joining in the slime with the miners at Loucofilho; he wondered, rather, whether there might not be a solid commercial novel to be written about the fabled greed and gold at Loucofilho.

Bodan was an on-again, off-again scrounger for rare books to pick up a few extra bucks. The next morning, with Van Allen Bradley's *Handbook of Values* at his side, Bodan drove his rusting Toyota to Marin County to hit the garage sales in an area of wealthy baby boomers—this a last-minute shot at some pocket money for the trip. He gave old Van Allen an affectionate pat on the spine for good luck. While it was true that Bradley's listings merely recorded what a book had brought at auction and, like the prices quoted on the New York Stock Exchange, were worth squat without a buyer, Bodan didn't care.

Bodan's stomach began growling when he got to Larkspur; he was getting hungry. He aimed his car for an AmeRiBurger franchise, parked it, and went inside to order a plate of AmeRiBs—good ol' country gnawing, according to the window posters.

Bodan had an AmeRiB in hand, teeth firmly clamped on flavored bone, when he spotted Tigard Feed and Seed, Harold Johnson, Proprietor, an improbable store across the street. If it actually was a feed store and not a chic restaurant, it appeared that Harold had somehow decided not to progress past 1955. There were no cars outside, but a sign in the window told drivers-by that it was open for business.

He wiped the AmeRiCue from his fingers with a wad of paper towels. Picking sugar crystals from his teeth, unaware of any jinxes, hexes, or omens, he strolled across the street. Nicholas Bodan liked improbable stores. There were books and all sorts of surprises in improbable stores.

Bodan opened the door to Tigard Feed and Seed, Harold Johnson, Proprietor, and stepped inside.

Bodan saw two sacks of rabbit pellets in Tigard Feed and Seed but nothing else resembling animal feed and only one revolving wire rack of vegetable seed in faded envelopes. There were trails worn in the wooden floor which was swept, sort of, but not truly clean. There was a dulling layer of dust over everything from the wire seed racks to the shelves, which were covered with butcher paper. The shelves were divided into bins: plastic shoes next to artificial-smoke additive, cooking oil alongside a bin of lipstick; there were pruning shears, lopsided softballs, and charcoal in yellowing paper bags.

To the right of the entrance, past the seed rack, was a large shelf of both hardcover and paperback books. What was more, these books looked old, some of them really old.

He casually pulled H. Rider Haggard's *King Solomon's Mines* from the shelf. The dust jacket wasn't the best but it was there. Bodan opened the book: London, 1885, first edition. That was worth a few hundred bucks for his voyage to Loucofilho. Yes, sir! Was this a beginning of some kind? Had his luck turned for the better?

Indeed it had. Bodan blinked. There sat Charles Darwin's *On the Origin of Species.*

Bodan knew a first-edition *On the Origin of Species* was worth major bucks. He also knew he wouldn't be selling it to anybody. He didn't care how damn broke he was; Bodan liked to listen to the music of amazing minds. *On the Origin of Species* was a keeper.

A bespectacled man, whom Bodan hadn't seen, was sitting behind one of the glass cases. He wore a bright green baseball cap with a Rabbit Breeder emblem on the front.

"Are you Mr. Johnson?" Bodan asked. He resolved to remain calm about *King Solomon's Mines* and *On the Origin of Species.* Any sign of interest could kindle an untoward suspicion that the books might be valuable.

"What's that?" The old man turned his head and cupped one ear.

"I said, are you the proprietor?" Bodan said loudly. He was envious of the man's Rabbit Breeder hat.

The tall man narrowed one eye. "Proprietor. Big word. Yes. Harold Johnson. They call me Hal. Pleased to meet you. Looking for a little feed, are you? I've got stuff here for chickens if you want." He shook Bodan's hand.

"Just killing a little time," Bodan shouted.

Hal smiled. "Well, take your time. There are some real deals in here, believe me."

He had to draw Hal's attention from his interest in H. Rider Haggard and Charles Darwin.

He picked up a long, faded box and pulled out the insides. There were mahogany parts of a model boat, that much was obvious from the brass smokestack and deck fittings. But the accompanying plans—six sheets of detailed drawings folded into fourths—were not for a model; they were for the riverboat *Barco Igaranha,* which had what appeared to be fish's eyes painted on either side of the bow. The *Barco Igaranha* was the name of the boat on which Bodan had booked passage to Loucofilho.

Hal said, "I've had it in here for a little while, ever since I moved over from my old store."

"When was that?" Bodan shouted. He held the box up, unable to believe it. The same riverboat! In his mind's eye, he saw the fish-eyed riverboat rising and falling slowly in the mist of the Purus on the way to Loucofilho. The *Barco Igaranha* was real *African Queen* stuff. He had to have that model.

"It was 1957," Hal said. He looked thoughtful, dangling his reading glasses by their frames. "Or was it '58? I swapped a fella a sack of oats for that model, I remember. You are going to buy it, aren't you? Sure you are. I see you like books. Buy yourself some books too; I've got some good ones here."

Bodan inadvertently licked his lips.

Hal ran his finger along a handwritten note in Portuguese in one corner of the plans. "You know, some Mexicans came in here one day, Hispanics I believe they call them nowadays, and they said they could sort of figure it. This is a copy of the marine architect's plans for the boat, together with the parts for a model. It's from Fernando Candido, see there, to Armando Olympio, there. They couldn't tell me about the fish eyes, though."

"Father to son!"

"What's the price there? Sixty dollars? I'll give it to you for forty. A model like that would cost you a hundred and fifty today. That's mahogany there. You go to a hobby shop and see if I'm not right. I might as well be giving it to you. Let me see if I can find the box with the hardware and fittings, solid brass all of it."

Bodan, glancing at the books, watched him paw through a large drawer. "Why'd you keep it all this time?" he shouted.

He straightened. "Nobody wanted to buy it."

"But you knew someone would someday?" Bodan wondered if people might not be able to hear their conversation out on the street.

The tall, bald man grinned broadly. "Oh sure, I knew. One day, I knew, someone would walk in that door and take one look at that riverboat and just have to have it. I'll tell you a little secret." He leaned toward Bodan and cupped his hands around his mouth. "Take it from me, if you buy that boat it'll take you on an adventure like you won't believe. This boat can see, what with those eyes there."

"Really?" Bodan grinned.

Hal Johnson winked; he was a joker.

Bodan sighted down the keel of the model, which was a full yard long. "The keel is crooked."

"You can straighten it out when you build the hull. You pull it around there with the sheaves. Is that what they call them? Is that how it's done? You'll have to have an X-acto knife, maybe a little saw there, and some glue."

Bodan glanced across the street at his Toyota.

"Some of these are pretty old books, but they still read. Four bits each. You know, I knew somebody would walk in one day and buy that model. All I had to do was be patient. Say, I'll tell you what I'm going to do. I've got a little old Portuguese-English dictionary in this pile of books somewhere doing nothing but collecting dust. If you buy the kit,

I'll throw in the dictionary so you can figure out what the note says. You were wondering about that."

"You talked me into it. Done."

Bodan bought the kit of the *Barco Igaranha* for forty dollars and *King Solomon's Mines* and *On the Origin of Species* for a buck. He sat in his car to check them out. The Haggard was genuine. He turned to Darwin. He did this slowly, savoring the suspense as a chef savors a sauce. Was this a little ha ha? A fake cover? Someone's idea of a joke? He licked his lips. He turned the book slowly to the title page:

The Mealy Bug Man, poems by Alfonso Stevens.

"Aw shit!" Bodan slumped wearily on the seat.

When he got home he took the Portuguese-English dictionary which hard-of-hearing Hal had thrown into the deal and sat down to translate the handwritten note on the plans of the *Barco Igaranha.* It had to be the same boat on which he was ticketed to Loucofilho. How many boats on the Amazon could there possibly be named the *Barco Igaranha*? It was the same boat. Had to be.

Bodan knew a little Spanish, but no Portuguese, so it took him a couple of hours of work with the dictionary to get the note down to what he thought was an accurate translation.

> *For my dear son, Armando Olympio,*
> *When the ship's architect said he was going to build me a model of what Igaranha's boat will look like, I asked him to give us the parts so we can put it together ourselves. He says the model is as faithful to the real boat as he could make it. We'll put an electric engine in her and sail her on a lake early in the morning with wisps of vapor rising like ghosts of sailors past. Can't you see her there? Won't she be a beauty? So graceful. The rounded lines of her stern. The languid rise of her bow. An ark of learning bearing biologists and botanists and zoologists up the Xingu, and the*

Tapajós, the Maués Guaçu, and the Madeira. Such lovely names, don't you agree?

With affection, your father,
Fernando Candido Padim

4

HE LISTENS WITHOUT

INITIAL COMMENT

❋

Dr. DeeDee Sarant had just gotten off a long stretch in the emergency room stitching up knife wounds and sewing shooting victims back together—her mind less on her driving than on her upcoming duty of hosting an AMA cocktail hour honoring a good friend—when for no reason she had a hankering for squid.

Her friend, Dr. Robert Gibson, was a cardiologist and such an anomaly as to have literally given away his services, both in Zaire and Ethiopia; it was a yearly ritual for the doctors to haul forth such an oddball and show him off, his payoff for admirable but unprofitable behavior.

The green-eyed DeeDee stopped at a fashionable little fish market down the street where they always had fresh young squid. When she got home she soaked her five-foot-four-inch frame in a tub of hot water. She dried her black hair and was sitting slumped, relaxed on her kitchen stool with a glass of white wine, cleaning the squid, when her ex-husband's friend called with the long-expected news.

For months her ex-husband had been wasting away until he was a skeleton in diapers. She was nevertheless numb as she listened to the news. She had tried to prepare herself for this, but that was impossible. No matter that he turned out to like men more than women, the fact remained that DeeDee had once been in love with Walter.

She cried softly there, sitting on her kitchen stool, thankful that he was dead at last, spared more suffering.

DeeDee felt the truth was that if the medical profession had been more honest about AIDS from the beginning and less motivated by profit—a life is a life, she believed, whether homosexual or not—then tens of thousands of lives, if not more, might have been saved, possibly including Walter's. For months during which the plague virus spread silently through the gay population, the responsibility-dodging medical system showed only a token interest, allowing a generation of homosexuals to be taken under.

The irony, she felt, was that the male doctors liked to go to San Francisco because of all the sex available there, although they were forced to register for boring seminars and workshops to have this activity approved by the IRS. They liked to cruise Polk Street like everybody else to watch the gays in their colorful costumes and take photographs of the Hard On leather store.

However, in her opinion, none of the physicians of the year, including Gibson, were about to be so foolhardy as to complain about any ethical uncertainties or moral hesitation in practicing medicine for the absolute maximum profit. If he bitched publicly about the money machine, the tribal elders would find some way to quietly isolate him.

She decapitated her squid with a paring knife and pulled out the flexible spine that looked like a translucent collar stay. She stripped back the skin from the squid, pinning the skin against her thumb with the edge of her knife and pulling back. The skin came off *vvvvvvttt*—quick and simple as you please. Squid was underrated, in DeeDee's opinion, but you had to know how to cook it.

She stripped the innards of the squid with her fingernails, and what she wound up with was four thin tubes of white squid meat. She sliced the tubes into rings about a quarter of an inch wide.

She lowered a handful of squid rounds into the hot oil with a slotted spoon. She watched them pop and sizzle.

There must be something she could do to shake up the AMA a little. She was surprised some creative gay man hadn't come up with something flamboyant already.

DeeDee thought, *Wait, Robert's cocktail hour. The cocktail hour is my chance.*

She knew Gibson wouldn't care if she used the occasion to have a little educational fun. Gibson really didn't give a damn for silly honors, she knew. He was as annoyed by excess as she was, but resigned.

Her squid rings were done. She dipped them out of the hot oil with a slotted spoon and dumped them on some paper towels to soak up the grease. She poured herself another glass of wine and got out a pad and pen. She dripped a couple of drops on the pad but didn't rip the top sheet off. She thought for a second the drips looked like teardrops, but decided to start with a clean sheet.

What, then, would she feed them?

She remembered a few months earlier this young man dressed like a Princeton undergraduate had wandered into the ER at the hospital where she was working late one night and asked if he could have a cup of coffee with her when she got a break. DeeDee had regarded him as essentially a kid; he was in his late twenties at best; she herself preferred a man with a couple of gray hairs on his balls.

After they'd settled down to coffee the kid told her, in as roundabout and oblique a manner as he could manage, that he dealt in drugs and human organs. When he saw that she wasn't going to immediately flip out and run for the telephone, he told her that he had gotten into the profitable transplant business after a strung-out doctor offered to barter a minutes-old set of primo teenage kidneys for two ounces of Venezuelan pink—that being a variety of cocaine then currently popular.

"You can't save every mangled body they haul in, can you? When the cause of death is obvious, nobody is going to audit the corpse to make sure the liver and kidneys are still there, are they? I assure you, we're not talking pocket money here, Dr. Sarant."

"So all I have to do is go snip, snip here, snip, snip there, and slip the goodies into the refrigerator. Is that it? I think you're probably talking to the wrong doctor."

The kid hadn't said anything, but had scrawled a number on a business card, telling her if she ever changed her mind . . .

This, then, was the dealer in human organs and chemical highs that DeeDee called. The entrepreneur agreed to meet her at a hangout for young San Francisco professionals toiling in the hives of the commercial and financial districts.

Two hours later they settled in on both sides of a booth and ordered Tanqueray on the rocks. The dealer was feeling good because he never expected to be doing business with DeeDee, who was still rocked by the news of Walter's death.

"You know, Dr. Sarant, when I was walking over here, I got to thinking about junkies. When a junkie needs a fix, he comes to me. Junkies never say 'strung out' or anything like that. They say they're sick. When they get their fix, they say they're well. Those are the words they use: being sick and getting well. So when they're sick they come to me . . ."

". . . the people's doctor."

"That's it. Very clever." He grinned. "The people's doctor. I write these sick people a prescription that's guaranteed to make them feel well again. I fix them every time."

"Guaranteed, eh?"

"If a person feels sick enough, he'll pay anything to get well, no questions asked." The people's doctor grinned, feeling clever.

"You keep them sick and make them well at the same time. A nice little practice."

"I'm not mercenary about it either; if a deserving patient doesn't have the bread, I can sometimes help him out. I have this one little blonde secretary, you know, who's always broke and coming in saying how sick she is. I sometimes let her give me a little blowjob for a fix so she won't have to hustle."

"A successful doctor has to have good bedside manners."

The people's doctor laughed. "I don't have to spring for malpractice insurance, you know, and I don't have to advertise for patients in the newspapers. Don't you find that practice boorish and unprofessional?"

DeeDee smiled.

"What is it you're after, Dr. Sarant?"

"I'm going to serve my AMA colleagues a rare dish called *les petits calmars noirs et blancs de Atlantide.* I need some very special ingredients. I thought perhaps you could help me out."

"The little light and dark squids of Atlantis."

DeeDee was surprised and it showed.

"I majored in French at Williams. You have to do something with a French degree," he said, shrugging the shoulders of his expensive blazer. "I always told my dad not everybody's cut out for the Foreign Service, but he'd never listen. My old man's father was in the Foreign Service. My old man was in the Foreign Service. I was supposed to be in the Foreign Service."

The people's doctor, sucking on a cocktail onion, listened without initial comment to Dr. Sarant's request.

5

SHE FEEDS THE DOCTORS

LITTLE SQUIDS

✳

Dr. DeeDee Sarant arrived at the hotel for the big do in the Ford Mustang convertible that her father had given her more than twenty years earlier—just two weeks before she had participated in the 1967 gathering of the human tribe and exorcism of greed in Golden Gate Park. She had put a few miles on the Mustang over the years, but it turned out to be a classic, just as her father said.

She arrived two hours early—she wanted to have plenty of time to dress and mellow out—and pulled her Mustang into a line of Mercedes-Benzes, BMWs, and Volvos waiting to be parked.

She glided through the lobby, all carpeted and mirrored, polished wood and pretense. She went directly to her suite, where she rolled herself a joint for old times' sake; she figured if wild DeeDee was going to make one last wonderful, crazed hippie run, it might as well be a dinger.

In deference to her grandmother Hanna Doherty's stubborn and contrary genes, infamous in her family, she poured herself a tidy shot of Irish whiskey to go with the cannabis and drank a private toast to Walter and all of those men like him who were now dead because a medical establishment geared up for profit instead of public service responded to the AIDS plague with cowardice and inaction. And there were even those, takers of the physician's oath and enjoyers of its material blessings, who refused to have anything at all to do with an AIDS victim.

One thing a woman wants to do when she's a hostess of a grand party is to look right. DeeDee decided she should look feminine, but not dangerous; she certainly didn't want to wear some harsh suit. Simplicity was the mark of sophistication, her mother had always said; DeeDee wanted to be sophisticated, but with just a hint of demure milkmaid, settling, finally, on a baby-blue dress of thin cretonne cotton, a filmy, gauzy thing with a snug waist and a skirt that flowed when she walked. There were no ruffles or flounces here— this was sophistication. The short sleeves covered her biceps but showed off the dimples of her elbows; the collar points lay out in a nice V, exposing her throat and the hollows of her collarbone, but with only a suggestion of a plunge toward her sternum.

walked across the street to have a beer. They could have carried them discreetly in their jacket pockets, but they didn't want to be confused with medical supply salesmen.

DeeDee watched the doctors at the bar, laughing.

"Oh, *Doc-tor!*" a woman called. This woman was not a doctor herself, DeeDee knew, but was attracted to doctors in the generic sense; a physician with the eeensiest, weensiest, most listless dick imaginable likely had a wallet stuffed to bulging with credit cards.

DeeDee heard her name called. "*Doc-tor* Sarant." She turned. This would be Snorry Finnegan, a blade and gynecologist who could remove a uterus quicker than a butcher could gut a chicken and so found alternative treatments beyond his imagination, the consequences be damned.

It was the blades who annoyed DeeDee the most, casual removers of body parts.

"Why, *Doc-tor* Finnegan," she said. She turned that special word like ice cream in her mouth. "It's so good to see you." Wondering just what kind of name Snorry was, she shook his hand and gave him the suggestion of a private look. She glanced at Billy Hults over Finnegan's shoulder.

Hults, who was wearing a bright red sweatband around his forehead and a small ponytail, moved in to record the fun.

DeeDee let her fingers linger slightly on the top of Snorry's hand.

Snorry liked being the center of attention of a photographer who wore a ponytail; it was obvious that he liked the pretty brunette too. "You're looking fine tonight, Dr. Sarant."

"So are you, *Doc-tor*. I was admiring your suit." Finnegan seemed unaware that his suit was impossible to admire. Almost every male in the room—there being only a scattering of women—was dressed identically, so cloned and conservative, so afraid of being an eensie bit different, that from a distance the room looked like a convention of tall Japanese.

She brushed her hair up, then let it cascade down her back. She gave herself just a hint of properly expensive perfume—enough to make the evening's guests want to lean just a silly millimeter closer—and discreet earrings that begged for examination.

In the end, Hanna Doherty's black Irish granddaughter looked like the softest, most innocent angel who ever settled onto a queen-sized bed. Smart, charming. Such black hair. Such green eyes. Such pale white skin. Dr. DeeDee Spankable.

A trifle stoned and feeling as if she were seventeen again, wahoo, she glided on down the hall to the ballroom to host her very special do on behalf of her dead ex-husband. She had hired two photographers, Michael Burgess and Billy Hults, to videotape the fun so that memories might be preserved. The babble and hubbub of happy doctors had already begun, the early gatherers wanting to get the most drinks possible for their fee.

DeeDee gave her friend Gibson a big hug. Gibson had been Walter's friend too and so was going along with DeeDee's prank, but he was still curious.

"Come on, DeeDee, tell me what you're up to."

"No, no. Better you find out later, Robert. Just lay off the squid."

DeeDee joined in the hoo hoo and nonsense of introductions. They all "doctored" themselves. She thought they almost broke the word into two syllables, almost smelling it, swirling it like wine in a goblet—there being a hint of credit card about its bouquet, a suggestion of new-car smell, with just the tiniest *soupçon* of freshly trimmed putting greens. They seemed to sip it and roll it in their mouths, savoring the pungent *dakt,* the sweet *tohrr.* All introductions were prefaced with this succulent password; convention participants were doctored with plastic name tags in order that outsiders did not horn in on the goodies.

In the hospital where DeeDee worked the young doctors wore their call beepers clipped to their belts when they

DeeDee brushed the inside of Snorry's wrist with her fingers.

"Have you tried *les petits calmars noirs et blancs de Atlantide?*"

"The little squid rings? No, I haven't had a chance yet."

She tapped him softly on the hand; his eyes glazed. "Well, you must try one." She guided Snorry to the squid.

She selected a good one for herself and gave Snorry a little squid from Atlantis. "Do have another," she said.

"They're just delicious, DeeDee," said a man behind her.

What, plain DeeDee, is it? No *doc-tor?*

DeeDee turned. Another blade, Dr. James Gitter, a professional snipper of breasts from frightened women. "I'm so pleased you like them." She lifted a squid ring from the tray and put it to his mouth, with Billy Hults following it all the way with his lens. "Do have another," she said.

Meanwhile, Snorry nibbled his squid and looked thoughtful, the model of a gourmet. He'd eaten in a lot of pretentious restaurants in his day and knew well the proper drill.

"I believe I prefer the dark ones," Gitter said.

At Gitter's declaration Snorry's confidence surged visibly. "I prefer the dark ones myself, a bit more taste, I think. They're very, very good."

Hults had this action neatly framed.

"Michael, Michael, would you please make sure you include a good shot of Dr. Gitter here," DeeDee said. Burgess hardly took his eye off the camera as he slid toward her through the crowd.

They shook, with Michael looking at Gitter's feet saying, "Wow, I like those shoes, dude. Cool."

Gitter looked at his wing-tip oxfords and blinked.

"Have another squid, Dr. Gitter," DeeDee said.

"Oh, thank you." He pursed his lips and sucked in his cheeks, savoring the squid for the benefit of Michael's camera.

"I wanted to have something special for Robert's cocktail hour."

"This is exquisite, truly exquisite." Gitter put a heavy accent on the middle syllable, ex-*quis*-it.

"Oh, I'm so pleased you like the squid, truly pleased."

She saw a tall older gentleman with a stout stomach and leisurely, measured walk. He was eating a large olive and drinking a Shirley Temple. DeeDee wondered how something as pedestrian as an olive ever made it onto this spread. She saw him adjust his spectacles and glance at the doctors gathered around the trays of *calmars*. She reminded herself to keep an eye on him; if he headed for the *calmars* she'd have to help him make a proper selection.

This was Dr. E. E. Lindell, a small-town doctor who had spent most of his life practicing medicine in a sweltering little agricultural town south of Fresno. He was officially retired but still practicing, she knew. He really was here to keep as up-to-date as possible.

There were those of Lindell's patients, Mexican illegals many of them, who could only afford to pay him with produce, often stolen from their employers' fields. He had been paid artichokes for delivering babies, grapes for removing tonsils, and cantaloupes for setting broken bones. Those patients who paid from their garden—or their employers' fields—often ran a tab for most of the year. Come harvest time they delivered more produce than Lindell and his wife could possibly eat, leading her to complain that in July and August their house smelled like a fruit stand.

DeeDee remembered that the wire services once ran a photo of him arriving home from work struggling under the weight of two huge baskets of sweet corn.

Oops, he was heading for the *calmars*.

"Dr. Lindell," she called sweetly. "Yoo hoo, Dr. Lindell!" She caught Michael's eye and shook her head: no pictures of this one.

Lindell turned, grinning. He was flattered at having a pretty woman call his name. DeeDee led him to the tray and selected an okay squid for him. He tasted it, looking thoughtful.

"Well?" she asked.

He looked perplexed. "I guess I just don't see what the fuss is all about."

She led him away from the squid in case he had second thoughts.

Of course Dr. DeeDee Sarant saw to it that there were leftover squid to accompany the videotapes in a little press kit she prepared before she fled to Brazil. She sent the press kits to the networks and wire services and caught a taxi to the San Francisco Airport.

By the time the news was on television in the United States, DeeDee—having made her statement and vowing to henceforth call herself Hanna Doherty in honor of her unstoppable Irish grandmother—was in a Varig airliner descending to the airport at São Paulo, where Walter's Uncle Desmond lived.

6

SHE BUYS A TICKET TO

LOUCOFILHO

❋

Walter's Uncle Desmond was an expatriate American who years earlier had successfully started a loudspeaker manufacturing company in Brazil that grew to be the largest in the southern hemisphere. He and his wife now lived in a wealthy São Paulo neighborhood not far from the football stadium.

Although DeeDee Sarant now called herself Hanna Doherty, there was no reason to expect Desmond to call her that; he never knew her grandmother Hanna of the wild genes.

It was from Desmond in his living room—surrounded by stacks of American books and magazines—that Hanna first heard the extraordinary story of the missing miracle fish of Father Machado. "What makes this story interesting is that it can be traced to the West African coast of the fifteenth century when a Portuguese priest, Father Antônio Machado, was serving lepers on the west coast of Africa. This would be in an area that is modern-day Liberia."

"Like Father Damien."

"The man who served lepers in Hawaii; yes, he was a similar case. The priests who served in Africa had the practice—as they later did here—of attaching Christian identities to pagan deities. In this case the local deity Obatala was held to be Jesus. Father Machado was interested in representations of local deities made of clay by local holy men and each month fashioned and fired one six-inch-long fish each month, using a local catfish for a model. As he fired each new fish—called Obatala's fish by the lepers he served —he destroyed the old."

"That's a story!"

"It's just beginning. When Father Machado died of leprosy after twenty-two years of service, his flock claimed that the remaining fish had miraculous healing powers and they held it enshrined until 1497, when Vasco da Gama happened by on his way to India and took the fish, which eventually found its way back to the church vaults in Lisbon. It remained there, except for periodic display and for an examination by a committee studying the possibility of sainthood for Father Machado, until two years ago, when it made its way to São Paulo as part of a collection of African religious artifacts."

"I see."

"São Paulo was the first stop, actually. It was also scheduled to be shown in Rio de Janeiro, Atlanta, New Orleans, and New York."

Hanna said, "You say da Gama *took* it. Stole it, don't you mean?"

"Well, that's not what the church says. Catholic official-dom says the fish was made by their priest, so it belongs to the church. But Mae Janaina would most certainly agree with you."

"Mae Janaina?"

"A *Candomblé* priestess in Bahia, but I'll come to her in a minute. First, I have to tell you that when the fish got to São Paulo it was stolen and the man charged with stealing it was later murdered."

"Whoops."

"Yes! A priest on the sponsoring committee charged that it was stolen by a fellow committee member, Dr. Armando Olympio Padim. Padim was locally famous for his interest in fish and was the patron of the German wildlife artist Hans Weckert. You may have seen some of Weckert's calendars of fish paintings in the United States."

"I think I may have, as a matter of fact."

"Well, this was a big affair locally. The police blocked off the streets leading to Padim's huge estate. On the news they showed smocked police technicians on their hands and knees and hanging from under eaves and emerging, frustrated, from storm drains and laundry chutes. The police searched the apartment in Rio de Janeiro where he entertained his mistresses. They searched his beach villa north of Salvador, his fishing retreat in the Andes, and his riverboat on the Amazon. Nothing. Two days after the searching was completed and Padim held innocent, he and his wife and daughter were found murdered in their home."

Hanna blinked. "And the murderer?"

"Nobody ever found out. One of the chief suspects—but with no proof to indict her—was Mae Janaina, whose cult in northeastern Brazil worships Obatala and who maintains that the fish correctly belongs to the people for whom it was originally made by Father Machado. It was after this that Lloyd's, with whom the church had insured the fish, offered a $2.8 million finder's fee."

"Almost three million dollars?"

"It's supposed to be priceless, which means it ought to fetch something on the market. The reason I've been following all this so carefully is that my son-in-law Henrique has a nephew, Pedro, who was on the army detail that searched the boat. Pedro told me the effort wasn't anything like the search of the estate on television. He said his captain obviously thought the hidden fish business was nonsense, and owing to a scheduling error, the television people didn't show up, so they opened drawers and gave a thump here and there and that was it."

Desmond asked Hanna if she'd like to see his orchids. Of course she did, and they went for a walk among the orchids at the rear of his villa, accompanied by two bounding Dobermans, all sinew and sculpted muscle, jet black, their ears pinned neatly back.

When she first met them, the Dobermans were in a rage, jaws of killer teeth open straight to quivering, murderous gullets, and with a growl that would make a pit bull cower; she almost wet her pants. But once she received her frail host's approval, the dogs were nothing but puppies. Then she was their friend. Then they bounded along merrily with her and Desmond—nuzzling, cuddly Dobermans, tongues flapping, happy, happy.

Let them frolic beside Desmond was the way Hanna saw it; she did her best to keep her distance.

As she walked with Desmond, she watched two large tortoises sunning themselves in the front yard by the high fence that bordered the street. The metal pickets were like heavy spears or lances set into the ground. The tortoises were well over a foot long and weighed six or eight pounds. They seemed like amiable pets to Hanna; at least they didn't dance around trying to ram their noses up her crotch.

As she listened to Desmond explain the origins and habits of his orchids, she noted that there was no dog manure on the estate's well-tended lawn. She mentioned this to him.

He adjusted his cap. "The tortoises eat it."

"The tortoises?"

"We've had them twenty years now. They love it. We feed them melon rinds and table scraps."

"That and dog leavings?"

He smiled. "They clean it up."

"It's a form of dessert, then. They have a nice dinner of mango skins and top it off with chocolate mousse à la Doberman."

"That's about it."

"After it hardens, I suppose you could call it fudge."

"I suppose you could."

"Well, I don't feel nearly so bad about feeding little squid to my colleagues. Can we look at the tortoises?"

He laughed. "Sure," he said. They strolled across the clean lawn to the front. There the tortoises were sunning themselves.

"How can you tell male from female?"

He tipped a tortoise on its side; its bottom was concave. "This is so he won't fall off." He tipped the female on its side. She was flat on her stomach.

Hanna thought tortoises must have conventional sex lives. The lady would have a hard time round-backing it, poor thing. She wondered about their sex life. Had nature provided them with some form of internal clock that told them when it's time, or were they a passionate pair at night, their armor making a sexy *ka-klunk, ka-klunk, ka-klunk* sound, as concave stomach bashed against convex back?

Through the black pickets of the metal fence she could see a guard at the residence across the street. He was armed with an automatic rifle. It was a hot day and quiet; he squatted on his heels, slouched against a delicate tropical tree.

She thought of the tortoises, of their placid faces stoically eating dog shit, their jaws working methodically, their eyes blinking.

Now the tortoises, their bellies apparently full of melon rind and dog manure, rested in the shade, their heads and feet tucked inside their shells and out of harm's way.

At her shoulder, Desmond pursed his lips. "You know, I've been thinking about that business of the missing fish. You know, the *Igaranha* is a kind of fish. Weckert has been using the boat as a studio to paint fish and his companion studies them. What more logical place for a fish fancier to hide a six-inch-long prize." Desmond stopped to cough weakly. "I get all these ideas, but I'm too damned old and sick to do anything about them. I was thinking, you know, that if a person were to book passage on that boat, with a little luck, why . . ." Desmond's voice trailed off. He stared into space for a moment, then said, "Weckert's a fabulous artist, by the way. I have a whole book of his prints."

"I'm not too old and sick to go on a riverboat ride."

Desmond raised an eyebrow. "Walter always said you were a little adventurer. What are you thinking?"

"Well, I was thinking, what if I booked passage on that boat? You never know, maybe I might stumble onto something the army overlooked."

Desmond straightened. "Good for you. I just wish I were younger, I would go along with you just for the ride."

"You can help me do a little research."

"I can indeed. Would you like me to call and see if it's possible to book you on a trip?"

"Certainly. Thank you."

"And what would you do with three million dollars?" he asked, giving her a curious little grin.

"I'd give you part of it for helping me out, but most of it I'd use to build a clinic down here in one of these awful slums. They wouldn't stop me from doing that, would they, even if I am a fugitive?"

Desmond laughed. "I can't imagine they would. You

can add my share to your clinic money. In the morning we'll go downtown and I'll have my travel agent see if she can't book you on that boat. Hah, adventure! I love it."

The next morning, Desmond ferried Hanna through the traffic to get to his travel agent downtown. When they finally got there, with Desmond casually driving the wrong way on one-way streets—a São Paulo custom, he said—Hanna learned the reason why he didn't find a travel agent closer to home. Our lady of tickets was a doe-eyed beauty who had Desmond charmed out of his socks. She spoke English and was a hard and persistent worker, however; she earned her commission. After a half hour of relentless calls to Belém, she got through to the agent she wanted.

"Ah, Jorge!" she said. Her face lit up. She told him her problem. She made a note on a pad. She smiled. She put her hand over the receiver and turned to Desmond and Hanna.

She said, "There's an astonishing waiting list for the *Barco Igaranha,* but there's been a cancellation. My cousin Jorge is the booking agent for Amazonas Transport, and he says if you can be there in the morning, you've got a spot. You'll sail from Belém to Loucofilho on the Purus River, with stops at Santarém on the Amazon and at Manaus on the Rio Negro. You'll have to decide now, Jorge says, or he'll have to take somebody from the list. Do you know about Loucofilho?" she asked Hanna.

Hanna blinked. "Loucofilho?"

Desmond said, "Oh, oh, you lucked out. Loucofilho is where they're mining that mountain of gold. You may have read about it in the United States. That'd be something to see."

"I certainly have read about it, and yes, it certainly would be something to see."

"You'll take it, then?" the travel agent asked.

"Sold. Absolutely. I'll take it."

Gold was excavated openly in Loucofilho. The miners dug side by side, *mano a mano,* appetite on appetite, in pits of piss and rainwater; a cheated party knew precisely who was responsible and might well respond with a knife. Even if she didn't find Obatala's fish on the *Barco Igaranha,* DeeDee Sarant, AKA Hanna Doherty, wanted to see those inspired diggers in action.

7

WHERE PRESIDENTE VARGAS
GAVE HIS CHARGE

❋

The sign in the airline toilet told users not to throw paper towels and other articles into the stainless steel toilet. Nicholas Bodan punched an aluminum button and the toilet flushed dark blue; he unlatched the plastic door and walked down a pitching aisle as bells dinged and seat buckle lights flashed: the Varig airliner had hit a stretch of turbulent air.

Bodan stepped over the stylish Brazilian couple who sat next to him, and buckled himself in, thinking how awful—no, how Dantesque—it would be to have to use an airliner toilet for the rest of your life. He remembered sprinting through a trail in the snow to an outhouse when he was a kid, and of sitting perched over one side of the two-holer, cold air straight out of the Canadian arctic swirling beneath his behind, sending goose bumps down his legs.

The greatest joy of growing up on a farm was the primal freedom of being able to walk outside in a warm summer breeze and take a wholesome piss with the wind caressing his balls. He even liked the word *piss,* a straightforward, honest word. He liked to watch his piss sink into the earth, and believed that people forced to bounce their piss off porcelain or metal all their lives missed this most essential of life's connections.

As the Varig airliner circled over the Amazon delta for its approach to Belém, Bodan leaned his forehead against the window and looked down at a river, reflecting the light, twisted silver, rootlike, into the dark green of forest.

Belém itself was one of those places, like Irkutsk, Port Moresby, and Rangoon, which had always jumped right off the atlas at Bodan, demanding to be visited. Belém was the principal seaport at the mouth of the Amazon, but it was actually on the Pará River, connected to the main channel of the Amazon by the Breves Strait. The reasons why Bodan had always wanted to go to Belém were as unclear to him as his recent obsession with shelter and beauty. These obsessions inevitably had to do with a story bumping around in his subconscious, demanding to be freed and put on paper.

The city—situated south of Marajó Island at the confluence of the northwest-flowing Guamá River and the eastward-flowing Pará—was itself one of the most exotic shelters on the globe, the port city at the mouth of the great Amazon basin, which contained one third of the planet's trees, which helped supply one half of its oxygen. On the northern flank of Marajó, the Amazon—after receiving last-minute hits from the southern-flowing Jari and the northern-flowing Xingu—emptied into the Atlantic.

He stepped off the Brazilian Varig flight into the moist, tropical air of Belém, thinking of shelter—or was it shelters?—in the abstract. And of beauty. Shelters and beauty.

In shelter there is beauty, as a house has beauty and a church. From beauty—a painting, a lovely woman—there is shelter. Shelter is beautiful because it is comforting. From shelter follows beauty, and from beauty comes shelter.

This was where Nicholas Bodan's obsessions began, the sowing of his seed, each story a child, *spurt, spurt,* lest future generations forget that he was alive, here, now, and working passionately, however blindered, toward the truth.

There were the lost shelters of childhood, and adolescence, the shelters of schools and institutions; there was the shelter of religion; the shelter of companionship; the shelter of marriage; the shelter of ideology.

Bodan mopped sweat from his face with the backs of his arms. The taxicabs were gathered in front of the open-sided passenger terminal. As he rode a Volkswagen cab to the Avenida Presidente Vargas and the offices of Amazonas Transport, he very carefully composed a note in Portuguese —using an English-Portuguese dictionary—inquiring just where he might find the *Barco Igaranha.*

The name plate on the desk of the Amazonas Transport booking agent said his name was Jorge Blanco. Senhor Blanco studied Bodan's note for a moment, then said, "You did quite a good job with your note actually."

Bodan felt foolish. "The verbs are the hardest."

The Brazilian smiled. "English isn't so easy either. You're scheduled to sail on the *Barco Igaranha* tomorrow morning, Senhor Bodan. Lucky you. There are a lot of people who would pay you handsomely for your ticket. You know about the *Barco Igaranha?*"

"Yes, I read about it in the United States just before I came."

"You were booked before Dr. Padim and his family were murdered. We've had at least a couple of hundred calls asking if there was a berth left on her next trip."

"All wanting to look for the missing miracle fish, I take it."

"I'd just bet every single one of them," Blanco said. "Are you interested in selling your space, by the way?"

Bodan wondered if he should tell Blanco about the plans of the boat he found in Hal Johnson's feed store, but thought better of it. "Oh no. I think I'll claim my spot."

"I could get you some real money."

"No thanks," Bodan said.

In his occasional weekend forays with his friend Herb Goldberg, scrounging for rare books in San Francisco, Nicholas Bodan had learned that the most memorable and valuable finds were in places like the Tigard Feed and Seed —that is, where he least expected to find them. It was part of the lore of the business that dusty streets in provincial

American cities sometimes contained junk shops with equally dusty shelves and on those forgotten old shelves, sometimes, not often, maybe, but sometimes, there lay wonderful, forgotten old books.

There were the inevitable stories, of course, most of them hyperbole. Nevertheless, Bodan had heard of legit hits made in the most ridiculous backwater towns.

As Bodan saw it, there would have been botanists and horticulturists going through Belém on their way to Manaus for the 1896 rubber boom, and a later wave in 1929 to oversee Henry Ford's rubber plantation at Santarém. Botanists and horticulturists took novels with them to pass the time on long voyages into the interior, didn't they? Manaus is a thousand miles from Belém; the plantation owners certainly didn't charter airplanes for them in 1896.

He entertained a momentary fantasy, however stupid, of scoring a first edition of *Huckleberry Finn* in Belém, left there by an adventurous American botanist who rode a raft down from Manaus after serving out his contract. Belém was an old town; by the standards of the Americas, it was old-old, founded in about 1615. He stopped at the base of a thirty-foot-high octagonal gazebo to consult his map and check the possibilities of an adventuresome walk. Bodan thought it was a handsome gazebo; the domed metal canopy was supported by columns of uncertain classical origin and stamped with decorative laurel at the eaves, delicate curls of wrought iron rising from the sides.

Bodan stopped at a news kiosk near the edge of the park and tried to find something to read, only to discover, curiously enough, that Brazilians, speakers of Portuguese, read books in Portuguese, not English.

Bodan carried a shoulder bag that contained a Japanese laptop computer plus a printer with a combined weight of under ten pounds, and an expandable valise that looked proper and civilized but which had a hidden frame and shoulder straps turning it into a utilitarian backpack. Bodan, with the computer and printer slung over one shoulder, and with the plans for the *Barco Igaranha* tucked safely into his valise—now in its backpack mode—began a hike down Avenida Presidente Vargas from the offices of Amazonas to the Pará River.

The grand *avenida* was flanked by forty-foot-wide tree-lined promenades that were tiled white with a black decorative strip on each side. The thick-trunked, high-branched trees were also painted white at the bottom, so that the avenue was starched white, in formal attire; the umbrella of limbs overhead and the palm shrubs in the gardens seemed greener than green to Bodan, a romantic, unreal green.

Farther down the avenue—to the north—the promenades narrowed to wide sidewalks and Bodan passed banks, travel agencies, money changers, and hotels. At the end of the Avenida Presidente Vargas, the Presidente himself—or at least a statue of him—stood grandly atop a pedestal.

The Presidente had a chin-up, visionary look about him. His stern gaze was fixed on the *café au lait* of the Pará, a river that seemed to stretch forever to the north, an ocean of a river. The soil was as red as Georgia's worst, the city greenery and surrounding jungle so green as to leave Bodan open-mouthed.

He unshouldered his backpack and surrendered the weight of the computer and printer.

Now, so much yellow-brown water!

Bodan dug his guidebook out of the backpack. It was in Belém, according to the guidebook, that Presidente Vargas made his "March to the Amazon" speech in 1940, urging his countrymen to take advantages of the riches of the Amazon. It was at the mouth of the incredible drainage of Amazonia that any such march into the green would logically begin.

The Presidente's special circle at the end of the avenue was surrounded by a metal fence; uniformed guards with automatic rifles watched the gates that led to the wharf on either side. The cranes and industrial gear needed to load and unload oceangoing freighters lay downstream from Presidente Vargas. The freighters could go a thousand miles into the interior to Manaus, where the Rio Negro and the Rio Solimões met to officially become the Amazon.

The shallow-draft riverboats required to trade in the oftentime shallow and narrow arteries of the Amazon were moored upstream from the Presidente in the direction of Belém's famous outdoor market.

Bodan shouldered his backpack and computer bag and started hiking toward the riverboats and his voyage to Loucofilho on the fish-eyed *Barco Igaranha.*

8

THE FISHERMAN WHO GOT

TOO GREEDY

✳

Nicholas Bodan thought he recognized the *Barco Igaranha,* but he wasn't sure. He turned up the first street which paralleled the river, hoping to find a bar or café where he could look at the riverboats. He found one with tables on the sidewalk and an awning that afforded some shade. The door was open. Overhead, a lazy fan screwed listless air.

Bodan decided on the sidewalk, plopping down in a chair that had originally been white but which, like the table, had turned gray from age and the knicks and scrapes of café life. The Pará was so wide here it was impossible to see the far shore. On the other side lay Ilha de Marajó—the largest island in the world built by the accretion of effluent —built by topsoil which had been washed down the Amazon basin and which continued to flow seaward, suspended in the *café au lait* water.

A waiter in baggy black trousers and soulful face came out to take Bodan's order. The waiter's jacket had been white, but now matched the veteran tables and chairs. Bodan ordered coffee, moved his feet to one side to get them out of the heat, and turned his attention to the riverboats.

Most of the riverboats were single-deckers, although double-deckers were not uncommon; Bodan couldn't spot one that wasn't painted white, with either red or blue trim. They were long and narrow so that the traders might reach the most isolated outposts in the interior, and owing to the need for protection from the heat and tropical rain, it was the fashion to leave no square inch of deck uncovered; it was under these roofs that hardy travelers of the Amazon slung their hammocks.

Bodan wondered if the riverboats might not get a little top-heavy when they were loaded, but they were oh, so very, very lovely; the lines of their white rails moved in an elegant slope from bow to stern. Only a sailboat or a human female could compete with their beauty, he thought. In the distance Bodan could see a small single-decker coming into Belém, loaded, white rails low to the water, the narrow hull sliding gently through the water.

He got his small binoculars from the pocket of his cotton vest and scanned the lineup of boats. Then he spotted her, a sleek single-decker, white with blue trim and a rust-red roof, the *Barco Igaranha*. The *Barco* was a classic Amazonian riverboat with one important exception: there was a rounded glass fish eye as wide as a dinner plate on either side of her bow.

Bodan shifted the focus of his glasses from the *Barco*'s fish-eye bow to her bridge, which was on the top front of the forward cabin. Then he saw two men emerging from the front cabin. One was a tall man in his late fifties wearing a floppy cotton hat, short-sleeved shirt, faded blue jeans, and running shoes, and with a small knapsack slung over his shoulder.

The second, in his mid-forties, was a stout fellow, broad of shoulder and back, with powerful arms and massive thighs; he wore military shorts, tattered tennis shoes, and a *Cock's Inn, Lagos* T-shirt stretched tightly over an enormous belly. He topped this off with a white-billed cap of the sort Bodan associated with effete golfers. His belly hung so far over his belt that it was obvious he could not see his genitals without a mirror. But it was a stout gut, with no fat or flab, Bodan could see that even through binoculars. This was a powerful man bellied out by gravity and beer.

The two men checked the tackle from which the single lifeboat was hung suspended on the port side near the bow, then disappeared into the cabin that was low and forward on the riverboat. The stout man did the heavy chores; the man with the knapsack seemed in charge, but both men pitched in and worked hard.

Having completed their chores, they hopped onto the wharf and began walking toward the café where Nicholas sat. The slender man had the loose amble of an academic on his way to the library. The stout man walked a slow, stately walk, his back ramrod-straight, chest and belly sticking proudly out.

In the horizon of the Pará, a storm, moving in what seemed like a wall of rain, swept over the water, heading for Belém. It was as though a wall of angry gray was being pulled steadily, evenly across the horizon of the river by an enormous paintbrush.

The men looked back at the boat and stood for a moment watching the approaching storm. They turned and walked faster, then began jogging. The man with the knapsack had a loose gait; the stout man moved smoothly, his feet rolling heel to toe, his back square to the earth, his solid belly forward, so that he resembled a huge fluid, human ice breaker.

As the rain swept over a freighter anchored at a distance, drilling straight for the harbor, they suddenly altered their course and headed for the café where Bodan watched.

The rain swept across the moored riverboats, bouncing off the roof and decks of the *Barco Igaranha*. The two men began running toward Bodan, the big-bellied man moving with astonishing ease, his elbows pumping smoothly, never once leaning forward.

Bodan stashed his binoculars, gathered his coffee up, and followed the man through the door. No sooner were they inside than the rain was full upon the city. The sky opened as though it were a heavenly faucet and the water came. Bodan had never seen anything like it, had never seen so much rain coming so fast—or heard it come so fast, for that matter. The doors to Oscar's remained open as the rain ripped and hammered, beat and roared, came down hard, hard, hard, in a thundering unearthly din, lashing roof and window, trees and awnings, street and parked car.

The two men chose a table and sat. The blond man hung his knapsack on the corner of his chair and flopped his wet hat on the floor. The stout man hung his cap on a hook on the wall.

The blond man had a long, handsome face, lined and leathered from the sun. He wore utilitarian eyeglasses and had pale blue eyes. There was something scholarly and studious about his eyes, Bodan thought. The stout man looked as if he might have been a rugger player in his day.

Bodan made a bet with himself that these men were the German artist Hans Weckert and the naturalist Lenny Humphries. He walked over to the bespectacled man. "Excuse me," he said. "I was watching you on the riverboat there, the *Barco Igaranha.*"

The man put down his book, which was in Portuguese. It was obvious he understood English. "Yes, can I help you?" He had the barest hint of a German accent.

Bodan said, "I'm to be one of the passengers and I was wondering if you might not be going with us tomorrow."

The German grinned and leaned to shake Bodan's hand. "I certainly hope so. Officially I'm the captain, I guess, Hans Weckert, and this is my friend, Lenny Humphries. And you would be?"

"Nicholas Bodan."

"You're the author, then. The gentleman from San Francisco."

"Yes, I am." Bodan shook hands with Weckert and Humphries, whose roast beef of a hand dwarfed his own.

"Pleased to meet you, Mr. Bodan," Humphries said, his voice a deep, resonant murmur. "Won't you bring your coffee over and join us?"

Bodan settled in at their table. He offered a little toast with his cup. "Well, here's to Loucofilho," he said.

"Certainly, here's to Loucofilho," Weckert said. "Are you going for the gold in Loucofilho, Mr. Bodan?"

Bodan grinned a grin which said yes, he was going for the gold at Loucofilho.

Humphries said, "Well, good luck. Even if you come out broke it's a sight you won't be forgetting soon, I assure you."

"I'm going in broke, so I suppose it doesn't make a whole lot of difference if I come out broke as well. Do you two go there all the time? Is it part of your regular schedule?"

"No, no, Mr. Bodan. We have two loads to deliver, one for the AmeRiBurger Corporation to Santarém and a second to Loucofilho for a river trader, Senhor Kobayashi, who'll be with us on board the *Barco*. This is an unusual job for us, as a matter of fact. A bloody mercenary run, I'm afraid."

"How's that?"

"Well, Hans and I really only care about painting and studying fish, not making money, but his art and my articles on fish aren't enough to keep the *Barco* fueled and maintained. If we take cargo rather than passengers, we get to run the boat at our pace and paint and think in peace. We've been able to take smaller loads to isolated villages and outposts because if we ran low on money we always had Dr. Padim to bail us out. Things are different now; when Senhor Kobayashi asked if we could take a load to

Loucofilho, we went for it. We knew there'd be no problem booking passengers."

Weckert said, "Senhor Kobayashi loves boats. For about the same price he could have flown his boxes into Loucofilho; they have an airport there and make regular runs."

"What on earth could a fast-food hamburger chain be sending to Santarém?"

"We have no idea. They delivered the boxes yesterday afternoon. They've got 'AmeRiBurger Corporation, Los Angeles, California,' on the side, and we're supposed to be met in Santarém by a certain Senhor Buenovena, that's all we know."

"Maybe they're opening a franchise in Santarém."

"Santarém seems an unlikely place for an AmeRiBurger franchise, but you never know, Mr. Bodan. Stranger things have happened down here, believe me."

"So there won't be a lot of painting for you this trip, I don't imagine."

Weckert shook his head. "Not this trip, I'm afraid; we've booked her solid. But after Loucofilho, we can afford to find ourselves another out-of-the-way river and see what kind of fish we can find there."

"Good for you. I'm lucky to have booked this trip, I see. Have you ever been to Loucofilho?"

Humphries groomed the bottom of his mustache with his fingertips. "I'm afraid not. Of course, I'm curious about what it looks like, the same as everybody else. A literal mountain of gold swarming with fortune hunters."

"Nature at its rawest, from what I've read."

Humphries nodded. "Pretty tough stuff."

"Look, it's stopped raining." The sky was blue once more and the sun was out. "So tell me about the *Barco Igaranha,* Captain Weckert. What does that name mean?"

Weckert brightened. "An author's question, eh, Lenny?"

"I would think."

Weckert said, "The man who had the boat built in the first place . . ."

"Dr. Padim's father."

". . . Padim's father, correct, was a zoologist at the University of Pernambuco. He spent most of the last twenty years of his life on the *Barco,* which he regarded as an ark of learning, and loved to hear various explanations of how the world works. I spent two years on the water with him before he died. The name *Igaranha* comes from a story of greed and a mythical canoe told by the Kamaiura people who live along the Batovi River, a tributary of the Xingu."

"Which is a tributary of the Amazon."

"A clear river flowing northward from the Mato Grosso. This is all part of a national park now, by the way."

"And the story is?"

"The story is that a man made a canoe out of *jatoba* bark, but he'd no sooner finished it than his wife had a baby, so he couldn't try it out. Several days later he went back to the *jatoba* tree where he had left it, but it was gone. Then he heard noises and the canoe, which had turned into a spirit, was crashing its way through the underbrush on its way back to the tree. The man climbed inside the canoe, which had eyes on its bow, and asked it if it could take him somewhere, and it did. The canoe carried him to the lagoon. As soon as it was on the water, fish began jumping inside."

"A helluva canoe!"

"The canoe ate those fish. Then more fish jumped inside. The *igaranha* gave these fish to the fisherman, but not until after it climbed out of the water and returned to its place in the forest. The man went home and told his wife he had found a fabulous place to fish. A few days later he went back to the boat's place under the *jatoba* tree. After a while the canoe appeared and beckoned for him to climb in again, which he did. As before, the canoe went to the lagoon and the fish began jumping in, only this time the fisherman tried to keep all the fish for himself."

"I see. What happened?"

"He so angered the *igaranha* by his greed that the canoe swallowed him up. His wife waited for him in his house, but he never returned."

Bodan sat back. "Well! A lesson of appetite."

"Lenny and I have heard people on the Xingu call it the boat of nervous dreams."

"I've seen your fish calendars in bookstores for years. If you've got any of your paintings aboard, I'd like to see some of them if that would be possible. But I suppose all your passengers ask the same thing."

"Of course they do. And I'm always pleased to show them my work. I'd be delighted to show you my little studio. And I'm sure Lenny wouldn't mind getting out the old scalpel and slicing open a few stomachs if you'd like." Hans Weckert signaled to the waiter for another cup of coffee.

"There's a remarkable passion. I believe I'll pass for now."

Humphries grinned. "You can learn a lot about a species by looking at their stomachs, Mr. Bodan. Fish are only 20 percent less evolved than we are, by the way. Their behavior is adapted to keeping their stomachs full, just as ours is. It's always interesting to find out what they eat."

9

A MAN WITH BOXES OF APPLES

❋

Hanna Doherty got up with the sun as usual and looked out over the swimming pool and the river beyond that. She remembered telling the travel agent in São Paulo about how she wanted a hotel with a view. What she got was the French-owned Novotel, which had been awarded a *good view* symbol by her Brazilian guidebook, said to be the final word on travel in a country which was larger than the continental United States, excluding Alaska.

Indeed, the back, or view half, of the Novotel did over-look the water, the Guamá River, which formed the south-western flank of Belém, and which flowed into Guajara Bay on the Pará.

However, just across the street from the entrance there was a large ditch in which human turds floated low in the water, looking like comfortable old logs or the backs of lazy crocodiles. They were part of a layer of garbage—old boards, empty bottles, melon rinds—that floated on the wa-ter. The human residents crossed the ditch on rickety foot-bridges, but she imagined the local rats just walked across the water like little tailed Jesuses.

A dirt path on the far side served open-fronted shacks that were bars and grocers and barbershops. Along stretches of the ditch, in the shadows of the bank, a certain pale green moss made a happy home, forming narrow, lush islands that floated on the dreck.

She took a long hot shower, standing with the water sliding over her shoulders and down her breasts and back. *Mmmm.* The water felt good. She thought, the woman stands on the burning deck, letting water run down her neck. From neck to breast the water runs. On down the spine, up over her buns.

She went downstairs to get herself some breakfast. There was a buffet of ham, boiled eggs, cheese, fruit juices, and papaya in the dining room. There was a swimming pool between the dining room and the river. As she sat sipping watermelon juice, she saw that the water in the pool was clear. Was it filtered from the river, she wondered. She supposed it was. She wondered what kind of filter it took to turn brown water clear. What kind of filter did it take to screen the turds from the sewer across the street?

She finished breakfast and went back upstairs to get her gear together. As she started to pack, it began to thunder. Black clouds rolled over Belém as she settled her bill. Just as her taxi started moving through the slum surrounding the Novotel, it started raining, and at the end of two blocks the driver stopped at an intersection that had turned into a lake; the driver put the car in low, and they started again at a crawl.

In Portuguese that she didn't understand, the driver explained to her that there was no way for the rain squalls to drain. The cab forded the first intersection only to confront a second. The rain stopped as the driver slowed for a third, until he finally hit a stretch where the streets had miraculously drained, possibly into the canal of floating turds.

He sent the cab careening through a series of lefts and rights through colonial buildings still bearing up to the tropical heat. At last the cab entered what was obviously a main drag. They passed a gorgeous octagonal gazebo and slowed for a commercial district. As the cab drew near the river, there were government buildings on Hanna's right. The driver turned left. There she saw riverboats lined up all sleek and grand. The *Barco Igaranha* would be somewhere among them.

The driver slowed, glancing at her in the rearview mirror for a signal that she'd spotted her boat. Then she saw it because of the fish eyes on the bow; it was the only boat in the lineup with eyes.

She didn't know the Portuguese word for eyes, so said, *"Peixe* eyes." She put her hands over her face to represent giant eyes. Then she pointed to the boat. The driver saw the *Barco* and smiled; he pulled the cab to a stop. He gestured to the bow and asked her a question in Portuguese. He obviously wanted to know about the eyes.

"I don't know what they're supposed to represent either, but I'll find out shortly," she said, repressing a giggle because he couldn't understand a word of what she was saying.

A tall blond man in his fifties with a good-looking weathered face opened the door. She stepped out into the full heat of the sun and understood immediately why Amazonian riverboats had roofs running the length of the deck.

She wondered how these people took it, living in heat like this.

"Hello, I am Hans Weckert," he said. "You must be Ms. Doherty. Welcome, welcome." He glanced briefly up at the sun and mopped his forehead with the back of his arm.

"Call me Hanna, please." She shook his hand. He seemed not to have recognized her as the fugitive prankster.

"And I'm Lenny Humphries," said the deep-voiced second man.

Weckert and Humphries helped retrieve her bags from the trunk and they carried everything aboard the *Barco Igaranha.*

Rolls of mosquito nets were neatly tied to the bottom of the eaves of the boat's roof which ran stern to bow, a necessity for protection against the equatorial sun and tropical rain squalls.

"She's eighty-two feet long, twelve feet wide, and has a five-foot draft," Weckert said.

All this meant to Hanna was that it was a pretty big boat. There was a cabin forward and a cabin aft. Weckert led Hanna and Humphries around the open hold midships that contained cabinets, a large gasohol engine, a fuel tank, a toilet, a curtained shower, and a cargo area already half-filled with neatly stacked boxes.

They went down a short flight of stairs into the aft cabin, and Weckert showed Hanna her quarters, a two-bunk private compartment at the stern end of the cabin.

"You can sling a hammock up top, if you wish. I believe Mr. Bodan will do that. The passengers ordinarily eat their meals on top of the cabin rather than down below. I run a generator off the gasohol and store juice in batteries so folks can have light up here to swap stories and play cards at night." Weckert squeegeed sweat from his forehead with one finger.

"I bet people even sleep up here if it gets hot enough."

"This is the best place to sleep, if you want my opinion.

I've got hammocks for everybody and there's plenty of room to sling them."

After the business of stowing her gear was finished, Weckert invited Hanna for a forward tour with Bodan, the man who would be sleeping up top.

Hanna followed him up to meet Bodan, who turned out to be a blue-eyed, curly-haired man in his mid-forties, who scoped her good-naturedly as he shook hands. "Pleased to meet you, Hanna."

"Mr. Bodan is a novelist."

"A broke novelist," Bodan said.

"Taking a little flyer on Loucofilho," Hanna said.

"Trying to survive."

Hanna and Bodan followed the affable German artist.

Bodan, ever the gentleman, trailed, eyeing Hanna's butt as they went down the stairs. "What got you interested in Loucofilho?" he asked.

"I read a magazine article about it." She started down the steps of the companionway.

"I don't have to watch what I eat or anything like that? It's safe to be around you?"

She paused in the companionway and looked back at him. "I thought you were a writer."

He shrugged. "Sorry. I'm not a bounty hunter or anything like that. You have a memorable face."

"If you stare at it every day on the front of magazines at the checkout stands."

"The way I see it, if Cassius Clay wants to be Muhammad Ali, do I care? Hanna Doherty's a perfectly good name."

"It was my grandmother's. Thank you, Nicholas. I appreciate the privacy, and no, you don't have to watch what you eat around me."

"Everybody knows the greedy bastards had it coming. Somebody ought to give you a medal."

Weckert and Humphries had divided the middle section of the forward cabin—the space between hull supports—

into a combination studio and laboratory. Weckert kept his brushes and paints and an easel on one side; Humphries had a small dissecting table on the other. They slept forward of their studio and laboratory, each having a modest compartment on either side of a ladder that led to a trapdoor in the floor of the bridge. Humphries's galley occupied the rear of the cabin.

Weckert paused before the easel and picked up a brush. He studied what were the beginnings of a portrait already taking on an uncanny likeness to a small fish pinned neatly to a smaller table easel. "Actually the light is awful down here, so I have to go up top to do detail work."

Weckert sat and moistened a brush, his eye on something wrong. "You two climb up in the bridge if you want. We've got the best gear on the market just about. A first-rate fathometer to tell us how deep we're running and a Japanese-made fish finder that gives us defined images. We know what they look like down there. Humphries has been entering these shapes into his computer so when we pass over a school, the names of the fish appear alphabetically on the screen. We've even got a floodlight mounted on the underside of the fantail so we can pop on the light and surprise the night feeders. Lenny can take photographs in a clear river."

"What happens with shapes you can't identify?"

"There's the fun part. That happens all the time. Lenny and I try to catch them and identify them, of course."

Hanna followed Bodan into Humphries's galley, which was as compact and efficient as the boat's architect could make it. No space was unoccupied by a cabinet or was otherwise unused. The gas refrigerator was flanked by a four-burner stove on one side and a stainless steel sink on the other.

Bodan climbed the ladder to the bridge, peering up at the steering wheel and pilot's instruments. He retreated down the ladder and Hanna took a turn. When she came down again, Weckert started to rise.

"No, no," she said. "Finish what you're doing, we're in no hurry. At least, I'm not."

"I'm not going anywhere," Bodan said.

"The bridge also opens onto the top of this cabin," Weckert said. He ran a rim of yellow around the eye of the fish; he did this just so, a delicate touching of brush to paper. He narrowed one eye and tilted his head slightly to one side, judging his effort.

"Beautiful work," Bodan said.

"You really think so? Thank you." Weckert washed his brush in a jar of muddy water and blew gently on the paper. He took a smaller brush and then, on the yellow, just so, he painted two round spots of red. He washed the small brush and added a green spot. These were identical to the spots around the yellow eyes of the dead fish.

Weckert straightened, looking satisfied. "He's a colorful one this, a parrot of a fish."

"He likes his color." Hanna could hardly believe the artistry of Weckert's touch. The realism of the painted fish was amazing.

"Some of these species might not be around in another hundred years. I thought it would be nice to at least honor them with their own portrait."

"I see."

"I want them to look their best, which is how they look when they're out here by themselves eating and being eaten." Weckert scooted his chair back to get a different look at his fish. Then he leaned over, studying the fish on the table.

"Incidentally, there may be more species of fish in the Amazon than any other river in the world, did you know that?" He leaned to one side so Bodan could have a better look.

"No, I didn't know that."

Weckert retrieved a portfolio of paintings and hurried through the pile of carefully rendered tropical fish, pausing at one manure-colored fish.

"Here's a predator. You can tell the predators because they tend to have protective coloring so they can lurk, invisible to their victims." He flipped some more pages, stopping at a painting of a small leech painted alongside a wristwatch to give an indication of its size, which was about a half-inch long.

"Lately I've been working on a collection of leech paintings. There're amazing leeches down here, small ones like this that are also found in Europe and America, and one, the giant Amazonian leech, that grows up to a foot and a half long."

"Oh no!" Hanna said.

Bodan stepped back. "Leeches?"

"Oh yes. The Ch, a tribe that lives on the Ist, a tributary of the Amazon, have doctor-gods who use the leeches to draw bad blood from sick patients. The Ch swear by its healing powers."

Weckert got up and opened a small sea trunk from which he removed a portfolio of leeches rendered with his characteristic lifelike realism. In one of the paintings, an enormous, bloated leech, greenish black in color, was shown feeding between the ribs of a human being. In a second painting a cluster of thirty or forty glistening leeches, each one looking like an inch-long armadillo, clung to an adolescent breast.

Bodan said, "Uuaagg."

"That's a giant Amazonian leech," Weckert said. "The one on this man's ribs is eighteen inches long. It's feeding out of a proboscis one-third the length of its body."

"That's enough!" Bodan backed away.

"It appears not to bother you, Ms. Doherty. Do you have the heart of a scientist?"

Hanna's stomach fluttered. Did he know she was DeeDee Sarant? Bad enough that Bodan should know. "We women can take more than a man," she said.

Weckert closed the portfolio of paintings. "The doctor-gods are called leechmen, by the way."

"Leechmen?" Bodan looked amused.

"The Ch live inland from a marsh near the mouth of the Ist River. I've been there, in fact stayed there for a while looking for specimens in the Ist. It's not far actually, about halfway between here and Santarém."

"Are we going to stop there?" Bodan paled.

Weckert said, "If everybody wants to." Weckert stood and pulled a portfolio from the shelf which he opened to a painting of an amazing fish. "This is istu, the death fish, a cousin to the piranha, of which there are about ten known varieties in the Amazon, the most familiar being silver-colored with a red belly. But piranhas travel in schools; the istu is a loner."

The mottled gray istu rather resembled a swimming jaw. There was only a suggestion of room for intestinal organs on its underside, and its efficient little tail and fins seemed muscular beyond necessity. Nature had designed this swimming jaw as a single tensed muscle, streamlined so that it might spring through the water. The jaw, obviously only content while eating, was lined with needle-pointed band-saw teeth. The istu's rather large eyes were a metallic gold with blood-red irises, the only colors on the fish.

"Ooof!" Bodan's mouth hung in open amazement.

Weckert said, "A good boxer usually has a short stout neck, and not much of a chin, functional for taking a hit. A good marksman has good eyes and reflexes."

"And this thing does what?" Hanna asked.

"Chews up everything in its path, according to the Ch. But you have to remember this is not a painting of a real fish, just the istu as the leech people describe him. I've made him look like a rock here, but he has the chameleon-like ability to blend into the background even in the Ist, which has remarkably clear water. The Ch say the death fish can look like a rock if he wants. He can look like a rotting log. He can look like clay, like moss, like anything under-water.

"What's even worse from the standpoint of his fellow

fish, the istu can assume their colors as well. If there is a school of catfish traveling by, he slips in with them, unseen, a swimming jaw with their exact coloring except for his gold eyes with the red pupils."

Hanna Doherty was on her bunk napping when she heard Hans Weckert up top calling to Humphries. Humphries boomed back, "Yes, Hans, I got it." Hanna shook the sleep from her head and went up top to find out what the fuss was all about.

She saw the sonorous-voiced Humphries on the dock talking to the lead driver of three aged pickup trucks loaded with what appeared to be brand-new wooden boxes. Bodan was with Humphries, looking over Humphries's broad shoulder. The driver peered up, listening, the uneven idle of his engine shaking the chassis of the pickup. A second man in the pickup listened carefully but said nothing. Humphries gestured at the *Barco Igaranha* with his right hand; he put his hand on the pickup.

The driver stuck his head out of the door and looked back.

Hanna hurried down to the dock and joined Bodan and Humphries. Weckert followed closely behind.

A taxi suddenly appeared behind the procession. Two Asian men got out. The younger man, dressed in a stylish sport shirt and yellow slacks, shook the older man's hand, bowing in respect. The older man, pulling a handkerchief from his hip pocket, mopped his brow with his left hand. He gestured toward the boat with his handkerchief.

The man in the yellow slacks got back into the taxi and sat back; the taxi drove off.

The man with the handkerchief, a stout Japanese-Brazilian in his late forties or early fifties, hurried toward the lead pickup where Humphries waited.

The driver asked him a question, holding the steering

wheel with one hand and motioning to the boat with the other.

The Japanese man spoke briefly to Humphries, and the big-bellied man said, "This is Senhor João Kobayashi, who is a river trader of some years experience, although this is the first time we have carried merchandise for him."

"To Loucofilho," Kobayashi said.

"This is Ms. Hanna Doherty from the United States, who is going with us to photograph the activity at the Loucofilho gold strike. This is Nicholas Bodan, an American author who'll be with us to Loucofilho also. And this is Hans Weckert, who is the captain of our vessel."

"I'm very pleased to meet you all," Kobayashi said. "Shall we get on with loading my boxes, Senhor Humphries?"

"Well, of course." Humphries nodded his head yes again and stepped back; the driver, his eye steady on the rearview mirror, backed the truck to the loading plank, and turned the key off, giving its rusting body a rest from the shaking.

Humphries, deferring to the instructions of the Japanese, unlatched the tailgate. The drivers of the remaining two pickups killed their engines and joined the group at the boat.

Kobayashi then told them what to do. He was apparently concerned about the safety of the boxes, going so far as to demonstrate to the men how the boxes should be carried. He held his end of an imaginary box and talked at the same time. Their heads bobbed yes; they understood what he wanted done.

Hanna walked around to watch the loading of the wooden boxes. There were two kinds of boxes, one about six feet long by a foot and a half wide, another about two feet by two feet. Both kinds were heavily spiked and reinforced by metal strapping. They had no label or identifying mark of any kind.

Humphries hopped aboard the riverboat, laughing

deeply. "Bloody sod doesn't want me to help. I don't think the bugger trusts me."

"With his boxes?" Hanna asked.

"He says he knows it's possible for one man to carry one of his boxes, but he wants two men on one bleeding box at all times. They are to be very, very careful, he says."

"What's in the boxes?"

"I don't have any idea. Would you take a look at this?"

Two of the drivers were loading one of the long boxes. The boxes didn't seem heavy, but the contents were apparently fragile. One man backed up, taking small, tentative steps, the other—taking equal care—felt his way forward. Kobayashi followed closely behind, concerned that the box might be bumped or whacked on its way to the security of the cargo hold where they were stacked neatly against the AmeRiBurger Corporation's shipment to Santarém.

His boxes stowed and secured, Kobayashi rejoined the other travelers, digging business cards from his wallet. "I'm sorry. I forgot to give you my card. Very bad manners." He gave Hanna and Bodan each a card, which listed a post office box and a phone number in Belém. It identified the bearer as Senhor João Kobayashi, Imports/Exports.

"I see. Well, what are you importing here?" Hanna tapped the edge of the hold with her foot.

Kobayashi, glancing at Weckert, considered the question. "Apples."

The boxes obviously didn't contain apples. "Apples? Really? What kind of apples?"

Kobayashi hesitated. "Crisp red ones."

"I see, Rome Beauties or Delicious, or something like that. I like those boxes. All those nails: pound, pound, pound. That strapping tape. You don't see fruit boxes like that anymore."

Kobayashi smiled. "If you'll excuse me, I think I better check their work again. The weather can get stormy this close to the Atlantic." Kobayashi bowed politely. "Miss Doherty, Captain Weckert, Mr. Humphries, Mr. Bodan."

10

MORE FISHERMEN ARRIVE

✸

Equatorial heat was unkind to wearers of full penguin black, so Father Franco Ferrua had modified his clerical costume for conditions on the Amazon. The man from São Paulo, who looked hardly over five feet tall, wore neat black shoes, light tan chinos with a black belt, a white dickey, a turnaround collar, an off-white cotton jacket that had paperbacks bulging from both pockets, and light cream Panama with a wide black band.

He carried a large valise, a stuffed nylon travel bag slung over one shoulder, and a small leather briefcase. He wore round-lensed spectacles with cheap clear plastic rims.

Bodan went with Lenny Humphries to meet the tidy little cleric. After introductions, Ferrua said, "My, my, what a lovely boat, Dr. Humphries."

"Why don't we get your belongings stowed away, Father. I'll introduce you to our Amazon trader, Senhor Kobayashi, and our American guest, Hanna Doherty."

"Here, here, let me help you," Bodan said. He started to grab Father Ferrua's heaviest bag, the valise.

Ferrua gave him the stuffed travel bag. "Thank you, Mr. Bodan. But the best one to take is this thing digging into my shoulder."

Bodan, following Humphries and the priest, was astonished at how easily the stout-gutted man negotiated the narrow passages and doorways of the *Barco Igaranha.*

Hans Weckert called after them. "Also, Lenny, the *candomblé* folks will be arriving in a few minutes. We'll have to help them stow their gear and show them where everything is."

Humphries said, "We'll clear a space next to Senhor Kobayashi's apple boxes."

Ferrua looked surprised. *"Candomblé?* Will there be *candomblé* followers on this trip? How many?"

"Four. Two women, a man, and a girl."

"These wouldn't be followers of Mae Janaina, would they?"

"Mae Janaina's one of them. They won't be with us for long, though; they're not going anywhere near Loucofilho." Humphries tucked in a loose shirttail and hitched up his belt with massive hands, the backs of which were covered by a forest of black hair.

Father Ferrua looked surprised. "They're not?"

"They'll be getting off at Monte Alegre just before Santarém."

"Monte Alegre? I see."

"She told Hans and me she has a sister in Monte Alegre."

Bodan started down the stairs into the aft cabin.

Ferrua followed, saying, "Mae Janaina is a *yalorixa,* which means a high priestess and diviner; she can talk to spirits and can raise the dead. *Candomblé* is a Yoruba religion."

"From Nigeria?" Bodan asked.

"It means more than that actually. The Portuguese first took African slaves to Brazil in the sixteenth century. These early slaves were taken from an area that extends roughly from Nigeria to Liberia and which is sometimes called the Yoruba nation of tribes. Bantu slaves later taken from the Congo took *macumba* with them to the areas around Rio de Janeiro and Minas Gerais. Say, this is a large cabin!"

Humphries said, "Any free berth's yours, Father. It's been first come first served, but they each have a curtain for privacy, as you can see. Ms. Doherty will have the private compartment to the rear there."

*   *   *

Hanna Doherty retreated briefly to her little compartment and checked the pile of newspaper clippings about Obatala's fish that Desmond had helped her collect. Sure enough, Father Ferrua was the São Paulo priest who was in charge of bringing the miracle fish for exhibit in Brazil.

And Mae Janaina was the Bahia priestess who claimed the fish belonged to her people. Hanna wondered if there was anybody on board who wasn't looking for the fish.

She joined Father Ferrua up top. Lenny had left a pitcher of iced tea for Nicholas and Hanna to enjoy as they watched Lenny and Hans clear a modest space in the hold for the Bahians to store their extra belongings. Senhor Kobayashi, apparently concerned that his boxes of apples be somehow jarred, or opened, paced the deck at the edge of the hold.

"In the United States all we hear about are voodoo, hex dolls, zombies, and *macumba,* Father Ferrua. Is this genuine stuff or hocus pocus?"

"I suppose one can argue that if one's faith is genuine, there is little to choose among religions, whether they're primitive or sophisticated. But I won't go into that." Father Ferrua smiled pleasantly. "A *candomblé* is both an African religious cult and commune of sorts. The leaders of most Bahia *candomblés* are women, *yalorixas.* The *yalorixa* is both a healer who prescribes medicines of Yoruba deities called *orixas*—intermediaries between mortals and the supreme god, *Olurun*—and a religious figure."

"Eye of newt, ear of bat," Hanna said. "Simmer six hours."

Ferrua smiled. "The *yalorixa* communicate with spirits and the dead in an *acheche* ceremony, in addition to their participation in Salvador's carnival celebration. I can guarantee they'll miss Mae Janaina on television this year. The folks in Salvador will be wondering where she went."

"On television? Why is that?"

"The prestige of the *candomblé* is at stake in the carnival parades, and Mae Janaina and her sensational women followers stop the show every year in Salvador. Most of the televised coverage is of the commercial spectacular in Rio, but every year they switch to Bahia when Mae Janaina makes her entrance. There have been rumors that outsiders have paid fortunes to be allowed to witness one of her *batuque* dances where there is much rubbing of bellies."

"Ahh, the inevitable scam."

Ferrua held up a finger and waggled it gently. "No, from all accounts, if Mae Janaina does charge a fee, she uses the income to benefit her *candomblé*. Believe me, there are a lot of mothers in Bahia who would just love to have a daughter be one of her assistants."

Hanna looked skeptical. "No invented touches to make it a teensy bit more spectacular?"

"There could be some of that, I suppose. But as a matter of fact, of the whole complicated range of African religion and Catholicism in Brazil, the Bahia cults appear to be the least contaminated by Christianity. The early Jesuits were forced to mix Indian religion with Catholic practices because there were so few priests to teach and so many Indians to be taught. Priests later did the same thing with the religions the black slaves brought with them. Anything that could easily be combined with Catholic rituals was accepted, including African fraternities and brotherhoods."

"A person would be well advised to stay on her good side, I take it."

Father Ferrua smiled. "At least on the good side of the *orixas*. Mae Janaina speaks through the spirits."

11

A Chicken for Exu

✳

Father Ferrua and Hanna Doherty watched with interest, as the Bahians unloaded from the back of a decrepit old truck. A tall, statuesque woman rose grandly above her companions, looking serenely at the *Barco Igaranha*.

Hanna assumed this was Mae Janaina. She was six-five if she was an inch, with a great butt and boobs that moved like sleek, frisky colts under her white dress. Hanna could see perfectly well that there was not a hint of cellulite on her anywhere. She had a long neck; her skin was blacker than black, seemingly reflecting no light whatsoever; she had high, broad, almost Asian-looking cheekbones; she wore a red bandanna on her head.

Around her neck she wore a cluster of baubles and doodads.

She waited as her gear was unloaded. Her chin was up, her back straight.

She looked at the crew and passengers with mirrored sunglasses.

"What's that thing around her neck?" Hanna asked.

Father Ferrua said, "That's called a *balangandan.* It has the *figa* of the ancient Romans, the Jewish Star of David, the symbolic fish of Christianity—in this case represented in the shape of Father Machado's catfish—a dove of peace, African horns to protect against the evil eye, *candomblé* drums, keys, and the four-leaf clover of European sorcery."

A second woman, also impressive but no Mae Janaina, and a shy, lovely girl no more than thirteen or fourteen, gathered behind the tall one. Their dresses were identical to hers, but they wore white bandannas, not red. A man in a white trousers and scarlet shirt appeared to be the fourth traveler.

When their gear was unloaded, Mae Janaina began leading a procession toward the boat. Well-wishers, maybe two dozen believers, bore the travelers' bags, hammocks, mosquito nets, a tall drum, a squat square drum, a little round drum, a cardboard box, a lidded basket, a small wooden cage, and a metal bucket.

The procession stopped and Mae Janaina waited as the young girl stood ready with the bucket.

Mae Janaina was given a newspaper and a paper bag.

The second woman in white took a small wooden bell, which she held high and struck with a rod. Owing to the bell's odd shape, the report was high-pitched, quivering, and spooky:

Toook-toook! Toook! Toook-Toook! Toook-toook!

Hanna said, "Father Ferrua, you know about *candomblé*. Can you tell us what's going on?"

Father Ferrua said, "I suppose you would call this a form of *candomblé* bon voyage. The woman striking the bell is most likely Mae Janaina's assistant and heir apparent, Mae Pequena. She's using the bell to get the attention of the *orixa,* or spirit, of Exu, who in Christian terms would be the devil. He's also a go-between, the messenger who delivers human prayers to the spirit world. He opens and closes gates. This is why all sacrifices are offered to him first. Cocks' blood and entrails are offered to him at the doorsteps of every house, also in the main square of every village or at its approaches and at crossroads."

Toook! Toook-toook! Toook! Toook-Toook!

The *yalorixa* sat cross-legged, adjusting her skirt as she did, and began folding the newspaper in her lap. Three of her well-wishers gathered with the three drums, which were painted with part-animal/part-human figures and bright dabs and swirls of reds, greens, and yellows.

Father Ferrua said, "The square drum is called an *adufo.*

The man on the big bass is the *alabe-huntor.* He'll probably do the singing if there is any."

Toook! Toook-toook! Toook! Toook-toook!

The drummers joined in with rhythmic patter.

The ensemble got into it; the Bahians moved to the rhythm of the drums. The man in the red shirt opened one of the cages and retrieved a black rooster and tucked its head under its wing. The chicken relaxed in his grip.

Bodan was forward with Hans and Lenny, having volunteered to help the Bahians get settled in.

"A black chicken! This is to be a *pade,* then, a sacrifice to Exu. The man in the red shirt must be a *babalaô,* or male diviner. In the *macumba* sects around Rio, a priest or priestess might be hired to make a *despacho* against a rival politician or football club. The giving of *despacho* through the use of dolls is a debased outgrowth of Bantu, rather than Yoruba, origin. In Bahia it's found among *canboclo candomblés* such as Mae Janaina's, meaning other religions are mixed in."

"Dolls and pins stuff," Hanna said.

"A good *yalorixa* can let an *orixa* enter her body and in the form of this spirit she can travel the night wind and enter your body and steal your soul. Mae Janaina's *despacho* is the most feared in Brazil. If you believed the stories about her, I can't imagine you'd want to be on the same riverboat with her." Father Ferrua looked contemplative. "She's said to possess the most formidable *despacho* of any *yalorixa* in memory."

When Mae Janaina completed folding the newspaper, what she had was a paper boat.

"I think the cage contains guinea pigs, by the way, which means the young girl must be an *abian,* a novice who is undergoing her training. One four-legged animal must be sacrificed to her *orixa* each day for seven years, a long and expensive training."

The *babalaô* offered the rooster's neck to the *yalorixa,*

which Mae Janaina accepted—all the while moving her body to the drums.

The rooster, now awake, began to struggle.

She took a small knife and held it high, blade up.

She walked toward the boat, holding the jerking bird by the feet. She looked up at the passengers and Hans and Lenny.

She held the bird over the water at the stern.

She walked back to the paper boat. She turned. With a neat twist of the knife, she severed the bird's neck.

Mae Janaina aimed the squirting blood at the paper boat, lashing it with red.

Father Ferrua said, "Exu's a mischievous god. He likes to play pranks and tricks. He'll make trouble between friends or create havoc in meetings, but helps those who feed and respect him. He's a patron of magicians."

The initiate gave Mae Janaina the metal bucket and the *yalorixa,* dancing, moving to the rhythm of the drums, went to the water. She threw the bucket over the edge of the dock.

She pulled a full bucket of water up with the plastic rope and used both hands to balance it on top of her head. Her sweating face was ecstatic. Her head was upright and unmoving beneath the load of water, but her body moved in drumbeat fluid shimmers.

Mae Pequena mopped Mae Janaina's face with a hand towel.

Mae Janaina, at last reaching the paper boat, turned and used the bucket of water on her head to slosh the boat in the direction of the river. That done, she returned to the edge of the dock for more water.

Father Ferrua said, "Did you know, Hanna, that if you add the entire weight of all the water borne by women on this planet each day, they carry more foot pounds of sheer burden than all other load-bearing chores combined? I say again, more weight in water each day than the total of all other burdens lifted by human muscle."

"They do?"

"More accumulated weight in water than all the boxes lifted, bags moved, and wood stacked," Father Ferrua said.

"You're talking about water carried in jugs and pots. Water carried on women's heads and shoulders. Surely you don't mean that's all the water they carry, Father?"

He looked surprised.

"When she's pregnant, a woman carries a couple of pounds of extra water in her amniotic fluid, a couple of pounds in her blood, and two or three pounds in her body tissue. A pregnant woman's like a tankard, if you think about it. And in the first month of her pregnancy the human embryo looks precisely like a fish."

"A woman with a fish in her belly," Bodan said.

"Aquarium belly is just about it," Hanna said. "I've long had an interest in this, as it happens. Do you know, Father Ferrua, that in hours and days evolution is replayed in miniature inside this fluid? The fish begins to change. In a fish embryo the gill arches become gills. In a human embryo, the gill arches become the beginnings of a jaw, tongue, and larynx. Until a month is up, the embryo could be a chicken, a rabbit, or a human. Anyway, I got to wondering once just how much water the women of the world carry around inside them."

"What's the answer to that one?" Bodan asked.

"I figured out a rough calculation once. If you take current population growth times seven pounds of water it comes out to more than 550 million pounds a year; that's more than 140 million gallons. Women carry water on their heads and in their bellies and there's no calculating the tears of their burden of caring. You men hardly give a damn. How many pounds of water do women shed in tears annually, do you suppose? How many gallons were required to wash away all the accumulated hurt?"

With one last bucket of water, Mae Janaina sloshed the

paper boat into the Amazon. She turned her back on it and the ceremony was finished. The Bahians were ready to board.

12

A RUMOR OF BOCAGRANDES

❋

Hans Weckert, looking slightly worried, asked the passengers to gather on the observation deck for a brief word before the *Barco Igaranha* started across the Pará River for the southern shoreline of Marajó Island.

Nicholas Bodan helped Lenny Humphries raise the table that folded flush to the deck atop the aft cabin. The tabletop —surrounded by benches on three sides—was lifted from the deck by a recessed handle at either end. The handle wells were covered by hinged lids, and judging by a smaller, matching set of lids, this was actually two tables in one.

Humphries chose the larger table. He and Bodan each pulled a lid back, grabbed a handle, and pulled; sturdy legs followed, locked reassuringly into place by large stainless steel hinges. These were legs that admitted of no wobble.

"What a table!" Hanna said.

Weckert said, "No, two tables in one. The *Barco's* a cleverly designed boat. If you look underneath you'll see the legs of the smaller table tucked up under there. There'll be times when you'll want to move around a bit and still have a table for cold beer and some snacks."

Weckert and Humphries had bottles of Brazilian champagne in buckets of ice when Mae Janaina and her three companions arrived from their quarters atop the forward cabin.

Adjusting his spectacles, Weckert first spoke to Mae Janaina and her company in Portuguese, then addressed the rest of the company in English. "First of all, let me say that Lenny and I sincerely welcome you all aboard the *Barco Igaranha.* Before we drink a toast we have to decide whether we want to push off tonight as planned or risk waiting a couple of days. The weather people are predicting an Atlantic storm due here in Belém in ten hours. That should give us more than enough time to get to the protection of Marajó's lee. From there we go west upstream to the Breves Strait, which will take us to the main body of the Amazon.

"The *Barco Igaranha* is a riverboat, remember; she has a shallow draft and virtually no keel, so she can scoot if she has to, but there's always a chance she could turtle if we let her get caught sideways in a hard wind. Riverboats have a history of doing that in storms this close to the Atlantic."

Father Ferrua said, "Perhaps you should also remind your passengers that those boats are almost always found to have been overloaded and top-heavy. And most of them are double- or triple-deckers rather than the single deck of this boat. She seems like a well-designed boat to me."

"I think she is too, thank you, Father Ferrua. Lenny and I did have the engine overhauled for the trip. The alternative is taking a chance on a two- or three-day wait in Belém; it's courting disaster to deliberately sail into one of these storms. Lenny and I value our boat too much to attempt that, not to mention our skins. Hanna?"

"From my experience if there isn't one storm out there, there'll be another on its way. If we wanted to avoid all storms we'd never leave dock. When you see your chance go for it. I say we push off as planned and hightail it across the Pará."

"I agree," said Ferrua.

"Let's see what the next chapter is!" Bodan said.

João Kobayashi seemed momentarily concerned, perhaps for his cargo, then nodded his head in agreement.

Weckert said, "Good. Lenny and I have a schedule worked out where we'll push off at six o'clock every morn-

ing. I'll take the first four-hour shift so Lenny can fix breakfast, which he'll serve here on the observation deck at ten.
Lenny will take the helm from ten o'clock until two. I'll
take over from two until six o'clock, while Lenny serves his
grand meal of the day at four, after which he'll retake the
helm from six until ten while I fix and serve a light supper.
We'll drop anchor and roll down the mosquito nets at ten
o'clock.''

"But tonight's an exception, I take it," Father Ferrua
said.

"We won't stop tonight until we're in the shelter of
Marajó. Incidentally, if any of you are interested in learning
how to pilot the boat, most of the time we'll be staying
close to shore where the current's less swift, so there's no
trick to navigation. If you're able to take a turn at the helm
now and then, Lenny and I'll have more time to fix you
some decent meals.''

"Well, that's an incentive. I'd like to learn," Hanna said.

Senhor Kobayashi said nothing.

"Mr. Bodan?" Weckert asked.

"Oh sure, of course. Sounds like fun.''

Father Ferrua licked his lips apprehensively. "I take it
clerics aren't forbidden from steering the vessel.''

"Not at all, Father. Not at all," Weckert said. He was
pleased. "Good, then. Lenny and I will take turns showing
you how everything works tomorrow. Now then, as to our
schedule. When we reach the shelter of Marajó sometime
early tomorrow morning we will turn upstream and get as
far west as we can before the storm hits. We'll stop for a
short rest later in the morning, then push on. On the fifth
day we'll be stopping at Santarém, where Lenny and I will
deliver our AmeRiBurger shipment for Rancho Olivieres.

"Finally, Mae Janaina asks our indulgence in the matter
of Obatala's fish. She says she knows that we don't believe
in *candomblé,* but she asks for our understanding and patience for the irregularly spaced drum calls we'll be hearing
over the next four nights.'' Weckert consulted with Mae

Janaina. "She says whether you find the fish, begging your pardon, Father Ferrua, or whether a fortune hunter finds it, or even if it remains lost, the decision is in Obatala's hands, not ours or hers. She says she needs four nights, beginning tonight, to properly consult with Obatala. She and her companions will disembark on the fifth day at a village a couple of hours east of Santarém, where her sister lives. Does anyone have any objections? Father Ferrua?"

"I have no objection at all," Ferrua said. "She should certainly perform all the *candomblé* rituals as may please and reassure her."

"Fine," Weckert said. "The day after our Santarém stop, we have an opportunity to visit the Ch, the folks who worship leeches. I've had lobbying for this one from Nicholas and Hanna, also from Father Ferrua. We'll have to spend the night but it should be worth it." Weckert waited for objections. "Good, we'll visit the Ch, then. Lenny and I have traded with them; they like us and will treat us well.

"The day following our visit to the Ch, we'll be arriving in Manaus and there we'll find out whether they'll let us navigate the Purus as we have planned. There've been unsettling rumors on the river about a leviathan catfish named Bocagrande, which you may have heard about. But I think Lenny should be the one to tell you about Bocagrandes. He's more of a catfish man than I am. Even if the government allows us to proceed, it may be prudent for us to go up the Madeira instead. If you like, you can travel west by bus from Pôrto Velho to the strike at Loucofilho."

Hanna said, "I think you should give Lenny the go-ahead, Hans. I say we open the champagne, kick back, and enjoy the sunset. We'll beat the weather tonight and worry about Bocagrandes later."

Weckert spoke briefly to Mae Janaina in Portuguese and she too agreed. They would push off for Marajó.

Weckert and Humphries opened the champagne and they all toasted the successful voyage of the *Barco Igaranha.*

After receiving the go-ahead from Weckert on the intercom, Lenny Humphries set the engine into an all-slow *mmmwam-mmmwam-mmmwam,* screw in reverse, and eased the *Barco Igaranha* from the dock.

When the boat was moving forward, engine increased to a leisurely *mwam-mwam-mwam* as he piloted the boat out of the Bay of Guajara.

Weckert, checking the harbor traffic on both sides, spoke into the intercom again. "I think we're clear now, Lenny. You can start winding her out if you want."

Lenny Humphries's reply was so deep and reverberating it made everybody grin. "Ayyye, ayyye, skippperrr, bound nor' by nor'west for Marajó. You folks have a good time back there now, drink a little champagne for me."

Humphries jacked the engine up to a galloping *mom-mom-mom-mom,* and the hull seemed to rise on the water.

13

THE EVOLUTION OF CATFISH

❋

With Hans Weckert pushing the engine in a hard-driving *ma-ma-ma-ma-ma* that vibrated the hull, the *Barco Igaranha* all but skipped across the surface of the Pará, which was flat save for little dapple waves—goose-bump shudders sent by skitters of wind—and save for the primal, roiling muscles of the river current.

The passengers on the cabin top drank iced tea and watched the twilight stroll of old sol through rain clouds ripped lean and thin across the sky: streaks of white, slabs of black, meadows of cool blue, orb of blazing orange, a warming blush on the surface of the water.

As the last orange edge of the sun disappeared below the horizon, the *babalaô,* sitting squat-legged on the bow with the three *candomblé* drums before him, gave the fat drum a hard thump, and then sat meditating.

The call to Obatala had begun.

Ten minutes later he gave the square drum two quick squats, followed by a knock on the little drum.

Lenny Humphries, bringing with him a quart of rum in each hand, joined the passengers aft as the *Barco Igaranha* pushed farther and farther into the broad expanse of the Pará—the shorelines of the river were invisible fore and aft. He poured himself a tall glass of rum over ice and settled back with his hand on his stout belly and his feet on the edge of the table.

He said, "Well, their drumming won't be too bad. It's not like they were playing in a rock band or something."

The passengers waited minutes that stretched with anticipation of the *babalaô*'s next call, and eventually it came. This time, three evenly placed strokes on the smallest drum.

In the dim glow of the running lights they could see the profile of the *babalaô* on the bow.

Bodan said, "Hans said you'd tell us about something called Bocagrande."

Humphries looked surprised. "He didn't tell you about Bocagrandes?"

"No, he said you know more about catfish."

"Left the chore to me, did he! There's leadership for you. Some captain." Humphries's voice rumbled up, volcanolike, from the deepest regions of his massive chest. "Bocagrande is the name which was given to rumors of the fish by early Spanish explorers and which has generally stuck. It literally means 'big mouth,' but the fish is known by a variety of Indian names as well. Most of them might be loosely translated as He Who Eats Everything. The latest reports are from the Purus; the fish in the Purus and in the Juruá, which is also fed by rain-forest upwellings as well as runoff from the Andes, are the least studied in Amazonia, so we never know what to make of a report until it's properly checked out.

"The Purus is the crookedest river in the world, a pilot's nightmare. Sometimes the forest thins a bit, and you think you can see through it to the other side, but you never know. There are times when the southern-flowing Purus is flanked by the northern-flowing Purus about fifty yards away. The number of islands makes things confusing, and if you go up the river far enough there are sandbars in the dry season."

Humphries refilled his glass of rum. "If the stories are true, the Bocagrande is a siluroid, that is, a catfish. Catfishes are among our oldest fishes. Most of them have some form of armor and they have naked bodies—by that I mean skin, not scales. And of course they have the familiar whiskers. In Amazonia there are several varieties of enormous catfish, including one that grows to fifteen feet long. There are minute parasite catfish that live in the gills of their larger brethren. One catfish can walk from pond to pond on its fin spines. There are catfish that can spend months living in dried mud until the next rain. There are catfish in the feeder streams in the Andes that use their mouths to work their way from stone to root in rapid water; they can even go up waterfalls. There are catfish that graze on algae in the water, and others are equipped to strain it out of mud. Some catfish eat insects. Some eat other fish. One variety of catfish, the Candiru, is said to be attracted to urine, and stories abound about the consequences of what happens to the unwary who relieve themselves in Amazonian streams."

Hanna Doherty said, "Stories about both sexes, I take it."

"Oh yes. Both sexes. Incidentally, there are reports of slaves bringing species of catfish with them from Africa. In fact, Father Machado used an African catfish as a model for Obatala's fish."

"That's right, he did," Ferrua said.

"From early reports, if they aren't hysterical nonsense, the Bocagrande, if it exists, is very likely an overgrown pimelodid, an unarmored catfish, of which there are two hundred fifty species in Amazonia. The *Pimelodidae* greatly resemble the *Bagridae* in Africa and Asia, which is the basic stock from which many other catfish families are derived. One of these, the colorful fish eater Sorubi, gets to be six to eight feet long. The *Brachyplatystoma* can grow to fifteen feet and there are stories about fishermen in canoes being pulled under.

"Reports that Bocagrandes are albino and blind aren't unusual either. There are documented accounts of catfish that have evolved at the bottom of deep springs or wells and so are colorless and can't see. The Bocagrande is said to have evolved in the bottoms of the great depths, the largest sinkhole in the Purus."

"Just what is it Bocagrandes are said to have done?" Hanna said.

Humphries cleared his throat. "The riverboat people back in Belém said riverboats have been disappearing on the Purus."

"What?"

"They're blaming it on Bocagrandes, but you have to realize rumors can get pretty wild on the river. We'll want to check the stories out for ourselves at Manaus."

"A catfish is pulling riverboats under now, not mere fishing boats?"

Humphries shrugged. "If the stories are true. We've got a week to go before Manaus, where we can sort fact and rumor. For example, we may be encountering the banjoman, a kind of catfish known by the noises it makes at night. They're widely distributed in this part of the world."

The passengers, contemplating the Bocagrande and its many catfish cousins and rocked by the gentle motion of the boat plunging forward, watched the fading lights of Belém. With the coming of dusk, the river changed colors. The quality of yellow went first, followed by the brown, as the cold grays of night water took over.

The reassuring lights of Belém faded until they were pinpoints and then were gone.

Then the water ceased to have any color at all; it was a

great black void and the passengers of the *Barco Igaranha* were alone, pushed off like Thor Heyerdahl.

There was a heavy cloud cover overhead, so there was no moon, no stars. Nothing. No thing.

The *Barco Igaranha,* which had been as white as a bridal veil in the full sun, now traveled spiritlike in the blackness, a hard-driving ghost vessel slipping *ma-ma-ma-ma-ma* through river smells and night bugs patrolling the primal waters of istus and Bocagrandes, far, far from the comforts of shore.

On the bow, Mae Janaina, who had taken over from the *babalaô,* cuffed the small drum twice and the fat drum once and waited for Obatala's reply.

Above the aft cabin Nicholas Bodan lay slung in his hammock, feeling the warm air slide by, remembering the faraway year when he was eighteen years old and worked as deckhand for Tidewater-Shaver on the Columbia River, saving money for school.

Twenty days on, ten days off; usually oil upstream and wheat down.

While he hadn't stayed on the barges long enough to be any kind of veteran, he worked long enough to experience the poetry of four seasons on the water. He remembered moving through the water in a snowstorm, the shores invisible on either side. In his mind's eye he once again plowed through the darkened water late at night watching the dappled lights of passing towns and the beacons of isolated farmhouses.

The winds were especially memorable. In the summer there was the hot east wind blowing up the Columbia River gorge, and in the winter, the hard, cold winds blowing down from Canada and across the high plateau of eastern Washington. And once in a while, in late February or early March, a warming Chinook would race across the snow, melting it literally in minutes. Bodan could not imagine anyone forgetting the embrace of a Chinook.

If it was not the wind that had fascinated him, it was the tan bluffs rising from the river east of the Cascade Mountains, those bluffs looking like women's butts lined up side by side. Just east of the Columbia River gorge, the wonderful rows of lovely earthen butts flanked both sides of the river for almost eighty miles. Bodan could not imagine any sexier passage on the planet.

The Columbia River was a living presence for Bodan; he had grown up with it and identified with it and its seasons as people do home. When he worked for Tidewater, there had been one hydroelectric dam, Bonneville, between his hometown and the sea. Now there were four: McNary, John Day, The Dalles, and the great Bonneville of which even Woody Guthrie sang the praises in 1936.

The Columbia might have rolled on in 1936, but forty years later it was a geographic corpse.

Windsurfers enjoyed the corpse, it was true, and new kinds of fish—shad and pike, not dishonorable fish, but not the original either—had been introduced to the parts of its body constricted by hydroelectric dams.

Proud as he was of the Columbia, Bodan had to admit it was nothing, a piss-ant trickle, a creek, a joke compared to the astonishing Amazon, whose turn, inevitably, he suspected, was next.

Lying there, Bodan thought of his daughter, his only child, who was a sophomore at Dartmouth College. He felt he had been run over by one slightly crazed woman, *ka-whack,* like a passing truck and was cheerfully lied to by a second. Still he had endured, never quit, never gave up, and through it all his daughter, who was a female version of himself as far as he could see, had been his special fan, tolerant of his faults and appreciative of his generosity.

When he had it, she got hers; when he was broke, she didn't. She was his biggest fan, nonstop.

Thus, thinking of his daughter, Nicholas Bodan fell asleep on his first night aboard the *Barco Igaranha.*

14

AND BE LED BY THE

YELLOW-BROWN WATERS

✳

Hanna Doherty awoke suddenly but didn't know why. The boat was rolling. The engine was silent. She heard a man mumbling, then Humphries swearing. Something was wrong. She hopped off her bunk and slipped into jeans and a blouse. She pulled back the canopy of the companionway but quickly shut it again when she heard the wind.

She went back to her cabin and put on a jacket. She slipped through the dark cabin and up the companionway again. She stepped out on deck and found Nicholas Bodan.

"I woke up and the engine was stopped," he said.

"What is it? What time is it?"

"One o'clock."

The *Barco Igaranha* wallowed in heavy waves, plumes of spray shooting off her rails.

Weckert and Humphries were down with the engine, talking, swearing.

"When I get my hands on that bloody little Brazilian mechanic you can bleeding bet I'm going to show him a bleeding thing or two about how to take something apart and put it back together," Humphries muttered. "Sod must have shit in the engine to foul it up like this."

Hanna followed Bodan down the short flight of stairs into the cargo hold, where Mae Janaina and her followers had gathered to get in out of the wind, watching the drama taking place around the *Barco*'s gasohol engine. Humphries, squatting by the engine, a dim light bulb dangling above his head, examined a length of copper tubing. He blew down it.

Humphries's shoulders slumped. "Nothing in there. Our best shot. Hans, that's not it either. My bleeding arse."

Weckert—seeing Bodan and Hanna grabbing for support as the *Barco* plunged into another trough—said, "We've got a couple of problems here, I'm afraid."

Humphries began replacing the length of tube with an open-end wrench. "We're in a bloody king-sized tub of manure without any bleeding water wings, if you'll pardon my frankness, ma'am." Humphries's ordinarily low, booming voice had somehow moved an incredible register lower and vibrated as though he were electrified, plugged in.

Weckert said, "Hanna, the problem is we've got ourselves some blocked fuel somewhere. Remember me telling you that I had the engine overhauled before the trip? Well, the gentlemen who . . ."

"Bloody sods," Humphries said.

"The short of it is that the mechanics apparently put it back together wrong and the fuel is blocked. That means our generator's down too, so the only electricity we have left is in our batteries." Weckert tapped the light bulb with his finger.

"If it were just the mechanic's brains in the line, the gasohol would go right around it, no problem," Humphries said. He braced his stout body against the roll of a storm wave. "I thought that was it, Hans. I really did. I'm sorry."

Weckert said, "Our second problem is that the weather people were a full seven hours off on the ETA of this storm."

"Is it going to get worse?" Hanna asked.

"It's a sea storm blown in from the Atlantic. We're not into the hard part either. This is just the advance fun. A sudden shift in the storm, they're saying on the radio." Weckert bit his lip anxiously.

"They fucked up is what they did," Humphries said.

"Have you told anybody what's happened?" Hanna asked.

"Oh yes, I radioed a mayday, but Belém's three hours behind us and we could be into it any minute. Hanna, would you please go wake everybody in your cabin, and help Nicholas dig out the life jackets, please. I want everyone in a life preserver. They're in a box by the lifeboat."

Hanna followed Bodan up the stairs on his way to his life preserver chores. Holding on to the rail, rain blowing hard in his face, he eased his way up the port rail. While he fumbled with the latch on the storage locker, the storm descended on the *Barco Igaranha* with a fury.

The boat rose on a storm wave and plunged bow first into a trough, and a tremendous wave washed across the deck. Bodan gripped the rail hard to keep from being washed overboard. Hanna ducked down the companionway only to find that everybody was up and stirring. She retreated to help Nicholas with the life jackets.

From forward, she heard two sharp drumbeats. She looked and there, head bowed, lashed to the railing, was Mae Pequena with her legs wrapped around the heaviest drum.

"They're still calling Obatala," Bodan said.

From behind her, she heard the quivering *toook-toook* of the *agogó* bell.

When she got back to the hold, head turned against the driving rain and arms looped round wads of life preservers, she tossed the preservers below and turned to see Mae Janaina. She stood on the deck between the hold and the forward cabin, wet dress plastered against her awesome figure, wielding a hot stick on the *agogó*.

She faced straight into the wind, legs spread wide and braced against the pitching and swaying of the deck. She held the bell with her left hand and struck it with her right. She chanted, shouted a song into the storm, challenging the storm with her song, attacking it.

Bracing her legs, Hanna yelled, "Yes! Yes! Yes!"

Mae Janaina knew Hanna was with her but she was also in a trance, giving it her all.

Bodan joined Hanna in cheering Mae Janaina on. Even Kobayashi had his fist doubled in support. Father Ferrua was downstairs praying.

Mae Janaina hung in there, duking it out with Exu or whatever errant spirit had gotten the *Barco* into this fix.

The boat plunged into another trough; water rushed across the decks and into the hold, taking Mae Janaina by surprise. She grabbed for support with her stick hand but missed, her head whacking the edge of the companionway to the forward cabin. She sat on the wet deck hardly conscious.

Hanna looked down at Mae Janaina, who was nearly knocked out. Still stunned, she retreated to the hold, the side of her face bleeding from a bruise.

Hanna took Mae Janaina's place on the deck, facing squarely into the wind, feeling the rain whip against her face. As hard as she could and with all the emotion she could muster she winged it *a cappella.*

> *"Last night as I lay by the river*
> *And looked up at the stars in the sky*
> *I wondered if ever a woman*
> *Would travel up that sweet by and by."*

"All right, DeeDee!" Bodan shouted from below. "Give it to 'em, lady! Sing to the bastards."

> *"Roll on, roll on;*
> *Roll on, little Barco, roll on.*
> *Roll on, roll on;*
> *Roll on, little Barco, roll on."*

Mae Janaina, sitting spraddle-legged, braced now by Mae Pequena, was coming round. She saw Hanna singing and grinned.

She got on her feet again and faced the wind and joined Hanna, whacking her *agogó* bell as Hanna sang.

> *"To travel up to those bright mystic forests*
> *Up there in green foliage to lie*
> *And be led by the yellow-brown waters*
> *To the home in the sweet by and by."*

Father Ferrua, who had emerged from the cabin, apparently having exhausted Christian remedies, joined in. "Yes, yes, sing, do sing, Hanna."

> *"I often look upward and wonder*
> *If the green forests will seem half so fair,*
> *If ever the wrong river I have taken*
> *Will fail to get me over there."*

The engine coughed once. Hanna looked at Mae Janaina, who nodded, still striking the *agogó*.

"Yes!" Bodan cried.

> *"Oh, bring back, bring back,*
> *Bring back my Barco to me, to me."*

The engine coughed again. Mae Janaina gave Hanna a clenched fist for support.

"Don't stop," Bodan yelled.

> *"Oh, bring back, bring back,*
> *Bring back my Barco to me, to me."*

Another cough. Mae Janaina really banged her magic bell.

"Yes. Sing to it, DeeDee," Bodan said. "Sing real sweet to that engine." He whacked an imaginary bell to encourage Mae Janaina.

> *"They say there'll be a great voyage . . ."*

Hanna Doherty didn't have to continue. She got her answer.

The engine rumbled to life with a solid, healthy *mmm-*

wab-mmmwab-mmmwab, which was met with a whoop and a bellow from Humphries and celebratory shouting from bow to stern.

The *Barco Igaranha* was to survive the storm.

Weckert scrambled through the forward cabin to the bridge with Humphries bellowing deeply, "We've got it! We've got it! We've got it! Good and solid. Put her straight into the wind, Hans! Straight into the wind!"

They reached the lee of Marajó Island at 4 A.M., and after a short nap Nicholas Bodan awoke wondering if Mae Janaina and her companions were still calling Obatala, and was finally rewarded with a single blow on the square drum. They were. Then he fell asleep again, awakened an hour later by the faint tapping coming from somewhere on the deck above.

He opened his cabin window. An orange rim of sun was rising above the tropical trees of Marajó Island.

He listened for the *candomblé* drums, but there was nothing.

Tap, tap, tap.

Tap, tap, tap.

He listened to the tapping, which at first seemed to be coming from the stern of the boat. This was puzzling. If the tapping were coming from midships, it could conceivably be Lenny Humphries working on the balky engine. Bodan fell back on his bed, listening, remembering Hanna's version of "The Cowboy's Dream," and composed a little poem of his own—perhaps more in line with Edgar Allan Poe.

> *As I lie back exhausted from the storm,*
> *Risen from a gentle slumber,*
> *I hear a little tapping on the deck above,*
> *A little tapping, nothing dumber.*

As I lie back exhausted from the storm,
Risen from a gentle slumber,
I want to tap the tapper on the head
With a little piece of lumber.

As though he had heard Bodan, the determined tapper responded:

Tap, tap, tap.
Tap, tap, tap.

Bodan slipped out of bed and into his jeans. He slid back the curtain to his berth. Senhor Kobayashi was still in bed. Father Ferrua was not. The curtain was back on his berth and his bed was neatly made. As Bodan emerged from the deck of the companionway, he heard the sound of wrench against metal. Lenny Humphries was below working on the engine.

The tapper, who was on the stern, continued his work: *tap, tap, tap.*

Bodan hopped up the stairs to the observation deck: the tapper, Father Ferrua, was on his hands and knees systematically sounding the decking of the fantail. He straightened on his knees, still holding his spoon.

"Oh, I hope I didn't wake you, Mr. Bodan."

"No, no, Father. I forgot my sleeping mask and unless I wear it the sun always wakes me up. My mind's freshest then and that's when I get my writing done."

"Dr. Humphries has a large pot of coffee on the stove in the galley. He says we're welcome to help ourselves. I believe Captain Weckert went into town to see if he can't get something for Dr. Humphries to use as a fuel filter."

"Well, I think I'll go get a cup. Would you like me to bring you one, Father?"

Father Ferrua stood, putting his spoon in his pocket. "I'm afraid I really did wake you. I apologize. I'm just like you; I find it difficult to sleep in the morning. Also I was excited about the prospect of finding Obatala's fish."

"If you're that thorough you'll find it if it's here."

"It's here somewhere, you can be sure. I'll sound every inch of the *Barco Igaranha* before I'm through, Mr. Bodan. I won't let any portion of her hull or gear go untested. It's merely a matter of finding it, nothing more." Father Ferrua followed Bodan around the hold.

Bodan paused, looking down at Humphries, who worked with an empty cup at his side. "Mr. Humphries, we're going below for coffee. Would you like a fresh cup?"

"Indeed I would, Nicholas, thank you."

Bodan, stepping through Weckert's studio, said, "How can you be so certain the fish is aboard this riverboat, Father? I'm afraid I don't understand."

"First, we know that Padim stole the fish, Mr. Bodan. We know that. We know, to their everlasting shame, that he was protected by the police. This fish is priceless. An ordinary thief doesn't steal a fish he can't sell. Padim stole for different reasons; he was, as the Spanish say, an *aficionado* of fish, a fancier."

Bodan understood Ferrua's argument. There were some books that collectors wanted to own that had nothing to do with the larger market for books. These were books that people simply wanted to own for private reasons; Bodan knew of a man in Oakland, a former eagle scout, who collected books written by former eagle scouts.

Bodan, having reached the galley, found cups and poured coffee from a pot on the gas stove.

"Obatala's fish belongs to the church, Mr. Bodan, and we'll have it back, you can be sure of that. I will see to it. God does work in mysterious ways, I suppose. Listen, I believe Captain Weckert is back from his errands."

15

THE RUBIES OF RUBIU

※

After the *Barco Igaranha* had passed the Breves Strait—the narrows, as it was referred to locally, according to Lenny Humphries—Hans Weckert kept the boat tight along the southern shoreline of the broad Amazon; shortly after noon they passed by a crude hand-painted sign above a small dock in front of what looked like an abandoned lumbermill. The word *Loucofilho* was prominent in the message.

"What's that say?" Hanna Doherty asked as they passed by.

Father Ferrua smiled. "It's asking the river traffic why go all the way to Loucofilho when there is a mountain of rubies at Rubiu. They're offering a one-hour ride to the rubies at a reasonable rate."

Hanna, looking back at the dock and the sign, said, "Why don't we go there? Have you ever heard of a place called Rubiu?"

Ferrua said, "I haven't, but that doesn't mean it isn't possible. They're constantly making mineral strikes in the interior. Have you heard anything about there being rubies at Rubiu, Dr. Humphries?"

Humphries bunched his face, trying to remember. "I've heard the name somewhere. It's possible. Do you want me to ask Hans to check it out?"

"Sure," Bodan said.

"I agree," Hanna added quickly.

Humphries, grinning, flipped on the intercom to the bridge. "Our passengers are all curious about those rubies advertised back there, Hans. Do you suppose we could take a few minutes to check it out?"

"Of course," said Hans, and he eased back on the power

and let the current carry the *Barco* down the shoreline. Weckert eased the boat next to a small dock by the sign and Humphries, his great belly no obstacle at all, was quite the riverboat *danceur* as he hopped lightly ashore, bowline in hand. "We're in luck, I think there's somebody here," he called back over his shoulder.

An old man and his companion, barefoot and in his late teens or early twenties, walked very slowly toward the boat, crossing a compound that had long since surrendered to weeds. They walked slowly because the old man had stiff joints and could barely move.

Weckert and Lenny Humphries held the powwow in thigh-deep weeds by the edge of the dock, their conversation clear to Father Ferrua and Senhor Kobayashi, who listened with Hanna and Bodan on the cabin top.

Weckert and the old man exchanged greetings and introductions in Portuguese. Everybody shook hands; the old man, turning one ear toward Weckert, told him about the rubies of Rubiu in high-pitched, squawking Portuguese.

"What did he say?" Hanna said.

Weckert said, "He said last summer they discovered a mountain of rubies at a place called Rubiu, which is not far from here. He says Loucofilho is too famous; there are too many people there. He said they have a system at Rubiu where you pay the owners by the minute of gathering rubies. He says you put up a deposit and they give you a piece of paper with the time written on it and they calculate your tab when you come out. He says the roads aren't the best, but it isn't far from here—fifty to sixty minutes, he says. He says his nephew Antonio can take us there in his Volkswagen bus, but he'll need a few minutes to unpack a load of wood and bolt the seats back in."

Bodan said, "Does he get a lot of business with his sign?"

Weckert grinned. "I asked him that and he said we'll be his first customers."

"I say we take him up on it," said Bodan.

Hanna said, "Me too."

There being no objections, Weckert told the old man yes, which pleased both him and Antonio, who shook everybody's hand again and loped off to a pale blue VW bus parked behind the abandoned mill, and fired it up.

Antonio returned in something less than five minutes with seats bolted in place and they climbed aboard—minus Lenny Humphries, who stayed at the boat to do chores, and the Bahians, who preferred to concentrate on the *orixas* although the call to Obatala could only be made at night.

Antonio drove them to a small café next to gasohol pumps so he could service the Volkswagen for the trip. No breeze stirred, but the afternoon rain was due soon, and they were grateful the concrete slab had a roof but no walls. They sat on rickety chairs and drank Brama Chopp as a barefooted boy, his eye on the gathering clouds, helped Antonio with the van.

The boy filled the tanks and used a stub of two-by-four to knock off the chunks of red mud that had collected under the tire wells. This labor was due to pride rather than optimism, because the last bank of clouds had turned the road into two parallel streams of watery mud.

Antonio did his best to affect an air of an experienced and responsible man-in-charge; he eased the bus from the front of the café and gasohol pump, and the travelers were on their way. As the bus struck the first pothole with a thump, it began raining again.

Father Ferrua said, "Captain Weckert, that old man back there told you when they first found the rubies at Rubiu they thought they had found XuXu, but I couldn't hear all of his story. Did he have a XuXu report?"

Weckert said, "Surely you don't believe those stories, Father Ferrua?"

"XuXu?" Bodan said.

Ferrua said, "We're talking about a lost colony of evolutionists that is said to exist isolated somewhere in Amazonia supported by a mother lode of minerals of some kind."

Weckert turned from his seat up front. "Father Ferrua! XuXu's a myth, a joke, everybody knows that."

Ferrua smiled. "I'm not so sure."

"I'd like to hear the stories," Hanna said.

"Me too," Bodan added quickly.

Weckert shook his head as Antonio slowed for a wash-out.

Father Ferrua said, "It was raining like this the day when a blind man told me about the geographer of XuXu, which is what made a believer out of me. We were on the train going south to Pôrto Alegre and he told his story with such obvious sincerity and feeling that I knew here that he was telling the truth." Ferrua placed the palm of his hand over his heart. "Since then I've never ignored a report of XuXu, never. Some of the claims seem pretty far out, I agree, but I'm convinced that XuXu's out there somewhere."

Father Ferrua paused in his narrative as Antonio gunned the engine and the bus fishtailed out of the washout. As it settled into the ruts again, Ferrua continued.

"The old man told me he was born in XuXu, but was taken downriver to Belém when he was four or five years old and sent to a school for the blind in Rio, his fees paid by an unknown benefactor. He said he remembered clearly that nobody understood what he was saying; he had to learn Portuguese from scratch. This was doubly hard since he couldn't see. Not only is there a XuXu, he says, but barring scourge or pestilence, it should be a thriving community to this day.

"He said the community dates to 1662, when an eccentric naturalist named Emilio Gonzalvo was hired to lead one of scores of cartographic expeditions up the tributaries of the Amazon. The problem then as today is that nobody knew for sure what is out there. Oh my."

The passengers bounced as Antonio rammed a deep pothole.

The road seemed constructed of potholes, ripples, and gullies. Antonio would have to make a choice: he could

creep at a civilized speed, easing the vehicle from one pothole and mud wallow to the next, inflicting noise and bore-
dom on the passengers; or he could put the accelerator to
the boards and get it over with, take a chance, go slam bam,
hard-core, hoping the axles and suspension held up.

Antonio chose momentarily to ease the bus carefully in
and out of the potholes, a ridiculous demonstration of responsibility and everybody knew it; the bus might as well
have been standing still.

Hanna said, "Please continue with XuXu, Father."

"The old man showed me photocopies of an account
purportedly written by an engineer contracted by Emilio
Gonzalvo to design a water and sewage system for a community supporting a diamond mine in the interior of the
Amazon. The blind man was on his way to see the original,
owned by a man in Montevideo."

Father Ferrua stopped, remembering. "The old man had
the document memorized and recited it as I read it. The
engineer related how the pay was generous for employees
in XuXu—Senhor Gonzalvo returned all profit from the
diamonds to the self-governing community—but the employees had to agree to spend one half of their day attend-
ing to their professional duties and the other half studying
XuXu, the official language of the community. They agreed
to speak only XuXu at work after six months and if they
wanted to stay past a year, they had to speak XuXu entirely.
They were free to go at any time.

"The voyage to XuXu began in Belém, but after a few
hours, the engineer was taken to a windowless cabin where
he stayed for the remainder of the trip. The secrecy didn't
seem extraordinary; mine owners were plagued by bandits
and pirates. The captain and his crew drank rum and played
dominoes with the engineer every evening. Sometimes at
night, he was taken for a walk on deck. He saw stars and the
gloomy profiles of a jungle shoreline. He saw no communi-
ties or settlements."

Father Ferrua, holding on to the edge of his seat, said,

"In about ten days the engineer thinks—he was never sure; he lost track of time—the boat arrived in XuXu, a community built around a spring-fed lake. He was pleasantly surprised. Emilio Gonzalvo had built a thriving community peopled by handsome Europeans, as well as Asians and prosperous-looking black men, both male and female.

"The engineer said the greatest charm of XuXu was that it was a fabulous lover's language; there were hundreds of evocative words expressing physical passion and romantic love. Gonzalvo's love of women was obvious throughout the language. For example, the geographer remembered one remarkable word, the XuXuian equivalent of the Portuguese *adeus,* the Spanish *adiós,* or the English *goodbye,* that was rendered differently according to sex and the speaker's intonation. To a man it could mean, 'Next time we'll go drink rum and talk about women,' and to a woman"—Father Ferrua, coloring, nodded to Hanna—"and to a woman —if you'll pardon me, Hanna, this was said to be a graceful sentiment in XuXu—it could mean 'Next time we meet I'd love to lick your, ah . . .' " Father Ferrua, looking uncomfortable, left the rest of the sentence to his listeners' imaginations. He shifting his rump, looking out through the rain.

It was obvious that Antonio's creeping was getting them nowhere. He looked at Weckert as though to acknowledge the consequences of the absurd attempt to deliver a smooth ride.

Hanna, reading Antonio's look, said, "Why don't we tell him to do it, Hans. Go for it. It will take hours at this speed."

Weckert said something to Antonio in Portuguese, and Antonio, turning to grin at Hanna, increased the rhythm of attack: *thump, whump, thump, whump!*

Weckert, who was holding tight to the handholds on the dashboard, said, "I told him you said for him to go ahead and do it Brazilian style."

Antonio, taking the American lady at her word, plunged the bus recklessly into a chasm of water and the bus emerged with the engine still blasting. The elated Antonio gave a shout and grin and a thumbs-up for victory.

"All right," said Weckert.

Bodan joined in. "Attaboy, Antonio, you rascal you. Let's drive this thing. The Amazon Grand Prix."

Antonio didn't understand a word of what Bodan said, but grinned and gave another victorious thumbs-up.

The suspension system absorbed a wince-inducing *whack, whack, whack* pounding, bouncing and slamming the passengers about as though they were rag dolls.

After a few more minutes of *whump-thumping* in and out of potholes, Antonio's face suddenly brightened, the reason for which he explained to Hans Weckert, who listened and turned to Hanna. "Antonio says he remembers this stretch on account of he drove over a boa along here once while delivering a van load of marijuana to Rubiu."

Antonio said something more.

Weckert grinned. "He adds that this was before he went into the army. He's not in the marijuana delivering business anymore."

The bus passed a small abandoned hut, then another.

"We're getting into the burbs," Bodan said.

They passed several more abandoned huts before Antonio, laughing, goosed the van for the final, triumphant curve before the rubies of Rubiu.

Then he stopped the van.

Before them was the end of a vast potato-shaped lake, traces of which spilled across a scar of red that cut into the forest apparently for some miles. To the right of the lake's tip lay what was left of a sprawling shantytown—a swampy wallow of rusted scraps of corrugated tin and broken boards sticking out of the mud, these the remnants of a hive of huts and shacks that had been trashed and salvaged and abandoned.

Antonio said something to Weckert.

Weckert said, "Antonio says he is astonished. He apologizes. When he was here three weeks ago, they were selling tickets just like his grandfather told us. He said he was told the strike would last a hundred years. The end of this lake was one end of the ridge that extended about six miles, which is probably how long this lake is."

Bodan blinked. "They eliminated the entire ridge?"

Weckert shrugged. "It looks that way. Antonio apologizes again and says by way of consolation, how would you like to see the fields where the Aguid Corporation lost fifty million dollars trying to grow rice? He said you might find it interesting. It's on the way back, a detour of just a few minutes, he says."

16

APHIDS, NEMATODES, AND

STINKBUGS GOT THIS RICE

✳

As they set forth on what Hans Weckert said would be a six-mile detour, he told the travelers they were going to experimental farms originally financed by a British-French-Dutch consortium which worked for two years until they were taken under by problems that had been predicted by agronomists before a tree had been cut or a match lit to clear the fields.

Father Ferrua, at the urging of Bodan and Hanna, continued his discussion of XuXu, picking up where he had left off, with XuXu's unusual language.

"Considering the charms of the women hired by Gonzalvo, the engineer—who already spoke Portuguese, Spanish, and a little Italian—undertook the language assignment with enthusiasm. It turned out to be an arduous if ultimately rewarding chore.

"In fact, it was a language unlike any other that the engineer had heard or read about. There were rules, but in

XuXu the whole point of rules was that there must be need-lessly complicated and unreasonable exceptions. There were exceptions to everything and exceptions to exceptions. Adjectives and adverbs took on new meanings depending on the nouns or verbs they modified. Any one rule of spelling held true for only a handful of the tens of thousands of entries in the XuXu dictionary. It seemed like everything had to be committed to memory by brute repetition; otherwise nothing made sense.

"The engineer persevered and once he understood the subtleties of XuXu's elusive logic, he realized that it was a perfectly lovely language, a tongue for poets and storytellers, however wasted on mechanics and shopkeepers. Emilio Gonzalvo hired editors to learn the language and publish a newspaper, periodicals, and books by XuXuian authors.

"The engineer, encouraged by the sensuous aspects of the language, immediately fell in love—unfortunately to a young woman attracted to another man. There was nothing in the comforting XuXu vocabulary that could console him. He began roaming on his days off and one weekend followed the narrow XuXu River from its source at the lake. He was shocked to find that only twenty miles away it emptied into a main tributary of the Amazon, a heavy, broad tropical river. In one of those oddities of nature, the channel of the XuXu passed through an overgrown swamp and into the larger river at such an angle as to be invisible to a casual riverboat observer."

Father Ferrua paused in his narrative.

Weckert said, "You really don't believe all that nonsense, do you?"

Ferrua shrugged. "I'm not sure. The engineer couldn't stand to live in XuXu without his love and so asked to leave. He was taken out in a windowless cabin just as he had entered, and after another week to ten days he was put ashore at a fishing village on Marajó Island. He returned to Rio, but nobody believed his story. He wrote passages in

XuXu and provided translations, but nothing about the language made sense to other people."

Antonio slowed the van.

A relieved Weckert said, "Ah, we're here."

They had come to the corner of a vast rectangular lake, clearly man-made—carved in straight lines and right angles out of the forest. The shallow water of the lake, which was filling with sediment, was held in place by low dikes that divided the lake into rectangles. Antonio drove the VW two miles down the water-covered road that flanked one levee, then turned right and went straight through the middle of the abandoned enterprise. The lake ended somewhere past the horizon.

Weckert said, "I remember reading about this. Aguid flattened a ten-mile-long by four-mile-wide stretch of forest to plant a miracle-variety long-grain rice developed in Asia. They had wonderful yields for just two years, then the problems set in."

"Problems?" asked Hanna.

"An old story, really. The rice suffered from iron poisoning which resulted in sludge collecting on its roots. Then the plants were hit by plant diseases: rice blast, brown leaf spot, and leaf scald. There were insects too: mites and aphids, nematodes, stinkbugs, and army worms. Aguid had had success with African feed grass in other areas, but by the time they gave up on the rice, it was too late for feed grass. Until they can figure out what to do with the fields, they're keeping the forest back with a perimeter of defoliants."

Antonio eased the bus through the six-inch-deep water that covered the road. He addressed the fording of the artificial lake as he had first confronted the potholes; he started off carefully, but little by little speeded up. The faster he went, the greater was the anxiety among his passengers.

Three miles into the lake, the bus stalled.

Antonio swore. He tried the ignition. The bus grunted healthily. He brightened. He tried the key again.

A good grunt.

Again.

A modest grunt.

The passengers looked stricken.

Hanna said, "Do we really want him to run the battery down?"

"Maybe we'll have to wade," Bodan said.

Unblinking, listening to the engine, concentrating, Antonio leaned on the key: *gruunnt.*

Antonio laughed nervously, then swallowed visibly.

Gruuuuunnnt, gruuuuuuuunnnnnnnnnnt. Antonio, swallowing visibly again, suddenly yanked his hand back as though the key were made of hot metal.

Antonio and Weckert stepped outside and waded to the rear to have a look at the engine and a little palaver. When they came back, Antonio checked his clipboard by way of demonstrating that he was still captain of this vehicle and was about to make a decision. He cleared his throat and spoke to Weckert.

Weckert said, "Antonio says we've gotten water in the electrical system somewhere and we'll have a short wait while it dries out. He has to make sure the engine is completely dry before he tries to start it again or he risks running the battery down." Weckert looked at the bank of dark clouds gathering in the west. "It's probably best to stay by the bus here. Looks like we'll be having even more rain. This, uh, is an unforeseen circumstance and we do apologize for the wait."

The travelers, mopping sweat from their foreheads, watched darkening clouds gather in the distance. A few seconds later they could see the rain ruffling the water as another bank of rain clouds swept their way.

Lightning flashed as the leading edge of the rain swooped across the stalled bus.

Hanna Doherty said, "What happened to the blind man you met on the train, Father Ferrua?"

A crack of thunder sent Father Ferrua to his feet. "Oh,

that was right on top of us. He agreed to meet me in a week to share his find. I went to his apartment in São Paulo only to find that he had been robbed and murdered. I received permission to search for the engineer's story, but the original document was nowhere to be found."

"Did you really think you would find anything?" Weckert said.

Hanna shook her dark hair. "I'll just bet Senhor Gonzalvo was clever enough to omit that lake and short little river from his map of tributaries, wasn't he?"

"It's not on any map or chart."

Bodan said, "If it's not on any maps that you can find, perhaps it doesn't exist. Modern maps are made from high-resolution satellite photography, aren't they?"

"Good point. Remember, this is a broad system of continental rivers. These are broad rivers, extending hundreds of miles. Some of the branchlike headwaters extend to the slopes of the Andes; on satellite photographs these ever-forking and ever-more-delicate branches are obvious down to twiglike rivers hardly larger than creeks. The mapmaker's eye is trained to trace larger rivers into ever-smaller streams. The blind man said he was told, and I have corroborated this, that a narrow twenty-mile-long river sheltered by a canopy of tropical forest could easily be mistaken for a quirk or anomaly if it emptied into the Amazon or one of its larger tributaries."

Bodan said, "Okay. But even then, that was more than three hundred years ago. They'd have to have some kind of contact with the outside world in order to market their diamonds."

"The blind man had considered that. Emilio Gonzalvo himself never lived in XuXu, but visited the colony frequently with his daughter, who was fluent in the language. The engineer said Gonzalvo had come up with an arrangement for the XuXuians to have permanent secret contact with the outside world. A gentleman in Pernambuco recently told me an interesting theory that XuXu has been served all these years by a series of riverboat captains who pass the secret on to a hand-picked successor."

Weckert said, "I assure you, Father, Lenny Humphries and I are not serving as XuXu's contact with the outside world. We paint fish and we study them." Weckert punctuated his sentence by tapping on the ignition key.

Antonio tried the key and the VW roared to life.

17
CATFISH THAT PLAY BANJOS

✳

It was after dark before the travelers got back to the *Barco Igaranha* where Mae Pequena sat squat-legged, trancelike, contemplative, the *candomblé* drums between her knees. Humphries had not spent the afternoon sleeping. While the travelers were enduring the jolting return from Rubiu, he had fixed a special treat of sweet and sour fish on rice—the sauce made from papaya and containing colorful hunks of both purple and white onions and green peppers.

Each traveler received three unusual fish. To the passengers' astonishment—and to Humphries's amusement at their reaction—no two of the small fish at the table were of the same species. He also served small bowls of olives and marinated hearts of palm for a salad, plus cold bottles of Antarctica beer—a special treat after a hard day of travel.

The travelers had settled down to enjoy some port when they heard a banjo playing in the darkness of the marsh.

"What's that?" Hanna asked.

"You want to tell them, Lenny?" Weckert said.

Humphries laughed. "Well, that's a banjoman, Hanna."

The phantom banjo player gave them a few more notes. Then he fell silent.

The travelers waited. Nothing.

"What the hell is that?" Bodan asked.

Father Ferrua was amused. He knew exactly what the eerie banjo was all about.

Weckert said, "What do you think, Lenny? Do you want to have a little go at him?"

"Certainly I'll give it a try. We just may have ourselves a little fun," Humphries said.

"We just might."

The travelers watched with curiosity as Humphries went forward. He returned a few minutes later with an ancient banjo that had seen better days.

"What's this?" Hanna said.

Humphries was pleased. "I bought this in a pawnshop a couple of years ago on a trip to Rio for just this reason. In a few minutes we'll get some action."

Weckert said, "Lenny can't do much with a song but he sure can talk to catfish."

"Catfish?" Hanna was goggle-eyed.

Humphries said, "Sure, and he'll be back in a few minutes too. There are catfish that grunt and catfish that bark, catfish that growl and catfish that hum. There's even a catfish down here that can drum or mew as it chooses. The banjoman is a widely distributed *bunocephaline,* a dorsoventrally flattened species. His air bladders are divided into sections by membranes, and his first four vertebrae are very thin, in fact functioning like elastic springs. One end of each thin vertebra, or spring, locks into strong muscles at the base of his skull; the other end fits into the air bladder nearest his head. He vibrates the springs, and the partitions in the air bladder act as amplifiers. And there you have it: banjoman. Humans are able to talk and have language because we can make a wide variety of sounds. He can only sound like a banjo."

Hanna said, "Give him a note, Lenny."

Humphries grinned. "We'll see if he's worked up his nerve. Here I am, little catfish. Let's jam."

Pluck.

The banjoman remained silent.

Pluck.

Nothing.

Pluck. Pluck.

Bodan said, "Keep talking to him, Lenny."

Pluck. Pluck.

And from the darkness the banjoman, perhaps an introvert, responded:

Pluck. Pluck.

"Oh wow! This is like birdcalling. Fishcalling," Bodan said.

"Isn't it a kick," Humphries said.

Humphries played: *Pluck-pluck. Pluck.*

Banjoman replied.

Pluck-pluck.

Then from the other side of the boat, a second catfish musician joined in:

Pluck-pluck. Pluck.

"You're getting some action, Lenny," Weckert said.

Bodan bit his lower lip with excitement and slapped his thigh. "All right, Lenny, you've got 'em jamming."

Father Ferrua said, "That's wonderful, Lenny. Wonderful."

"Sing to 'em, Lenny. Make that banjo sing," Hanna said.

Pluck-pluck. Pluck. Pluck-pluck.

This earned a single *pluck* from the first catfish and an excited triple *pluck-pluck* from the second. Then there were banjomen catfish everywhere, on all sides of the boat *pluck-plucking* their vibrating spines and air bladder amplifier both *allegro* and *fortissimo.*

Humphries showed his best stuff, his thick fingers actually quite nimble, his call to the fish hopping from his instrument.

After several minutes of frenzied playing, the banjomen in the water lost interest as quickly as they had first gotten excited.

"Keep after 'em," Bodan said.

Humphries did, offering his *pluck-pluck* calls.

But the banjomen weren't listening. One by one the players fell silent, until one last catfish, perhaps the original musician, offered a plaintive *pluck* and rested his vertebrae. Humphries did his best. He tried. He called and called with his banjo, *pluck pluck-pluck,* but no fish answered.

The quiet of the night returned.

Bodan said, "They're hip to you, Lenny. You're not one of them and they know it."

Hanna said, "Give it another try, Lenny. See what happens." She cuppled her hands around her mouth and called, "Yoo-hoo, banjoman! We know you're out there, you rascal little jammers."

Humphries played:

Pluck. Pluck-pluck.

Nothing.

On the bow, Mae Pequena called long, quick-quick, echoing Humphries's last call.

With the catfish silent, one by one the party left the cabin top for bed, Weckert and Father Ferrua first, followed closely by Humphries and Senhor Kobayashi, leaving Bodan to sleep topside in a hammock. "I like the *candomblé* drums," he said.

As Hanna started to go below he hauled out his laptop computer and turned it on.

"Gonna do a little writing, then," Hanna said.

"Probably not tonight. I found the architect's plans for this boat in a feed and seed store just north of San Francisco." He giggled. "I put them into my computer so I can turn them this way and that to see if all the space is accounted for."

"You don't expect me to believe that, do you?"

"No," he said. He giggled again. He'd had too much to drink.

Hanna went down below and slipped into her bunk, wondering about odd Bodan and his computer. She opened the window. She heard a clicking of his keyboard, then silence, then more clicking. She whispered loudly through the open window. "Nicholas?"

"What is it?"

"You were telling me the truth about having plans for this boat in your computer, weren't you?"

"Oh yes. I'm able to trace the lines onto the screen with a stylus."

"Are you really up there turning the boat plans around in that machine of yours?"

"That and listening to the *candomblé* folks calling Obatala."

"Is the Obatala's fish on this boat, do you think?"

"Not so as you could tell from these plans," he said. "Got the nets down and the coils burning, though. Why don't you come up and see for yourself? You can play with the computer if you want."

"Maybe I'll give it a try," Hanna said. She slipped back through the cabin as quietly as she could and back onto the cabin top where Bodan stared at the computer. He had the plans of the *Barco Igaranha* on a graphics display facing left to right on the screen. For Hanna's benefit he turned it upside down and, using an attached mechanical mouse, he shook the plans back and forth on the screen.

"See there, empty," he said. "No special place for a miracle fish in this boat. Find a place for your rump."

Hanna found a place to sit, looking at the complicated architectural drawing of the *Barco Igaranha* on the screen of Bodan's computer.

Bodan gave her the mouse, using the occasion to establish a hint of thigh contact. "Here, try your hand. Do you know how to use one of these things? When I got used to it I couldn't go back to keyboard software."

"Got one at home," she said. She slid onto the bench beside him to try her luck, turning the plans this way and that on the screen, even standing the boat on its bow and its stern. The insides were revealed with astonishing clarity.

On the bow, the call to Obatala went forth once more:

Baoom. Baoom-baoom.

"Isn't this something? Calling African gods in the Amazon. You're in no hurry to go below, are you?"

"I'm in no hurry at all," she said. She turned the plans for the *Barco Igaranha* upside down and gave them a little shake, rattle, and roll, but her effort didn't produce any revelation either.

"I like the smell of river water," Bodan said. "African gods, the smell of river water, and thou. Who could ask for more?"

Baoom.

To which a banjoman replied:

Pluck. Pluck.

Hanna said, "Mighty big river."

"I grew up on what I thought was a mighty big river. By this standard, I gotta admit it was pretty much of an ordinary river."

"Where is that? Where did you grow up?"

"On the banks of the Columbia River in eastern Oregon. I grew up way out where there was nothing but plateau desert. In the night, I could hear the coyotes howling across the river in Washington State and in the springtime, in June, the water rose from the spring runoff and the willows by the river were transformed into a wonderful swamp. I used to float downstream on rafts, pretty scary stuff."

"Regular Huck Finn."

"That's just about it. They fucked the river up, of course. They built a string of hydroelectric dams along it, the idea being to stop flooding and provide water for irrigation. Also the power was useful. They used it to process the plutonium for the bomb they popped over Nagasaki and to smelt aluminum, but they also destroyed the salmon runs. In the stretch of the river where I grew up they discovered all that wonderful unused sandy soil on both sides of the river; it was perfect for growing potatoes, so they came up with a system whereby enormous aluminum pipes are used to suck water out of the dammed-up river. The water is pumped to sprinkler systems mounted on large wheels that cover a quarter-of-a-mile circle of former desert. From the air the bright green circles stretch from horizon to horizon."

"It must be really something."

"Oh yes. It takes a hell of a lot of french fries and jo jo potatoes and hash browns to supply the AmeRiBurger franchises."

"Really? That's where AmeRiBurger gets its potatoes?"

"That's exactly it. The very same folks with the cargo bound for Santarém. They figured out a way to turn sand into cheap potatoes. They rattle the potatoes around in peelers, then mash them up and crap them out through machines like skinny white turds so the french fries are neat and slender with no uneven pieces or skin. A form of progress, they say."

18

GOGOL COMPLAINS OF LEECHES

✳

The next day was a long, long day on the river as the passengers began to appreciate the incredible size of the Amazon. The *Barco* struggled doggedly against the current, the jungle rising without stop on the shoreline. Forward, the Bahians slept after their exertions of calling Obatala in the night. In the afternoon, Nicholas Bodan, restless for fun, asked Lenny Humphries if he might not tell them something about leeches in preparation for their upcoming visit to the Ch and the leechmen.

Humphries went forward and in a few minutes returned with Weckert's paintings of the leeches attached to worshippers—which he passed around to the passengers.

Humphries rubbed his palms together with excitement.

He loved talking about animals and had brought a lapful of reference books in case they were needed. "I'll do my best. If you've got questions, ask 'em. For starters, there're four kinds of leeches based largely on differences in their mouths. They have suckers around their posterior as well as their anterior, you see."

Hanna Doherty said, "Back and front. That means they're capable of sucking with both their assholes and their mouths."

"That's right."

"The little devils!"

"Medicinal leeches, the five-eyed *Hirudo medicinalis,* are part of the family Hirudinidae. That is, five pairs of eyes for a total of ten."

"Heavens, two faces I've heard of," Hanna said. "But ten eyes?"

Bodan was impressed. "Ten eyes and they can suck with their assholes!"

"Down here they use their assholes to hang from the brush where they wait to attach themselves to the first animal that brushes past."

Hanna said, "Isn't that something? They hang by their assholes and wait for unsuspecting passersby?" She looked thoughtful, her finger poised on her lower lip.

"Oh, oh, just a second. That's just starters. There's more," Humphries said. "Leeches've got two brains, a larger brain for the forward sucker, and a smaller one for the asshole sucker. They're also hermaphrodites. Each leech is half male, half female. They've got both kinds of privates too, the sexy little buggers."

"Hermaphrodites? Really?" Bodan asked.

"That's right, two sexes, although we're assured that a male of one leech doesn't get it on with his attached female."

Bodan said, "She's just sort of like a buddy. Like a sister or something."

"That's right, but it is possible for two leeches to collide and all four partners get it on at once."

"Ohhh! Ohhh!" Hanna cried. "So they're swingers, the wicked little things. Shootie patoot!" She shook with laughter.

Lenny Humphries was pleased with the response to his impromptu lecture. "Leeches move through water in a vertical rather than a horizonal position. They can be very delicate about this, almost hovering in the water while they search out a nice spot to plant their suckers. The medicinal leech is commonly found in ponds and ditches. The rage of medicinal leeches was between 1820 and 1850, with the French being the principal champions. For example, a certain enthusiastic Dr. François Broussais, if you'll pardon my mangling his name, is said to have attached fifty to sixty leeches to himself each day for two weeks as a cure for indigestion."

"Did it work?" asked Father Ferrua.

"He apparently survived. I have a book that claims medicinal leeches sucked about 350,000 liters of French blood each year, although how the author arrived by that figure is unclear. We do know that Europeans collected leeches by walking around bare-legged in farm ponds and that leech gathering became a profession. The gatherers used sharp knives to scrape the leeches off their legs into buckets of cold water."

Ferrua shook his head. "Wherever there's a market."

Humphries opened one of his reference books, reading as he talked. "I found this one article here that says a hard worker could collect as many as 2,500 leeches a day from a good pond. In 1824, the yield from the legs of wading peasants allowed the Germans to export five million leeches to England in a single shipment. When the leeches began to get scarce, the French and Germans tried farming them. They forced old horses to stand in farm ponds as leech feed, but the horses bled to death."

Bodan winced.

Humphries laughed deeply. "Ah, but there's more, Nicholas. It says here that leeches almost became extinct in Europe, so the buyers followed the farm ponds to the east, following them all the way to Russia. So many leeches were collected in Russia that the government put a season on gathering and levied a tax on their export."

Hanna said, "Nobody ever said the Russians were stupid."

"Here's one for you, Nicholas. Do you know the story about Gogol and the leeches?"

"Gogol?"

"Gogol was a hypochondriac, forever worrying about illness of both the spirit and the body. He went to a priest seeking solace of the spirit. The priest convinced him his work was evil, so Gogol burned all his as yet unpublished manuscripts. All this did was ruin him financially. He was plagued by bad health as well, and in Moscow he turned to physicians and science for treatment." Here Humphries used his finger to trace along the lines as he quoted directly from the article:

> The physicians subjected Gogol to prolonged sessions of leeching in which six leeches were allowed to feed in each nostril. Gogol had to be restrained. He twisted and screamed, "Take the leeches off my face. Take the leeches off. Take them off. Nyet! Nyet! Nyet!" When he passed out from the ministrations of leeches squirming in his nose, draining his blood, the physicians doused him with cold water. When he was revived, they returned the leeches. They kept this up, determined that Gogol should be healed, until he died.

Father Ferrua closed his eyes.

The company fell into a momentary silence.

"We've long had a fascination with leeches," Humphries said. "There's something about the business of sucking blood." He closed the book. "The medicinal leech extracts blood through an opening cut by three cutting plates, each of which has sixty to a hundred teeth. Under a microscope these plates look like the blades of a circular saw. They're arranged radically and cut with a back-and-forth motion so the flesh is opened in three directions at once."

"Ouch!" Bodan said.

"When the leech bites, it releases an enzyme that kills everything in the blood in the immediate vicinity of the wound. This acts as an anesthetic, so there's no sting. Leeches can collect on your legs, but you don't feel anything."

Hanna said, "They're there sucking away contentedly and you don't have any idea."

"Not a hint."

"Why, the little devils!"

Humphries leaned forward, grinning. "Here's a good one. A sucking leech makes a wound that medical researchers call the Mercedes mark because it's shaped like the hood ornament of a Mercedes-Benz automobile. And so it is. Look here."

Humphries opened a second book to a marked page that contained a photograph of freshly sucked flesh, a raw and inflamed circle with a triangle in the middle that indeed looked exactly like the hood ornament of the Mercedes-Benz.

19

A VIRGIN FOR OBATALA

❋

With Hans Weckert in the bridge piloting the *Barco Igaranha* and with Lenny Humphries in the galley preparing supper, the passengers gathered on the cabin top for rum and talk; because of Humphries's little lecture earlier in the afternoon, the talk was mostly about leeches.

The river, rendered into a splendid mirror by the dying minutes of old sol, seemed forever and six leagues to the other side, its polished surface broken only by floating islands of limbs, branches, and snarls of foliage. In the noonday sun the islands were bright green patches floating on yellow-brown, now they were mysterious dark forms on the brooding surface of the river.

The boat had first encountered the islands—they were often nothing more than a single floating limb, sometimes elaborate rafts of snarl ten to fifteen feet across—after passing through the narrows and into the Amazon River proper, the north channel of the delta. The green islands, rare at first, became more frequent as the boat moved upstream, sometimes floating in isolation, sometimes in congenial groups that looked like colorful tourists on a leisurely outing.

The passengers, anticipating the coming night smells, rode in contemplative silence. The *Barco* passed a primitive sawmill as the softening darkness of night closed in on the river. The mill—established in a clearing by the riverbank —consisted of a large machine, presumably a saw, under a thatched roof, plus a shack, and a pile of freshly cut lumber.

As the sun set, a luminescent white moon rose slowly over the river. The boat, still close in to the shore, slipped through eerie shadows of the tall forest at a rapid *mom-mom-mom-mom* clip. There was no blocked fuel now; the gasohol engine was running free and easy.

At a few minutes before ten, Lenny Humphries emerged from his chores in the galley just as Hans Weckert slowed the engine to a *mawm-mawm-mawm.* Humphries called up to the observation deck, "Mosquito drill coming up. You lads ready up there?"

"We're ready, Hans," Bodan said.

"Father Ferrua, Senhor Kobayashi. Let's everybody take their places, please." Humphries called something forward in Portuguese and received a reply from the *babalaô* who shouted orders to the others. Humphries seemed to be in a good mood.

The passengers—save for one Bahian obliged to remain always with the *candomblé* drums after dark—gathered around the mosquito nets rolled up and tied under the eaves of the boat's roof. Everybody on the boat had an assigned spot.

"Cut her, Hans!" Humphries boomed.

There was a splash forward.

Humphries boomed, "I've got her, Hans."

The boat drifted momentarily.

The passengers, gathered at the rails, waited expectantly. The line stiffened. The boat held, bow into the current.

"Okay, let's drop 'em," Humphries called.

The passengers sprung into action, untying the mosquito nets and sending them furling to the deck. They quickly tied the weighted bottoms to the special deck stays, then turned their attention to tying gapless seams between the panels. They did this with enthusiasm because the mosquitoes always closed in when the boat stopped.

The nets tied, the Bahians built themselves a fire on their decktop stove and the passengers repaired to the cabin top for supper and talk before they went to bed in the ringing silence.

Hanging belly up like a netted shrimp, Nicholas Bodan listened to the *candomblé* drums on the bow, which were far more agitated and passionate than on the previous night, the drum calls now coming in heated, excited riffs. It seemed to Bodan that the players were clearly becoming more emotional in their exhortations for Obatala to speak.

Bodan could see the ragged black silhouette of rain forest through the panels of mosquito netting. Beyond the *candomblé* calls, there was an awesome silence, a yawning chasm of no sound, yet Bodan knew that this vast world was no void, knew that it was teeming with bugs and little four-legged animals and snakes and bats that fed and foraged and flew by darkness. The river seemed even more silent than the previous night, if that was possible. It was as though the farther they traveled from the shelter of Belém, the deeper into the rhythms of Amazonia, the more silent the night somehow became.

Then Bodan heard somebody talking in the hold, a chant almost or poetry of some kind. It was English, that he made out clearly.

He turned out of his hammock and went down the stairs to have a look. He peered over the edge of the hold just as the drummer up front ran another call. Senhor Kobayashi was under the light bulb intended for users of the toilet. In his careful, measured English, he read aloud from his faithful red book:

> "Delaying and straying and playing and spraying,
> Advancing and prancing and glancing and dancing,
> Recoiling, turmoiling and toiling and boiling,
> And gleaming and streaming and steaming and beam-
>   ing,
> And rushing and flushing and brushing and gushing,
> And flapping and rapping and clapping and slapping,
> And curling and whirling and purling and twirling,
> And thumping and plumping and bumping and jump-
>   ing,
> And dashing and flashing and splashing and clashing;
> And so never ending, but always descending,
> Sounds and motions for ever and ever are blending
> All at once and all o'er, with a mighty uproar—
> And this way the water comes down at Lodore."

Kobayashi studied his little red book again, which Bodan saw was marked by several slips of paper. Kobayashi took a deep breath, looking thoughtful. He opened the book at another mark and began reading aloud again:

"I wind about, and in and out,
With here a blossom sailing,
And here and there a lusty trout,
And here and there a grayling,

"And here and there a foamy flake
Upon me, as I travel
With many a silvery water-break
Above the golden gravel,

"And draw them all along, and flow
To join the brimming river,
For men may come and men may go,
But I go on for ever.

"I steal by lawns and grassy plots,
I slide by hazel covers;
I move the sweet forget-me-nots
That grow for happy lovers.

"I slip, I slide, I gloom, I glance,
Among my skimming swallows;
I make the netted sunbeam dance
Against my sandy shallows.

"I murmur under moon and stars
In brambly wildernesses;
I linger by my shingly bars;
I loiter round my cresses;

"And out again I curve and flow
To join the brimming river,
For men may come and men may go,
But I go on for ever."

Bodan watched, astonished, as Kobayashi read the lines again, his voice ringing with drama. Having gone out twice to join the brimming river, he turned to yet another bookmark.

Kobayashi studied the book. Pushing out his lips, he

said, very rapidly, "No man, no mind, no man, no mind, no man, no mind, no man, no mind, no man, no mind." Then, pausing, checking the book, he said, "So—we—do—see—across—the—lea. So—we—do—see—across—the—lea. So —we—do—see—across—the—lea."

Looking satisfied, Kobayashi turned to another marker; this time in a falsetto woman's voice, he said, "Nothing is small! No lily-muffled hum of summer bee but finds some coupling with the shining stars; no pebble at your feet but proves a sphere; no chaffinch but implies the cherubim. Earth is crammed with Heaven and every common bush afire with God, but only he who sees takes off his shoes."

Kobayashi returned to his normal voice and said, "Lovely Lolita drifting along in the moonlight over the murmuring lagoon." He repeated that sentence twenty times, then closed his book, and—with Bodan watching from the shadows—he returned to his berth in the cabin.

Hanna Doherty woke up to surreal screams. She'd been fast asleep, drifting in that old and mysterious slough where memory and desire swim entangled as passionate eels.

She opened her cabin window and she could hear everything clearly.

A girl or young woman was screaming.

"Holy shit!" Bodan said from his hammock up above.

Hanna heard the canopy of the companionway open and close.

Humphries shouted an unintelligible oath. Weckert said something.

She screamed again, moaning this time.

Hanna slipped on jeans, a blouse, jumped into some rubber go-aheads, and took off, her eyes not yet accustomed to light. Up and out of the companionway she went, fumbling and groping her way along the port rail.

Ahead, she saw Weckert and Humphries. In front of them Mae Janaina loomed in the darkness, standing with her feet apart and her arms folded under her breasts. Just behind her was Mae Pequena. It was the girl who was screaming, then.

Behind Hanna, Bodan arrived and Father Ferrua.

Somewhere behind Mae Janaina, the young girl, the *abian,* continued her moaning and wailing.

Weckert was having an earnest discussion with Mae Janaina in Portuguese.

"Yes, what is happening?" Hanna asked.

"We don't know for sure," Humphries said. "The only thing we know is this bloody woman's not letting us pass, and I don't know whether I'd want to tangle with her or not."

Weckert listened, his face grave. He nodded his head in understanding to whatever it was she said. He passed this on to the rest of the passengers:

"She says she doesn't understand why we're getting so excited. She says she told us she and her three companions would be calling Obatala with regard to Father Machado's fish and so they have been. She says the passing of five hundred years since the theft of the fish is nothing to Obatala, who remembers it as if it had happened a minute ago and is still unspeakably angry. The young girl, who is an initiate and a virgin, was brought along in case something like this happened. Obatala is known to be a lusty god, she says, and when he goes too long without sex he gets irritable same as we do. The girl's virginity was offered as a means of calming him down. She assures us that the deflowering was correctly performed by the *babalaô* according to prescriptions of the *candomblé.*"

"I guess what matters is she's not hurt," Hanna said.

"Mae Janaina has assured me the girl's fine and has agreed to let you and me and Father Ferrua talk to her a few minutes in private, but I don't see any need for that."

A white dress walked toward them along the narrow deck between the port rail and the forward cabin. Then they saw her face and arms and feet; they were so dark as to be invisible in the night light. She stepped under the yellow glow of the companionway light, sweat glistening on her face and arms. She was a pretty girl with large dark eyes. She wore a necklace of large red wooden beads that were themselves covered with a sheen of perspiration. She stood by the *yalorixa,* her eyes fixed on the deck between her feet.

Mae Janaina said something to the girl, who looked up at the passengers with large brown eyes and a hint of a smile. Shyly, she said something to Weckert, who listened carefully. He thanked her with a slight bow.

Weckert said, "She says she's just fine. She apologizes for waking us. She assures me her outcries were not due to pain."

The initiate's Mona Lisa smile grew just a hint. She then returned forward to join Mae Pequena and the *babalaô.*

Mae Janaina, looking at the passengers, whispered something more in Hans Weckert's ear.

Weckert seemed puzzled by her question. He said something more and she repeated what she had said, looking at Nicholas Bodan. Weckert said, "She is curious about your laptop, Mr. Bodan. They can see the screen glowing back there. She asked me what it was and I said a computer. She wants to know what you're doing with it."

"Tell her I'm keeping a journal of the trip, a form of notes."

Weckert translated for Mae Janaina and looked as though he could hardly believe her reply. His face was ashen.

Humphries said, "What was it, Hans? What did she say?"

"It was nothing."

"Nonsense."

"Really, it was nothing." Thus Hans Weckert ended the conversation. He didn't want to talk about it.

20
THE CURSE OF HICCUPS
✳

Lenny Humphries hauled in a set line the next morning, pulling in a string of bewhiskered fish intended for lunch. The *Barco's* original schedule for rotating turns at the helm had deteriorated, with some of the passengers taking odd turns and naps and playing cribbage and gin to while away the time.

When lunch came Weckert was in the bridge piloting the *Barco Igaranha* about a hundred yards off the northern shore.

The Amazon flowed slightly northeast from Santarém to the delta, so that while the travelers could have enjoyed shade from the forest rising high on the southern bank, Weckert kept the boat on the northern bank. This was because while the mornings are tolerable after a cooling evening on the water, it is during the late afternoon, after a searing, sweaty day of tropical sun, that the cooling shade is the sweetest and most welcome. Crossing from bank to bank to follow the shade was time-wasting because of the incredible width of the river.

In the morning the sun rose to the *Barco's* left rear above the horizon of trees on the southern bank; this cast an elongated shadow of the *Barco's* profile that ran nearly to shore, preceding the boat upriver.

With the blazing sun directly overhead, Hanna helped Humphries prepare the meal: well-peppered catfish fried in crisp chunks and mixed with browned onions.

Weckert anchored the *Barco* and joined Humphries and the passengers on the aft cabin top. After they were settled down to Humphries's catfish and onions, steamed chayotes, a pale green vegetable somewhere between a zucchini and a yellow squash, bread, butter, and cold Brama Chopp, Father Ferrua noticed activity on top of the forward cabin.

He wiped off his mouth, and took a sip of coffee. "It looks like we have activity of some kind up front."

As indeed there was. Mae Janaina's *candomblé* followers were building something on the tabletop.

Hans Weckert paled. He stopped chewing mid-bite.

"What's the matter, Hans?" Humphries asked.

Weckert continued chewing. "We'll see."

Eating their catfish, they watched as Mae Janaina and her followers, using pins and needles and thread, assembled an object that very soon began taking on a human form.

Hanna, watching Weckert's reaction, said, "Tell us, Hans."

Humphries said, "This has to do with what Mae Janaina told you last night, doesn't it, Hans? You can't hide anything from me. You know that."

Weckert cleared his throat. "She told me Obatala had in fact asked for two things: a virgin and one of us, because it was we white people who stole the fish in the first place."

"What? Are you bullshitting us?" Bodan said.

Father Ferrua sat up straight. "Dear me. *Despacho* from Mae Janaina, pretty strong stuff if you go along with *candomblé.*"

"Who is it?" Hanna said.

Mae Janaina, looking aft behind her sunglasses, put the finishing touches on the doll, which identified the intended sacrifice. This took the form of curly hair and a mustache.

Obatala had asked for Nicholas Bodan.

Bodan's knee whacked the bottom of the table. "Me?"

Weckert's lips tightened. "Yes, I'm afraid so, Mr. Bodan."

"She told you that last night?"

"Yes, she did."

"No shit? Did she say me, specifically?"

"Yes, she did."

"And why was that? What did I ever do to her?"

"She said Obatala doesn't give reasons why. He merely requests and his wishes must be fulfilled. They've been watching you writing at night and think you're talking to Exu with your computer."

"With my computer?"

"She believes that's why Obatala asked for you."

"What?"

"I'm afraid that's it."

"Why didn't you tell me this last night?"

Weckert said, "Perhaps I should have, Mr. Bodan, but I was hoping nothing would come of it."

The *yalorixa* and her followers, ordinarily silent during the day, brought out the *agogó* bell. The muscular *babalaô* squatted by the Nicholas Bodan doll and began striking the *agogó* with quick-quick, slow, slow beats, the rhythm of the *agogó* making a hollow, riveting sound: *Toook-toook! Toook! Toook!*

"What do we do now?" Hanna asked.

"We do nothing," Bodan said. "A doll and a bell, let them have their fun." He stood, stretching. "I think I'll go below for a nice nap."

Weckert returned to the bridge and pulled anchor and the *Barco* was on its way again, Humphries with the aft passengers, except Bodan, drinking coffee and listening to the *mom-mom-mom-mom* of the engine mixed in with the unearthly *toook toook toook* of the *agogó* summoning Bodan's spirit.

Bodan came up a half hour later, shaking his head. "Never could sleep during the day."

"You can't possibly believe this nonsense, Nicholas," Father Ferrua said. "That's a pile of rags and underwear; it has nothing whatsoever to do with you."

"I agree with you that it's nonsense, but is there any logical difference between believing in the divinity of Christ and believing Mae Janaina can somehow do me in with a doll?"

This wasn't put as any kind of challenge to Christianity

or the Catholic church. It was a serious question, although Bodan was amiable as usual in the way he asked it.

Ferrua said, "Well, the ever-logical Mr. Bodan. What can't be proved by physical evidence must be taken on faith alone."

"So where does one draw the line on the limits of faith?"

"I believe as I do and Mae Janaina believes as she does. God provided us with a range of imaginations, just as he provided us with a wealth of birds and the fish that interest Captain Weckert. This wonderful stew includes my faith, and your apparent lack of it."

The repetitious quick-quick, slow, slow beat of the *agogó* was hyponotic, spooky in its calm insistence. Only the most deaf *orixa* could fail to hear that determined call:

Toook-toook! Toook! Toook!

Mae Janaina herself, wearing a white cotton dress, stepped up to the bow. She took the bell from the *babalaô* and began striking it harder, faster. Senhor Kobayashi was obviously impressed with the lady's body, as was Father Ferrua, evidence that his hormones functioned the same as noncelibate men's.

Watching Mae Janaina, Bodan took a swig of Brama Chopp and went *hic.* "Excuse me." He went *hic* again. "Got the hiccups." He took a deep breath and held it. He let go, exhaling through puffed cheeks. *Hic.*

Mae Pequena took her turn at the *agogó.* When one Bahian got arm-weary, another took a turn.

Bodan watched this, unable to shake his hiccups. What started as a mere *hic* advanced to a *heeaaak* that jerked his diaphragm, and every time Mae Janaina took a turn on the damnable *agogó,* his hiccups came faster and harder, twisting his exhausted body.

As it got dark, Weckert piloted the boat farther offshore, but not so far out as to fight the main current of the river.

Humphries, who had been in the galley working on supper, appeared from the darkness and seized Bodan, and boomed, "Fuck Mae Janaina!" in his ear, and crushed Bodan's diaphragm with a twisting bear hug that swept Bodan off his feet, legs dangling. Humphries slammed Bodan hard to the deck. Bodan, grateful for Humphries's attempt, got up wincing, holding the side of his head.

Heeaaak!

Bodan went downstairs to his bunk for a second time in the futile hope of escaping the *agogó,* but it was impossible. The passengers listened to him below, the wracking increasing in frequency and severity, Bodan's body barely having time to relax between each *heeaaaaak!*

Hanna went to her compartment and pulled out her medical bag and the issue of *People* magazine with her photograph on the cover. Then she went back to Bodan's bunk, where Father Ferrua and Humphries had gathered, wondering what could be done to give the poor man relief.

She handed Father Ferrua the magazine and started digging into her medical bag. "Nicholas already knows about me. Recognized me the first day. Hanna Doherty was my grandmother's name." She found a tranquilizer. "I was getting to enjoy the privacy."

Father Ferrua said, "I rather admired what you did in San Francisco, although I can see why the physicians got upset. You'll still be Hanna Doherty when you're finished."

"You came aboard as Hanna Doherty," Humphries said. "This is Brazil, remember."

Hanna loaded a hypodermic and slid it into Bodan's arm. "This may not cure your hiccups, but it should help you relax a bit, Nicholas."

From forward, the *agogó* stopped.

The silence that followed was broken only by Bodan: *Heeeaaaaak! Heeeaaaaak! Heeeaaaaak!*

Bodan's hiccups were suddenly worse than before the bell stopped. He was wet with sweat.

"Pl-*heeaaaaak*-lea-*heeaaaaak*-ase. *Heeaaaaak,* do some-*heeaaaaak*-th-*heeaaaaak*-ing."

Hanna mopped the sweat off Bodan's face. His face bunched in pain with each hiccup.

"I think I should talk to Hans about putting in somewhere," Hanna said.

"We have to do something for him," Ferrua said.

Father Ferrua and Humphries stayed with Bodan while Hanna took the *People* magazine with her to the bridge to consult with Weckert.

On the way through the galley, she stole a boiled egg she found in the refrigerator and climbed halfway to the bridge and knocked on the trapdoor above her. It opened. Weckert looked down at her.

"Yes, Hanna."

"May I come up for a moment."

"Of course."

She climbed the rest of the ladder and started peeling her egg. Inside the bridge, Weckert was drinking coffee. A reassuring glow of gauges and dials told him how the engine was running, how much fuel he had left, plus the latitude and longitude of the boat, the depth of the water, and how far he was from the shoreline.

"Are Bodan's hiccups better?" he asked.

She gave him the magazine which he looked at. It took a moment for him to match her face with the cover. He looked up at her, then down at the magazine again. He grinned. "You!"

"Me."

"Wonderful, Hanna. I thought they had it coming to them."

"How far are we from a town with an airport?"

"A day and a half if I push it and the engine holds up."

"Do you know anything about frogs down here, Hans?"

"Oh, sure. Some. I take notes on just about everything, but concentrate on fish when I paint."

She asked him about a certain small green tree frog that exuded a toxic sweat.

21
FROM THE BACKS OF FROGS
✸

With Nicholas Bodan below on his bunk surely dying of the hiccups, the travelers found themselves in an uninhabited stretch of the river that ran for miles upon endless miles. Before, there had been scattered huts along the river, a single shack here, two or three there—often on stilts with the family boat tied to the front door—but now, with Bodan desperate, there were none to be found.

Lenny Humphries was in the bridge pushing the boat as hard as it would run, with Weckert beside him using binoculars to look for a settlement along the banks. The river was so wide that it was impossible to make out the details of the far shore with the naked eye.

Bodan was curled up in the fetal position to ease the pain in his ribs and stomach that accompanied each twisting hiccup. Hanna stayed with Bodan, kneeling beside his bed and mopping the sweat from his forehead.

"*Heeaaaaak* I am going to die here of the *heeaaaaak!* fucking hiccups. I don't believe *heeaaaaak* this is happening to me. *Heeaaaaak.* I'm going *heeaaaaak* up top. *Heeeaaaaak.*"

"Maybe if you just stayed here and did your best to rest, Nicholas?"

"*Heeeaaaaak.* Rest? *Heeeaaaaak.* Are you *heeeaaaaak* mad?"

Bodan sat up on his narrow berth. "My dad-*heeaaaaak*-dy would never *heeaaaaak* have ap-*heeeaaaaak*-proved of a son who *heeeaaaaak* died wallow-*heeeaaaaak*-ing in *heeeaaaaak* pity. I will *heeeaaaaak* not *heeeaaaaak* quit. No. *Heeeaaaaak.*"

Bodan stood and headed for the deck, his body yanked by the terrible hiccups. Refusing to surrender, he struggled up the steps onto the observation deck. Father Ferrua and Senhor Kobayashi stood to applaud his appearance.

The boat turned suddenly, *mom-mom-mom-mom,* as Humphries piloted the *Barco Igaranha* across the river. Weckert had obviously spotted a settlement on the far side.

Both Ferrua and Senhor Kobayashi looked at Hanna, wondering what on earth she could find in one of these isolated shacks that could possibly relieve Bodan of the affliction that gripped him.

Hanna put her arm around Bodan. "Listen, Nicholas, I want you to know I'm playing the longest of long-shot hands. All I have to go on is a dim memory of an article in the *New England Journal of Medicine* about the toxic qualities of a substance found in the skin of almost all frogs. A dog or cat will kill a frog but spit it out for this reason. This poison, used by some Indians in Amazonia, is actually a powerful muscle relaxant of a kind that may make it so Hans and Lenny can get you to a proper hospital."

"Let's *heeeaaaaak* try it."

With Hanna's arm around him, Bodan held on to the bench, his body jerking. After a painful twenty minutes of this, Humphries began slowing the boat; the travelers could see a settlement of four or five shacks around a small dock sticking well out into the water.

As they drew closer, they could see brown-faced Indian children peering out from a shack, then an old woman in a yellow dress.

The old woman came out to the dock to greet the visitors, but the children remained in the safety of the shack, looking out.

Humphries slowed the boat even more. Weckert took the bowline in hand, and Humphries piloted the boat skillfully alongside the end of the dock.

The travelers watched from the observation deck as Weckert talked to the old woman.

Weckert returned with his report. "The woman says there are plenty of *igitos* in this area. She says the adults are at a weekly market held at a village about ten miles from here, but the children are better at catching frogs anyway. She says certainly you can hire them to catch some for you."

"How many children are there?" Hanna asked.

"She says two boys and five girls. They're all between ages four and eleven."

"Please tell her the rich gringo lady will buy all the *igitos* the children can find in two hours or whenever you give a whistle at one hundred American dollars for each frog."

"Are you serious?"

"We've got a life at stake here."

"She's spent most of her life thinking *cruzeiros,* which has three more zeros than the current *cruzado.* That's about a five-million-*cruzeiro* tree frog."

Weckert told the old woman about Hanna's offer; her mouth opened and she looked at Hanna in disbelief.

Hanna opened her handbag and flashed a wad. She looked the old woman straight on so the woman would know she was serious. She meant damn well what she said. Five-million-*cruzeiro* tree frogs.

The old woman nodded at Hanna, agreeing to the deal. She turned and shouted at the children in her Indian language.

The children, who had been peering out from the doorway and windows of the little house, were suddenly gone, skedaddling into the bush.

There was no doubt that the *candomblé* believers were affected by Bodan's outcries, as they had ceased striking the *agogó.* Mae Janaina, masked as always behind her mirrored sunglasses, looked back impassively toward the stern once in a while, but otherwise showed no particular interest in Bodan's agony. This was Obatala's show, not hers.

When Humphries and Weckert finished securing the boat, they joined Senhor Kobayashi on the aft cabin top to await the harvest of tree frogs—if there were any to be found. They sat in silence save for the terrible *beeaaaaaks* from below, setting their teeth on edge, and the murmuring of Father Ferrua, who was on his knees on the privacy of the fantail, deep in earnest prayer that his new American acquaintance might live.

Bodan's eyes were now moist bags of pain, and worse, he was now too weak to resist his affliction. With Hanna wiping sweat from his face, he lay on his bunk at the mercy of the demonic tic in his nervous system. It was as though each hiccup yanked a little more life out of him and he was incapable of fighting back.

He was most assuredly dying.

At the end of an hour Hanna could stand it no longer. She called Father Ferrua down to soothe the rapidly declining Bodan and told Weckert he should call the children in.

"He doesn't have long left. We'll have to make do with what they've found . . . if they've found any."

Weckert hopped off the deck and ran to the shack at the end of the dock where the old woman was prowling the nearby underbrush to see if she too might not lay a hand on a five-million-*cruzeiro* frog.

The woman hurried back to the hut where she talked to Weckert, and after hearing what he said, she turned and called the children in a loud shriek, which she repeated several times.

Seconds later, the first child arrived, a little girl. No frog. Then another little girl. This one, beaming, held high a small bag. Yes. One by one the children came in. Some with frogs, some without. In the end Weckert held up all fingers on both hands than added a thumbs-up for victory.

They'd found eleven frogs.

Weckert waved Hanna off the boat and she too ran to the river shack, peeling eleven hundreds from her handbag as she went.

She said, "Hans, I want you to tell her the money is to be used to benefit the children. They're the ones who found the frogs."

Weckert told the old woman, with Hanna watching her face.

She understood.

Looking at Hanna, she told Weckert that yes, the money would be used for the children. She'd see to it, she said.

The frogs were in a basket. Hanna lifted the edge of the lid to peer inside. The children had lined the basket with leaves and she didn't see anything at first. Then she realized that the frogs were there all right, motionless, blending in with the leaves.

She reached in and touched one and it jumped, startling her.

Hanna said, "I just can't bring myself to use one of Lenny's metal pots. For some bizarre reason it seems more civilized to use a clay pot if there's one around."

"I'll ask her," Weckert said.

"Well?"

"She's got one."

"Better to do it here than on the boat," Weckert said.

"I think so."

"I take it she has a stove I can use."

The old woman did have a stove, one that was originally a metal drum, but altered creatively so as to provide a flat surface for cooking and a space for an oven of sorts.

"Shall we get on with it?"

Weckert, watching the woman build the fire, said, "How hot do you want it?"

"How hot does it take for something like this?"

"How about a small one?"

"It's all barbarous."

Weckert squatted beside the woman as she tended the fire.

Standing behind him, Hanna peered in again at the frightened frogs, who had managed to make themselves almost the precise shade of green as the leaves in the basket. They did their best, the frogs did. They did what they could do, which was to make themselves green, green, green, oh please, gods of frogdom, green, green, and they hoped against hope that the beast peering in at them would somehow let them go.

Hanna said, "Hans, I'll need a knife with a sharp blade."

He dug into his pocket and came up with a Swiss army knife. He unfolded the large blade. "Will this do? I try to keep it reasonably sharp."

She ran the edge of the blade across the pad of her thumb, feeling the crisp edge of the blade. "It is sharp. You efficient German," she said.

Weckert grinned. *"Ja."*

As she waited for the stove to heat, Hanna examined the frogs: they were little beauties; they had slender, graceful legs. Long, streamlined legs. Looking at them, she didn't believe she'd ever seen such gorgeous creatures. They had smooth, flawless skin, an almost translucent skin that seemed to radiate greenness.

When the stove was hot, Hanna got on with it. She opened the lid just above the pot and tilted the basket sideways. The frogs hopped quickly out, going to what they thought was freedom only to land plop, plop—eleven little beauties—on the bottom of the clay pot. They immediately began turning a dun color to match their new surroundings. But there was no escaping because the pot—which must have held two or three gallons—was one of those classic numbers, rounded wide at the bottom and curving up to a smaller mouth. The frogs bounded and hopped like popcorn or bouncing Ping-Pong balls, leaping as high as they could and trying for higher, only to rebound off the shoulders of the pot.

The pot on the homemade stove began to warm.

Hanna watched, saying nothing. In the distance she and Weckert could hear Bodan on the boat hiccuping: *Heeeeaaaaaaaakkkkk! Heeeeeaaaaaaaaakkkkk!*

The hiccups were getting worse if that was possible. Weckert heard them too and ground his jaws in anxiety and sympathy for Bodan.

The frogs began to hop.

Hanna expected the old woman to leave, but she didn't. Neither did Weckert.

As the stove got hotter, the frogs hopped faster, seeming to roll in the air like tortured gymnasts coming off a trampoline, kicking their slender legs in a futile effort to slow their descent onto the heat. Slowly, they began turning color, sliding from their protective dun to first a sandy color with the barest hint of yellow.

They leaped open-mouthed. The hint of yellow gradually became banana yellow. Then they were entirely yellow, with tracings of apricot.

Weckert was wide-eyed.

"It's Nicholas's only chance."

Slowly the frogs turned orange. Their bodies seemed almost to glow as they turned, rolling in the air on their return to the blistering heat.

As Hanna watched this, she heard Bodan's terrible spasms:

Hhhheeeeaaaaaaaakkkkk! Hhhheeeeaaaaaaaakkkkk!

"Hanna, I . . . ." This was a hard business for Weckert.

"Turn your face. It's either the frogs or Nicholas."

The frogs screamed silently, turning from orange now to red.

She again ran the edge of the knife blade across her thumb.

"I'll need a small dish, please," she said. She was unable to take her eyes off the tortured frogs.

The old woman, whose eyes too were on the frogs, pressed a dish into her hand. The leaping, kicking frogs were now turning an ugly purple, and a fine sheen of sweat began to appear on their backs.

"I said dammit turn your back, Hans."

Hanna folded a handkerchief in the palm of her hand and scooped out a frog and slammed it on the table, back up. She used Weckert's Swiss army knife to scrape the layer of secretion off its inflamed back. She waited while the tortured back secreted more fluid. She scraped that off too. She waited again and the back responded with more sweat. The fourth time there was nothing. The frog was dead and she discarded it.

She scooped out another frog and likewise scraped its back until it died.

Grinding the enamel on her teeth, she repeated this ghastly ritual eleven times, with Bodan *hhhaaaaakkkkking* on the boat. Then she was off and running for the boat with her saucer of sweat, leaving Weckert behind her, vomiting.

Nicholas Bodan looked up at Hanna with haggard, moist eyes. *Heeeaaaaakkkkkk!*

She said, "Nicholas, I . . ."

". . . *Heeaaakkkk!* Do it."

"The idea is to total everything but your respiratory system. I remember reading an article about this stuff in a medical journal. They're trying to develop an artificial version of it in a biomedical lab at MIT."

Heeeaaaak.

"It may very well kill you, but if it doesn't work you'll surely die, Nicholas."

Heeaaakkkk! He answered yes, with his eyes. He knew he would die unless the frog sweat worked.

"Give me a fist," Hanna said.

Hiccuping, Bodan gave her a fist.

She sank the needle home.

22

THE WOMAN ON THE

TWENTY XUXU BILL

❋

The *Barco Igaranha*'s fourth night was a warm, tranquil evening on the water. Nicholas Bodan lay on his bunk, barely breathing, while on the bow, Mae Janaina and her companions—having delivered a virgin and about to deliver a white man to Obatala—set about to complete their last night of appeals.

The passengers, by now accustomed to the irregular drum calls, set about preparing their nightly defense against mosquitoes. They wore long-sleeved shirts, but there were still hands and wrists to be protected, not to mention necks, ears, and faces. Here the passengers resorted to petroleum distillates given a sweet-yuck smell for the wearer's enjoyment. The combination of burning mosquito coils and insect goo gave the observation deck a distinct *eau du* repellent, a chemical stench that hung, unmoving, mingling with the dead-fish smell of the river air.

Accompanied by an orchestra of excited crickets trilling on the shoreline of the Breves Strait and the irregular drum calls of the *candomblé* drums, the travelers settled into Lenny Humphries's feast to help keep their minds off Bodan lying in an apparent coma below. Lenny served them *feijoada completa,* a Brazilian specialty of black beans, sausage, and ham.

After dinner, they settled back with coffee, wondering whether Bodan would survive the night and recalling Mae Janaina's promised revelation about Obatala's fish, which was due in the morning. They all had had plenty of opportunity to roam the boat at will, poking and prying, thumping, and knocking, everyone except Father Ferrua pretending they were not poking, prying, thumping, and knocking.

Now all save Ferrua were as convinced as Weckert and Humphries that the three-million-dollar fish was not aboard the *Barco Igaranha.*

Humphries said, "Well, she'll tell us in the morning what the *orixas* think. One way or another, there's nothing we can do about it tonight."

"The same is true for Nicholas," Hanna said. "He's either going to live or die down there, and there's not a whole lot I can do for him. I say Father Ferrua should tell us some more XuXu stories. He promised some more."

"Oh no, not more of those," Weckert held his hands to his ears.

Hanna said, "You might get tired of them, Hans, but we're new to the Amazon. They're still fun for us."

Using the toe of his shoe to edge his burning mosquito coil along the deck, Father Ferrua scooted his chair forward. He turned his head at the telltale hum of a winged vampire and slapped his neck. "Got him!" He took a tidy sip of rum.

"There are hundreds of XuXu tales. If one assumes that there *is* such a place as XuXu, then one can conclude that at least some—but certainly not all—the stories may be true. Because of the isolating language, my usual standard is that the story contain some credible XuXuian source. The exception is the story of the president who wore no clothes.

"About six years ago, I read an article about a well-known fashion designer in Rio de Janeiro who believes she had dealings with XuXuians for years without knowing it. The woman was a respected, educated designer, and was originally skeptical about XuXu stories, regarding them as myth. The magazine copy was entirely sensational and lacking in detail, so I went to see the woman, who was pleased to receive me.

"She said some years earlier she had received a visit from a man who asked if she spoke Dutch, which she did not. He claimed to represent the residents of a fashion-conscious community of expatriate Europeans who had lived for several generations on an island which he declined to name, but which he said was a former colony of the Dutch. These people were isolated from the mainstream of fashion and were determined to remain that way; they weren't interested at all in the latest line from Paris or New York or Tokyo. They had been fashioning their own styles, but now wanted to work with a professional who could market their clothing for them.

"The woman in Rio was an artist by temperament and a romantic at heart; the proposal appealed to both instincts. She entered into a relationship which lasted ten years and which she says was the most beautiful thing that had ever happened to her. She received perfectly lovely questions that were both naive and practical, together with some of the most imaginative, stylish designs she had ever seen. Her correspondents even sent her folders of drawings of people dressed in costumes of their unnamed island. In one of these folders, an artist had included a watercolor of a fashionably dressed crowd—eclectic, tropical, Bohemian, and flagrantly sexual best describe the costumes—at what appeared to be a reading of some kind. The designer sent her mysterious correspondents their fair share and ended up making a small fortune for herself.

"She told me she just loved it when her friends began to get restless with one fashion. One day, her intermediary enclosed a piece of paper with gibberish words typed in the form of a neat letter. The designer assumed that the intermediary had inadvertently enclosed the results of a child playing on a typewriter. She threw the paper away on her way to have lunch with a friend. Halfway to the café she had a flash, and turned her car around. By the time she had gotten home, however, her maid had emptied the trash.

"That was the last time she heard from the intermediary. She was convinced that the intermediary had inadvertently enclosed a letter in XuXu. She believed that the intermediary was fearful she might have taken her XuXuian letter to a university to have it analyzed by computers; he had withdrawn without a word to eliminate the possibility of discovery.

"Robbed of the source of their vitality, the fashion designer's styles began to lose favor on the market. She sent letters to the intermediary begging, pleading for a response. Nothing. All she could do was watch and wonder which of her competitors, if any, were receiving inspiration from the artists of XuXu.

"Of course, there are all kinds of problems here. For one thing, she was working through an intermediary who may have rewritten the correspondence from both sides. Also, it's possible that the lost letter was just what it appeared to be: the result of a child whacking on a typewriter. It was still fascinating, however, and became even more so when I came upon the story of the naked president of XuXu.

"I heard this story from an old man in Pernambuco, who said he heard it from a drunk who spoke barely intelligible Portuguese. Ordinarily, I wouldn't have paid much attention to it, but it had a couple of interesting details.

"In this story XuXuians were portrayed as being stylishly dressed and sexy. Also, they were said to be artistic by temperament, lovers of literature. There were no television sets or radios in XuXu; in fact, XuXuians were almost entirely ignorant of the outside world. They knew other people were out there, because almost everything in XuXu was imported, including high-tech mining equipment. They had repeatedly attempted to make contact with the outside, but had never been able to communicate with anybody. One result of this was that everybody in XuXu seemed to be working on a novel or a poem, and there were nightly readings after which XuXuians groped one another or engaged in playful philosophical arguments. Also XuXuians loved their marijuana; alcohol was looked down upon because too many drunks got boorish and aggressive. Other drugs were out of the question.

"Over the years, however, XuXuians had become distressed over the behavior of their presidents, who were given to making all kinds of outlandish, undeliverable promises in order to get elected.

"Furious by the flooding caused by a promised but undelivered diversion dam, XuXuian congressmen met in an epic session of marijuana smoking to put an end to the nonsense. In the end, the stoned delegates passed a law requiring candidates for president to submit six specific promises one year before the election; an incumbent president faced a similar requirement, his promises to be delivered at his annual State of XuXu Address.

"According to the new law, for each promise undelivered at the end of one year, the president would have to make all public appearances the following year minus one designated article of clothing of his or her choice. For a man, the articles were shoes, trousers, underwear, shirt, jacket, hat. For a woman, they were shoes, skirt, underpants, blouse, bra, hat, or shoes, trousers, underpants, bra, blouse, hat. The idea was that sensible, deliverable promises would replace hyperbolic nonsense, which was the usual standard. The president vetoed the bill, but the determined XuXuian congress overrode the veto.

"A candidate willing to forgo the wearing of a hat during the second year of his administration could make one grandstanding promise. If he wished to wear sandals rather than shoes and socks, which was the practice of most XuXuians, he could include two undeliverable promises on his platform. If he was willing to be an informal president and not wear shoes, say, he could allow himself three worthless promises. A woman's sacrifices depended on whether the occasion required a dress or trousers."

"What happened?" Hanna asked.

"The drunk told the old man that the occasion of the first presentation of each candidate's list of six promises was much awaited in XuXu. There had been a problem with democracy as practiced in XuXu and the imaginative XuXuians had confronted it with reform; now, they would know the results of their new law.

"A crowd gathered as the candidates and their platforms were announced, although the details would be published in one or another of XuXu's six daily newspapers. One of the candidates, one of the sexiest single women in XuXu, entered the race unexpectedly and at the last moment."

"Promising what?" Hanna asked.

"She promised more romance for XuXuian women; more sex for XuXuian men; less rain in the rainy season; more rain in the dry season; the passage of a bill subjecting members of Congress to submit six questions of their own; and a domed chess pavilion."

"And?"

"She won in an apparent act of irresponsibility by the playful XuXuian voters. Although she was only able to deliver on one official promise—luckily the rainy season turned out to be drier than usual—her first year was marked by an impressive list of legislative successes. When the penalty year arrived, the president made her first appearance in a one-piece dress; this was entirely legal according to the law. For more casual appearances, she wore stylish trousers and went naked from the waist up. For parades and other outdoor appearances under the blazing sun, she wore a wide floppy-brimmed hat and nothing else. XuXuians loved all this, of course; they themselves wore as little as possible, and their president had a gorgeous figure. Her appearances in the nude almost always made the front page of the XuXuian newspapers.

"Of course, XuXuian women copied the sexy fashion, and the public was forced to acknowledge that through her influence the president was able to deliver, however belatedly, on two more of her original promises—a better sex life for men and more romance for women. In the end, she turned out to be one of the most sensible and civilized presidents in XuXu history.

"From this experience there evolved a XuXuian theory that any candidate with the ego to run for president was the very last person any responsible voter would want to elect. Of those who did run, seriousness and high purpose should be the most suspect of motives, almost always being a front for egomania and appetite. The function of XuXuian democracy is not to elect the best possible candidates—really worthwhile individuals won't allow themselves to be nominated—but to deal with the inevitable bad luck, that is, to reject the most insufferable politicians. Lacking the ideal candidate, one who refuses to run for office, the next best choice is whoever promises the most charm and fun with the minimum cost to the rest of us.

"The unusual reform was repealed by the legislature after the president made five outlandish promises in her second State of XuXu Address, ensuring near nakedness during her fourth-term campaign for reelection. There just weren't any politicians as fun to look at as the president. According to this story, a picture of the reclining president, naked save for a floppy hat, now graces the stylish twenty XuXu note."

23

WATER THAT IS NOT FROM

THE WELL

✳

After a long night of listening to the night sounds and Nicholas Bodan's labored breathing on the bunk opposite her own, of thinking about Father Machado's miracle fish and Mae Janaina and Father Ferrua, Hanna Doherty finally fell asleep.

She awoke, wet with sweat, and listened to the drum on the bow. She checked her travel clock. Seven in the morning. She got up, sleepy-eyed, to check Bodan. They'd died on her before and she didn't hold any expectations in particular, just hope. He was, in fact, still breathing. She took a deep breath and exhaled slowly.

So far, so good.

She mopped her face and breasts and armpits with a towel and crawled back into bed. She lay there listening to Bodan breathe. She knew she wasn't going back to sleep, so she slipped out of bed and got dressed to see how far they were from a settlement with hospital facilities.

She went straight to the bridge, where Weckert was at the helm pushing the *Barco* as hard as he could. The engine had by now taken a lot of punishment, another worry on top of everything else.

"How is he?"

"Still breathing, but we need to get him in a hospital."

"We've been pushing the red line all night. I figure about two hours to the Mae Janaina drop-off and another three to Santarém where they'll have a good hospital."

The engine made a *mom-mam-mom* sound.

Hanna said, "I can't remember that little *mam* sound in the engine before. What's that?"

Weckert didn't know what she was talking about. Or pretended not to know.

"That little sound in the engine. Hear it there?"

"I don't hear anything."

Indeed, the engine suddenly seemed to run smoothly.

"My imagination, I guess."

"No, I heard it too, I confess. It comes and it goes away."

Hanna went back to the aft cabin top and leaned against the comforting shoulder of Lenny Humphries. Humphries had a big pot of coffee on the table as well as slices of ham, cheese, and halves of papaya.

Kobayashi excused himself to go below, little red book in hand.

After he closed the cover of the companionway, Humphries said, "I assume he'll let us know if Nicholas's dead."

The engine hit a *mom-mam-mam-mom* that sugared the travelers' stomachs.

Hanna said, "What do you think is in Senhor Kobayashi's little red book, Father?"

Father Ferrua said, "I would like to think it's a religious text of some kind; that's the only kind of book that would command such attention. He's got his mind on moral order and on questions of origin and existence."

Mom-mam-mam-mam-mom.

The engine sounded scary.

"Well, what about his boxes?" Hanna said. "Don't you find them interesting?"

"The boxes are harder," Ferrua said.

"They could be anything," Humphries said. "He sure is fussy about them."

Hanna said, "Something valuable surely, perhaps hard-to-get mining equipment for the gold fields at Loucofilho."

"Maybe he's going to establish a brothel at Loucofilho," Humphries said. "Those boxes are filled with gilded bidets."

Father Ferrua laughed at this. "Then I'll stand fast too. I say the boxes contain the equipment necessary for Senhor Kobayashi to establish a religious mission in the jungle. He's a modest man and doesn't want to talk about it."

The *mam-mam* sound disappeared after about ten minutes. Then the canopy to the companionway slid back.

They heard Bodan sing:

> *"I know a girl in Kansas City,*
> *She's got gumdrops on her titties . . ."*

Bodan, pale and with perfectly awful eyes, made his way to the cabin top grinning and not hiccuping.

Kobayashi followed close behind, little red book in hand.

Hanna rushed over and grabbed Bodan and hugged him for all she was worth. "I won! I won! With an injection of frog sweat! I won and I didn't kill you. I can hardly believe it."

Over Hanna's shoulder, Bodan looked straight at Mae Janaina and casually gave her the finger. Then he hugged Hanna with all the strength his weakened body could muster.

Bodan said, "Hanna, have you ever heard a Jimmie Rodgers song called *The Woman from Liberia*? Probably not. It was popular when I was a kid." He gave Hanna the card.

"An amended version, as you see. I can only remember one phrase."

"I've heard it before but I don't remember the lyrics." Hanna read Bodan's little poem.

*"Well, there once was a woman
from Amazonia.
Well now,
She shouldered the water.
She carried the water.
She brought me the water
That was not from any well."*

When he was finished with the poem, Hans and Lenny and Father Ferrua and even the pleased Senhor Kobayashi gathered around Nicholas Bodan and joined with Hanna in giving a big hug of congratulations for having survived to be with them for the rest of the run to Loucofilho.

24
WHAT OBATALA SAYS

❋

Lenny Humphries, almost running around the hold, motioned with his hands for the aft passengers to come forward. The passengers could tell by the expression on his face that it was time for Mae Janaina's report on her communication, by *candomblé* drum, with the African god Obatala—Father Machado's designated pagan stand-in for Jesus—with regard to Obatala's long-missing clay fish.

"It's time, Father Ferrua, Hanna, Senhor Kobayashi. Mae Janaina has asked us to gather on the bow, please." Looking at Hanna, he gestured to the cabin. "Shall I go below and get Nicholas?"

"I'll go take a look," Hanna said. "If he's up to it and wants to, I'll bring him on along." She went below and found Nicholas sitting up on his bunk.

She gave him a big hug and stepped back and gave him a round of applause. "All right, Nicholas! Looking good."

"It worked. Thank you again, Hanna."

"It could have killed you."

"I suppose it could have, but it didn't. Sleep was what I needed. I think the drum stopped."

"Time for Mae Janaina's report on the will of Obatala. Would you like to be there for the drama or will you pass?"

"I think I'll pass, thanks." Bodan obviously felt good, pleased to be alive and to be rid of the damnable hiccups. He stood and flexed his knees. "Injected with frog sweat. How about that?"

"I don't think going to Loucofilho is the smartest thing for you to do. Your system is weak now and there are enough exotic diseases to catch down here as it is. I've got my medical bag with me but there's a limit to what I can do with it. Rest is what you need most. If I were you I'd think about checking into a hospital in Santarém or at a minimum finding yourself a comfortable hotel for a few days."

"I'll be okay. Really. They're going to drop the Bahians off somewhere along the line, aren't they?"

"That's the plan, as I understand it."

"It'd be better for me with them off the boat, I'll admit."

The *Barco*'s engine stopped and the boat began to drift. From on the bow there came a *toook-toook, toook.*

"It's time," Hanna said.

"I've had enough *candomblé* and black magic to last a lifetime. I'll pass, I think."

Hanna gave Nicholas a kiss and went forward where the others were gathered around Mae Janaina, who was wearing a white dress, red beads, and a red scarf.

When Hanna arrived without Bodan, Mae Janaina understood that the party was complete. She nodded to Mae Pequena, who was whacking the *agogó* bell, and Mae Pequena ceased. Speaking first to Weckert, Mae Janaina removed the lid from a wide-bellied basket and, by a string tied to its tail, removed a six-inch ceramic catfish, which she held high.

Weckert said, "She says this is Obatala's fish and she asks us not to touch it."

With the engine off, the passengers drifted in complete silence, which itself was a bit spooky. There were no insects or bugs out. Just the passengers, alone with their thoughts. They drifted. They listened to the gentle lap of water against the hull.

The *Barco* began to turn sideways to the current.

The Amazon Mae Janaina, looking down on the aft passengers and crew from that great height of hers—dangling the ceramic catfish in front of her by the string—paused in front of Weckert, then Humphries, then Senhor Kobayashi, and finally Hanna Doherty. She walked by each of them, giving them each a good look.

Then she laid the fish on the deck and stood to talk to Weckert. It was clear that Mae Janaina liked Weckert and trusted him.

Weckert considered his translation for a long minute as his passengers squatted on the deck to have a closer look at the fish. Father Ferrua, who already knew what she had said, got down on his hands and knees, tilting his head to examine the fish through the bottom half of his bifocals.

"Mae Janaina says she and her companions have taken the proper four nights to communicate to Obatala with the *candomblé* drums in addition to offering him a virgin, and Obatala has responded as she knew he would. Obatala told her the healing powers of Father Machado's fish have long been lost from its sitting in cathedrals and museums rather than being used to help people.

"First, she says, the Christians took her fish. Then they took her people. She says it is a mistake to call it Obatala's fish, for Obatala now denies and scorns it. The fish has taken on the attributes of its Christian owners, Obatala says, and rather than being a healing fish it now knows only appetite. Call it Christ's fish, if we wish, but Obatala doesn't want to have his name connected to it. It consumes without thinking. It eats without seeing. It devours without enjoying. It only wants more and more and more." Weckert used the tips of his fingers to wipe sweat from his brow.

"She says what was once Obatala's fish has become Bocagrande, He Who Eats Everything and who lives in the great depths of the Purus." Weckert blinked and wet his lips with his tongue.

"She says when Dr. Padim and his family were murdered that the police came to Salvador and asked her if she was responsible for their deaths. She says it was forbidden to touch the fish when it was brought to Brazil for exhibit—this to preserve its miraculous Christian powers. Well, she says that's not the reason at all. The real reason is that the fish is cursed, which the church knows perfectly well. She says Padim's death is proof that he was the thief. The police asked perfectly silly questions, in her opinion. Who cares who planted the bomb? The murderer was not to blame. Padim was killed because he handled the fish when he stole it. The fish killed him."

Father Ferrua, who of course understood her Portuguese perfectly well, was still on his hands and knees peering at the fish. "Bocagrande, my word." He looked disgusted. "Cursed! Captain Weckert, can Mae Janaina tell us where she came by this so-called Obatala's fish?"

Weckert asked the question. "She says Obatala told her if she wanted to know the truth she should look Igaranha in the eye, and so the *babalaô* unscrewed the glass eyes from the bow; this fish was stowed in the left eye."

"I don't believe a word of it, not a word of it," Father Ferrua said. He asked Mae Janaina a question directly in Portuguese.

Weckert said, "He's asking her if he might not examine the fish and she's saying yes, he can if he chooses, but he should know that the fish is contaminated. It's bad luck to hold it directly."

Father Ferrua, looking up at Mae Janaina, took the fish and turned it in the palm of his hand. He examined it, adjusting his spectacles. He offered it to Hanna.

"I'll pass, thank you. I'll take the lady's word for it." The fish looked precisely like the photographs of the miracle fish in Desmond's magazines.

Father Ferrua looked at Kobayashi. Kobayashi shook his head no.

"What do you think, Father? Is it genuine?" Weckert asked.

"It certainly looks like Obatala's fish, but it has to be a fake. She surely must know we'll find her out once we have it examined in Manaus." Father Ferrua said something more to Mae Janaina in Portuguese.

Weckert said, "He told her the fish is a fake and that she'll be found out once we reach Manaus, where there are proper police laboratories to determine its authenticity."

Mae Janaina stepped back, her face hard.

She grabbed the string and with one quick yank of her wrist whipped the clay fish off the deck and sailed it into the water.

Splash!

The *Barco*'s passengers and crew stared, disbelieving.

Mae Janaina looked triumphant. She spoke briefly to Weckert, clearly mentioning the word *Bocagrande* several times.

Weckert said, "Mae Janaina says if we're so anxious to learn the truth about Obatala's fish, then we should ignore whatever she says and whatever we're told in Manaus and go ahead and face Bocagrande on the Purus."

25

THEY WATCH THE ORANGE

EAT GREEN

✳

The *Barco Igaranha* stopped at a tiny village at ten o'clock and without ceremony Mae Janaina and her *candomblé* troupe packed up their belongings and were gone, together with their bells and drums and virgin sacrifices and calls to Obatala.

By noon, the passengers saw the town of Santarém in the distance, houses on a bluff with the heat nearly visibly rising from its streets and white buildings. They were met at the dock by an athletic young man in a high-crowned cowboy hat and by a man in his fifties with a pitted face, hawk nose, and square jaw. Behind them there were pickup trucks and young working men, who waited patiently, in no hurry because of the heat.

The young man in the cowboy hat and the man with the extraordinary face were in charge; these were the gentlemen from the Rancho Olivieres, who were to receive the boxes from AmeRiBurger Corporation, of Los Angeles, California.

After the routine of docking and securing the boat, Weckert and Humphries conferred at length with the two Brazilians, gesturing toward the *Barco Igaranha* as they talked.

At last Hans Weckert, struggling visibly to restrain his amusement, returned to the aft cabin while ranch workers unloaded the AmeRiBurger boxes from the hold. Lenny Humphries, obviously in a good mood, joked with the two ranchers on the dock.

Weckert, on the aft cabin top, said, "We've got what I

think is an unusual request. Oscar Buenovena, the elder gentleman there, is the superintendant of the Rancho Olivieres. The young man is his nephew Luis, who was educated in the United States and who speaks good English. They're about to place a very important bid to supply AmeRiBurger with a substantial amount of beef for their hamburgers. These boxes contain fat from American beeves and AmeRiBurger condiments. Senhor Buenovena is anxious to give the AmeRiBurger buyers what they want. He asked me if there were any Americans on board and I said yes, there were two. He wants to know, Hanna and Nicholas, if either of you have eaten an AmeRiBurger and if you have, would you consider a small day trip to his ranch to sample one using his beef. He seems quite sincere in this; he wants to know your opinion. This is very important to him and he promises an educational, entertaining outing for us all. He says all he has to do is make a call and the ranch will dispatch an air-conditioned bus to take you out."

Bodan's mouth fell. "So that's it. This is where they get their meat! Tell Senhor Buenovena that I'd be delighted. Tell him I grew up along the river where AmeRiBurger gets its AmeRiFries and AmeRiPotatoes. Nothing better than a quick burger with an order of fries."

Weckert looked amused. "How about you, Hanna?"

"Oh yes, although I'd be embarrassed to claim I'm any sort of expert. That is if it's okay with you and Lenny and Senhor Kobayashi and Father Ferrua."

In spite of his terrible struggle with the hiccups, the idea of a day trip perked Bodan up. "Hey, we'll be like wine tasters. Gourmets of the highway."

"The idea, as I understand it, is for Senhor Buenovena to call cabs to take you to a café for refreshments while you wait for the bus. They promise to have you back here this evening. There being no objections, I'll tell them yes. This is quite fortunate actually, because it gives Lenny and me an opportunity to buy fuel and groceries and have some work done on that engine. We've been pushing it awfully hard the last couple of days."

"We don't want to run out of rum and beer," Bodan said.

"Certainly not," Weckert said. "Or gasohol either."

The decision made, within minutes two Volkswagen taxis pulled onto the dock with the hospitable Oscar Buenovena—enthusiastic about having found two experienced eaters of AmeRiBurgers, one even hailing from the origin of AmeRiPotatoes—shouting orders least their smallest concern be left unattended. The travelers divided into the Volkswagens and were summarily whisked to the nearby Casablanca Bar to wait for the Rancho Olivieres bus.

The Casablanca turned out to be a large balcony or verandah above the Casa Ponto Verde, a curio shop, and Electronica Souza, which sold television sets, miniature radios, and digital wristwatches. The building was painted white with neat blue trim and CASABLANCA BAR in large red letters above the verandah.

There was a hammock factory across the street with the doors and windows open for fresh air. Bodan and Hanna each had a tall rum and Coke and watched young men work hand looms, tapping each woof neatly into place, hands and fingers flying. The hammock looms, devoid as they were of electrical devices—plugged to no line that hummed, buzzed, or crackled in the spheres—went *cl-click, cl-click, cl-click:* muscle against wood, wood upon cotton.

A few minutes later, a large blue Mercedes bus pulled in front of the Casablanca and parked with its diesel loping. They boarded, under the supervision of the smiling Oscar, who comprehended almost zero English, and Luis, who started to use a tiny electric microphone but put it down; it was cool, quiet, and comfortable in the big Mercedes. The passengers all rode at the front so there was no need for Luis to even raise his voice.

Luis told the passengers that he had polished his English at San Diego State University, where he studied business administration and where his cousin was married to an assistant registrar. He said Rancho Olivieres was financed by French, Swiss, and Japanese capital.

"I will begin by telling you that American consumers have been led to expect grain-fed beef from the midwest. They know marbled fat in a steak makes it taste good. The housewife in the supermarket wants marbled fat inside the steak, but not a big wad of fat on the outside. You take a big old T-bone steak of Kansas City grain-fed prime. All you do is give it a blast of heat on either side and you've got yourself a first-rate piece of meat.

"For the feed lots in Kansas City to get that fat on the inside of the carcass there has to be fat on the outside, there's just no way around it. The American meat packers have discovered that this extra fat's easily whacked off and flash-frozen. They've got machines that follow along the beeves' carcasses like a giant razor blade and peels the fat off in great big white curls. When you add flash-frozen Kansas City fat to flash-frozen Brazilian lean, your machine pops out patties with Kansas City flavor at the other end. As I said, it's the fat that gives meat its flavor. If we at Rancho Olivieres receive the AmeRiBurger contract we will literally mix Amazonian lean with Kansas City fat."

The bus was air-conditioned, and unlike the dilapidated VW van the passengers had ridden in to find rubies at Rubiu, this one had shock absorbers that smoothed out the *bumpity bump* of the road out of Santarém.

Weckert looked at Bodan a moment, studying him. "Are you sure you're strong enough for all this?"

"I'll be okay, stronger by the hour," Bodan said.

Luis said, "I should tell you that this very road was used by workers going from Santarém to Boa Vista in 1927. The rubber market was then dominated by *Hevea* trees that had been transplanted to Asia, and Mr. Ford decided to grow his own trees along the Tapajós River. The Brazilians gave him a plot of land the size of Connecticut in return for 7

percent of the profit after twelve years. The plantation at
Boa Vista was called Fordlandia.''

"Fordlandia?'' Bodan asked.

Luis grimaced. "Five years later the United States was in
a depression. Ford had spent seven million dollars clearing
seven thousand acres, and the trees that were planted on
Fordlandia were stunted or died. The *Hevea* is native to the
rain forest and couldn't stand the pelting rain and blistering
sun of cultivated fields.''

"Oh, poor Henry,'' Hanna said.

"There were other problems too, but Mr. Ford didn't
give up. Two years later, he tried again at Belterra, which is
just up the road from here. He gave the government one
third of the Boa Vista land, and used the rest to experiment
with grafting techniques and insecticides. He kept losing
money though and gave the whole thing to the government
in 1945.''

"And then what happened?'' Hanna asked.

Luis turned serious. "The weeds grew at Belterra as they
had in Boa Vista. But you see, Ford was in the wrong business.'' Luis said something to Oscar; the elder Buenovena
nodded his understanding and addressed his guests in Portuguese.

Luis listened and said, "Uncle Oscar says people don't
seem to understand that farming schemes like Henry Ford's
are almost always doomed to failure. But what you do have
once you get rid of the trees and brush is land that will
produce a lot of protein.

"The Amazon can accommodate Japanese-built super-
freighters if necessary. We can supply more beef at a
cheaper price than anybody else in Brazil or in Argentina.
And as for the hides? It's no secret that Brazil is the number
one producer of leather shoes in the world. Look at your
own shoes. The odds are they were made in Brazil.''

Oscar Buenovena had something to say to his nephew.

Luis said, "Uncle Oscar says there's no secret to our

success. Rancho Olivieres is properly financed and organized just like AmeRiBurger.

"All this used to be open range, you know. All we had to do was cut and torch the forest and seed it by helicopter, but we kept getting hit by rustlers, so we had to fence everything off. About three years ago, a shipment of barbed wire was hijacked. We've never been able to trace the bandits."

"Barbed wire?" Bodan asked.

"It never did make any sense. We're the only outfit around here large enough to need that amount of wire. We never did find out who wanted it or why."

Hanna sniffed. "What's that?"

"Something's burning."

"The weather's given us a break the last few days; it's surprisingly dry for this time of year."

The flames, snaking skyward, smoke billowing high, appeared on their left, orange eating green.

There were smoldering snags and black stumps at roadside, and beyond that a pall of blue smoke hung low, seeming to caress the ground, and, having consumed a valley that had been forest, advanced upon a high canopy of trees a half mile away. Black smoke rolled toward the sun, muddying a calm sky sprinkled with happy fluffs of clouds.

The passengers watched the fire in silence for several long minutes.

"Isn't that something to see?" Luis said. "This land isn't worth a damn the way it is. What we do is clear cut it and bulldoze it and let it dry for three or four months. Then we burn it, which kills insects, parasites, nematodes, fungi, and pathogenic bacteria. The ashes contain rich stores of nutrients and we've created sanitary conditions to sow our grass by helicopter. We get some pretty big fires going sometimes. The front on this one should be about eight or ten miles long."

"What happens then?" Hanna said.

Luis considered the question before he answered. "The

soil poops out is the best way of putting it, then the weeds take over. To hear the environmentalists complain, you'd think we were destroying the planet. The truth is something grows back. It may not be exactly the same as before, but something grows back.''

Bodan said, "If you're going to cook a hamburger, I suppose you've got to build a fire.''

"You should be here when we get a really good one going,'' Luis said.

Miles after they had passed the fire, the passengers could still smell the acrid smoke.

26

CONVERTED FOREST OOZES FROM

THE BLADES

❋

The driver of the Mercedes geared down to cross the crown of a steep hill, and before the travelers lay a valley of stripped forest four or five miles wide. Nicholas Bodan and Hanna Doherty sat up straight, almost in unison: below them there lay an incredible vista of thousands of cattle grazing in lush grass growing up between stumps and snags and charred logs.

"Rancho Olivieres. We're here,'' Luis said. "Isn't it a sight? A pretty little spread.''

Bodan leaned his forehead against the window.

From the top of the hill, the cream-colored beeves looked like Texas longhorns without the horns. As the bus descended into the valley and slowed to part a herd of curious bovines, it turned out the cattle indeed had bony ribs and bony flanks and bony shanks—lots of leather for Brazilian-made shoes. Their big ears flopped out at crazy angles.

The driver beeped his horn.

The cattle parted with reluctance; chewing their cuds with indifference, they peered in at the travelers.

"They're range-fed," Luis said. "As you can see, they can't carry a lot of fat in this heat, but they don't taste bad and we can clear all the land we want to graze 'em."

Luis said something to Oscar, then listened intently to Oscar's reply. "My uncle says Americans can't eat enough hamburgers to keep up with us. It can't be done."

This is when the travelers saw them coming up the wide valley—wasps as big as a house judging from the distance and their profiles.

"Whatever the hell are those? Blimps?" Hanna asked.

There were five of them, yellow and black, flying in V formation, with what looked like great long legs trailing beneath them. They were clearly angling in the direction of the bus.

"Wasps," Bodan said.

They did indeed look like wasps.

Luis said, "They're Japanese versions of what we call air trucks. They're quite unusual. In a minute you'll be able to see how they work."

The air trucks had revolving bodies. There was a foil on each fuselage that turned into a giant screw. There was a stationary cockpit on the front plus exterior supports—top and bottom and on both sides—and an airfoil and rudder at the rear. Instead of being pushed by a traditional propeller, Rancho Olivieres fleet of air trucks literally screwed themselves through the air.

Two long yellow-barked logs dangled from the skids of each air truck, looking like giant wasp legs. The colors were spiraled onto the body of each wasp and spun, spun, spun, yellow and black, yellow and black, yellow and black as the fuselages turned like slow-motion bullets.

Luis conferred with Oscar, then said, "My uncle wants you to know these are the only air trucks now operating in the southern hemisphere. They were originally designed in your American state of Oregon to remove selected old-growth Douglas fir without the expense of building roads and clear-cutting. Their revolving fuselage makes them both fast and stable. What they do is spot a prime tree and hover over it. The pilot lowers a faller. The faller topples the tree and knocks the branches off with his chain saw and cinches a cable around the top. The pilot reels in the tree and the faller, and they're off to the mill. One air truck can take up to eight logs a trip, depending on their size. These logs, Tupilipas, grow farther north in the rain forest where we have lumber and hardwood operations. That's where these air trucks normally work, although they've been doing chores around here the last few days. The Tupilipa's yellow bark makes it an ideal target, by the way. It looks like we're here," Luis said.

The bus slowed before a compound of ranch buildings surrounding a huge stone house.

As the travelers stepped out of the bus, one air truck broke formation, and rose high above the ranch. The Buenovenas stood tall, pleased that their impromptu demonstration was going off without a hitch or snag.

The travelers watched intently, knowing this was for their benefit.

The pilot, two hundred yards high, released the two logs, which tumbled lazily through the air. They landed with a pop and shattered, shuddering the ground and sending great splinters of lemon-colored wood sailing in every direction. By comparison, the eye-catching bark had only a hint of yellow.

Oscar Buenovena, yelling enthusiastically in Portuguese, punched his fist into the air.

Luis said, "Isn't it beautiful? We thought you'd like it. My uncle says wait until you taste its smoke. There's nothing in the world tastes like Tupilipa smoke. Nothing."

While the AmeRiBurger barbecue was being set up by the Rancho Olivieres employees, Oscar and Luis Buenovena took their visitors on an impromptu tour of the ranch buildings, detailing the esoteric and complicated system—arrived at, apparently, by years of trial and error—in which forest was leveled to produce cheap beef.

The rancho's sprawling buildings were situated on a hill with cattle to the front and untouched forest to the rear.

After a half hour of touring corrals, slaughtering facilities, and a system whereby the meat was flash-frozen for export, the travelers were told it was time for the tasting. They were taken to a flagstone verandah to the rear of the main house. The verandah was shaded and pleasant and had a large brick barbecue with a neat pile of yellow Tupilipa wood on one side and a box with chunks of charcoal on the other. Rancho Olivieres even produced a portable bar with a tuxedoed bartender.

But it was not the lovely verandah itself which was the main attraction, and not the barbecue or the bar or even the view. Rancho Olivieres had somehow come by an antique meat grinder made of cast iron and with legs decorated with flowers and all manner of Victorian nonsense and frivolity that was just wonderful. The elder Buenovena had obviously had the grinder polished up, and it was easy to see why. What a beauty! There was a wooden hopper on top to catch hunks of meat which were pushed through cutting plates by a six-inch screw, the operator supplying the power by turning a five-foot-wide flywheel.

Bodan and Hanna squatted to examine the yellow Tupilipa wood, which turned out to be laced with delicate red lines, almost like roots or blood vessels.

Luis said, "After we mix the fat and beef, we'll try AmeRiBurgers without and then with Tupilipa smoke. After we finish the first round, we'll clear out the firebox and start again."

"Is this a local favorite for barbecue?" Hanna asked, picking up a piece of yellow wood.

Luis said, "It's a local delicacy, actually, ordinarily hard to come by, but not with our air trucks. The AmeRiBurger people are interested in a new smoke flavor to compete with mesquite and this may be just what they're after. Of course, they wouldn't use the actual wood in their franchises; we'd have to process the wood so they can brush it on."

"I see."

"My uncle says we can furnish AmeRiBurger with all the Tupilipa they can use. With our air trucks we can just spread out and pluck 'em out of the forest. He wants to know what an American might think of the taste."

The travelers sipped cocktails and watched as a box of Kansas City fat was brought to the flywheel, while boxes of AmeRiSauce, AmeRiPickles, and other ingredients were assembled on a long table for the inspection of the company. The Rancho Olivieres cook, a swarthy man with great mustachios, was pleased to be the center of attention and took great pride in his display of AmeRiBurger condiments— jars of pickle chips and AmeRiSauce.

However, it was Oscar Buenovena who exercised the right to open the first can of fat for his guests to see. Oscar jabbered at his nephew. The nephew shouted orders at a yes man and within seconds the senior Buenovena was fitting Hanna with a Rancho Olivieres apron, letting his hand linger a trifle as he tied the bow at her back. Senhor Buenovena liked his women and would have let his hand linger even longer had not Bodan been standing there.

"Oh, thank you," Hanna said.

She watched over Oscar's shoulder as he used a screwdriver to pry open the first of six cans of fat that was so white it was extraordinary. Oscar gave a little oooh of admiration at the whiteness.

"Isn't it beautiful," Luis said. "Such marvelous fat. So wonderfully white."

Two manservants, impeccably attired in black trousers and white shirts, brought large hunks of fresh red meat on silver trays. With solemn faces they went from guest to guest, so that everybody might inspect the meat. In his turn,

Bodan opted to reward Oscar Buenovena with a little drama. Furrowing his eyebrows in concentration, he poked the meat with his finger. He smelled it. *Sniff, sniff.*

"Very good," he said.

Oscar knew enough English to understand that and was pleased.

After the meat had been examined, the manservant dumped it into a stainless steel tub on the table beside the grinder. A second manservant issued rubber gloves so the guests might toss meat into the hopper without having to wash blood off their hands.

At Oscar's bidding, the bartender poured fresh drinks all around, after which he held his glass high.

Luis translated: "My uncle says here's to the mixing of Amazonian lean with Kansas City fat. May we both prosper."

Bodan said:

> *"Jack Sprat could eat no fat*
> *And his wife could eat no lean,*
> *So between the two*
> *They licked the platter clean."*

Luis translated this for Oscar, who was delighted. The wisdom of a child's rhyme.

Hanna said, "There's a dainty dish to lure hungry travelers off the interstate highway."

Luis, brandishing a videocamera, said, "My uncle bought this antique meat grinder at an auction in Buenos Aires. He wants tapes of everybody helping mix the meat. So we'll begin with our American hamburger tasters, and then if you, Father Ferrua and Senhor Kobayashi, would be so kind as to take a turn."

"I'd be delighted to participate," said Father Ferrua.

"I would be honored as well," Kobayashi said.

"Good. My uncle says he will begin turning the handle. He wants to know if you, Mr. Bodan, would like to add the lean and if you, Ms. Doherty, would like to assist by adding the fat. He is very charmed by you, Ms. Doherty."

"Of course and thank your uncle for his compliment," Hanna said.

"Two handfuls of lean to one scoop of fat," he said.

Oscar took his place at the flywheel.

Hanna took her place at the table by the fat. She scooped out a giant white curl of fat with a large stainless steel spoon.

Oscar, seeing everybody was in place and enjoying his toy, started turning the heavy flywheel, slowly at first then gaining momentum, faster and faster.

Bodan dug into the cool meat with a gloved hand and tossed in two quick handfuls of lean.

Luis said, "A little smaller handfuls next time, I think."

"Gotcha," Bodan said.

Hanna whacked the spoon on the edge of the hopper, sending a wad of fat onto the screw.

Bodan replied with two small handfuls of meat and watched them screwed into the blades.

Luis said, "Don't be afraid to toss in the fat, Ms. Doherty. We like to sell beef, but we've got to come as close to the AmeRiBurger taste as we can."

Thus the travelers watched converted forest ooze from the blades in red-and-white ropes that piled up in beautiful little curls.

27

PARTIERS AT THE SANTARÉM DOCK

✳

Nicholas Bodan and Hanna Doherty ate their hamburgers somewhat self-consciously, knowing the importance Oscar Buenovena attached to their reaction. Buenovena could not refrain from biting his lower lip just a trifle in anticipation of their reaction, but he managed not to outright stare as they tasted Rancho Olivieres' bid for an AmeRiBurger contract.

Bodan, still chewing his first bite, sat his AmeRiBurger down and rose applauding. "Bravo, bravo, Senhor Buenovena. I think you've done it."

Buenovena slapped his thigh with excitement. He didn't speak English, but he didn't have to wait for his nephew's translation to know the news was good.

Bodan said to Luis, "Do tell your uncle that this AmeRiBurger is perfect. Exactly like the ones you buy in the United States. But you know, I don't think it's wise for me to eat too much of this one before I try one smoked with Tupilipa."

"I agree," said Hanna.

"We stand to do very well indeed if Tupilipa smoke catches on," Luis said. "I'll tell my uncle."

As Oscar turned to give the cook instructions to start preparing the smoked AmeRiBurgers, a man wearing a pilot's sunglasses came to the verandah to whisper in the ranch manager's ear. Buenovena listened, keeping one eye on his guests.

Oscar's eyes widened momentarily. He whispered something in the man's ear. Nodding, the man left.

Suddenly, the visitors caught their first whiff of something exquisite—it was the smoke of the Tupilipa, the first wisps of which rose lazily above the grill.

Oscar did not fail to see their reaction and was pleased.

As the guests inhaled the exquisite odor of Tupilipa smoke, Oscar conferred briefly with Luis.

Luis said, "My uncle says you might be interested to know that this afternoon the air-truck pilots spotted a religious ruin about two hundred yards off the road between here and Santarém. My uncle is having a trail cut through the forest so that you might be able to visit it on your way back."

"We should see it by all means," said Father Ferrua.

"That's wonderful," Hanna said. "Thank you."

Senhor Kobayashi nodded his agreement.

"The pilots hovered just above it and would have lowered somebody to take a look but they were running short on fuel and had to get back to the ranch. They say it's overgrown with brush and looks like a string of beads each about the size of a car."

Oscar Buenovena, nothing if not a lavish host, served his Tupilipa-smoked AmeRiBurgers on a silver platter.

Bodan examined his as though it were a rare topaz or opal, while Hanna was a more straightforward eater.

Bodan said, "It's best to let it cool just a tad, otherwise the heat drives out some of the taste." He held his hamburger up and studied its profile.

Oscar watched this intently, pleased by Bodan's little show.

Bodan picked up the sandwich and took a bite. He chewed thoughtfully, his eyes narrowed in concentration. He took a second bite, chewing thoughtfully. To Hanna he said, "Do we tell the truth?"

Luis looked concerned and so too did his uncle.

Hanna shook her head. "They taste too good to get away with a lie."

Bodan's shoulders slumped. Still chewing, he said, "Tell your uncle that AmeRiBurgers smoked with Tupilipa are perfectly delicious."

The way back to Santarém went quicker than the way out for some reason, and before the travelers knew it, they saw a Rancho Olivieres wasp hovering in the air just off the road.

"These are the ruins," Luis said.

The bus driver pulled to a stop alongside the road behind an old pickup and his passengers stepped out onto the red soil. Four Indians—tiny bronze-colored gentlemen with cereal bowl haircuts and machetes—rose from the shade.

They conferred with the ranch manager, who talked to them in their language. Then Oscar briefed his nephew.

Luis said, "The Indians have hacked a path to the ruins as they were told, but they didn't examine them close up. They're afraid they might be taboo. There are some things better off left alone, they say."

Without further ado, they started. Oscar went first, machete in hand, although he didn't need it. The Indians—who had worked while the travelers sampled AmeRi-Burgers—had whacked a regular turnpike, actually more of a tunnel because the light barely filtered through the foliage above. Oscar was followed by Luis, who had a machete, then Hanna—entertaining visions of dangling spiders, vipers on the ground, and boa constrictors hanging from limbs—followed by Bodan, Father Ferrua, and Senhor Kobayashi. The Indians were content to remain with their pickup until further orders.

The travelers arrived at the ruins after a five-minute walk. The Indians, guided by the hovering air truck, had wound up confronting a large metallic object overgrown with underbrush. Oscar and Luis attacked the remaining few feet of brush left by the Indians.

For the first time, the travelers could see the ruins clearly.

The object was apparently an automobile wrapped round and round and round with barbed wire forming a metal cocoon of sorts.

Hanna and Bodan gathered with the others and cupped their eyes and mashed their faces against the wire to peer between the strands, which wasn't easy because of the barbs. Whoever wrapped this car had really done a job.

There was a skeleton in men's clothing in the first car, the bony wrist wearing a jewel-encrusted wristwatch. There was a pistol too. A skeleton beside the man, a female's, had a six-strand lapis lazuli necklace lying with the vertebrae that had been her neck. There was a ruby-encrusted anklet and a roll of gold chains where each wrist had been.

Seeing the inside of the first cocoon, Father Ferrua fell to his knees and began praying.

Nicholas said, "Whoa!" and grabbed Hanna by the hand.

Kobayashi blinked, then backed off. He didn't bring his little red book, so there was no solace there.

Luis cleared more brush with his machete so that everyone could get a clearer look at the barbed-wire cocoon.

At the front of the automobile, sticking up between two strands of barbed wire, was a Mercedes-Benz hood ornament.

"A Mercedes," Luis said. He began whacking forward in the brush to a still larger cocoon. "This one's a truck."

Oscar said something in Portuguese and began swinging his machete at the wrapped form to the rear of the first automobile. "Mercedes!" he yelled. He cut his way to yet another form. "Mercedes!" he yelled again.

"How many did they count from the air?" Bodan asked Luis.

"They said thirty small ones with two larger ones in the front."

"The trucks," Bodan said.

"It looks that way," Luis said.

Oscar, still chopping his way from automobile to automobile, shouted "Mercedes" at each one. Then he stopped and yelled something longer in Portuguese.

Luis said, "He said there are one or two skeletons in each Mercedes. He said some of them shot themselves and others apparently starved to death."

They waited as the elder Buenovena returned, sweating heavily. As he talked to his nephew he gestured back toward the wrapped cars with his machete.

"Does he know who they are or where they're from?" Hanna asked.

Luis said, "He doesn't have any idea who these people are, but suspects they might have been taking stolen Mercedes to sell to the miners at Loucofilho. This used to be a shortcut to a road that would get you there. There's no other place out here to market cars like these.''

Bodan said, "Who did it?"

"He doesn't know for sure, but if they weren't such a gentle people, he suspects it might have been the tQuati, a small band of vine worshippers who have moved farther back in the forests. Anyway, he says at least now we know what happened to the shipment of barbed wire that was stolen from us a couple of years ago.''

The travelers got back to the *Barco* after dark and Lenny Humphries set about preparing them a real spread, having toured the local produce markets while they were on their day trip to Rancho Olivieres.

Bodan said, "Well, did you and Lenny have a day of peace and quiet without us underfoot? They have a saying back in the United States that fish and guests stink in three days. I'll bet you were glad to have a little privacy again.''

Humphries said, "We're used to our privacy, it's true. We had plenty of errands to run, provisions to buy, and that sort of thing, so we kept busy.''

"Are you feeling better, Nicholas?'' Weckert asked.

"Oh yes, I seem to be coming round. But now I'm concerned about Father Ferrua's future. After what happened to me, I'm not certain I would have handled that fish if I were you, Father Ferrua.''

"The fish was an obvious fake,'' Ferrua said. "She wouldn't have tossed a fish worth three million American dollars into the water, *kerplunk,* merely to prove some kind of point, let's face it.''

"No, no, no. It wasn't an obvious fake at all. I saw you on your hands and knees giving it a careful examination. You don't know it was a fake at all. Not really. It could have been genuine. It's possible they found it in *Igaranha's* eye, just like she said. She's a high priestess, remember, a *yalorixa;* maybe she doesn't care about the money.''

Humphries said, "I checked the *Igaranha* fish eyes on the bow. For whatever it's worth, they've been unscrewed and screwed back on recently."

"Of course they were removed and put back on," Ferrua said. "The army searched the boat, however inadequately. Dr. Humphries, I don't expect to lose a lot of sleep over Mae Janaina's claims, opinions, or predictions. Bocagrande! My word. Good heavens, listen to these folks."

The passengers on the *Barco Igaranha* all turned in unison at a peal of laughter coming from four revelers, speaking a strange, fluid language, returning to their riverboat.

As they approached the *Barco,* one of the men—there were two men and two women—suddenly displayed a small flutelike instrument with a slide, rather like a trombone. He held the slide high and began playing the "Colonel Bogey" march while his companions, whistling, giggling, fell into step.

As they drew parallel to the *Barco* they could see everybody clearly on the well-lit cabin top—even behind mosquito nets.

One of the two men, looking in at the folks on the *Barco,* said something in his fluid language.

The revelers stopped momentarily, then hurried on, glancing back in at the riverboat.

Hans and Lenny glanced at one another. Hans paled slightly and Lenny bit his lip.

Senhor Kobayashi did a perfect double take, then stood, leaning, to watch them walk down the dock.

It was perfectly obvious that both Hans and Lenny had heard that language before and probably knew the foursome.

Kobayashi, too, clearly recognized the language. For the first time on the trip, the quiet salesman was moved to emotion. He was momentarily discombobulated.

Bodan, having taken all this in, threw Hanna a glance that said: *What do you make of it, Hanna?*

She gave him a beats-hell-out-of-me shrug of the shoulders.

The revelers' boat was moored several down from the *Barco Igaranha.* As the travelers began eating their steamed fish, fried bananas, and hearts of palm salad—with Hans, Lenny, and Kobayashi trying to pretend nothing curious had happened—one of the party, a man, began an impassioned speech in English, which was interrupted by hoots of derision and howls of laughter from his three companions. However, when he finished, they all applauded and whistled. Then a woman took over and made a speech in English, which was also the subject of much merriment.

Bodan gave Hanna another look: *Can you hear what they're saying?*

She shook her head no, she couldn't.

Then the celebrants began singing in their language. The trombone-flute player played "It's a Small, Small World," and after more giggling, the partiers fell silent.

28

A JOURNEY INTO CLEAR WATER

❋

After a long day on the water from Santarém, the *Barco Igaranha's* rejuvenated engine was in a loping, almost jovial *mwam-mwam-mwam* mood late in the afternoon as Hans Weckert, squinting his blue eyes against the late afternoon sun, piloted her about a hundred yards off the wall of green that rose high on the starboard.

Weckert was looking for an opening in the marshland, leading to a passage that ran parallel to the river before coming to a stop at the border of Ch country.

Nicholas Bodan was with Lenny Humphries at the bow when riverbank forest jungle gave way to the marshland.

Humphries yelled up at his mate. "I think this is the one, Hans. Remember those two trees back there?"

"Those were the trees, I'm sure of it, Lenny." Weckert slowed the boat, shifting *mwam-mwam-mwam* to a measured *mo-wab, mo-wab, mo-wab.*

Weckert aimed the boat toward an opening in the tall reedlike grass that hung out over a narrow stream that was the reason for the marsh. He slowed the engine to a lazy, low-pitched *wob-wob-wob* made by the exhaust burbling through water.

At the bow, Humphries yelled, "Slow, Hans. Slow. Slow."

Weckert forced the *Barco Igaranha* through the narrow channel, swamp grass and reeds brushing the boat on both sides.

The passage suddenly narrowed even more. The boat popped into a clear spot and drifted for a moment, *ker-runching* through marshland undergrowth, then came to a stop. The passage was too small for them to continue. Weckert nipped the *wob-wob-wob* of the idling engine and they were alone with the heat and the buzzing and clicking of insects. The air had an earthworm odor of mud and the sweet-rancid smell of decay.

Lenny Humphries parted the reeds that hung over the deck rails and lowered the anchor into the shallow water.

A few moments later, Weckert joined the group atop the aft cabin. "We can't go any farther in the riverboat, but the leech people use this passage to the river. They'll know we're here by and by. We'll just relax and have a nice supper after all this hard running today."

"They won't be frightened?" Hanna asked.

Weckert laughed. "No, no. Lenny and I have traded with them before. The other river captains are put off by the leech business and stay clear. But the younger men come out into these marshes every afternoon setting leech traps, and they know my boat. I always bring them metal pots or salt or something they can use, and I don't cheat them."

"Do we just wait then or what?"

"There's nothing we can do but wait. It may be five minutes, may be five hours, but they'll come. Meanwhile, if anybody wants to do a little fishing to help with a fresh dinner, Lenny's got the gear."

"Do the leeches wait around on reeds?" Father Ferrua asked. "Don't anybody brush against the reeds."

Hanna cleared a spot in the reeds for herself. It was cooler out on the river than in the swamp. The heat built up in the reeds.

Weckert grinned. "Lenny, can you bring up a case of Brama Chopp?" he called. "And some rum."

"Yes, rum," said Hanna. "And ice! Good thinking, Captain. We'll drink rum and contemplate leeches."

"Hans, visitors forward!" Humphries yelled.

Weckert stood. "If you folks'll stay here for a few minutes. We don't want to spook them until they know we're friends." He scrambled down the steps and hopped lightly around the boiler on his way to the bow. A few minutes later he returned to the cabin top.

"Apprentice leechers," he said.

"Apprentice leechers?" Hanna asked.

"I guess that's what you'd call them. Collecting leeches is restricted to priests. The apprentices are put to work setting leech traps in the swamps and marshes. This is all secret stuff. Even the traps are secret. They have a certain, uh, identifying mark that identifies their status."

"Really?"

"You'll see it all tomorrow morning. I told them how many of us there are and he says we're welcome to visit, no problem, but they have to go back for more canoes. They like visitors but few people ever visit them. I've agreed that we'll be up and ready to leave at dawn. They'll go back and get Ralph and pick us up late tomorrow morning."

"Ralph?"

Weckert smiled. "Ralph's a master leechman who serves as an interpreter. He speaks a few words of Portuguese and is a good mime, which is mostly how he communicates. It's his responsibility to deal with outlanders, as the Ch call their visitors. He's sort of their secretary of state."

Nicholas Bodan was entering a record of the sixth day into his laptop—his mind abuzz with *candomblé* and ceramic fish and killer hiccups and Bocagrandes and burning forests and oozing ropes of lean and fat—when he heard laughter coming from the main channel of the Amazon, which, Weckert.had said, lay less than a hundred yards away.

After a brief silence, there was more laughter.

A man with a megaphone or loudspeaker began making a speech. Although he was too far away to be heard, his delivery was distinctive. Bodan recognized the orator; he was the one on the docks at Santarém who had been holding forth grandly but without the megaphone.

Bodan slipped out of his hammock and leaned over the edge of the cabin to the open window of Hanna's compartment. "Hanna!" he whispered.

"I hear them. I'm awake," she said.

"The partiers. The same ones moored down from us at Santarém."

"Only now they've got themselves a megaphone of some kind. Just a second, Nicholas. Nicholas?"

"I'm still here."

"Everybody down here's awake too. They're all listening."

"It's impossible not to. Hans, Lenny, and Kobayashi all know them."

"Are they following us, do you think? Is that why they're waiting out there?"

"Beats hell out of me. I can't imagine why." Bodan listened to the partiers until they fell silent, then he himself fell asleep, worn out from a long day on the water.

Nicholas Bodan was awakened by the rising sun and lay there in the hammock enjoying the extraordinary quiet and the pungent river smells. The swamp was especially exotic viewed through the double gauze of the enveloping mosquito net. He turned in the hammock: the mosquito coil beneath him had long since burned out, leaving concentric circles of fine gray ash on the deck. His Zippo and one unlit coil remained.

They were in a swamp on the Amazon at the mouth of a mysterious river and Nicholas, fast recovering from his bout with the hiccups, felt good to be alive. This was real Jacques Cousteau stuff. In his mind's eye Bodan heard a solemn narrator, in the manner of a television documentary, setting the scene:

"Nicholas Bodan awakes at dawn to enjoy an Amazonian sunrise." Bodan, the great adventurer, swaying slightly in his hammock, imagining the eyes of public television watchers everywhere, narrowed his eyes and grinned at his fantasy.

The sun was a rosy glow, barely visible through the wall of reeds on either side of the boat. Bodan realized that the swamp's bugs were in the middle of changing shifts. The graveyard zoomers were finding places to hide from the sun. The day crew was not yet fully awake. He slapped his neck. A little bastard had found its way through the nets.

Bodan got up to enjoy the sunrise. Senhor Kobayashi, Hanna Doherty, and Father Ferrua came up later for coffee and breakfast. They were still eating boiled eggs and fruit when word came back from the bow that the leechmen had arrived as promised.

Weckert led Hanna and the travelers forward to the bow where three slender canoes waited. The canoes, sculpted from the trunk of a single tree, were each about eighteen feet long, but were most remarkable for their identical bow and stern, both of which rose gracefully from the water to a prow of a most horrible visage—in fact, as was clear, the face of an open-mouthed leech.

There were two leechmen for each canoe. They were broad-cheeked, tiny young men, something less than five feet tall, with jet black hair cropped into a perfect circle, as though their barber had followed the rim of a large bowl. All hair beneath the circle was shaved to the skin. They had copper-colored skins and looked enthusiastic, communicating happily in a language that lapsed into odd yelps that sounded like the barking of articulate dogs.

But the most remarkable thing about these happy little gentlemen was that their lips were stretched to resemble a suckerlike mouth. The insides of the suckers were stained a pale red, as were their teeth.

Weckert used his hands, arms, legs, and body in addition to his sketchy knowledge of Ch to communicate with the interpreter Ralph, a full-blown leechman judging from his flamboyant sucker. The sucker's outside had been kneaded and pushed into a tiny rim of uniform size. Whereas the interior of the suckers on the apprentices was a pale pink, his sucker was a bright crimson, as were his teeth and the tips of his fingers.

Weckert palavered with Ralph—their invented lingo involving charades as much as anything else, while the apprentices gossiped in their barky language and used their paddles to point at their curious visitors.

Weckert turned to explain the situation. "Ralph says he and his apprentices take three in a canoe. I'll go in the lead canoe with Hanna and Nicholas. Father Ferrua, you and Senhor Kobayashi can ride in the second canoe. They'll bring our cooler of food in the third. We'll be on Ist River all day, Ralph says, but we'll be in the land of Ch in plenty of time for a treat tonight: we get to watch a leechman wedding."

"A wedding?"

"Ralph says it's a colorful ceremony, although I can't understand his explanation of it. He does assure me the canoes will stay close on the way through the swamp so we won't get separated. We'll be several hours on the water, so if you get thirsty or need to take a leak or something just speak up. There's very little traffic out here, so you won't have to yell."

And so the outland travelers were loaded into the leech canoes and were off, their enthusiastic little hosts digging their paddles into the water with powerful strokes.

Weckert said, "The stretching of a leechman's lips is a long and complicated business. It's done by leechman elders who have studied the technique for years. Their lips are stretched tightly around a large wooden disk that has to be removed when they eat and which has to be replaced once a week with a slightly larger one. The replacing of a disk is in itself an ordeal because the apprentice must undergo a painful massaging of the interior of his sucker with the red dye.

"As the lips are stretched and massaged, the sucker gets redder and redder on the interior, and the outside is pushed into an even little rim. The idea is to end up with the widest, brightest sucker possible. Ordinarily these young apprentices would be wearing their disks, but we're outlanders; they want to show off their lips for us.

"You can tell a full-blown leechman by his fingertips. They'll be bright red, meaning he has reached the status where he is allowed to massage an apprentice's lips. He charges a stiff fee for this service and the stretching and coloring, which can take as long as ten to fifteen years. As I understand it, this stretching of the lips is a ritual form of initiation into the brotherhood of They Who Suck.

"Although the sons of Ch pinks, or commoners, aren't prohibited from having their lips stretched, the fees are so expensive that most apprentices are the sons of leechmen. The long and painful and expensive stretching is the justification for the fees and tithes levied for blessings and healings."

Hanna said, "What does Ist mean, Hans? Is it a Ch word?"

"It's a Ch word and it means That Which Is or the Clear Water of Truth, depending on the context. Incidentally, the word *istu*—Ist with the *oo* sound added—in addition to the killer fish, means eyes of darkness or death fish, also depending on the context."

29

EATERS OF THE RIVER IST

✳

The four canoes left the *Barco Igaranha* late in the morning, proceeding single file and at a leisurely pace through the swamp of tall grass and reeds. Merry birds chattered and hopped on either side, showing flashes of green, and yellow, and red.

Nicholas Bodan could feel cool shadow and hot sun alternately going *flit-flot-flit-flot* against the side of his face as the canoe slipped past the reeds. He closed his eyes and smelled the swamp air, sweet rot, rising methane, and listened to the birds and insects, felt himself being carried away in time and place.

Then the canoes left the reeds and tall glass, and the outland travelers were ushered into a primordial gloom of shade under a high canopy of branches, the homeland of such bugs and creatures as previously existed only in the dreams of the outland travelers.

The leechmen's paddles dipped *fooup-fooup-fooup* into the water, setting canoeist's rhythm. Insects with wicked sticks handled percussion; one drummer then another flashed its stuff, one sedate, the next manic, a passing *cl-lic-ic-ic-ic, cl-lic-ic-ic-ic* replaced by a measured *tic-tak-tak, tic-tak-tak.* Up ahead, a bird on French horn responded *fortissimo* to the swampmaster's baton: *ka-oooop! ka-oooop! ka-oooop!*

The tangle of trees grew directly out of the murk, white bark spiraling to a canopy of amazing green high overhead; branches of roots grew out of the crud and were doubled by their reflection on the water. A seedpod that looked like a parachute floated by. A bluish green insect that looked like a helicopter gunship hovered, turned, darted, stopped, hovered, turned, zipped off. An excited bug with a raspy sax replaced the French horn as the principal herald, *zzzziiizzziizzing* with a frenzy as the canoes approached.

Oblivious to the chorus around them, the leechmen paddlers calmly turned their file of vessels into a confusion of trails through the undergrowth. They followed a passage that branched unexpectedly, then turned back on itself, then circled an impossible stand of trees growing out of the water.

The leechmen, unconcerned, aimed their craft this way and that to negotiate islands of brushy snarl, paddling in silence, pleased that the outlanders were enjoying the ride. The outlanders peered into towers and spires of cobwebs as birds yakked and jabbered overhead. They saw a beehive that looked like a grand piano with no legs. They were inspected by a pair of yellow eyes poking up from the water.

After two hours of this, the procession entered a shaded clearing, and Hans Weckert's lead canoe pulled to one side and waited for the remaining three to catch up. "They say a napping place is coming up and it's close to nap time," he said. "The leechmen say it's stupid to do any work in the afternoon. It's too hot." Weckert produced a three-liter thermos of iced tea while the leechmen took a short break.

A half hour later, the lead canoe headed for an island and landed where a trail met a tiny beach. The leechmen happily set about collecting hammocks and their lunch, which they had brought in small baskets. The travelers disembarked, spraying and oiling themselves with another layer of insect repellent as they stepped ashore.

With Weckert and Bodan carrying food and hammocks,

the outland travelers followed the leechmen through the trail of cobwebs to a traveler's wayside. A pentagon of logs surrounded a neat firepit. A scrap of tin atop four stones made a neat stove. The thicket of slender trees behind the firepit seemed made to order for the slinging of hammocks.

Ralph started a fire and got a pot of water heating, as Weckert got leftover rice and bits of cooked fish out of the Styrofoam cooler and fried it quickly in a skillet. When the water began boiling in his pot, Ralph went into the stand of trees and returned with two heaping handfuls of dried leaves, which he crushed and tossed into the boiling water, stirring it with a stick. Thus prepared, they dined, the outlanders on fried rice and cold beer, the leechmen on raw fish, boiled root, and their special tea, which they drank out of wooden cups stored on the branch of a nearby tree.

Weckert insisted they all try some of Ralph's tea. This was a special brew, he said. They had to try it. To the outlanders the tea tasted like warm beer and numbed the insides of their mouth and throat, but Weckert insisted they all have at least one cup. Bellies full and sated by the tea, they retired to hammocks slung in the shade of the canopy of branches high above, pulled bug nets carefully around them, and fell into a dreamless sleep.

When the outlanders woke, the sun was low in the west. They had slept four hours! All the outlanders except Weckert were astonished that they had slept so long; it would be getting dark soon.

"The leechmen don't believe in fighting this heat," Weckert said. "Besides, they've been told to time your arrival for the leechman wedding. We'll be leaving this swamp shortly and entering the Ist River. There are yellow rivers, black rivers, and clear rivers in the Amazon basin. This will be a clear river, like the Xingu."

"Four hours! That's some tea," Hanna Doherty said.

"It's use is restricted to leechmen or their guests. It is taboo for the pinks."

"Well! I see," Hanna said.

The leechmen, refreshed by their nap, returned to the paddles in earnest, and minutes later the outlanders heard a distant high-pitched *bok-bok, bok-bok-bok* of a leechman's drum. The *bok-bok, bok-bok-bokking* got louder and louder until the canoes abruptly entered the clearest, purest-looking water that any of the outlanders had ever seen.

Hanna literally sucked in her breath at the clarity of the water in the river Ist. Hanna and Bodan leaned over the edge of the canoe and looked down at stones and rotting logs on the bottom, all magnified in startling detail by the clear water.

Bodan said, "Wow! Look at that. Water for a beer commercial."

Weckert said, "We're going to be having some pretty soon. Now, they'll all be wearing pink loincloths as compared to the bright red of our friends here. This color comes from a medicinal herb, which the leechmen rub on the suckers of their apprentices. If you drink the stuff it'll make you drunk, which is what all the men seem to want. The women want to dye their clothes with it. Unfortunately the bark is of the leech gods and may only be removed and boiled by leechmen. You either have to be very wealthy or a leechman to have a crimson loincloth. Ordinary people are called pinks from the pallid red of their loincloths. Look over there."

One, two, then three canoes slid toward them from the shadows of the narrow river. Still more canoes followed, until a flotilla fell in behind the apprentice leechers and their guests. The canoes contained all manner of little Ch in pink loincloths: women, children, old people—none of whom had their lips deformed in the manner of the leechmen. The pinks had high-cheeked, handsome faces. They waved shyly at the newcomers, but were obviously eager to be part of the welcoming party.

Bodan waved back, saying, "Well, would you look at this. The jolly pinks."

"My heavens," Hanna said. "They're a handsome little people."

"The pinks are beautiful, they really are. We'll soon be coming up to some barriers of sorts. They're actually woven fences hung from floating booms. They're built to protect the pinks from the istu. They say the istu blends in so well you can't see it; you look for the red on gold of its eye, but by the time you see the eye you're being eaten. It's ordinarily safe enough to wade and swim in these rivers; the usual piranha travels in schools and is attracted by blood. Istus travel alone or in schools and they don't need a nick or scratch to attract them. Just boom, one's on you and you're gone."

"So they built these elaborate barriers."

"That's right, they built these elaborate barriers."

"Wow."

"If you believed the stories of the istu you'd want a stainless steel barrier between you and them. Those woven barriers rot and have to be replaced. What if there was a rip or tear that nobody saw?" Weckert lowered his hand into the clear water.

"What are you doing?" Bodan said.

Weckert laughed. "I'm not convinced that the istu exists."

"You aren't?" Hanna said.

"I asked the leechmen for a sample death fish so I could paint it. They said no, it couldn't be done without endangering lives. I said surely there must be a way to safely trap one. They said no, an istu would chew its way through the trap to get at flesh, would spring for the eyes of its captor. I said I didn't want to paint a live one. I said I had a special fishing machine that could fool fish into eating bait that concealed metal barbs attached to an almost invisible line. They scoffed at the idea of fooling an istu. I said, well then, wasn't it possible to poison a section of the stream; the water would clear later? They said no poison can kill an istu."

Hanna said, "I thought you said they were fishermen. How can they fish and contend with something like that?"

"They tithe one tenth of their catch in return for the leechmen's blessings against the accursed istu."

"A religious tithe?" Hanna turned her head.

"Ten percent. But the pinks are satisfied because they're getting their money's worth. The blessing works—at least there's no record in memory of one having failed."

"No fishermen getting gobbled up."

"No."

"But some real horror stories from the past, I'll bet."

"Some real beauts." Weckert smiled.

They rode in silence for twenty minutes, listening to the dipping of paddles and the occasional cry of a bird.

Then Weckert said, "We're coming up to the barriers. They're actually woven baskets floating from log booms."

The lead canoe approached the first of the istu barriers. This one extended fifteen feet from the shore and ran parallel to the shore for forty or fifty feet before it made another right-angled turn to the shore again—forming a neat rectangular safe area that was safe from the death fish. A few minutes later they passed a second barrier that was a hundred yards or more long. As the canoes proceeded upstream, these fences became larger and more frequent; building them must have been quite an engineering feat for these tiny people.

Weckert said, "It'll be getting dark soon and it's a little hike back to the village, but I've been here when these enclosures were filled with children playing and women washing their clothes."

As the fences became more common, the paddlers, eager for the finish, seemed to have found a second breath, and the canoes slipped through the water at an accelerating pace.

When the leechman saw a plume of smoke up ahead the apprentice leechmen began barking excitedly: they were coming home.

Up ahead little pinks had gathered on a beach beside the entrance of a small stream. The procession of canoes paused at the enclosure surrounding the main landing. While one apprentice leechman stared into the water looking for the telltale flash of red and gold of istu's eyes, a second apprentice opened the gate in the floating boom. He did this quickly to prevent istu from slipping by unseen; the leechmen dug their paddles as hard as they could, and the canoe zipped inside.

The paddlers straightened with pride, tilting their chins back the better to display their deformed lips: by these suckers so painfully and expensively earned let it be known that we are mighty leechmen; look upon these leech lips, ye mighty, and despair.

The apprentice leechmen entered the protected area triumphantly, paddles stroking in unison. These leechmen came bearing outlanders from beyond the great swamp; they were heroes.

30

A Leechman Takes a Bride

❋

A crowd of several hundred pinks had gathered around what the outlanders saw clearly was a percussion band of fifty or sixty excited musicians. They each readied a rod or tube, a stick or triangle, or some kind of drum. Even from a distance the outlanders understood that the pinks loved drums, there being little and big drums, fat and skinny drums, and one mother of a drum so large it had to be steadied by assistants.

The apprentice leechmen canoeists lined their craft in a

single rank and, on the word of their leechman commander
—and keeping their leech lips at a proud angle—paddled
straight and hard toward the beach.

A little pink stepped up to the big bass drum.

The line of canoes hit the beach almost simultaneously
and as they did . . .

. . . the pink with the club leaned into the first blow:
WH-UNG!

At the sound of the drum, the spectators began stamping
their feet furiously and the rest of the band started jamming.

The big bass—deep, rich, jarring, jungle stereophonic—
set a resonant, majestic cadence, the stuff of the king's elephants. The little pink with the club swung from the heels
with each blow, sending tremors to the spheres, and shaking the pinks attempting to hold the drum steady:
WH-UNG! WH-UNG! WH-UNG!

Around this stolid beat, the pinks were jazzmen, some
inspired, some elegant, some obvious fuck-offs. There was
the familiar *bok-bokking* sound to which was added—
through no-bullshit one-of-a-kind instruments carved from
tropical hardwoods—creative variants of traditional *pik-pik-
king, pak-pakking, wak-wakking, wok-wokking, dik-dikking,*
and *dum-dumming.*

"The stamping of feet is the Ch way of applauding,"
Hans Weckert shouted over the music. He hopped off the
bow of the canoe, followed by Hanna and Bodan. "I'll find
out what's next."

In the midst of the din of the band and the stamping of
feet, Weckert began talking and gesturing to Ralph, who
held up his hand to stop the band so they could concentrate
on the difficult business of trying to understand one another.

After a minute, Weckert turned to his charges and said,
"Ralph says we'll proceed directly to the village. The band
will go first, then us, then the foot stampers. We're just in
time for the wedding."

Hanna said, "Have you seen one of their weddings before?"

"This will be a first for me, too, I assure you. I'll tell him we're ready to go." Weckert spoke to Ralph, who nodded his head at the apprentice leechman in charge of the band. Six bearers hoisted the bass to shoulder level, and were staggered by the first blow. The band, with the *wh-ump* bass at point, proceeded down a broad thoroughfare of a trail leading into the underbrush. The outlanders followed, and the courteous pinks brought up the rear.

The trail followed the stream that emptied into the Ist, and twice they crossed the stream on bridges that required them to walk on one large vine while they held on to two others strung at shoulder level. About a hundred yards after the second vine bridge, they heard a mammoth *wha-omphhh* of an even larger drum up ahead, presumably one too large to be borne by mortals.

A few minutes later the outlanders stepped into a round clearing in the forest. Inside this circle there was a smaller circle of fires. In the center of these fires sat a stationary drum that was a full ten feet across.

The pinks, who had packed themselves into a ring at the edge of the circle, began stamping their feet when they saw the outlanders.

Weckert again conferred with Ralph, who flipped the lower half of his sucker with his forefinger as an aid to concentration.

It was obvious it was beyond Ralph's ability to calm the welcoming din that now included the *wha-omphing* stationary sousaphone drum, the *wha-umping* portable bass that now seemed like a mere baritone, the *clicking, clacking, pik-king-pokking-bokking-wakking* of wood upon wood, and excited foot stamping by both the beach welcoming party and the pinks who awaited their arrival in the plaza.

Weckert motioned his charges to gather round him so he could explain the program above the racket; he had to speak loudly in order to be heard. "That main drum is the drum-god Boogah, and it vibrates the faraway waters, talking to the leech-gods. Ralph says the brotherhood of They Who Suck welcome us to Ch. He says the bride and groom consider it lucky to have the wedding witnessed by outlanders.

"The wedding will begin with something called the squealing; at least, I think that's what he's saying. After the squealing will be the parade of the bride. Or maybe it's just the walk or stroll of the bride, it's hard for me to make out."

Weckert held up his hand, halting his explanation. "Just a second, Ralph's got more."

Weckert watched and listened to Ralph's mixture of charades, Portuguese, and Ch. "He says we're outlanders, so it's proper for us to sit during the squealing. He says they have mats for us on the far side of the circle. When the ceremony begins we are cautioned that it is forbidden to turn around. Shall we follow him?"

"Indeed," Hanna said, as she fell in behind Ralph and Hans Weckert.

Father Ferrua too fell in, grinning broadly. "Thank you very much for bringing us here, Captain Weckert."

The party settled squat-legged on a semicircle of woven mats that faced the circle of fires with the drum-god Boogah in the center.

Suddenly the pinks in the plaza, whose backs were all turned in the same direction, fell silent save for Boogah, whose player—he was a leechman—took a small padded mallet and brushed the drum-god ever so lightly, keeping a low, stately cadence.

Suddenly, from behind them, a young woman, grieving, cried, "Ooooooooooooo! Aaaaahhhhhhhh!"

This was followed by squealing and giggling of other young women. The pinks, backs turned in their places around the circle, stamped their feet in reply to the squealing and giggling.

There came another grieving cry followed by more

squealing and giggling. The pinks stamped their feet vigorously. Whether the bride's crying out had to do with pain
or sexual excitement was uncertain. She screamed again,
followed by merry giggles and foot stamping. The ordeal
continued unrelenting; each time her agonized outcries
grew more intense and passionate.

None of the shocked outlanders thought this could possibly last long, so at the beginning nobody thought to count
the outcries. Bodan and Hanna looked at each other. What
on earth were they doing to that poor woman? Father Ferrua crossed himself. Senhor Kobayashi, unmoving, blinked.

How many times had the bride cried out? Twenty?
Thirty? Nobody knew. There were times during this trial
when the poor girl screamed as though she were being tortured beyond endurance, but these outcries were inevitably
followed by the loudest and merriest squealing and giggling from what were either her tormentors, attendants, or
spectators.

Finally, mercifully, it ended.

The pinks stood still around the circle.

The leechman on the drum-god gave his instrument two
hard licks:

WHAA-OMPPHHHH!
WHAA-OMPPHHHH!

In the silence that followed, the first of the apprentice
leechmen entered the circle, the head of a single file that
included the apprentices who had paddled the outlanders'
canoes from the *Barco Igaranha.* The apprentices were followed by the master doctor-gods, judging from the size of
their stretched lip-suckers and the deep red of their loincloths. It took a few minutes for the outlanders to realize
that the leechmen were entering the circle according to size
and redness of sucker, the newest apprentices first, their
appetites limited by lips as yet hardly maimed or stained.

The Order of Leechmen paraded slowly around the circle, their leech lips turned for inspection by the pinks, who

looked on in reverence. Then the leechmen made a circle of their own, squatting around Boogah.

The drummer gave the huge drum a whack:

WHAA-OMPPHHHH!

A doctor-god with a spectacular sucker stepped into the circle from the right rear of the outlanders. In his right hand he held high a Mercedes-Benz hood ornament. He turned the ornament so that the reflection of the nearest fire danced off the chrome. The leechman elder moved slowly around the circumference of the circle, passing the ornament over the heads of the assembled pinks. The outlanders waited their turn patiently, feeling the warmth of flames dancing against their faces.

The leechman, barking his chant, slowed as he came upon the outlanders. He farted loudly, his eyes solemn. He passed the ornament over their heads.

Boogah spoke again: *Whaa-uummph!*

The bride stepped from the edge of the circle to the right rear of the outlanders, as had the leechman, and the reaction from the gathering of pinks was an instant, sharp communal *oooooohhhhhhhhhhhhh!*—a mixture of awe, admiration, and envy—at the sight of leeches sucking blood from the bride's breasts.

While the leechman elder waved the hood ornament above her head as though he were trying to snag invisible cobwebs, the bride walked slowly around the circle, *oooooo-ing* as she wiggled her breasts in the faces of the pinks, who *aaahhhhed* in response.

She performed this dramatic exhibition in a counterclockwise direction so that the outlanders would be among the last to be treated.

As she approached them, the outlanders could see the wriggling, wormlike leeches covering her breasts, their blue-black, moist skins reflecting the yellow light of the fire.

As the bride grew closer to the outlanders, the leechmen in the center of the circle suddenly began shouting their support. The pinks, who had previously been restrained to foot stamping, immediately joined in.

The bride stopped in front of the outlanders and faced them. She thrust her breasts toward them, standing with her feet wide, knees turned out. Then she set about wiggling and shaking her breasts so that the leeches flopped this way and that on her body.

Behind her both leechmen and the pinks cheered and stamped their feet vigorously.

The cheering subsided when the bride, having paraded her leeches, went to the center of the circle where her leechman groom stood waiting by the fire.

She stood before him, wrists behind her back, shoulders back, chin up, and proudly offered him her breasts wiggling with leeches.

The groom, fingering a leech lip with one hand, plucked a leech and threw it in the fire.

As the groom plucked, the bride responded with an *oooooo!*

The pinks echoed with an *aaaahhhhh!*

The groom threw the leech into the fire.

He plucked another leech.

Ooooo! said the bride.

Aaaahhhh! the pinks responded.

One by one, the groom plucked the bloated leeches off his bride's breasts and threw them into the bucket, *splat, splat, splat.* When her breasts were free of leeches, the *ooooohhhing* and *aaahhhing* was finished, and he began licking the blood that oozed from the Mercedes-Benz suck marks that covered her breasts like a crazy quilt. The pinks watched in contemplative silence as he attacked the tiny circles of blood with the *sluurrrp, sluurrrp, sluurrp* enthusiasm of a thirsty dog on a hot day.

Then bride and groom, smiling into each other's eyes, holding hands, disappeared into the night with the approving sound of stomping feet ringing in their ears.

31

SHE REMEMBERS THE DAYS OF

CAPTAIN PEACOCK

✳

The travelers spent the night on woven mats piled on the elevated floor of a large thatched hut that had very little in the way of walls. Hanna Doherty could not sleep. She lay wide awake, her system still jarred by the memory of the solemn leechman elder waving the Mercedes-Benz hood ornament over the bride whose breasts writhed with leeches.

She remembered that the two things in life that had really gotten under her father's skin were the IRS and people who trashed Mercedes-Benz hood ornaments. He regarded owning a Mercedes as both a perk and a requirement for a surgeon living in Marin County and he bought a new one every year until the day he died. Over the years he had replaced a lot of hood ornaments.

When Hanna was growing up, her father was willing to go to the mat screaming rather than surrender one extra nickel to the IRS, and if he had ever caught anybody trashing his hood ornament, he'd have wound up in jail for sure.

The child DeeDee and her father went round and round on the subject of hood ornaments. She said, "Dad, what do you expect? The stupid thing is sticking up there just begging to be ripped off. Why don't you buy yourself a comfortable old Peugeot with luxury everything or one of those cigar-shaped Citroëns that glides along on air. Those things are so ugly they're beautiful. You can cruise around secretly rich and let other people fume over snapped hood ornaments."

Her father's real answer—which she was forced to divine from what she considered his self-righteous rationalizing and outright bullshit—was that he couldn't figure out any reason for being rich if nobody knew about it. As he saw it, dollar bills were like points scored by the 49ers.

She remembered that on her seventeenth birthday, which was on January 7—a week before the universal human be-in, gathering of the human tribes, and powwow—he showed up driving a brand-new Ford Mustang. A convertible. Blood-red, it was, and she could see by the look on his face when he got out that it was for her. She knew he meant well, but she wished he'd think a little sometimes.

She said, "Do you expect me to drive around in that?"

"Isn't it sweet? It's a beauty," he said. "Better than the '66 models, I think."

"The point of a car is to get from point A to point B, not show off how much money you make. You're more than a car, Dad. I know you are. You have to be."

"Hey, DeeDee," he said. "It's a small Ford. What kind of showing off can that be?"

"A used bug would have been fine," she said, thinking, This is unreal; the gathering of human tribes is just one week away, and he gives me this.

"It's a beauty." He was bewildered.

"Give me a break," she said, thinking, Why does he not understand? How many daughters in this country drive around in new cars? She tried to imagine herself driving a Mustang convertible to the powwow. "Dad, somewhere along the way somebody had to pay just a little bit more to have a tumor removed so that I can drive a sporty convertible. Did you ever stop to think of that? Did you? If you were a banker, I wouldn't mind. At least that's up front."

"DeeDee, DeeDee, honey, just what do you expect me to do? I can't just go down there to the hospital and announce that I'm going to undercut everybody's rates. They'd throw me out on my ear. What good would that do?"

"Well, complain," she said. "Sign a petition. Go to the

newspapers. If it's impossible not to practice medicine without making a fortune, something's wrong."

"DeeDee, I'm a surgeon," he said. "I can't operate on people's hearts or brains without a hospital and all that equipment. I'm not the only one involved. There are people who make penicillin and people who manufacture operating tables, people who run the hospitals."

"The lawyers, the insurance people," she said. She'd heard it before.

"All of those."

"They're all leeches, I agree. But you have to admit you doctors are among the worst."

"We're just the most visible," he said.

"You've got your patients thinking you're little gods. If you really object, they'll listen."

"Are we supposed to work for free to demonstrate our charity?" he asked. "How much would you allow us to earn for all our training and apprenticeships? How much?"

"Nobody says you shouldn't be paid well," she said. "It's the Mercedes-Benzes that people resent."

"Oh, DeeDee."

"People drive Mercedes and BMWs and Jaguars to show they can afford to. If money didn't mean anything to them, they'd drive VW bugs. They don't think they're worth anything unless they drive a show-off car. You're worth more than that. You don't have to drive expensive machinery for people to respect you."

"Does it ever occur to you, DeeDee, that you and your hippie friends have your own uniform? Mine just costs more because I'm older?"

"Okay, score one. But you still don't understand what I'm talking about."

"DeeDee, when your generation gets to be my age, wait and see, you'll swap your feathers and beads for business suits, and dented bugs for BMWs. Same clan. New clothes. Now they don't want to get killed in Vietnam, so they march. Twenty years from now, they'll be worrying about their investment portfolio and locking horns with the IRS. Everybody operates out of his own self-interest."

"Not me. Them maybe, but not me."

"Oh, DeeDee. You're just like your Grandma Doherty."

"The truth is you doctors won't change the way you do business because it's so damn profitable. You use the same argument to prescribe public law that you use to prescribe medicine: namely, that everybody else is too stupid to know what to do."

"DeeDee, you're just seventeen years old."

"Ignorance costs, Dad. You've always told me to tell the truth, haven't you? When we avoid the truth, we pay. Isn't that right? Then shouldn't it follow that if the public willfully chooses to remain ignorant, then it will pay as well?"

"DeeDee, honey, you can't open your mouth without sounding like your Grandma Doherty."

Hanna remembered telling her mother about the outfit she had designed for the gathering of human tribes, universal powwow, and exorcism of greed at Golden Gate Park shortly after she got her Mustang.

There had been a long silence on the other end. If her mother had her way, DeeDee was convinced, she'd be sitting around watching *Gilligan's Island* or *The Beverly Hillbillies* on the tube. Or *The Monkees,* maybe. Some dumb situation comedy.

Finally, her mother said she was appalled at DeeDee's flower power poster advertising the powwow.

"At least I'm getting out of the house and doing something besides staring at a stupid machine. I don't have to have a man punching recorded laughter to tell me what's supposed to be funny. I mean, give me a break."

"A gathering of human tribes," her mother repeated with all the disgust she could muster. She'd read in the *Chronicle* that the date of the powwow had been chosen by consultation with the stars, this by the grandson of former President Chester Arthur, and that appalled her, or so she said. DeeDee's mother liked the word *appall.* She appalled easily.

"Mom, think. This isn't a prom. It's a gathering of the human tribe. A powwow. You don't wear high heels to a powwow. It's a celebration and exorcism. If you're going to exorcise greed you have to show people you mean business. You start by . . ."

"I've heard it before from your grandmother."

"Mom . . ."

"DeeDee," she said, with a tone meant to convey resignation. In person DeeDee's mother struck little poses, like an actress, her body saying, I'm bored; I'm frustrated; I'm resigned; I'm whatever. On the phone she tended to overdo it, like a silent film actress auditioning for a talkie.

DeeDee told her about her planned outfit, omitting nothing, imagining the look on her face as she told her about the fishnet blouse. She said nothing about her nipples sticking through. She left that for her mother to imagine. Dr. and Mrs. Philip Sarant's daughter, DeeDee the hippie, was going to run around half-naked in Golden Gate Park causing men's pricks to stand like a forest of pines.

DeeDee's father told her he liked her so much when she was born that he named her twice. But when her mother was pissed, she snapped her daughter's name like a whip: DeeDee! DeeDee! A Ping-Pong name, this was. DeeDee herself always thought it was the damnable *D's* that did the damage. Walla Walla would have been far less lethal in the mouth of an angry mother.

"DeeDee," her mother said. This time she used her stoic, put-upon martyr voice; what did she do to deserve a daughter like this?

Now, twenty years later, Hanna Doherty retraced in her mind's eye that long-ago march to Golden Gate Park.

After she hung up, leaving her mother freaked, DeeDee and her friend Sissy had mellowed out on Colombian and listened to Country Joe and the Fish and settled in to sew their fishnet blouses. Since their nipples in fact stuck through the netting, DeeDee got this idea of having them be the center of the flowers, and so they painted bright petals on the netting with Sissy's acrylics. DeeDee had brown flowers with yellow petals. Sissy had pink flowers with blue petals.

She used her dad's credit card to buy long-stemmed chrysanthemums for ammunition. They had two bandoliers each, which they crisscrossed between their breasts. It was about a thirty-block hike from the Haight to the polo field in Golden Gate Park on a clear and chilly morning, but the sun was out, promising warmth later on.

DeeDee had had a week to be amazed by her friends' response to her Mustang, which was that everybody put it down, herself included, but they all had a good time zipping around San Francisco in it. She lucked out and found a place to park the Mustang near Buena Vista Park; this was about eleven o'clock, and they joined the flow of walkers west on Haight Street. DeeDee could feel the marine air glide across her breasts under her fishnet blouse.

Their little part of the parade included a girl on stilts who was a long-stemmed rose, a squad of Vietcong with sacks of blossoms on their backs which they grabbed in fistfuls and threw at spectators, and a black man in a purple body stocking. He had an orange and green and yellow tail which he held in a coil to keep people from stepping on it. He said he was Captain Peacock, harbinger of peace, and he was smoking weed in a little white pipe.

It was in this manner that seventeen-year-old DeeDee Sarant had confronted appetite.

32

A STORY TO TELL THEIR

GRANDCHILDREN

✸

After they finished the breakfast that Lenny had packed for them, Hanna Doherty told Weckert that before they left, she wanted to swim unprotected and unblessed in the Ist River.

"Could you please inform the leechmen for me, Hans. I could wait until the last minute and just do it, but I think it would be more informative this way."

"Informative? They'll want to bless you first."

"No blessing. I want to swim unprotected."

"Hanna, I've had dealings with these people on a number of occasions. The leechmen won't like it."

"I don't care if they don't like it, Hans. I'm going to have myself a nice unblessed swim in the Ist River. Please, tell them."

"Go for it, Hanna," Bodan said. "A little swim in the Clear Water of Truth."

"That Which Is," Hanna said.

Bodan grinned and shrugged. "Whatever they want to call it."

Father Ferrua looked concerned, yet Hanna knew he was curious about what would happen.

"Oh, come on, Hans," Hanna said. "What's the worst that can happen? They're not going to get violent or anything, are they?"

"Hanna, I . . ."

"Just what does this blessing consist of, physically, I mean? What does a leechman do to protect a fisherman from the death fish?"

Weckert's shoulders slumped. "He waves the hood ornament over the blessed's head."

"And for this the fisherman forks over a tenth of his
catch?"

"It would more accurately be translated as a contribution, a tithe, I think, Hanna."

"Okay, for this blessing the fisherman tithes a tenth of
his catch."

"Yes, he does."

"Why, that's just like it is back in the United States!
Please tell them I will swim in the river unblessed."

Weckert rose, grinning. "It'll be interesting."

The leechmen, upon hearing of Hanna's plan, sent a
delegation to the outlanders' hut. They were all elders
judging by the size and vivid red color of their lips. Each
leechman carried a personal mat which he unrolled and
flopped on the ground just outside the hut. Once settled,
they began to powwow.

The leechmen were aware that this dramatic move had
caught the attention of pink passersby because they kept
their palaver somewhat muted. But the longer the leechmen talked, the more pinks gathered—keeping a respectful
distance. Neither did the leechmen give a hoot that the
travelers were sitting on an elevated floor a few yards away
watching them and eavesdropping through holes in the wall
as they sipped coffee and ate chunks of papaya. The close-
ness of Hanna seemed to make it easier for them as they
pointed frequently in her direction, making the subject of
discussion abundantly clear.

Finally, Ralph, looking very grave, rose from the midst
of the group and went inside to see Weckert. They went
through their mime, which was far longer than they had
ever taken before. Ralph pointed frequently at Hanna,
pointing apparently being acceptable in Ch.

Weckert turned to Hanna. "The long and the short of it
is that the leechmen don't want you to swim unblessed,
Hanna. It's foolhardy and irresponsible, they say. If you

choose to continue, however, they want you to know they won't be responsible for your safety."

"Do they sue one another here?" Hanna said.

Weckert laughed. "No, but they just want you to know where they stand."

"I see. That's it, then. I'll take my chances."

"Well, the leechmen have slandered our manhood for letting you kill yourself. They say we must not think very much of you. The other thing is, Hanna, they're still talking it over. Ralph says they could change their mind."

"They could? And do what? Kidnap me to protect me from myself?"

"I have no idea."

"Then let's do it now. Let's go, everybody."

"Let's go," Bodan said.

Father Ferrua rose. "I agree, Hanna."

The travelers began collecting their belongings. The leechmen, seeing this, showed some relief that the crazed outlander woman was going to kill herself now, rather than later when more pinks had gathered for the farewell foot stamping.

Thus, led by Ralph and followed by the enraged leechmen and nearly a hundred curious pinks, the travelers returned on the broad trail leading back to the landing on the Ist River. There was no fanfare this time. No drums. As the leechmen became more passionate they threw more barking sounds into their language. Soon they sounded like chihuahua jazzmen barking into trumpet mutes. They were discontented and barked bluesy. They didn't like this business one damned bit.

When the procession arrived at the floating istu barrier, Hanna started taking her clothes off.

As she was bent over taking off her sandals, a leechman brandishing a hood ornament made a rush at her.

"Watch out, Hanna!" Bodan stepped quickly in front of her like a football lineman to keep the doctor-god at bay.

The frustrated leechman glared at Bodan while still trying to pass the hood ornament over Hanna's head. Bodan, who was crouched low on the balls of his feet with his elbows stuck out to form a barrier, refused to budge. The leechman tried to go left; Bodan moved with him, elbows out. He tried to go right; Bodan slid right with his encapturing elbows.

The leechman stepped back, inches from Bodan's face, and barked loudly at him.

Father Ferrua said, "Those barking sounds are the emotional part of their language. Watch he doesn't bite, Mr. Bodan."

"He sounds like a Doberman."

Bodan said, "Hurry up and do your thing, Hanna."

Hanna got her jeans and blouse off and there she was in a pair of inadequate cotton underpants and bra. "If I'd known I was going swimming, I'd have brought my bikini," she said.

Bodan liked the display of underwear. "All right, Hanna! When you've got it, flaunt it."

Father Ferrua said, "My heavens, very fashionable indeed, Hanna."

With all the P. T. Barnum circus impresario nonsense she could muster, Hanna yelled:

"And heeeeeereeeeeeee sshhhheeeeee iiiiiissss laaadiessss annnndddd gennnntlemennnnnn. The deathhhhhhh deeeefyyyiinnnngggggg, Haaaaannnnnnnnnaaaaa Doherrrrrrrtyyyy!"

Hanna trotted around the end of the boom and slipped into the water for her little swim.

The pinks, who had not been told of her plans, erupted with foot-stomping applause.

She swam on her back, taking a leisurely pace. She floated lazily on her back. "The water's nice," she called to shore. She turned and slipped underwater for a short swim, coming up smiling. "The water's beautiful," she called back. "It's like I can see for infinity. So wonderful." She took her time, slipping easily from backstroke to breaststroke. Then she swam in, grinning, and walked ashore.

The leechmen, who moments earlier were furious that she should be so foolhardy as to dodge their blessing, joined the pinks in welcoming her ashore.

Ralph seemed especially joyous and did his best through Weckert to relay the feelings of the others.

Weckert listened, then said, "According to Ralph, the leechmen and the pinks are very relieved that you survived. They say they have never met a braver person in their lives."

"What?"

"The day the outlander woman swam unblessed in the Ist and lived. It will be a story for the pinks to tell their grandchildren, Ralph says."

"How did they think that happened, Hans?"

"They think you were just fabulously lucky, Hanna. There just didn't happen to be an istu in this stretch of the river this morning. The leechmen say you survived through sheer blind luck and they warned the pinks never, ever to attempt that themselves."

33

A BOCAGRANDE AT EIFFEL'S
FISH MARKET

❋

The *Barco Igaranha* left the Ch country the next morning and after breakfast the travelers settled down on the aft cabin top with Nicholas Bodan and Hanna Doherty playing cribbage and Senhor Kobayashi and Father Ferrua playing dominoes. As they played, the four took turns using Bodan's binoculars to watch a small white riverboat, the *Darwinia,* which seemed to be taking a course consistently astern of and parallel with the *Barco Igaranha.*

When Hans Weckert came back for a visit later in the

morning, Bodan said, "I think we may have somebody following us, Captain."

Weckert looked surprised. "Following us? Why would anyone be following us?"

"They are."

"Your imagination must be working overtime."

"No, look, back there. The *Darwinia*. You can see it on the bow there. They've been following us, really." He gave Weckert the binoculars. "We've been watching them. Isn't that right, Hanna?"

"Where we go, they go," Hanna said.

"It does appear that way," said Father Ferrua.

Senhor Kobayashi seemed less certain. "Perhaps they're just traveling in the same direction."

Weckert adjusted the binoculars and smiled. "They're hitchers. Senhor Kobayashi's right. They do it for safety's sake. Bandits are far less likely to attack a boat if it's traveling with another boat; bandits prefer loners."

Bodan said, "The old buddy system, is that it? You keep an eye on him. He watches you."

"Exactly. If one boat runs into trouble or runs into problems, the other is there to help. No harm done. Besides, it gets lonely out here."

"That must be it, then, hitchers," Hanna said. "We thought they were plain following us. Were you going to tell us about Manaus and the opera house, Hans?"

Weckert seemed relieved to be off the subject of the trailing white boat. "The real treasure of Manaus is not its famous opera house or any of its churches, begging your pardon, Father Ferrua. The opera house is a toilet compared to the fish market." Weckert delivered this opinion with resonant authority.

Bodan blinked. "The fish market?"

"There are more than seven hundred species of fish within twelve miles of Manaus, Nicholas, and more than one hundred species may be found in the market on any given day. The market uses a list of 195 names for its statistics; the main food fish there, *Arapaima gigas,* the Pirarucu, lives in shallow lagoons and surfaces about every ten minutes to take air into its bladder, which it uses as a lung. The closest relative to your banjomen friends is the catfish Acari, which is fifth in popularity. The catfish Dourado, *Brachyplatystoma flavicans,* which grows to fifteen feet long, is number twelve, and the nearly as huge Sorubim, *Pseudoplatystoma fasciatum,* is nineteenth. I have portraits of them both up front somewhere. Would you want me to dig them out for you? It would only take a minute."

Hanna said, "We'll be seeing them for ourselves in the market, won't we? Why don't we wait?"

"I can show them to you later, perhaps. Now for the fun part. Hanna, did you know that the fish market at Manaus was designed by Alexandre Gustave Eiffel, the same man who designed the Arc de Triomphe in Paris and the interior structure of the Statue of Liberty?"

"Oh, come on."

"Oh yes, it's true, he did. Alas, he didn't design it for fish but as an elegant riverside station for the tram which Manaus then boasted, said to be one of the first in South America. But I assure you, the building was meant for the fish it now houses. As far as I'm concerned, all of Monsieur Eiffel's monumental efforts pale beside this grand market. Once I did a little survey of the tourist pamphlets describing Manaus. They usually begin by pointing out how the city is a duty-free zone. This is usually followed by a description of the opera house, the botanical gardens, the zoo, and a rubber factory which may be visited."

Weckert paused, then said, "Eiffel's canopy honors the amazing fish inside, which are found in no other market in the world. The fish market is unspeakably beautiful; the opera house is a curiosity, an artifact of twelve years of frenzied rubber devouring."

He opened himself another bottle of beer. "Eiffel's fish market is a church of evolutionary music. Lenny and I like to go there and enjoy the miracles. In a few minutes the rivers will be coming together and we'll want to be at the rails. The black Negro and the yellow-brown Solimões travel side by side for more than a mile before they begin to mingle to become the yellow-brown Amazon. The reason it takes so long, they say, is that the rivers are of different temperatures and travel at different speeds.

"The fish in the Manaus market are almost all caught in the Solimões or Amazon, not the Negro, because the Negro, despite reflecting black, is almost as pure as distilled water. It's far older than the Solimões and the black color comes from vegetation rotting on the bottom; there aren't nearly enough nutrients in it to support a large fish population.

"One of the fish that does thrive on the Negro lurks along the banks under a tree that grows out of the shallow water. The tree drops its berries into the water; the fish eats the berries and moves along before he relieves himself of the seed, which grows into a new tree. And so on."

Humphries's deep voice murmured through the intercom that connected the aft cabin with the bridge. "It's coming up on our right, Hans. You better get them down at the rails. Make sure everybody gets to see it both in the sunlight and the shade."

Humphries slowed the boat to a leisurely *mwam-mwam-mwam.*

They watched and slowly, slowly, the water on the starboard darkened and was suddenly, astonishingly, black, although this was hard to see at first because of the way it reflected the light. But when they were upon it and able to look directly below them, they saw a clean, crisp line where the two rivers ran side by side, yellow-brown Solimões on the port, jet-black Negro on the starboard.

Humphries piloted the boat first on one side of the line, then on the other. Then he turned the boat to the northwest up the Negro, and the Amazon was behind them. The prop wash, whitish on the yellow-brown Amazon, was now a greenish yellow. But the undisturbed water absorbed all light and so was an astonishing jet black.

As the *Barco* approached Manaus, Weckert said, "We're at high water now, so you won't be able to see it as well, but the people here have built a remarkable system of ramps and docks to accommodate an annual drop in the Rio Negro of about forty-five feet. Seagoing vessels moor at a floating dock served by a 450-foot-long roadway that also floats. We'll be using the floating riverboat dock that simply sticks out into the water, rising and falling as necessary up a slope that leads to a plaza and the main market area of Manaus. The city's situated on a hill rising from the west bank. It should be coming up on our starboard in a few minutes."

Manaus did in fact appear in a few minutes; looking like an elegantly dressed Victorian lady gone to seed, she lay in soft repose on a hillock that rose from the river. Humphries piloted the *Barco Igaranha* straight for the riverboat dock, which looked like a traffic jam of fifty or sixty sleek riverboats, some nosed headfirst in the dock, and newcomers anchored bow to stern waiting for their turn.

"These riverboats serve the entire Amazon basin, including parts of Bolivia, Peru, and Colombia. If you'll excuse me, I'll have to help Lenny with the mooring. I know it looks impossible but they always seem to find a place to fit one more bow. They're all long and thin, just like the *Barco*."

Weckert headed for the bow, leaving the passengers to enjoy the view of the riverboats and the harbor at Manaus. To the left and downstream of the riverboat dock lay the seagoing ships.

And there, tucked in among colonial administration buildings and dockside warehouses, was Alexandre Gustave Eiffel's fish market.

Hanna trained Bodan's binoculars on the fish market, a long, rectangular canopy of delicately wrought iron and stained glass. "It looks like there's something going on there. Look at the people on the other side." She gave the binoculars back to Bodan.

"Why, yes, there is. Some kind of excitement." He gave the binoculars to Father Ferrua.

"Mmmm. I see what you mean," Ferrua said.

"It is a gorgeous building," Hanna said. "Shall we go up front for the action?"

On the way to the bow with Hanna, Bodan said, "I want you to take a look out there."

Behind them, the riverboat that had been traveling with the *Barco Igaranha*—*Darwinia* clear on its bow—hung back, as though uncertain of what to do next.

"Our friends from Santarém," she said.

"Following us. Have to be."

"They talked to Hans and Lenny while we went on that day trip to Rancho Olivieres."

Bodan looked surprised. "What?"

"It's just a feeling. I say they know Hans and Lenny and they've been following us from Santarém."

Humphries cut the engine to a slowdown *mmwah, mmwah, mmwah* as the *Barco* drew near the covered dock, and sure enough, there was a spot, sort of, open at the end of the dock.

Hanna and Bodan were at the rails as Weckert waited at the bow; Humphries cut the engine. The *Barco* drifted the final inches—hitting the dock with a slight *ka-wump* of car tire bumper against car tire bumper.

There was a commotion on the dock where a glut of riverboat workers and visitors pushed toward the plaza, where people were running to join the crowd on the city side of the fish market.

From the bow, Weckert shouted back, "Something's going on, Lenny."

Weckert hopped onto the dock and trotted alongside a T-shirted man hurrying to rid himself of a sack of rice. The man began answering Weckert's questions, then suddenly abandoned the rice on the dock with a plop and joined the crowd pushing for shore.

Humphries, Bodan, Father Ferrua, Kobayashi, and Hanna joined Weckert on the dock.

Hanna said, "What's going on, Hans?"

"He says they're going to open He Who Eats Everything. He says they were going to wait for the doctor, but the fisherman says no."

"A Bocagrande?"

"He took off before I was able to find out more."

The end of the dock was almost entirely empty, save for an old man who suffered from stiff joints and could barely walk in addition to being nearly blind. He wore thick eyeglasses with pink frames held together by tape; the left lens was slightly cracked.

Humphries glanced toward the fish market as he talked to the old man in deep resonant Portuguese. The old man had a squawky voice and talked with his hands; he seemed to know all about the excitement.

As Humphries got the story from the old man, the rest of the passengers watched the people push and shove their way toward the fish market, which was downstream from the riverboat docks.

"This gentleman is Senhor Correa. He says a man went with his uncle to fish for the giant white catfish that the local Indians have always claimed lies in the great depths of the Purus. His uncle lost his arm almost to the elbow to a Bocagrande last summer and swore to have his revenge. The uncle and his nephew went out again two days ago. This morning the nephew, sobbing uncontrollably, came back alone with a white catfish that was so big they had to load it onto a freight dock."

Senhor Correa, who was excited by the drama but far too frail to fight the crowd, enjoyed listening to his story being translated into English. He liked the attention. He added more details, his fingers fluttering like bird wings.

Humphries said, "Senhor Correa says when the nephew

returned he was wailing and babbling so much, nothing he said made any sense. They asked him where his uncle was. This sent him into hysteria. The doctor said the fish would have to wait and gave him an injection to calm him down. They covered the fish with ice—they used up all the available ice on the waterfront—and erected an awning over it to keep the sun off. Senhor Correa says the nephew has now recovered from the effects of the tranquilizer."

Senhor Correa beamed at the mention of his name.

"The nephew told the doctor that he and his uncle made homemade depth charges with dynamite. He said they spotted a Bocagrande on a fish-finder sonar. The first explosion stunned the catfish; the maddened Bocagrande rose in response to the second detonation and attacked the boat, taking the bow and swallowing his uncle. The catfish retreated, thrashing in the water, alive, but still reeling from the underwater explosions. The nephew threw one last charge that went off just beside its head; the fish rolled over, dead. The fisherman looped a line around its tail and towed it back here with his uncle still in the gullet."

Hanna said, "What're they going to do now?"

"He says they're about to remove the uncle. That's what all the excitement is about."

Suddenly a man shouting, pushing his way against the foot traffic on the dock, burst through the crowd and began running toward the *Barco.*

Father Ferrua said, "Good heavens, someone spotted my clerical collar. They need a priest at the opening of the fish."

"Ferrua on the spot. Okay!" Bodan said.

Weckert scooted aboard the *Barco Igaranha* to grab a large sketch pad—and Humphries his camera—before the party, lucky to have been in the company of a much needed priest, proceeded toward shore in the wake of the Brazilian, who shouted his mission as loud as he could and with as much importance as he could muster. The people parted respectfully, if somewhat reluctantly, to allow the servant of the Lord and his companions to pass as quickly as possible.

There wasn't room in Eiffel's fish market for the catfish that lay in the middle of the street under a mountain of ice and protected from the sun by five striped awnings, two green, two red, and one yellow, which had obviously been commandeered from the stalls at an outdoor market across the street.

The great white fish was eighteen to twenty feet long, its head larger than the Volkswagen squad cars the Manaus police used to block off the streets. In addition to its length, the Bocagrande was heavy-bodied. Its seven-foot-long snout was covered entirely with ice.

There was a hump behind the fish's head, and there—about six feet from the pavement—the first of two dorsal fins poked out of the ice; the first, a standard fin, was about four feet high by six feet wide; the second, shorter fin was fleshy and wavy rather than spiny and was nearly nine feet long. The Bocagrande's tail fin—the tips of which also poked out of the ice—was outsized, being eight to ten feet high. Just forward of the tail fin, the Bocagrande had two anal fins on its underside and a huge pectoral fin just behind its gills and low on its belly.

Upon seeing the Bocagrande, Father Ferrua turned ashen.

He Who Eats Everything looked precisely like Obatala's fish—exactly like the clay fish that Mae Janaina had thrown into the Amazon when Ferrua challenged her. There was no difference. None. It was as though the sainted Father Machado had somehow managed to sculpt the future.

Ferrua licked his lips and conferred briefly with the police officer in charge of the detail of keeping the crowd back. Ferrua, unable to take his eyes off the fish, listened to the officer.

The remainder of the party from the *Barco* knelt beside a dumpster used for trash from the fish market. Behind them, between the street and the river, was Alexandre Gustave

Eiffel's train station turned fish market. The market, which was without walls—being an ambitious Victorian canopy mounted on iron posts to allow the air to pass through—was graced by outlandish swirls and loops and swoops of delicate wrought iron and stained glass mosaics that colored the light falling on the exotic fish inside.

The market was now empty of all but fish, however. The fishmongers had joined the crowd on the street to watch the unfolding drama.

Humphries murmured, "God, what I wouldn't give to take a look inside that thing."

The officer, listening to Father Ferrua, turned to look at Humphries.

"Professor Humphries!" Ferrua called.

"Ahh, professor, is it. Bless you, Father, you're thinking all the time." Humphries went to join Ferrua and the police officer and the three of them had a chat.

Humphries rejoined his companions. "The policeman says we're waiting for the doctor to say the nephew is steady enough to witness the removal of his uncle. The nephew says it's his fish and he demands to be here. The policeman has taken Ferrua's word that I'm a biologist and has agreed to let me look at whatever's sticking out from under the ice as long as I don't damage anything. I can shoot some close-ups of the fins if I want, but I'm to take no samples or and make no incisions until the proper officials have arrived. The rest of you'll have to stay here, I'm afraid."

Weckert, who had already begun the task of sketching the Bocagrande, said, "This is the fish, Lenny. The stories were right."

"It appears that way." Humphries strode to the fish and began taking close-ups with his camera. He knelt beside one of the fish's wet whiskers, each thick as a man's arm, that lay like tangled wet ropes in the runoff of melting ice. He put his Oakland Athletics baseball cap next to a huge whisker for scale.

Hanna, watching Weckert furiously sketch in the broad outlines of the Bocagrande, said, "Father Ferrua's a bit shaken."

Weckert glanced up from his pad. "He has a right to be, I suppose. If you put yourself in his shoes, this must be an unsettling turn of events."

34

IN THE FISH'S GUT

✳

Hanna Doherty and Nicholas Bodan watched the giant fish in silence. There was a man in its belly.

Those closest to the fish sat squat-legged while those farther back stood.

Father Ferrua knelt in earnest prayer.

The policeman coughed.

A baby cried.

Hanna could hear herself breathe. She felt a trickle of sweat slide down her underarm.

Humphries came over and squatted on his haunches. "That it's albino is easily explained if it evolved in the bottom of the great depths. There's nothing unusual about that."

"Why is it so goddamn big?" Hanna said.

"Eats too much, I suspect. Remember what Mae Janaina said: a Bocagrande knows only appetite; it's blind to everything else. I don't know for certain, but judging from the skin, I think this one might be an immature specimen. I'll know more when we turn him on his side and some of that ice falls off. Can you imagine being the biologist who gets to open that thing's gut and see what's inside?"

"Don't forget there's a dead man in there, Charlie Darwin."

"Sorry."

There was a commotion down the street—a party coming toward the fish. The onlookers stepped politely aside as they had for Father Ferrua and his party.

Humphries's face brightened. "Good. They've got Ramos, Hans. Ramos'll let me do it for sure."

"Ramos?" Bodan said.

Weckert said, "He's the curator of the Manaus zoo, an old friend of ours."

The nephew, a skinny teenager in blue jeans and T-shirt, dropped to his knees before Father Ferrua. Ferrua knelt as well, appealing to their mutual God.

Meanwhile, the nephew's entourage, all officials of one sort or another, conferred with Humphries and the policeman in charge.

Weckert whispered, "Ramos is the short man with the bow tie. The man in the short-sleeved shirt is Carlos Coelho; he's in charge of the fish market. The man in the suit I think is the harbormaster. The other guy has to be the doctor. Look at those cuff links!"

The conference having concluded, the policeman gave instructions to his subordinates, who began pushing the crowd back from the opposite side of the fish. Humphries returned to his party.

"We're going to hook some ropes onto his fins and use police cars to turn him on his side. Ramos has convinced everybody that the fish should be preserved for science, but the nephew is distraught at the loss of income. The harbormaster says he's sure there's some kind of fund for cases like this."

"Oh crap," Hanna said.

"The kid isn't convinced either, but there's not much he can do, since he and his uncle brought the fish up illegally with dynamite. There are biologists and bureaucrats on their way from Brasília and São Paulo. Everybody agrees the body should be gotten out of this heat and preserved as soon as possible. Ramos said I'm a professional and I should be the one to open its guts to retrieve the uncle. They all agreed."

"The chance of a lifetime, Lenny," Weckert said.

"Part of the problem is there is no cold storage room in Manaus large enough to store him whole. Can you imagine skinning a fish like that?"

Humphries went back to the fish as policemen tied ropes to the fish's fins, which they then lashed to the front bumpers of Volkswagen squad cars. The cars backed slowly in reverse and the fish turned, to a collective *oooooo* from the crowd, sending chunks of ice tumbling.

The Bocagrande's vast belly was now turned toward the fish market. Humphries examined the belly as policemen began repacking the fish in ice and adjusting the awnings to make sure the fish was still in the shade.

Father Ferrua held the young man, one hand on his elbow, the other around his waist.

A man from the fish market brought Humphries a pair of black rubber gloves and a knife whose blade had been sharpened so often there was hardly anything left. Humphries tested the blade with a fingertip, then put on the gloves. He walked down to the fish's anus, an orifice that looked large enough to extrude cannonballs. He gave the anus a preemptory poke with the finger of his rubber glove. He took a photograph of the target and set his camera aside. He considered the task before him.

He walked the length of the fish's girth and returned. Then he began a neat incision. The hide was tough, but yielded; the knife was sharp.

Humphries ran the cut line neatly up the fish's stomach.

The white skin split, turning neatly in the wake of the blade.

The nephew stiffened. Father Ferrua held him.

Everybody leaned forward.

White fat.

Humphries stepped back and shot a picture of his preliminary cut.

He returned to the anus. He began again, cutting deeper, and being even more careful, if that were possible.

The fat opened deeper, split neatly, deeper, split evenly, deeper.

Humphries had now exposed a twelve-foot-long stretch of translucent white gut.

He ran the blade very, very carefully along the gut, careful not to graze or nick it, and stripped back a final film of fat.

He took a deep breath. He considered the gut, which bulged as though it were a huge balloon filled with fluid. This time the gut was chest-high to Humphries.

Humphries conferred briefly with the policeman, who moved the crowd back a little farther.

He went back to the gut, which he shot with his camera, first standing back, then close up. He removed his right glove and put his naked hand against the gut. He cocked his head to one side.

He looked puzzled.

He closed his eyes, hand on the gut, listening, concentrating, thinking.

He gave the gut a slight poke with his finger and conferred with Ramos. They both went to the exposed patch of gut. Humphries put a palm on the gut. Ramos did the same. They moved up and down the gut, putting a palm here, a palm there. Lenny left Ramos with his hand on the gut and fetched both Coelho, the fishmaster, and the man who was presumably a doctor, then went to Hanna.

"Hanna, I'd like you to please feel this fish's gut before I open it. I've told them you're a medical doctor but not who you are."

"Thank you, Lenny." Hanna followed him to join the others at the gut.

Humphries introduced Hanna in English and Portuguese, "doctoring" her as he did; the Brazilians were gentlemen, two of them experts on fish, a third a physician. They were anxious for her opinion.

Visible little bumps were being made from inside the gut, not in one place but rather all over the surface. Hanna placed the palm of her hand against the cold gut. She could feel the hits, which were much like the bumps of a baby kicking around in its mom's insides, only harder and more insistent, as though there was some kind of swirling turbulence inside the fish's gut. She moved her hand to another place, the same:

B—b—b—b—b —bbbb—bb—bb.

"Spasms? Gas?" she said.

"Gas seems to be the consensus of our Brazilian friends, but none of them have ever felt anything like it."

"Gas would rumble and gurgle. This is different. Something is hitting my hand. Something on the inside. But not the uncle, if that's what you're thinking. He's long dead."

"They're spread out over too large an area for Father Ferrua to have himself any kind of miracle out of his African fish. Gas, I suppose."

"Gotta be it," she said.

"Well, thank you, Hanna. If you'll step back, please, we'll find out what's in there."

When Ramos, Coelho, the Brazilian doctor, and Hanna were back in their places, Humphries stepped up to the Bocagrande's gut. He ran the point of his knife along the tightly stretched surface and jumped back . . .

. . . The stomach's contents tumbled in a rush: piranhas, jaws snapping; fish bones; a human skeleton; a metal hook.

The fish, dozens of them, perhaps a hundred or more, leaped and flopped on the street, jaws and needle teeth snapping. They were as white as their host. And like the catfish they were stone-blind.

The nephew dropped to his knees, praying fervently, with Father Ferrua beside him doing the same.

Humphries danced at the edge of the flopping fish, shooting pictures.

One of the fish reached a cotton guy wire holding one of

the awnings in place and severed it neatly with a buzz-saw attack and began flopping *snap-snap-snap-snap* in the direction of the startled onlookers, who scrambled back in stunned retreat, laughing nervously after they were out of harm's way.

The other fish did the same. They were freed from the fish's gut and they couldn't see, yet they wanted desperately to eat and they could somehow sense prey out there.

Several of the frenzied eaters flopped toward Hanna, their toothy jaws chattering and snapping with all the aggression they could muster. She hopped back a few yards to give herself a little space. Precisely like their leviathan host, these little eager eaters were driven by nothing but appetite. They weren't interested in the river behind Hanna. They wanted *her*.

There were eaters flopping in all directions—upstream, downstream, inland. Direction was not the point. Food was.

Suddenly Bodan, who had momentarily disappeared, was beside Hanna again. He'd slipped into the fish market and lifted a sack of fish. He threw a fish to the side of her attackers. They went for it, flopping with fury, yet hardly able to move. Hanna was forgotten as they concentrated on Bodan's offering.

Hanna and Bodan watched as one fish, having come within a tantalizing inch of a succulent prize, seemed to have forgotten how he had progressed as far as he had and stalled, jaws snapping at an incredible pace. He got close enough so that his teeth barely grazed his target, then he made a wrong flop and landed a heart-rending six inches away.

The onlookers, horrified, but unable to take their eyes off the incredible scene, scrambled back, giving themselves a ten-yard safety zone. The fish couldn't really go anywhere and they were hypnotic in their viciousness.

Suddenly Hanna was aware of a metallic clicking sound. *Cl-click, clack. Cl-clack. Click. Click. Click. Cl-ick, ick, ick.*
Camera shutters.

The press had arrived; it seemed as though every photographer on the planet had suddenly descended upon Manaus to take pictures of the Bocagrande. They had arrived just in time and they knew it. They shot pictures as if there were no tomorrow.

"DeeDee! Dr. DeeDee Sarant!"

Hanna turned out of habit; she couldn't help it.

The photographer was torn between whether to shoot her or the flopping fish. He shot Hanna once, twice, then returned to the fish.

Weckert saw this. "He recognized you."

"I think we should get out of town while the getting's good. Once they get tired of shooting fish pictures, they'll turn on me."

35

HOW A BOCAGRANDE DIGESTS

ITS FOOD

✳

Hans Weckert and Lenny Humphries both knew that once the photographers get bored with taking pictures of the catfish they would turn on Dr. DeeDee Sarant, notorious for serving the most infamous hors d'oeuvres of the twentieth century. So it was that Hans wound the gasohol engine as tight as it would go, humping the black water *m-m-m-m-m-m-m,* heading for the yellow-brown.

Lenny Humphries gathered the passengers together on the aft cabin top.

"We have to make a decision and Hans has asked me to take an informal poll. Senhor Kobayashi here has contracted with us to take his boxes to Loucofilho. It is possible to get his cargo to Loucofilho via the Madeira, which runs parallel to the Purus. In that event we would have to unload the cargo at Pôrto Velho and have it trucked west."

Senhor Kobayashi's jaw hardened. He did not like the idea of having his cargo trucked from Pôrto Velho.

Bodan said, "What do you and Hans think?"

"We've talked about this before. If it were left to us we'd take the Purus; if there are more blind white catfish up there we want to see what they're all about. But we can't endanger your lives without your consent and that's what we're asking here, yes or no. We have to decide now if we're to backtrack to the mouth of the Madeira."

"I'm for the Purus," Bodan said.

"Me too," Hanna added.

Father Ferrua said, "In view of Mae Janaina's charge about Obatala's fish, which I resolutely deny—the fish may look the same, but they most assuredly are not the same—I cannot in good conscience turn away from the river. I believe we should honor Senhor Kobayashi's contract and let the river give us our answer."

Senhor Kobayashi bowed. "Thank you, Father. I do thank you all for your support."

Humphries was pleased. "I'll tell Hans. Also, if we hope to outrun the media people we're going to stick with it all night. Right now, if any of you would like to watch me dissect one of those little finned eaters, you may."

Humphries left, taking Nicholas Bodan with him. Father Ferrua began studying his Bible with the concentration normally reserved for the assembly direction of children's toys.

Senhor Kobayashi got out a pocket calculator and entered some numbers. He furrowed his brow and entered some more. He thought this over.

Hanna said, "A *cruzado* for your thoughts, Senhor Kobayashi?"

He looked puzzled.

"What is it you're calculating?"

"Ahh. I see. I was thinking about that fish. How much will it weigh, do you suppose?"

"I don't know."

"I was thinking that they will have to skin that fish in order to mount it. They will most certainly want the skeleton and I take it they will save the organs for study, although Dr. Humphries could tell us more about that."

"Which leaves?"

"The meat itself, which would bring a fair enough price if it were just any fish. But this fish?" Kobayashi turned his palms up and made a face that said everything else should be self-explanatory. He bowed slightly to acknowledge his cleverness. "Smoked, I would think. How much water do you lose in the smoking, I wonder?"

Just then Humphries and Bodan returned, Humphries with an undissected fish lying in a bowl of crushed ice. He put the bowl on the table so everyone could get a good look at the fish.

Bodan said, "Man, you should have seen Lenny wield that knife. You're talking about a dude who knows how to take a fish apart. He separated every tiny tube and diminutive organ just so." Bodan demonstrated with his fingers, a pretend scientist. He shook his head in admiration of Humphries's skills.

Humphries liked the compliment. "Took a few thousand practice runs, Nicholas."

"Okay to pick it up?" Hanna said.

"Sure. Just treat him gently. I did the knife work on the other side. I'll freeze this one."

Hanna picked the eager eater up by the tail and laid it carefully in the palm of her hand. "It feels cool."

The fish was not silver; it was white, devoid of color. Like the piranha and the istu, it was heavily muscled for its tiny size—a little under two inches—and was mostly jaw and teeth. Only, its eyes were sightless; it was as blind as its catfish host.

"Father Ferrua?" Hanna offered him the fish.

He hesitated. "Yes, certainly."

She laid it in the palm of his hand. He flinched slightly.

He looked at the fish lying there, a miniature fish that lived in the gut of a leviathan. A fish that swam and ate, but could not see, knowing only the cavern of desire.

Humphries said, "Its entire existence is ordered around appetite, just like its host's."

Ferrua's lips tightened until they were white.

Kobayashi held the fish in his hand, but said nothing. He put it back in the bowl.

"Tell us what you're thinking, Lenny," Hanna said.

"I think there's going to be pictures of that catfish in the next issue of almost every science magazine in the world."

"No, no. I mean tell us what you think about this fish and about that thing back there in Manaus."

"I think there are all kinds of interesting symbiotic relationships in nature. We all know about the birds that pick bugs off the backs of buffalo. I already told you there are tiny catfish here that spend their lives living in the gills of huge catfish that lie on the bottoms of the rivers. In fact, I'd make book that that big fish back there had a couple dozen diminutive catfish in its gills hitching a ride.

"There are worms that live and breed in animal guts. I don't suppose there's any reason why a properly evolved piranha can't be dealt into the digestive action. A little help for the enzymes there. These little toothy guys have hardly any digestive system at all. Their job is to break the flesh down with their teeth; they absorb necessary nutrients as the minced pieces pass quickly through their system. Very roughly speaking, the host catfish lives off piranha excrement—but of a crude, undigested sort. When an Bocagrande eats, his parasites get both food and fresh water.

"When the chompers get hungry or need oxygen, they bang against the sides of his gut, signaling their host that it's time to give them a little attention. That's what we were feeling there before I opened him up. The little bastards were telling old Bocagrande that it was time for fresh water, but he was dead and not responding. It's the fate of overspecialization. If your host dies, you die."

"And how do the chompers get into the baby catfish's belly?" Hanna asked. "They can't be born in there."

"Judging from the Bocagrande's snout, I'd say mother accomplishes this mouth to mouth. She simply passes along some of her own chewers to her offspring's stomach. There are all kinds of animals where the mother masticates food for her young."

"Just vomits them in there."

"In a matter of speaking. The Bocagrandes have evolved to consume in a way that rivals the human imagination in its rapaciousness. If those little guys in a Bocagrande's gut aren't fed or given fresh water, they put up a helluva fuss, as you saw for yourself. I'll just bet it's possible for a Bocagrande to starve to death without losing weight; if the eaters in its gut don't get fed, sooner or later they're going to turn on their host."

Father Ferrua stood. "Well, if you'll all excuse me, I believe I'll take a brief walk."

A few minutes later Father Ferrua stood on the fantail alone, looking out at the brooding silhouette of the shoreline, his hands in his pockets, his shoulders stooped.

When Hanna Doherty awoke the next morning, she could hear Nicholas Bodan upstairs tapping on the keyboard of his computer as though he'd been working all night—which he just might have, she knew. She heard Father Ferrua hard at it too: *tap-tap-tap.*

Ferrua's quest for Obatala's fish seemed to have taken on a new urgency. His sounding of the *Barco* seemed to have risen in both frequency and loudness. *Tap-tap. Tap-tap-tap. Tap-tap.*

He had by now tapped each stair of the companionway leading to the aft cabin. He had tapped the entire interior and exterior of the cabin, the narrow strip of deck on both sides leading to the fantail, as well as the fantail itself.

He had examined the interior of the hold, having

pushed aside Senhor Kobayashi's boxes to get at every square inch of wood; he had checked the decking on either side of the hold, and the interior of the forward cabin, including every nook and cranny in the galley and bridge.

Amazingly, he seemed intent on sounding out the entire boat, which struck Hanna as a daunting task.

She went forward and found Ferrua tapping the bow with his instrument.

"Good morning, Hanna," Ferrua said. He stood stiffly, flexing his joints.

"Good morning. Examining the deck must be pretty hard work."

He rubbed his knees. "The labor is a pleasure, but I suppose I should make myself some knee pads." Ferrua looked a bit foolish. "I guess that would make sense."

"No use suffering when you don't have to."

Humphries called, "Breakfast, Hanna. Father Ferrua. Everybody."

Father Ferrua and Hanna were on their way aft when they first heard a soft *whop, whop, whop* in the distance. Almost before they could react, the helicopter zoomed directly above the *Barco* and hung like a metallic wasp, blades going *whack, whack, whack.* The blast of air buzzed through the mosquito netting and flattened the water around the boat, sending spray in every direction.

The helicopter zipped to the far side of the boat and hovered, trying to get a shot of Hanna under the roof.

Then it started her way.

"They're after me!" she yelled. She ran down the companionway to refuge inside the forward cabin. Through the cabin windows she watched it zoom off.

"They didn't see me," she said, still breathing hard from her dash from sight.

Bodan said, "Royal assholes."

Hans Weckert and Lenny Humphries piloted the *Barco Igaranha* west of the Solimões, which was really the upper Amazon and which ran straight down from the Peruvian

Andes. They were one day away from the Purus, which would enter from the south bank, which was where Weckert and Humphries kept the *Barco*—this also being opposite the village of Caldeira and the town of Manacapuru, both connected by road to Manaus.

It was by now apparent to Hanna and Bodan that—contrary to Weckert's conclusion—the *Darwinia* was in fact following the *Barco,* not merely hitching a ride. Father Ferrua was likewise convinced. Senhor Kobayashi maintained a discreet silence, refusing to speculate.

In the late afternoon the passengers were playing Scrabble on the observation deck, well past Manacapuru, when they saw two riverboats bearing toward them at an angle from across the river.

Suddenly Humphries was on the cabin top handing Hanna a pair of binoculars. "Would you like to take a look, Hanna?"

Hanna looked at the two boats, focusing in on one, then the other. "I don't think I've ever seen so many cameras in my life." She gave the binoculars to Bodan. "Can we outrun them, Lenny?"

"Hans and I talked about that. It's possible, although we've been pushing the old *Barco* pretty hard. It'll be dark soon, and if we could just buy enough time, we'll be coming to the Purus. I can't imagine they'll be wanting to follow us too far up the Purus after they took pictures of that Bocagrande in Manaus if that was an immature specimen. Unfortunately . . ." Lenny shook his head.

"The head start we have now isn't good enough?"

Humphries shrugged. "They've probably rented the fastest boats in Manacapuru . . ." His voice trailed off.

"What is it, Lenny?"

"On the other hand they're not armed. Supposing they do come alongside? What are they going to do, ram us? If we travel all night again we'll make the Purus in the morning."

"What do you and Hans conclude?"

"We think we ought to let them come for now and take our chances. There may be a way to shake them once it gets dark."

The passengers watched as slowly, slowly, the two boats gained on the *Barco.* When they were about a quarter of a mile aft, Hanna went below. "I'll be damned if I'll let them get any shots of me until I've made them work for it."

In another twenty minutes there were boats on both sides of the *Barco,* sliding right along, just howdy doody there partner, a little traffic jam on the south bank of the Solimões. Humphries, Nicholas, and Father Ferrua joined Hanna below.

Humphries said, "They've radioed Hans they want us to pull to. They want a press conference with you, Hanna."

Bodan burst out laughing at this. Lenny found it funny too. Even Father Ferrua was amused.

"A press conference?" Hanna was disgusted.

"That's what they say. They're demanding 'photo opportunities.' I believe Hans said was the phrase used."

"Well, I say we stick it up theirs."

"My bloody sentiments entirely."

Bodan said, "No, no. I say we let them have their way. Tell them we'll give them a press conference in the morning, but it's party time tonight. Invite them over. How can they resist? But when they're in the water in their dinky little boats there, we pull anchor and hightail it out of here with our lights out . . . say, what's this?"

The two boats suddenly turned away, heading back to Manacapuru.

Bodan punched the intercom button. "What is it, Hans? Are they talking to you on the radio up there?"

Weckert said, "There's been a coup in Argentina with fighting in the streets. A chance of civil war. They say they'll catch up with us on the other side of the great depths. They say good luck with the Bocagrandes."

36
MR. CARNEGIE'S ADVICE
✳

The next morning Hanna Doherty was awakened by a muted *thup, thup, thup* that had replaced Father Ferrua's determined *tap, tap, tap*—this new sound coming from the fantail. She slipped out of her berth and arrived topside still tucking her blouse into her jeans. Bodan's hammock was down and put away.

Father Ferrua, she soon learned, had returned to the fantail and now wielded a tiny padded mallet. Having unsuccessfully sounded the entire boat looking for the miracle fish, he had returned to the beginning of his search the first morning on the river.

Ferrua looked up at Hanna. "The other instrument was too harsh, I think. No wonder I missed the fish. If you'll note the nuances of this new report." He thumped on the deck three times:

Thup, thup, thup.

"What do you think?"

"That is a better sound. You're right. I see what you mean."

"An entirely different response, don't you think? I was just banging away before; largely a waste of time, I think. This mallet gives me a sound that lets me really hear what the wood is telling me. I have to let it speak. I was smothering it before. Also I was pushing myself; it's difficult to pay attention if you work too long at a time, a mistake, I think."

"A mistake, surely, Father. You should take it easy. It's not good being on your hands and knees for hours on end. You're getting too old for that kind of thing."

"This time I won't miss it. When I find it, I'll know it."

Thup-thup. Thup. Thup-thup.

216

"You'll find it in due time."

"Of course I'll find it," he said. He looked up, pausing in his labors. "By the way, Hans says we're on the Purus. We entered it a couple of hours ago."

The passengers gathered topside for breakfast as Weckert, keeping close to shore to avoid the heavier current in the middle, followed the river around a tight curve bearing to starboard. Then the curve seemed almost to reverse itself, bearing port as the river screwed around on itself. These were the infamous turns of the Purus.

Following breakfast, Humphries took the helm, piloting the *Barco* into a curve that turned into a circle of sorts, a circle within a circle, going round, round, round. Then he brought the boat out again round, round, round.

The *Barco* bore starboard, starboard, starboard along splendid green rising high, then port, port, port through yet more tropical broadleafs.

As the boat hugged the shoreline of yet another curve and with Father Ferrua, Nicholas, and Hanna playing gin topside, Weckert and Senhor Kobayashi fell into a low, heated argument in the hold.

The players on the cabin top resisted the temptation to put down their cards and leave the cabin top so they could hear the details. Weckert and Kobayashi argued in Portuguese, so Bodan and Hanna were forced to rely on Father Ferrua, who turned his good ear toward the argument and closed his eyes in concentration.

Weckert, in a rage, held his shaking voice just below the shouting level.

Kobayashi, who was clearly on the defensive, replied in a low, steady voice.

Ferrua whispered, "I can't hear everything, but it has to do with Kobayashi's cargo and someone or something they saw in Santarém."

"Those people on the dock," Bodan said.

"Possibly," Ferrua said.

Weckert swore in German, apparently not caring who in

the entire Amazon might hear him. He was clearly losing control.

Bodan and Father Ferrua rose out of concern for Kobayashi's safety, but the shouting suddenly ceased.

Weckert, red-faced, trembling, emerged from the hold. He looked back at Kobayashi, his eyes furious, and swore again in German. He stormed into the forward cabin, slamming the canopy behind him.

A moment later, Kobayashi emerged from the hold as well, hands shaking. He wiped his forehead with his handkerchief, his face tight, and, trying to act as though nothing had happened, joined the others atop the cabin.

"Dear me," Father Ferrua said.

"It was nothing," Kobayashi said. He licked his lips. "A small disagreement between gentlemen. A little temper. Everything's fine."

Shortly after lunch, the *Barco* was following the inside of yet another meandering circle, when Weckert, cooling his temper at the helm, came upon a small gunboat lying dead ahead, at anchor in the cooling shadows of the rain forest; its Brazilian flag hung limply in the hot, wet air.

Something went *splat!* off the bow of the *Barco* as a puff of smoke burst from the gunboat; a half second later the passengers heard a hollow pop.

Weckert slowed the *Barco*. He brought her to all but a stop in the current. The marine cable unreeled with a whir; the anchor went *plop,* the boat drifted, then held. On the deck of the gunboat, soldiers with automatic rifles at the ready kept a cool eye on the *Barco*.

As the soldiers boarded an aluminum launch, Weckert hustled back to the cabin top.

"This happens once in a while. There might be pirates in the area or other trouble or perhaps this is about Bocagrande. They might not let us proceed up the river."

Father Ferrua said, "Or these could be pirates themselves."

Weckert glanced at the military vessel, which was drawing close. "Thank you, Father. That's very true. Either way, I want you all to remain here on the cabin top unless you're told otherwise. If you're asked a question, answer truthfully. We're doing nothing illegal. If this is a legitimate army detail, we shouldn't have too much trouble. If they tell us to go back, then we go back. We don't argue. We go back."

"And if they aren't soldiers?" Bodan said.

"They look legitimate to me," Weckert said. "If you'll excuse me."

Weckert and Humphries threw a rope ladder over the side to assist the boarding of five privates, a sergeant, and one captain in the Brazilian army. They wore tropical combat fatigues and held their automatic rifles rather too proudly to make the boarding reassuring to those on the *Barco.*

The lieutenant, whose name tag identified him as one Souza, came aboard first, looking trim and fit. The sergeant who followed him stood with a clipboard and pen. The lieutenant took the clipboard and pen. "I speak English," Souza said with authority. He made a note. "Are you the captain?" he asked Weckert.

"Yes, I am."

"What are the nationalities of your passengers?"

"Two American citizens, Mr. Nicholas Bodan and Ms. Hanna Doherty. Two Brazilians, Father Franco Ferrua and Senhor João Kobayashi. One German, that's myself, plus my assistant, Dr. Humphries, who is a British citizen."

"Do you and Dr. Humphries have permits to work in Brazil?"

"Yes, we do."

"And you are both licensed to pilot the boat?"

"Yes, we are."

Souza made another note, then looked around. "And the owner of this boat is?"

"The boat belongs to the estate of a São Paulo physician

who died recently. I'm licensed to run it until the estate is settled."

"Where was your last stop?"

"Manaus."

"Did you get to see the catfish they caught?"

"We saw it."

"A Bocagrande. They got it in one of the big holes up ahead. Did they tell you that?"

"They told us."

Souza shook his head. "And before Manaus, where were you?"

"We started in Belém and we stopped at Santarém."

"And your destination?"

"Loucofilho."

"Loucofilho?" Souza smiled. He made another note. "Are you carrying any cargo?"

Weckert looked at Kobayashi. "Senhor Kobayashi here has . . ."

Kobayashi interrupted. "Lieutenant, I wonder if it would be possible to have a word with you in private."

Souza raised an eyebrow. "Of course. How about inside the cabin here?"

"Fine," Kobayashi said. He slid the canopy back and led Souza down the stairs to the aft cabin.

A few minutes later they emerged chatting amiably as though nothing had happened.

Souza said, "Captain Weckert, I'm obliged to tell you that I and my crew were dispatched here this morning to await orders from Brasília to stop all boat traffic on the Purus." Souza checked his wristwatch. "The orders should have come through hours ago but they haven't. Until they do, I don't have any authority to stop your boat. You should all know, however, that there have been reports of missing riverboats on the great depths. If you continue, you travel at your own risk."

"Would the missing boats be due to bandits or smugglers or what?" Weckert said.

"You say you saw the Bocagrande in Manaus. You know perfectly well what the suspicion is. Do you have weapons aboard?"

"Two shotguns which we carry for hunting."

"You'll need more than a shotgun if you run into an adult Bocagrande. I would like to examine the passports of all persons aboard this boat who are not Brazilian citizens. I would like to see your working permits and pilot's licenses as well." He nodded at Hans and Lenny. "If you could get them now, please. I would like the registration papers of this boat as well, Captain Weckert."

Lieutenant Souza gave his sergeant instructions in Portuguese. Then he said, "You're all fools."

Souza watched while the sergeant's men carefully searched every suitcase, handbag, drawer, shelf, and nook and cranny on the *Barco Igaranha*.

Only Senhor Kobayashi's sturdy boxes were spared.

Kobayashi spent the remainder of the day on his berth with the curtains drawn. At nine, he went up top. He stood unevenly for a moment, then said, "Good evening, everybody." He steadied himself with his hand before he tried to sit down, then bungled that by striking his knee on the arm of the bench as he flopped into place.

He noted the half-empty rum bottle on the table. His eyes were red. He rubbed his knee.

Bodan said, "Well, good evening to you, Senhor Kobayashi. Have a good nap?"

Hanna laughed. "You don't look like you've been sleeping to me, Senhor Kobayashi."

Kobayashi's face flushed. He blinked; his eyes were red. "I am sorry about my quarrel with Captain Weckert this morning. I . . ." He fell silent.

Father Ferrua said, "That's entirely between you and Hans, Senhor Kobayashi. You must remember that I'm a priest. If there's any way I can help . . ."

"No, no. That won't be necessary, Father."

Bodan said, "We've all been talking about ourselves one way or another. Tell us about yourself, Senhor Kobayashi; you haven't had a lot to say so far."

Kobayashi seemed pleased. "Since you asked, my grandparents came to Brazil with other Japanese emigrants in 1923 to work in the cocoa fields on the Pará near Belém, but it didn't work out," Kobayashi said. He looked at his wristwatch. "Supper's not for another hour. Are we drinking rum, then? No reason to quit so early in the day, eh?"

"No reason indeed," Hanna said.

Bodan poured Kobayashi an overly full glass of rum by way of encouraging him. "Here you go, Senhor Kobayashi. What happened?"

Kobayashi, concentrating momentarily on the rum, seemed to have forgotten the subject.

"You said your grandparents came to work the cocoa fields near Belém but it didn't work out."

"They were taken under by malaria and the soil quit."

"I see," Bodan said.

"They were interned at Tomé-Açu during World War II, and after the war, they grew black pepper there until disease hit in the 1960s. That's when my family and many others resettled in Bragantina. That's good rum."

Father Ferrua said, "Bragantina's on the northeast coast, Nicholas."

Kobayashi said, "If you'll excuse me, I'll admit that I've been drinking. My wife says I talk too much when I drink." He took another hit of rum and crossed his arms as though determined to remain properly silent.

"Oh no," Bodan said. "Please tell us about yourself. Continue."

Father Ferrua said, "Yes, please do, Senhor Kobayashi. It will be good for you."

Hanna Doherty gave Kobayashi's shoulder a slight squeeze. "I think Father Ferrua's right, Senhor Kobayashi."

"It's an interesting story, I think. You know, the Brazilians had tried to farm Bragantina before, shortly after the turn of the century. They cleared, then abandoned 300,000 acres, but we Japanese made it work. We grow oranges, cocoa, and melons there, and are experimenting with new varieties of pepper plants, but it isn't easy. Fertilizer is very expensive."

"But you're not a farmer?"

Kobayashi wiped some sweat from his forehead. "It's been a long time since I've gotten drunk. I'm ordinarily a temperate man. No, I am not a farmer, Mr. Bodan. I am the seventh of seven sons, unfortunately, so my future wasn't the best on my father's orange farm." Kobayashi glanced in the direction of the forward cabin. "First I got a job in a farm supply company in the town of Castanhal. Then I decided to push out on my own. I decided to apply myself assiduously to sales." He squared his shoulders.

"Sales?"

"That is why I am studying this little book. It was recommended to me by a successful Argentinian businessman who had spent years in the United States. You see, here." The cover was worn illegible from use, so Kobayashi turned the book to its title page and spread it on the table for the company to enjoy:

PUBLIC SPEAKING
AND
INFLUENCING MEN
IN BUSINESS

The Official Text of
New York Telephone Co.
Babson Institute
The YMCA Schools
American Institute of Banking
National Institute of Credit
Fordham University
Dept. of Civil Engineering,
Johns Hopkins University

And many other Universities,
Corporations, and
Organizations

Bodan looked surprised. "I overheard you reading poetry from it one night, Senhor Kobayashi."

"There's plenty of poetry in Mr. Carnegie's book.
Which poem did you hear me recite, by the way?"

"The ending of 'The Cataract of Lodore,' I think."

Kobayashi took a great slug of rum. "Ahh, Mr. Carnegie
recommends reciting that poem daily to get rid of the habit
of dropping g's of *i-n-g* endings in English words. English is
very important for a businessman these days. It has become
an international second language. I like the beginning especially." Kobayashi straightened and from memory recited:

> *"The cataract strong*
> *Then plunges along,*
> *Striking and raging*
> *As if a war waging*
> *Its caverns and rocks among;*
> *Rising and leaping,*
> *Sinking and creeping,*
> *Swelling and sweeping,*
> *Showering and springing,*
> *Flying and flinging,*
> *Writhing and wringing,*
> *Eddying and whisking,*
> *Spouting and frisking,*
> *Turning and twisting,*
> *Around and around*
> *With endless rebound . . ."*

Kobayashi stopped. "The waters of 'The Cataract of
Lodore' have a long way to travel."

The travelers applauded his recitation.

"Well done, Mr. Kobayashi," Hanna said. "Do finish
it."

"I think that's enough; it's a long poem and that's just a part of it, but note how I pronounced my *i-n-g* endings. My Argentinian friend said this is a classic book, unmatched by many imitations over the years. Always learn from the classics, he said, and I believe he is right. For example, Mr. Carnegie includes the full text of 'Acres of Diamonds,' a lecture given by Dr. Russell H. Conwell of Philadelphia each night for fifteen years; in all he made the speech more than 5,700 times."

"Do you have that memorized too?" Bodan asked.

Kobayashi smiled. "Oh, of course. I flatter myself that I may know it as well as Conwell himself. It begins: 'In 1870 we went down to the Tigris River. We hired a guide at Bagdad to show us Persepolis, Nineveh, and Babylon, and the ancient countries of Assyria as far as the Arabian Gulf.' 'Acres of Diamonds' is a long and difficult speech to learn, believe me, but Mr. Carnegie gives full instructions on improving one's memory. The one I like better is Mr. James Allen's essay 'As a Man Thinketh,' which Mr. Carnegie also includes."

Father Ferrua said, "Can you remember any of that, Mr. Kobayashi?"

"I remember it all, of course, but two paragraphs stand out, I think:

> *"Man is made or unmade by himself; in the armory of thought he forges the weapons by which he destroys himself; he also fashions the tools with which he builds for himself heavenly mansions of joy and strength and peace. By the right choice and true application of thought, man ascends to the Divine Perfection; by the abuse and wrong application of thought, he descends below the level of the beast. Between these two extremes are all the grades of character, and man is their maker and master.*
>
> *"Of all the beautiful truths pertaining to the soul which have been restored and brought to light in this age, none is more gladding or fruitful of divine promise and confidence*

than this—that man is the master of thought, the moulder
of character, and the maker and shaper of condition, envi-
ronment, and destiny."

Father Ferrua applauded lustily.

Hanna said, "Wonderful, Mr. Kobayashi."

"Extraordinary," Bodan said.

"It's complete arrant, utter horseshit is what it is and
everybody here knows it," said Hans Weckert, who had
suddenly appeared from the shadows.

Kobayashi, glancing up at Weckert, quickly took another
drink of rum.

Humphries, who was right behind Weckert, grabbed his
friend. "Please, Hans. No temper. You must control yourself. You must remember your promise. You must never,
ever, forget your promise."

Weckert swore at Kobayashi in German.

"Hans, please," Humphries said. "Your promise,
Hans." He took Weckert by the elbow and begin pushing
him forward toward their cabin.

"Ja, ja, ja," Weckert said. "My promise. My promise."

37

THE NATURE OF RICOCHETS

✸

For reasons that were unclear to him Nicholas Bodan
awoke in the early hours of the morning. He looked out
into the darkness in time to see a riverboat a half mile
upriver—revealed momentarily by the moonlight—floating
without lights and on a course parallel to the *Barco.*

Bodan slipped on his shorts and without bothering about
shoes ran past the hold and pounded on the door to the
forward cabin. "Hans! Lenny!"

The door opened. Humphries, squinty-eyed, stood in his underwear scratching his balls. "What is it?"

"There's a boat floating toward us without night lights."

"Hans?"

"I heard, Lenny." Weckert appeared in the shadows wearing the bottoms of running sweats and looking sleepy-eyed.

"What time is it?" Humphries asked Bodan.

"Three in the morning. A cripple, do you think?"

Humphries rubbed his eyes. "It could be, but this is the Purus, remember. There isn't anybody out here but us and them and a whole lot of trees. What do you think, Hans?"

"I think this is what we've been fearing. We better get the shotguns out."

"Shotguns?" Bodan asked.

"We've got two shotguns and a .22," Weckert said. He dropped to his knees and removed a shotgun clamped under his bunk.

"We'll wait and hope it's a cripple." Humphries dug at his testicles, then started pulling on his trousers. "It's been the fashion recently to ambush people while they sleep. Hans and I have thought about the possibility of this happening to us, believe me. We've had months to plan a counterattack."

"And we do what?" Bodan said.

"First we get everybody without a weapon into the hold and behind the engine." Humphries bent to retrieve the shotgun clamped under his own bunk and also a .22 automatic, which he gave to Bodan.

Weckert laced on running shoes, talking to Bodan at the same time. "Lenny and I have got a contingency worked out, Nicholas, our best chance, I think. I want you to go back to the aft cabin and tell everybody to hustle into the bottom of the hold. Tell them where we want them. Tell them to keep low and do it quickly. If we do this right, we might still have a chance."

Weckert bit his lip, considering the possibilities. "When

you get them on their way, I want you to take your .22 and lie flat on your stomach on the deck of the aft cabin. We'll tell you what to do when the time comes. Use him for the lights, do you think, Lenny?"

"If they have them."

"What?"

"Blinders. If they follow the pattern reported in the papers they'll ambush us and blind us with a torch at the same time so we can't see. Can you shoot a .22?"

"I shot jackrabbits when I was a kid. Wouldn't do it again."

"You can shoot. Good. You'll have responsibility for the blinder. You'll understand when you see it. You'll need your sunglasses, get your sunglasses. Shoot when you're told. I'll tell you when. Quick, quick. Go."

Bending low, Bodan took the .22 automatic and hustled to the aft cabin and shook Father Ferrua and Senhor Kobayashi. "We're in very grave danger, everybody. There's a boat coming our way. Hans and Lenny want you to go very quickly to the bottom of the hold and lie on your stomachs. Get behind the engine. Quickly now and keep low. Hanna!"

"I heard what you said," Hanna said from inside her compartment. Seconds later she appeared, still dressing, medical bag in hand, and joined Ferrua and Kobayashi on the way to the hold.

Bodan hurried quickly up onto the cabin top with his rifle and flattened himself on the deck.

In the darkness he heard Weckert whisper, "Hurry, hurry," to Hanna and Ferrua and Kobayashi.

"Dammit, get in place, Nicholas!" Weckert whispered.

Bodan saw Weckert glaring at him from the top of the stairs to the hold, a shotgun cradled in his arm. Humphries, also with a shotgun, was crouched just below him on the steps.

The riverboat held in the water about twenty yards off the *Barco*'s starboard, which was toward the middle of the river. The boat lay with moonlight reflecting off her white rails. Bodan studied the riverboat, which was smaller than the *Barco*—perhaps forty or fifty feet long. Then Bodan saw them standing clearly in the moonlight:

Four men with automatic rifles.

He watched, astonished, as they raised their weapons and opened fire full automatic on the *Barco Igaranha,* the cascade of bullets smashing glass and shattering wood before the sound of the muzzle report could be heard, both cabins nearly exploding from the impact.

A huge spotlight mounted on the roof of the boat began sweeping the decks of the *Barco,* caressing the destruction with a blinding blue-white light.

"Oh shit," Bodan said inadvertently, jerking his head away from the light as a hail of bullets all but brought the *Barco*'s roof down on the aft cabin top.

In a stage whisper, Weckert said, "We had them figured, Nicholas. The light's yours, but not until we tell you. Get your eyes ready. You'll have to fire right straight into the lens."

"Got it." Bodan put his sunglasses on.

The gallant ambushers then tattooed the *Barco* with short, playful bursts from their automatic rifles punctuated by giggling and laughing.

Weckert whispered loudly, "Nicholas?"

"Still here."

"Don't move. Lie perfectly still now." Both Weckert and Humphries had both hands over their eyes to retain their night vision.

It was impossible for Bodan to look directly into the light even with the sunglasses, but he worked at adjusting his eyes by easing around the edges of the torch.

The men with the automatic rifles were nowhere to be seen on deck, although Bodan knew they were there, watching in the darkness, waiting to flatten the slightest hint of resistance.

When they were satisfied there was nothing left living

aboard the *Barco*—but not so brave or gallant as to risk their boat in a direct approach—the four riflemen lowered a lifeboat, started an outboard engine, and headed across the darkness for the *Barco,* which sat, brilliantly lit, upon a stage of primal blackness. Two men remained, one in the pilothouse working the rooftop torch, and a second in the shadows with a weapon to cover the boarding party if necessary.

Bodan clicked the safety off on the .22. He forced his eyes to accept more and more light while the bandits negotiated the twenty yards that separated the two boats.

Bodan heard the *ka-bump* of the boat as it hit the hull of the *Barco.*

Working at adjusting his eyes to the light through the sunglasses, he thought, *Now, do it now, Hans, Lenny.*

A metal hook sailed over the starboard rail and held fast. There was a rope ladder attached to the hook.

He thought, *Let's do it.*

He heard the rope ladder slap against the side of the hull. His eyes were getting better. Getting better.

Weckert and Humphries, listening to the clump and bump of uninvited guests, still had both hands over their tightly squeezed eyes.

I can see the fucking thing. Let's get the sons of bitches!

"Now, Nicholas," Weckert whispered.

Bodan snuffed the lens on the first shot as Weckert and Humphries, their night vision intact, rose from the blackness of the hold, one tall, bespectacled, and determined, the other big-bellied but quick, and fired their shotguns—*boom! boom! boom! boom!*—point-blank at the occupants bumping against the hull of the *Barco.*

Just as quickly Weckert and Humphries retreated to the security of the hold to await the results of their ambush.

There was no reply from the party alongside the hull. Silence.

Then Humphries called, "Are you okay, Nicholas?"

"I'm fine."

"Stay where you are until we see what they're going to do next."

"You won't find me standing up."

A dangerous moment. Bodan wondered what would happen next. How many more bandits were on board? What would they do now?

The pilot across the way started his engine. Just as he did there was a thumping *ccrrruuunnnccchhhh!* as a third riverboat crashed bow first into the boat that had launched the attack on the *Barco.* This was followed by swearing in Portuguese from aboard the pirate boat. The boat that had used its bow as a battering ram—which Bodan knew instantly was the ever-present *Darwinia*—quickly retreated into the darkness.

There was more swearing aboard the rammed boat. There was one burst from an automatic rifle, then a second. The second time more bullets hit the *Barco*'s hull. The shooting stopped. The swearing returned. The swearing stopped. The silhouette of the boat disappeared under the water.

After a silence, a man's voice from the *Darwinia* yelled, "There are three of them in a lifeboat. Are you okay over there?"

From the hold, Hans Weckert yelled back, "Stay clear and leave them alone, eh? Our boat's been trashed but everybody seems in good health."

"We'll stay well clear. Do you need help?"

"We're not sure just yet. How about your boat?"

"We may be taking some water through our bow, but I think we can handle it."

"A perfect hit, by the way. Well timed. Thank you."

"You're welcome. You didn't do badly yourselves."

Weckert lowered his voice and called up at Bodan, "What do you think, Nicholas? Are you okay up there?"

"Untouched, thanks. I think you and Lenny must have gotten them."

"Let's take a look," Humphries said.

Bodan joined Weckert and Humphries at the rail where the artist and the scientist had bushwhacked the ambushers. They looked down at the water. A dead man clung to the rope ladder, hooked by his armpit, his head drooping from his neck. The small boat with his dead companions was gone.

Weckert cupped his hands around his mouth and called toward the *Barco*'s benefactor, "Everything's just fine here. I think we can take care of everything now. Thank you very much for your assistance."

"You're entirely welcome," said the man on the *Darwinia*. "What do we do about the man in the small boat?"

"Let him go."

"I agree."

Weckert unhooked the top of the ladder and let both it and the corpse sink into the water.

"How many were there?" Bodan asked.

"Four including this one," said Weckert.

"We fired right into their upturned faces. God!" Humphries said.

After a momentary silence, Weckert said, "We had to do it, Lenny. It was them or us."

Bodan said, "You know those people across the way, don't you, Hans? That boat's been escorting us since Santarém, not just hitching a ride."

Weckert shook his head. "River etiquette, just like I told you. This is precisely why boats travel in pairs—for safety's sake."

"Listen, they're the ones who . . ."

"Hans! Lenny!" Hanna called from the hold.

"Ah, Hanna." Weckert left without giving Bodan a chance to finish his question.

Bodan, glancing back through the darkness trying to spot the little riverboat, followed Weckert and Humphries into the hold, where Hanna knelt beside Father Ferrua with Senhor Kobayashi looking on.

Father Ferrua looked up with open, dead eyes. Hanna closed his eyes with her fingertips. Her shoulders slumped. "I had my medical bag with me. I had drugs. I had some surgical equipment. I had everything I could possibly expect in a place like this, but Father Ferrua took a ricochet in the cortex and bam, was gone, just like that. No return." She shook her head.

Humphries said, "Father Ferrua might have been smart to take Mae Janaina's bloody advice and lay off handling that clay fish."

"There was nothing I could do, Nicholas. Nothing."

Bodan squatted and put an arm around her. "Hey, Hanna, there was nothing anybody could do. This is the safest place he could have been. There's no accounting for either miracles or ricochets; his church bestows sainthood and builds monuments to honor miracles but pretends ricochets don't exist. He was killed by a bad angle. There is no shelter from ricochets."

With the rising sun lighting the water an electrifying orange, the weary travelers wrapped Father Ferrua's body in a sheet and loaded it onto the lifeboat. With a stolid Weckert at the oars and the *Barco Igaranha* anchored in the orange behind them, Hanna and Bodan listened to the dipping of oars and the chatter and jabber of birds awakening from the night as the small boat slid toward the wall of forest.

Weckert beached the boat at a narrow strip of red soil at the edge of the trees and the five stepped out of the boat, looking back at the *Barco Igaranha* silhouetted on the orange. The forest smelled sweet and dank.

Bodan and Humphries lifted Father Ferrua's body from the lifeboat. They laid it on the wet sand as Weckert used a machete to clear space for the burial. When he finished with his labor, Weckert stepped back and mopped his brow with the back of his forearm and watched in silence—breathing from the exertion of swinging the machete—as Bodan and Humphries took turns digging a shallow grave with the *Barco*'s folding camp shovel.

When the grave was deep enough to hold the wrapped body, Bodan stepped out of the shallow hole and said, "I can't imagine it'll be any more comforting to him if we dig it deeper."

Weckert said, "Do we have any believers here?" He looked at Hanna and Bodan and Humphries and Senhor Kobayashi.

"Well then, I'm the captain; I'll have to say something brief." Weckert ground his jaws together and adjusted his spectacles. "If you were right—if God created us in a week and in His image and the rest of it—then I'm sure you will get whatever reward it is the church promises, Father Ferrua. You did your best to return Father Machado's miracle fish; I assume your God must know that. If He asks for more, I can't imagine He was worth praying to in the first place."

Bodan bent to the task of spading dirt on top of Ferrua's corpse. Weckert used his Swiss army knife and some string to fashion a makeshift cross out of a branch, which, with Senhor Kobayashi's help, he poked in the ground at the head of the grave.

When Weckert finished, the party returned to the small boat. There was an outboard on the lifeboat but Weckert and Humphries, who hated the uncivilized racket it made, preferred to row. So with Humphries at the oars, stolidly bending and straightening, bending and straightening, the passengers set out for the *Barco*.

The oarlocks squeaked lightly as they bore the power of Lenny Humphries's deep, powerful thrusts. The muscles of his Buddhalike gut tensed with each push of oar against oarlock. The sun was now well above the vast and lonely forest on the far side of the river as behind them Father Ferrua, having honorably completed his turn, surrendered his corpse to the soil.

Resting at anchor downstream, as though waiting patiently for the voyage to continue, was the riverboat that had rammed the pirate boat in the night. The captain of the *Darwinia* had apparently given up any pretense of posing as a coincidental traveler and had anchored his crippled boat close enough that Hanna and Bodan could both see its name clearly without field glasses and make out the details of its crumpled bow.

38

A MAN IN A WHITE BOAT

❋

The travelers sat down to a three-way game of dominoes after breakfast and it became painfully obvious as the morning wore on that the plucky little *Darwinia* was struggling to keep up with the *Barco Igaranha.* At first Lenny Humphries slowed the *Barco* just a hint in the apparent hope that the smaller boat could keep up. No use.

The *Darwinia* began to lose ground at a more rapid rate.

As the *Darwinia* began to recede in the distance, a figure appeared on the rooftop waving a yellow flag.

Bodan punched the intercom button. "Lenny?"

"We see it, Nicholas, thank you."

Humphries slowed the *Barco* and brought her to a stop, staying even with the current.

A dark gray cloud of rainwater appeared off the stern, a near wall of water rolling up the river. The storm cloud swept across the *Darwinia* as though easing it from existence and bore down upon the *Barco* with the vengeance of apocalypse.

Wide-eyed, the domino players put down their tiles and in less than a minute the rain hit the roof with a shuddering whack and the boat was swallowed by water that looped and curled from the eaves of the roof in translucent sheets.

The water crashed onto the roof in such an astonishing downpour that the passengers could not see past the rails. They were enclosed, enveloped in water.

Bodan said, "Was that little boat still moving?"

Senhor Kobayashi said, "It appeared so, but I believe it was also taking on water."

"It looked like it was riding awful low to me," Hanna said.

It was impossible for Humphries to see in the rain, so there was nothing he could do immediately to help the stricken *Darwinia*. He waited, *mwab-mwab-mwab-mwab*, as the storm, eerily, seemed to have stopped directly above them. The passengers on the aft cabin top grinned foolishly at one another; the rain was spooky.

Hanna said, "When it lifts I bet we'll have to scoop these people up out of lifeboats."

"It'll be close," Kobayashi said.

The boat sat under the downpour for several long minutes before the storm moved upriver and the travelers were left with a bright sun in a cloudless sky as before . . .

. . . Only now, gaining slowly on the stationary *Barco*, bloated with water and riding low, was the *Darwinia*.

The pilot of the *Darwinia* shut off his engine as he drew alongside the *Barco*. Humphries did the same. The two boats drifted side by side.

Momentarily, an entourage of two men and two women appeared next to the destroyed bow, dragging with them sacks and baskets of belongings.

One man was apparently the maximum leader or main man; at his side clung a braless blonde in skintight shorts and translucent blouse.

A second man, with a full black beard flecked with gray, wore black shorts and a T-shirt with a tuxedo collar and tie imprinted on the cloth.

Finally a petite Asian beauty of delicate bones and features and large almond-shaped eyes—she was hardly more than five feet tall and not much more than a hundred pounds—was dressed in a stylish if skimpy outfit of combat camouflage. Her sleek hair hung to her rump and shone blue-black in the sunlight. On each hip she wore a long-barreled six-shooter.

The important one was so designated by the magnificence of his outfit; the scarlet uniform had wide yellow stripes on the sides of the trouser legs and large golden epaulets on the shoulders of the tunic. The handsomely tailored tunic featured large golden buttons that flashed and dazzled in the sun, and such numbers of colorful ribbons and medals on the breast as to be a Russian's wet dream. On his left hip there hung a sword whose handguard and scabbard were so loaded with gilt that the combined weight stretched the top of his broad belt.

The man in the scarlet uniform was tall, handsome, thin-faced, in his early fifties, with a leonine mane of silver hair and an air of confidence in his manner. There were huge ropes of gold above the bill of his World War II pilot's cap, which he had pushed back on his head at a cocky, jaunty angle.

He steadied the heavy sword with his left hand; with his right, he brandished an electric megaphone that warped his voice, giving it an unreal, warbling, echoing, tinny sound:

Ahoy. Yo soy Corporal José María Quixote de la Balboa-Grigsby, presidente de Bolivia.

In English, Weckert called back, "Do you speak Portuguese or English?"

Of course I speak English. What kind of question is that? said Grigsby in his strange voice. He looked scornful that Weckert had been so stupid as to ask such a silly question. Seemingly indifferent to the fact that he was standing on a sinking boat, Grigsby lowered his megaphone, made some adjustments, and put it to his mouth again, his voice tinny:

I will repeat it for you. I am Corporal José María Quixote de la Balboa-Grigsby, President of Bolivia in temporary exile. I see that you have encountered some problems on your voyage, as have we, as you can plainly see. Owing to pressing circumstances, my advisors have suggested that it is time to move up to a larger boat. Please allow me to introduce myself; I am an honorable man dispatched by merciful destiny to reclaim Sena Madureira, Rio Branco, Bôca do Acre, and other cities and territories illegally annexed, and insufficiently compensated for, by the Brazilian government in its imperialist expansionist aggression on May 16, 1896.

And this is my Minister of Culture, Rosa María Sancho-Vargas, my Secretary of the Treasury, Sanger Humpperman, and the heroic and brilliant head of my armed forces, Sergeant General Lola Corona, protector against the rapacious hordes . . . Grigsby introduced his cabinet with a grand wave of his hand. Rosa María Sancho-Vargas responded to the applause by rubbing her soft body against Grigsby's hip.

Sergeant General Corona's breasts threatened to spill out of the camouflage bra that served as the top of her outfit. In addition to the load for which it was designed, the bra was festooned with colorful campaign ribbons and medals. When she was introduced, Lola Corona grinned and gave a little wiggle. She bowed deeply, then straightened, smiling broadly. She twirled her six-shooters by the trigger guard.

The treasury secretary, Sanger Humpperman, adjusted his utilitarian spectacles and nodded gravely, one hand at his full beard.

The passengers on the aft cabin top, uncertain of what they were expected to do, applauded politely at the introductions.

First of all, I would like you to know that I am a fair man. I never do anything without warning. So I will tell you now that if you don't pay close attention to what I have to say, I will have Sergeant General Corona shoot you. Demonstrate, please, Lola.

The sergeant general wiggled her little frame, giggled, flipped her mane of glistening black hair, and fired a shot *boom splat* that skipped off the water.

There is a time when leadership is necessary and called for in the name of the tranquility of the people and justice for the common man and order in the Western Hemisphere. You ask why am I, José

*María Quixote de la Balboa-Grigsby, who have held every commis-
sioned and enlisted rank in the Bolivian army, reduced once again
to a corporal, am qualified for this uplifting task of history. As the
well-known Hideo Santayana once said, "If you don't live the
present as though it were past, you are doomed to repeat the future." I am here to tell you that if we remember the future we can
better understand the present, and the revolutionary distinctions
between present and past, and ontological and other discussions of
the future are called for and I support them without reservation. I
assure you, the ramifications of this extend not only to land reform,
but the role of the clergy in establishing guidelines for a properly
baked loaf of bread. And I promise you an army that will take on
the Israelis, the Poles, or anybody else who threatens Bolivia's sover-
eignty.*

The *Darwinia* shifted, obviously taking on water at a
faster rate. Grigsby wet his lips. Rosa María Sancho-Vargas
snuggled up against him, gripping him with both arms; the
other two members of his government looked solemn. The
boat was literally sinking beneath their feet. He returned
the megaphone to his mouth.

*I would like to relate to you an incident from my childhood that
you may find instructive. I am the son of an American engineer, in
case you may not know, and my mother was universally considered
the most beautiful woman in all of Bolivia, of such startling beauty
as to be famous throughout the Andes. From the very beginning, I
will tell you, my mother knew that I, José María Quixote de la
Balboa-Grigsby, was a child of destiny. She said this was obvious,
and to prepare me for my role in life, she taught me to be thoughtful
and considerate of others, which is necessary for dynamic and responsible leadership, the hallmark of statesmen, and she also
taught me to track a jaguar and make a slingshot. She told me,
"José, you must learn how to smile and to be tough at the same
time. We know that from our history books and the American
President Terry Roosevelt." This I have never forgotten.*

Grigsby lowered the megaphone briefly to demonstrate
his smile, which featured handsome white teeth. He held
the smile for five or six seconds that seemed far longer

before he raised the megaphone to continue his monologue:

*But of course you will want to know about the influences of my
childhood. As it turns out, I was born in a small room in a
dilapidated hotel in the village of Conquista, on the Madre de
Dios, a tributary of the Madeira River. I arrived in the world at
noon on a Thursday, an auspicious birth according to astrologers
in La Paz, and during which time my father was in the mountains
studying rock formations for Standard Oil, as it was called in those
days, leaving my mother in care of her maids and a midwife named
Rosa, who delivered me.*

Although the boat was sinking, Grigsby, the consum-
mate politician to the end, calmly continued his speech as
though ego and rhetoric would float all boats.

*This was all preparation for the time, later, when I made my
first tour of the great capitals of Europe and learned firsthand the
lessons of statesmanship that later served me so well. But I'm afraid
I digress. My father, who as you may know was a graduate of the
University of Colorado, at Boulder, Colorado, that's not too far
from Denver, my American university graduate father took me
aside and said, "José, I want to talk to you about honesty and
sincerity, two qualities no proper gentleman is ever without." He
said . . .*

The *Darwinia* shifted again, causing all four of her passengers to grab for support.

Where are you bound?

"To Loucofilho," Weckert called back.

*Ahh, Loucofilho. My advisors tell me that owing to a pressing
need to replace our current fleet, which is in need of some repair, it
is time to move up to something more compatible with our current
objectives. Judging from the looks of your boat, we have arrived just
in time. You can obviously use our help. The* Barco Igaranha *is
now the flagship of the new Bolivian navy, the most modern of its
kind in the world. You are all citizens of the New Republic of
Bolivia with all rights and privileges thereunto appertaining. We
are coming aboard.*

With that the newcomers accepted the help of Weckert,

Humphries, and Bodan in boarding the *Barco.* They watched in silence for a moment as the *Darwinia,* almost as though on cue, slid under the water and was gone.

"Who's the captain here?" said Grigsby.

"I guess that would be me," Weckert said, and if he knew Grigsby from before he showed not a sign.

Or did he? Neither Bodan nor Hanna could be sure.

Grigsby said, "You are now a forward admiral in the new Bolivian navy. We do not have, what was that again, Rosa María?"

"Rear admirals, Presidente."

"We don't have rear admirals in the Bolivian navy. Balboa-Grigsby and his officers are all forward-looking. We have rear ends perhaps, but no . . ."

"Boobie!" Rosa María said.

"Sorry. What's your name?"

"Hans Weckert."

"Are you German, Hans Weckert? That sounds like a German name."

"*Ja.* I'm still a German citizen," Weckert said.

"You are now Forward Admiral Hans Weckert, a Bolivian, and you shall take your place among great German-Bolivian admirals of history and rule the waves of Titicaca . . ."

"Yes, sir. I'll do my best."

Grigsby was pleased. "That's the spirit, Admiral. I want you all to take note of this man's spirit. You can tell by looking at him, the admiral of the new Bolivian army does not know the meaning of defeat." He checked his watch. *Mmmmmm.*

"Sir?"

"It's getting late and everybody's tired. We don't have to go through everything at once, do we? Why don't I give you the details of our mission in the morning?"

Having thus fled their sinking riverboat and made their introductions, Corporal Presidente José María Quixote de la Balboa-Grigsby and his colorful band retired to their

241

quarters atop the forward cabin where their hammocks lay waiting to be slung. They proceeded to open a basket and unpack a cold supper.

39

HOW BALBOA-GRIGSBY WOULD

CONTROL APPETITE

✳

Hanna Doherty lay on her berth thinking about Father Ferrua's death. Lying there on his stomach, a rain of bullets crashing onto the boat above, he had prayed, and Hanna remembered watching him—thinking how peaceful it must be to be a believer, to face the end with such grand, calm assurance—when suddenly he stiffened and was no more, taken under by a ricochet.

Who was the crazed presidente and his colorful band?

They had sacrificed their little riverboat in defense of the *Barco,* then stepped off their sinking boat like a troupe of jugglers and pitchmen what with blazing pistols and Grigsby's megaphone. She thought, *Forward Admiral Weckert! My God!*

She could hear who she now recognized as Grigsby up front making a speech as he had in Santarém and that night outside the entrance to the Ist River. And as before, his companions had their fun in the process.

Hanna couldn't sleep. She slipped into a blouse and some jeans and went through the insect repellent drill, wretched stuff. She cinched the laces on her running shoes, opened the door quietly, and eased soundlessly through the cabin. Senhor Kobayashi had the curtains pulled around his berth.

She went up the companionway as quietly as she could. She closed the canopy behind her, careful not to make a sound. She went up onto the cabin top, where, sure enough, Nicholas Bodan was hunkered over his computer, his fingers attacking the keyboard in short bursts.

He whispered, "Hey, Hanna!"

"I can't sleep for their laughing and carrying on up there."

"Grigsby's researching a speech of some kind. It's in English, but I can't quite make it out; they keep interrupting him."

"They've been following us ever since Santarém on account of Lenny and Hans."

"And Senhor Kobayashi."

"Shall we listen in? It's dark. Maybe we can find out what they're up to."

"Let's do it."

"You first."

He shrugged and led the way off the cabin top, keeping low. He stopped, considering which way to go.

"You go first," he whispered.

"Oh, come on, then."

"I don't want to be accused of being sexist," he said from behind her.

Staying in the shadows and keeping as quiet as they could, Bodan and Hanna negotiated the deck around the hold and soon were in the darkness at the base of the forward cabin, listening to the visitors up top. On the cabin top above, Grigsby held forth:

"In a dictatorship or totalitarian state the right to consume is controlled by one man, a few cronies, or a bureaucracy; what we're talking about here is democratic consumption. A democracy attempts to manage competing appetites so that favored devourers don't consume everybody else. Lawyers are one such class of favored devourers. You are a nation of litigation because politician lawyers reserve as much space at the trough as possible for their hungry brethren. Do you have to shine that thing in my eyes, Sanger?"

Sanger giggled.

Rosa María said, "You're going to have to get used to it, Boobie. You're going to have to learn not to screw your face up like that. When we practice it has to be under battle conditions or it doesn't do any good."

"Also you look less retarded when you relax," Sanger said.

"You've got a lot of room to talk."

"Gentlemen!" Rosa María said. "Okay, Boobie, go ahead. No squinting now."

"Your women complain that they are politically under-represented—that is, they are discriminated against by male predators—and so they are according to the numbers of their sex. Almost all other nonlawyers can make the same claim: fishermen, farmers, house painters, truck drivers, shoe salesman."

"Slow down, Boobie. Remember, speak clearly and maintain eye contact with the camera. That's what the books all say."

"The books. Sure, sure. Most of you defer to the lawyer, the eater who charges money for interpreting deliberately complicated and unintelligible rules by which others consume or are consumed. Okay, that's enough. My eyes."

"Boobie, Boobie! You've hardly begun. If you want women to vote for you, you first have to make them want to go to bed with you. Back with the light, Sanger."

"Undeniably the most serious underrepresentation is the lack of women in public office. If they're all like you, I don't know . . ."

"Boobie!"

"There are solid, undeniable studies that prove that men have evolved to be more violent and aggressive, while women are more loving and nurturing."

"Oh, you know I love it when you say that, Boobie."

"If half of the world's political officials were women, it's hard to imagine that the chances of a disastrous outbreak of war wouldn't be substantially lessened; I think that is a conclusion any objective zoologist or anthropologist would concur with."

"He'd say anything for sex," Humpperman said.

"Sanger!"

"The civilized answer to all this is to hold a political lottery to even out opportunity, to ensure an equitable number of women in office, and at the same time to ensure properly qualified candidates. This lottery would include an educational program that would—in the opinion of our finest scholars and thinkers—best prepare a citizen to be president, vice president, secretary of state, senator, and all other offices, down to the local level. These courses of study —the students would be paid, of course—would vary in length and difficulty according to the office at stake."

"Go for it, Boobie!"

"My eyes! Swine who now linger for years at the public trough justify their tenure on the grounds of experience. Under the Balboa-Grigsby system, this on-the-job training would be replaced by systematic, rigorous study to include consideration of ideals and ethics."

Humpperman tittered at the mention of ideals.

"Nobody expects *you* to have ideals, Sanger."

"Come on now, Boobie. We've got to get this right."

"We should always remember that even though we are mere animals, we can think. We can work toward ideals and ethics suitable to what we are, not what we imagine ourselves to be. I forget the next part."

"All local and national . . ."

"All local and national classes will be filled by lottery on one fabulous day. There will be, say, a fifty-student class of presidential aspirants, and the same for secretary of defense, governors, mayors, sheriffs, judges, and so on. All seats will be filled by lottery, plus a list of numbered alternates to account for felons and those who are in institutional care or otherwise unable to participate. A mere fraction of money now spent on emotional nonsense will be used to pay both

students and professors a full, equitable salary for their
work—"

Rosa María interrupted: "Let there be classes and
courses and ideas bubbling in every state of the union."

"Oops, forgot that part. Let there be classes and so forth.
The lectures will be televised and when possible held in
auditoriums so that people can judge for themselves the
issues being discussed. This way government becomes a
community enterprise, both on small issues, who pays what
kind of tax and how much and why, and large ones: what
amount of consumption is consistent with achieving some
workable harmony with nature. We cannot continue to casually defecate in our natural environment. Okay, hey, time
out."

"You're doing fine, Boobie!"

"You look like you have to go to the toilet," Humppperman said.

"Sanger, would you lay off him just a bit. The light is
hard on his eyes. Come on, Boobie, you don't have far to
go."

"I do have to take a leak, he's right. We casually consume everything in our path. For example, in Brazil we are
about to devour the forests of Amazonia, which contain half
the oxygen-producing trees in the world, but without oxygen we all die: those of us with big brains as well as those of
us who swing in trees and fly by night. This is the big medicinal river, my friends; it supplies life-giving oxygen to
the entire planet, we should never forget that. We *Homo
sapiens* are only one species. If we weren't here, life would
go on. Who are we to so presume that we are God's chosen
eaters, placed here to consume all other species?

"At the end of each course of study, students will take a
series of competitive examinations, the top scorers earning
one term as president, vice president, and so on. The finest
minds drawn at random, properly educated and freed of the
obligation to repay financial supporters, will be given the
opportunity to serve the public in the way rhetoric now

demands. But we must never forget one thing: the instinct to devour may only be managed, never suppressed. Predators long to consume; even predators chosen by lottery long to consume."

"I know what I like to eat. Yum!" Humpperman said. He made a slurping sound with his tongue.

"Let him finish, Sanger!" said Lola Corona.

"There'll always be arguing and quarreling and unanswered questions. Always. Our brains evolve because we ask questions. How? Why? What? Where? When? Who? Cheetahs evolved for speed; we evolved for intelligence. If we don't ask questions we go out of business. We do our best to equitably . . . Equitably?"

Rosa María said, "Yes, equitably."

"We do our best to equitably manage the urge to consume. When imperfections arise, we ask why and make adjustments that seem most sensible. People lament the lack of heroes; what they're really asking is: Where are leaders who don't behave like animals? Remember as you go to the polls, serious-faced, solemn eaters everywhere dress themselves with deceptive language as easily as they tie their neckties or apply lipstick in the morning. My eyes! *Whew!*"

His lips brushing Hanna's ear, Bodan whispered, "I think he's winding up. We better get on back while the getting's good."

"I agree."

They left slowly, easing through the darkness, while behind them the would-be candidate, released at last from the torture of having a flashlight shone in his face, was now laughing with his friends and they were all having a good time in the same melodic language they had used in Santarém.

When they get to the aft cabin, Bodan whispered, "Do you think Senhor Kobayashi would know or care if you should happen to spend the night up top with me?"

"He'll almost certainly know," she said. "But I don't give a damn whether he cares or not."

"Well then, after you, my dear." Bodan bowed low, a courtly gesture.

It didn't take them long to unroll the futon on the aft cabin top and scramble under a single sheet.

Bodan said, "I've never had a chance to thank you properly for saving my life. You like bartering?"

"Bartering?"

"How would you like a fun little story in exchange for your medical services? You saved my life, after all. The least we could do is be friends." He had his face buried in her hair and she could feel him inhaling. *Mmmmmm.*

"I like a little story now and then, you dream machine man." He casually breathed in her ear, which sent goose bumps up her body. *Oooooooo.*

"The first chapter is called 'He Addresses His Lady with Lips.'" He gave her a sweet kiss.

"You like that?"

She told him certainly-you-fool with her body and so was rewarded with his lips again.

"You want the next page?"

She said yes again with her body. She bent like a reed, vibrated.

"Chapter Two is called 'He Addresses the Mountains That Make Men Crazy.'"

He trailed his fingertips across one breast. He did this extremely softly, barely brushing her skin, which stiffened her nipple. "This next episode's called 'He Breathes Sweetly into Milady's Ear.'"

She took a quick breath and let it out. "Some author you are. Why don't you finish the second chapter?"

"I got your interest, didn't I? We can come back to that little drama." He trailed his fingers lightly across her breasts. His fingertips lingered at her nipple as though testing for ripeness. He breathed very gently in her ear. He caressed her ear with his tongue, then breathed coolly into the wetness. "Is that nice?"

"Oh yes."

"Then put your wrists above your head. This one's called 'The Kindling of Primal Fire.'"

She did what she was told and he pinned her wrists with his left hand, letting her twist sweetly as he attended to breathing in her ear, which she could hardly take. The longer he did it, the hotter she got.

Simultaneously, he attended to her breast with his right hand, being in no apparent hurry about this. He let his fingertips linger and tease, and when she reacted, he moved on, finding all manner of ways to torture her breasts while hardly touching them. "You build a fire the same way. You blow on it very carefully. You apply a little friction. You pay attention."

"*Ohhhhh shhittttttt!*" she breathed.

"Getting a little warm, are we?"

She pushed her breasts up for more.

"Tell me if this is too much, now. I don't want to put out the fire before I get it started." Watching her reaction, Bodan took her by one nipple and twisted it very gently from side to side, not too hard, just right, just so. *Yes,* she told him with her body. A straight talker was she. He held her close, breathing in her ear as he attended to the hot spot of her nipple.

The breathing and the friction really got her going.

She sucked in her breath. She arched her back again. *Yessssss!*

Bodan kept multiple subplots going, using his fingers, his lips, his teeth, his tongue, his big toe, his thigh, until he had her squirming beautifully. He took her through "She Offers Her Globes to Her Admiring Man;" "Exploring the Valley of Exciting Delights;" "He Who Likes Lapping Enjoyeth Sweet Fragrance." He topped it off with an action-packed ending, "He Mounts an Assault on Thunder Pussy," which left them both sweating and exhausted.

40

THE RIGORS OF INDIGESTION

✴

Hanna Doherty left the warmth of Nicholas Bodan's embrace in the early hours of the morning and retreated to her compartment, wondering, on her way through the cabin, if Senhor Kobayashi might not have had a sleepless night what with Bodan and her having such a good time on the roof above him.

Bodan leaned down from the cabin top and gave her a good night kiss through the open window, and if Cupid's arrow had lost its poop over the years, Hanna couldn't tell the difference.

She lay back hoping to get a couple of hours of sleep before facing the question of precisely what Grigsby and his friends were up to. She was sore at herself for not having stayed up top wrapped in Bodan's arms. That's what she really wanted: to be held and cuddled, and his needs were complementary.

When she woke again it was nine o'clock; she'd slept in. When she got up top, she found Bodan reading a paperback. Humphries had left her cheese, ham, bread, and a thermos of hot coffee.

"Hans didn't make his usual appearance this morning," Bodan observed.

"Maybe he just dozed off," she said, pouring coffee.

"I don't know about you, but I'm betting it has something to do with his quarrel with Kobayashi."

"You think so?"

"Maybe one of us should go see if he's okay."

"Let me, Nicholas. Maybe this needs a woman's touch. The good Dr. DeeDee Sarant or whatever." Hanna went to the forward cabin, where she found Weckert lying on his bunk, staring at the ceiling of the cabin. He'd been crying, although he'd mopped up in a failed effort to conceal it.

"Hey, Hans, what's the matter?" Hanna said. She gave him a hug.

Weckert's eyes looked defeated. He looked aged, suddenly, more like sixty-seven than fifty-seven.

"Everything's fine," he said.

"Don't bullshit me, Hans. Just look at you, for God's sakes."

"Really, Hanna. Everything's okay. I'll get it together. I really will."

"Then why aren't you up top telling us about oddball fish and beautiful birds? Lenny's having to pilot the boat."

"There's plenty of time for that, Hanna. This river always seems like forever."

"I want to know what's wrong with you, Hans. I know it has to do with Kobayashi and these people who came aboard. Nicholas and I both saw something going on back at Santarém. They didn't just follow the *Barco* out of some sort of buddy system. I'm a good listener. Come on now."

"It's nothing." Weckert fought to hold back the tears.

She squeezed his hand. "Go ahead, Hans. Flush it out. Nicholas and I've got eyes. We're not blind. We know it's all linked: Grigsby and those folks from the *Darwinia,* Kobayashi, you and Lenny."

Weckert still fought tears. "If you want to know the truth, Hanna, I don't know if I can go on."

"What do you mean you don't know if you can go on? Don't be silly, Hans. Of course you're going to go on. What on earth are you talking about?"

Weckert, holding her hand, fought the tears again.

"I don't know if I can go on. I just don't know."

"Nonsense."

"I don't know if I want to."

"We're born to go on, Hans. We don't have any choice. It's programmed in us, bred in the bone. We get up every day. We survive. We push forward. We fight the good fight.

Now tell me what's going on, Hans. It really will be better if you talk about it."

"Hanna, I . . ." He was taken under by the tears. He reached up and pulled her closer, looking her straight in the eye. "You must swear that you'll keep me away from Kobayashi? You must keep me away from him. You must. Swear it."

"I'll do my best. Who are these people?"

"Otherwise I just might try to kill him."

Weckert wiped the tears away again, but his chin still bobbed up and down.

"I don't want to hear that kind of talk, Hans. What's in Kobayashi's boxes—tell me?"

Weckert's lips tightened. He shook his head no.

"Tell me, Hans, what's he been doing? What's in those boxes? Drugs? Arms?"

He shook his head no again.

"These people have been following us since Santarém. They recognized you and Lenny and Kobayashi at Santarém. Who are they?"

Weckert's chin trembled again. "The worst part is . . ." He waited for his chin to settle, as though if he could control his chin, the rest of his face would follow. "He knew. God help us, Kobayashi told us. Apples, he said. Remember? When he first came aboard, he said his boxes contained apples. He's such a literalist. Who would have thought?"

"Apples? What on earth are you talking about, Hans?"

"He . . . I . . . Oh God, Hanna, it's hard to know how to start. For the last four years, he . . ."

Weckert wasn't about to tell her. He started to cry again.

Hanna held him tightly.

Somebody banged on the companionway with his fist. Bodan yelled, "Hanna, Hans, come up quickly! Quickly!"

Lenny Humphries cut the *Barco* hard to starboard and the middle of the river, slowing the engine as he did.

Weckert and Hanna scrambled up top, Weckert wiping

his eyes with his forearms as he went. When they got on deck they found everybody at the starboard rail pointing toward shore.

Bodan had his binoculars trained at the base of the forest. "You want to take a look at that?"

A Bocagrande perhaps a fourth again as large as the one at Manaus had rammed the shore and lay dead at the base of a tree, its back host for a gathering of vultures.

As the boat approached, the birds flew off with reluctant flaps of their awkward wings.

Humphries idled the boat to match the current and sent the anchor splashing into the water. The *Barco* swung around, a maneuver well done, as the boat rode the current opposite the dead fish. Hanna, Weckert, and Bodan watched it through binoculars, joined by Grigsby and his group, who had discarded the theatrical costumes of their entrance for more utilitarian garb.

The Bocagrande, which was a good six or eight feet longer than the one at Manaus, had plowed into the shore with such force as to gouge a huge scar on the riverbank. At least three fourths of its carcass lay on the ground, its progress stopped only by a tree. The fish lay on one side. It couldn't have been dead long; the plowed dirt was still fresh and the vultures hadn't had a chance to start their banquet.

The fish had a large, jagged hole in its stomach, and even from the river the passengers could see clearly a trail of miniature white piranhas on the ground, blind every one, who died while trying to flop back to the river.

"They got so hungry they ate their way out," Weckert said.

Grigsby ran the fingers of his right hand through his lank gray hair. "That's precisely what happened. A form of indigestion."

"Boy, those little floppers sure like to eat," Bodan said.

Grigsby said, "I was planning to give a brief talk about appetite this afternoon, as a matter of fact. Remember yesterday I promised to tell you what our plans are for the assault upon Loucofilho and after."

Weckert gave Senhor Kobayashi a look of undisguised, elemental, spooky rage.

41

THE SPENDING OF GOLD
FROM LOUCOFILHO

✳

When Nicholas Bodan and Lenny Humphries returned from doing the lunch dishes, the bearded Sanger Humpperman, running his fingers through his beard, rose to introduce Presidente Balboa-Grigsby. "We all agree that was a beautiful meal. Thank you very much. The Presidente promised to give you a full report on our mission this afternoon, and after witnessing that beached fish this morning, now couldn't be a better time. Presidente?"

Grigsby rose and cleared his throat. "I'm down here to begin a campaign for President of the United States. Since the American presidency is obviously up for sale every four years, my companions and I have decided to buy it with the gold from Loucofilho the next time around."

Grigsby examined his notes, then looked from face to face gathered around the cabin top. He stopped with the blue-eyed Weckert, looking him straight on.

"With your help, Admiral, I will ride this boat to triumph in the White House." Grigsby lowered his voice and bent low, again catching and holding eye contact with his listeners. "When I get to Loucofilho, I will swap guaranteed emigration to the United States to any miner who is willing to buy into my campaign; a miner can get rich in slime, then take his money to the United States, where there are blondes beyond his wildest dreams and every house has a microwave."

Grigsby grinned. "Yes, it's good, huh? Thus armed with a campaign treasury so enormous as to dwarf the opposition, we will proceed north to the Potomac River and capture the White House. We will have so much gold from Loucofilho that nobody will be able to outspend us—no coalition of industrialists or unions, no oilmen, no church of any kind, no cartel of lawyers, no doctors encamped outside Congress, not even the amassed television contributions to the Reverend Billy Gill. We will be everywhere: on television, in magazines, in newspapers, on billboards, written in the sky by airplanes."

"What do you think?" Rosa María asked Hanna.

"I think he'll look good on television."

Grigsby said, "Perfidy and greed are my true opponents, no matter what the name of the candidate. 'Perfidy,' is that the word?" Grigsby paused in his monologue to check the word in a small dictionary provided him by Rosa María.

"I was right. Perfidy is the word. It says: 'a deliberate breach of faith or trust; faithlessness, treachery.' The truth is that your senators and congressmen, elected to serve the larger interests of the country as well as the more narrow interests of their constituents, in fact blindly pursue just one objective: to remain at the public trough and in the public limelight as long as possible. To consume. To devour. To eat. You must have seen some of the bites taken out of the forest here on the Amazon."

Bodan said, "I think you may be on to something, Presidente."

Grigsby bowed. "Thank you, Mr. Bodan. Your voters profess surprise and rage at appetite, but would be a lot better off if they made an effort to understand the nature of who they are instead of stubbornly insisting—against all rational evidence—that they're special, not mere apes."

Grigsby shook his head, a gesture that said: *so very, very sad.* "Your voters allow themselves to be eaten as so many flavorful snacks, the most pious and self-righteous eaters having the largest appetites.

"Predator politicians use the federal treasury to please their predator voters, each of whom wants the government —that is, someone else—to pay for what he or she devours. Incumbent eater-politicians use the federal treasury to buy reelection. They spend, but don't tax because voters don't like taxes. This is economically disastrous and the elected officials know it, yet they spend, spend, spend, year after year. Isn't that so, Rosa María?"

"Nothing but honesty, Boobie. No bullshit."

"They put their own comfort and ego above the needs of their fellow predators. There's no secret to this. But if you believe that humans are God's special miracle, not mere apes, and therefore are immune to selfishness, then this has to be called perfidy. What was the other word, Rosa María?"

Rosa María had a bookmark in her dictionary. She opened the dictionary to the marked page and read:

" 'Un-con-scion-a-ble.' It's an adjective, Boobie. It means 'lacking conscience, unscrupulous. Behavior not in accordance with what is just or reasonable. Excessive.' "

Grigsby took a sip of tea. He wiped his lips with the back of his hand.

"In merely seeking office, a politician defines himself as a predator of potentially disastrous appetite."

"Right on!" Hanna Doherty raised her fist in support of Grigsby.

"We can't change the nature of an ape by the cosmetics of reform or by rhetoric. A predator may be shackled; he may be redefined, but his genetic programming remains the same. He is what he is: a smart ape, a cooperative predator. Those predators elected to Congress earn campaign money by selling public laws. This is a straightforward swap: legislation in exchange for more time at the trough. Unfortunately, the largest and wealthiest groups can afford the biggest helpings of the national treasury; individuals with only votes to spend get drippings and leftovers, a bridge here, a highway there, and your House of Representatives has become the House of Lords; it is nearly impossible for an incumbent to lose an election."

Rosa María said, "You are entirely correct, Boobie. One buys potatoes from a grocer. One goes to Congress to buy a law. The congressmen only lack a menu listing favors and laws that are for sale. The presidency itself is for sale."

"And the solution to all this?" Bodan asked.

Grigsby looked surprised. "A solution? A political lottery perhaps, but that is subject for another talk. All we need is money, Nicholas, an adequate campaign fund. The gold at Loucofilho ought to do just fine."

42

THEY TURN SLOWLY IN A
CLOUD OF BLOOD

✳

Nicholas Bodan and Hanna Doherty were sound asleep on their cabin-top futon when the shouting began. They sat up, fully alert, adrenaline pumping, because the shouting was truly scary. It came from the hold and was in Portuguese, so they couldn't understand a word of it.

They got up, grabbing for clothes, dressing. Bodan fairly jumped into his pants and bounded down the stairs in his bare feet. Seconds later, still buttoning her blouse, Hanna joined him at the aft edge of the hold.

Grigsby and his friends were gathered at the forward edge, likewise drawn by the shouting.

In the lit hold, Hans Weckert and Senhor Kobayashi were arguing face to face. Or rather, Hans argued. Kobayashi tried to remain patient.

Lenny Humphries went down the stairs into the hold. "Hey! Hey! Come on now, Hans."

Kobayashi was holding his little red book. Was he going to recite "The Cataract of Lodore" or a Dale Carnegie aphorism?

Weckert was in a rage. His eyes were feral.

"Hans, please," Humphries said. "This is not good, Hans."

Kobayashi abruptly decided to withdraw. Book in hand, trying to ignore Weckert, he started climbing up the stairs.

Weckert followed, with the stout-bellied Humphries on his heels, trying to calm his friend.

Kobayashi, who had nowhere to hide on the boat, opted for the stern.

Weckert, his face red, went after him, shouting, pinning him against the aft rail of the fantail, continuing to berate him. Humphries and everybody else scrambled atop the aft cabin. Bodan flipped on the fantail lights with the combatants stage center.

Rosa María Sancho-Vargas called, "Elongxa Quayloo! Elongxa Quayloo! Ooo. Ooo."

Weckert turned and looked up at her; the pain in his eyes was from the lower levels of Dante's dream; it was as though he were being flayed before her eyes—stretched on a medieval rack.

Weckert's face was suddenly flushed with tears. Looking up at Rosa María, he blubbered like a baby.

Kobayashi, sensing a break in Hans's mood, said something in a calming tone of voice.

But Hans was not placated. He wiped the tears from his eyes with his forearm and said something low and murderous in German, then rushed Kobayashi, ramming him low and hard with his shoulder.

Dale Carnegie's advice skidded to the deck as Weckert pinned Kobayashi against the rail.

Humphries rushed in and struggled with Hans, trying to

pin his arms, but Weckert wouldn't have any part of it. He elbowed Lenny and broke free.

That was when Weckert showed a knife.

He eyed Kobayashi down the corkscrew of a Swiss army knife.

Grigsby yelled at Weckert in the mystery language.

Weckert ignored him.

Rosa María offered some advice, pleading in the same language.

Lola apparently reaffirmed what Rosa María had said.

Humpperman tried to calm Hans.

Lenny took a turn. "He has a mind like a cash register, Hans. You have to look at it from his point of view."

Weckert was beyond calming in whatever language.

"Hans, please. We've been together too long. Listen to me, Hans. Your work. Think of your work."

Hans reached out and slashed Kobayashi's hand with the corkscrew, then raked the back of his own hand. Blood flowed on both hands.

The blood was scarlet, hypnotic in the dim light on the fantail.

"Oh, bloody shit, no, Hans," Humphries said.

"Ooo, Elongxa Quayloo," Rosa María cried.

"Ooo, ooo, ooo," said Grigsby. This was echoed by Lola Corona, whose face was wet with tears.

"Ooo, Ooo, Elongxa Quayloo," said Humpperman.

Weckert, taking Lenny by surprise, threw the knife aside and dipped, bending his knees, ramming Kobayashi again; he straightened with Kobayashi on his shoulder and Lenny struggling with his free arm.

"Hans!"

Weckert twisted at the rail, trying to free himself of Lenny, and the three men tumbled over the rail.

Into the water . . .

. . . which was alive with piranhas.

The shocked spectators scrambled off the cabin top and

Bodan flipped on the powerful water light mounted on the underside of the fantail.

The forms of what were once Hans and Lenny and Kobayashi, each covered with wiggling, eating fish, turned slowly in a cloud of blood.

Then part of a body emerged from the water. A head. Weckert's. In a horror, his body seemed to float in a vertical position, suspended, held there by the energy of frenzied fish eating him from all sides.

Weckert's corpse stared up at the fantail, snapping fish where his eyes had been. Humphries's near skeleton, writhing with fish, rolled in front of his old friend's sightless face and was gone.

Piranhas not only ate their way into Hans's eyes, they ate through his ears to get at his brain; fish ate through the place where Weckert's nose had been; they competed at his mouth, bent on eating as far down his throat as possible before everything was stripped, devoured.

Then they were gone, all three of them.

Nicholas Bodan and Hanna Doherty and the survivors of the sunken *Darwinia* stared at the cloud of blood that slowly blended into the water and was gone, part of the cycle of the river.

43

EULOGIES FOR ELONGXA

AND ELLURIA

✳

It was impossible for Nicholas Bodan and Hanna Doherty to fall asleep for the memory of Weckert and Humphries being eaten by Piranhas; trying at the same time to remember and yet to forget, they talked far into the night.

Bodan said, "Hans treated Kobayashi perfectly okay until we got to Santarém and we saw Grigsby and his little troupe; I'm betting all this has something to do with the boxes."

"Certainly not because Kobayashi's guru was Dale Carnegie."

"Hans and Lenny told me that Kobayashi was going to take his cargo to Loucofilho by boat rather than plane for the reason that he loved boats. Did Kobayashi strike you as especially fond of riverboats?"

"He wasn't on the *Barco Igaranha* because he liked riverboats; that's nonsense. He showed no sign of that whatsoever."

"The quarrel had to do with whatever's in the boxes, then."

"Whatever's in the boxes and Grigsby. And Father Machado's fish too. He was probably after the fish like everybody else."

"*Sssssh.* Listen."

The weeping ceased. Hanna and Bodan rose up on their elbows, and in the predawn light they saw Grigsby coming aft, followed by Rosa María, Lola, and Sanger Humppperman. Grigsby sniffled and blew his nose. Rosa María and Lola sobbed quietly. It was too late for Hanna and Bodan to do anything but stay under their sheet as their visitors gathered on the fantail, well aware that they were being watched from the cabin top.

Sanger Humppperman stepped up to the end of the fantail. He shook his head, then leaned with both hands against the rail. He studied the river. He held his spectacles in his hand, looking at them. He mopped his eyes with the back of his hand. He attended to his beard. He ran the palm of his left hand over the bald patch that ran halfway back of his head.

Then the tears came. He sobbed openly and without embarrassment, then cried out:

"*Elonnnnngxa Quaylooooo! Elooooooooria Quaylooooo!*"

Then he began his eulogy in earnest, gesturing dramatically with his left fist, then with his right, scoring this point and that, paying obvious tribute to Elongxa and Elluria Quayloo.

Hanna whispered, "Hans and Lenny."

"I think so," Bodan whispered back.

When Humpperman was finished, he put his hat over his chest and waved farewell to Elongxa and Elluria.

Then he stepped back, crying, replaced by Grigsby.

Grigsby was on hardly firmer ground emotionally. His eyes were red from weeping. He ran his hand across his hairy chest. He adjusted his floppy-brimmed hat at a rakish angle. He held his hat high and turned in a slow circle, repeating the names Elongxa Quayloo and Elluria Quayloo. When he finished, he knelt and kissed the fantail where Hans and Kobayashi had struggled. Then he kissed the rail over which the three men had tumbled.

Lola Corona and Rosa María Sancho-Vargas also took turns on the fantail, delivering passionate eulogies to Elongxa and Elluria Quayloo.

Finally, Grigsby took out a foot-long musical instrument that looked like a cross between a flute and a trombone—the same instrument Hanna and Bodan had first saw and heard at the dock at Santarém. He played an eerie, lonely tune, his left wrist moving the slide with a tremulous, soaring vibrato that spoke to the stars.

His companions linked themselves arm over arm and sang softly in their beautiful language.

When they returned forward they glanced up at Hanna and Bodan, who stared down at them from under their sheet.

"These are such sad times. A terrible day," Grigsby said.

"A terrible day, I agree," Bodan said. Beside him, Hanna was overcome by emotion and unable to talk.

Sanger Humpperman, with exactly forty minutes of solo experience at the helm, wheeled the *Barco* easily this way and that as the travelers entered a stretch of floating green islands, evidence of yet another storm upriver. Nicholas Bodan and Hanna Doherty were in the galley doing dishes when the boat bumped into something.

There was yelling topside. Bodan and Hanna raced up on deck in time to see an enormous tail fin disappearing into the water. A Bocagrande.

The Bocagrande, maybe a twenty-footer, rose and hit another island of debris, this one closer to the *Barco.*

Grigsby and Rosa María held on to the starboard rail, staring at the *café au lait* water where the catfish had disappeared. The Bocagrande didn't look large enough to actually damage the *Barco,* but it sure was willing to try.

Sanger yelled, "Watch for him! Watch for him! Help me out now."

Bodan ran for the stern, yelling, "He's behind us, Sanger. Aft and starboard!"

A huge white dorsal cut through the water, aiming for the *Barco*'s stern. The Bocagrande sank into the river, then broke water again, its mouth a chasm, giving a high-pitched, weeping cry.

It disappeared.

Bodan yelled, "Behind us, Sanger. Shit, oh dear, behind us, I said!"

Sanger cut to port with Bodan still yelling at him.

The starved catfish rose off the *Barco*'s stern.

"Goddam it, Sanger!"

Humpperman wheeled it starboard, swearing in his unintelligible language, then shouted, "I'm doing my best."

The Bocagrande slammed into the fantail, its jaws opening and closing pathetically, too weak to get any kind of grip on the *Barco.*

The fish fell back into the water, then rolled on the surface, weeping, its mouth wide, but making no sound.

"It's okay, Sanger. He's dying."

On the bridge, Sanger could see that the Bocagrande

was no longer a threat. He eased back on the throttle and held the *Barco* in the water near the leviathan, the engines going *ma-wab, ma-wab, ma-wab,* as the passengers watched its dying moments.

The Bocagrande, its mouth remaining open in a soundless scream, began screwing itself along the surface of the water.

Then it turned belly up.

The travelers gathered at the rail and stared down at the fish's belly, a thumping, quivering mass, alive with energy, a storm of hunger, a rebellion of craving.

Then the skin of the leviathan's long belly tore in one small spot and a blind piranha popped out, jaws snapping, just as, everywhere and all at once along the entire length of the fish's girth, the other eaters erupted. Out popped the twisting parasites, their jaws snapping and chattering with craving. They tumbled off the dying Bocagrande and into the Purus, their jaws never once stopping.

44

THE LEGACY OF EMILIO GONZALVO

❋

Gripping the rails with whitened knuckles, the passengers stared down at the shocking white corpse for a moment; then Sanger Humpperman goosed the *Barco* through a heavy stretch of debris, the islands of brush scraping the sides of the *Barco*'s bullet-ridden hull, and the giant fish was gone.

Grigsby's jaw was set, tense. He said, "Well, what do you think, do we continue or turn back?"

Bodan said, "I don't think either the fish in Manaus or the one we saw beached, or this one, is large enough to actually sink the *Barco* even if it was healthy. It'd have to get some kind of angle."

"Like this one tried to do," Rosa María said.

Hanna said, "You have to remember that Lenny thought the one at Manaus was an immature specimen. A twenty-five-foot fish could easily take a chunk of stern or bow. Let him try is what I say."

Bodan said, "I agree."

Grigsby raised his voice. "Have you heard all this, Sanger?"

"I'm having fun playing with the boat," Sanger said, his eyes on the debris floating toward the *Barco.*

"Okay, then forward," said Rosa María.

Lola nodded her head yes. She was in agreement.

"Well then, we continue," Grigsby said.

Five minutes later, with Grigsby, Rosa María, and Lola all in the bridge watching Humpperman maneuver the *Barco,* Bodan and Hanna took the opportunity to slip below to the hold. Both wondered just what in the hell was in the boxes, which were ultimately what got them into this mess.

"Without being disrespectful to the late Senhor Kobayashi, he's not here to object to a quiet inspection," Hanna said.

"At the very least we have a case of murder and suicide. Don't we have an obligation to investigate the circumstances? After all, the captain of the boat was involved."

Bodan scrounged through Humphries's tools until he found a pair of shears, then both he and Hanna knelt in the hold to address the question of Kobayashi's so-called apple boxes.

"Which first do you think, Hanna, a square one or a long one?"

"A long one."

Bodan selected a long box and leaned into the shears, popping one metal strap, then a second. He used the claw of a hammer to get a start under the wooden lid and slowly pried it open.

Hanna leaned close.

Bodan lifted the lid. There was a cardboard box inside

the wooden box. Bodan, frustrated, attempted to attack the lid with his fingers. When that didn't work, he used the hammer claw to get a start. He ripped the lid off. Styrofoam. "Crap," he said. He lifted the Styrofoam-encased contents out of the box. He parted the Styrofoam halves. There it was.

"What is it?"

"Beats hell out of me."

"It unfolds," Hanna said. "See here. Like this."

"Hah. Here're the directions. It's a television antenna. One of those scoop things. A dish is it called, or a disk?"

"Go for a square box."

"I'm betting a television set."

Bodan selected a square box and attacked it with shears and hammer. Sure enough, this time the Styrofoam casing parted to yield a television set.

From above them Grigsby said, "The antenna is capable of picking up channels from North America."

Bodan, glancing up at Grigsby, looked foolish. "Thought maybe I'd catch a ball game on the tube."

"You might as well set it up if you want. Senhor Kobayashi's not around to complain."

"Is that what got Hans so worked up, television sets?" Bodan asked Grigsby.

Grigsby's face tightened. "It's a long, long story, Nicholas."

"More than television sets."

"Far more than television sets, I'm afraid."

"Tell us," Hanna said.

"Well, you see, there was . . ." Grigsby sighed. "Perhaps later," he said. Then he turned and left, saying no more.

"I bet Hanna and I are both good listeners," Bodan called after him.

"I bet we are too," Hanna said.

It was hot that afternoon, and later—with Bodan on the cabin top drinking beer and watching the Golden State

Warriors and the Portland Trailblazers—Hanna lay naked on her bunk unable to shake the ghastly vision of Hans Weckert's corpse standing rigid in the water. She saw again those fish eating through his ears and eyes.

Kobayashi had called the television sets apples.

She scratched a trickle of sweat running down her rib.

The *Barco* began to slow. She grabbed for her jeans and bra. The boat stopped. Someone knocked at her door, a polite but firm knock.

"Yes?" she said, buttoning her blouse.

"Hanna. It's me, Grigsby. We, ah, we . . ."

"I'll be right out." She stepped outside.

"We've come upon a stream emptying into the river and Rosa María was thinking it might be nice to have a picnic. You and Nicholas and Rosa María and myself. Rosa María wants to give Sanger and Lola some time by themselves."

"A picnic?" Four people dead and he wants to go on a picnic?

"We have to tell you and Nicholas about ourselves, Hanna. Under the circumstances, I'm afraid we can't put it off any longer." Grigsby sighed. "Sometimes you just have to trust people; there's nothing else to do."

Sanger Humpperman anchored the *Barco Igaranha* near the entrance of the small stream and Grigsby, Rosa María, Hanna, and Nicholas Bodan—the men with small backpacks of food—put ashore a small boat and hiked single file up the left bank of the stream, which was about fifteen feet across.

The stream had receded from the previous day's rain, leaving space for them to pick their way along the edge. There was a flush of activity in the trees as they proceeded upstream. They saw a flash of yellow on a departing bird.

The two couples walked in silence admiring the rain forest. Finally Grigsby said, "Hans Weckert killed Senhor Kobayashi because he learned that Kobayashi has been peddling television sets and antennas to XuXu for more than five years."

Bodan said, "XuXu?" He looked amazed.

"Yes, we're from XuXu."

"The stories are true, then," Nicholas said.

"It depends on the stories." Grigsby smiled. "Some of them maybe are true. Some aren't. We have our ways of knowing. We are in fact XuXuians. We've been following you since Santarém, as I think you both figured out."

Hanna said, "You did a double take when you saw us at the dock in Santarém and we heard you practicing your speeches when we were at the mouth of the River Ist."

"You've heard stories about XuXu, I take it."

"The priest who was killed by bandits was interested in XuXuian stories. He told us several the second day of the trip."

"Did he tell you any story about Emilio Gonzalvo?"

"Yes, he did. He was supposed to have been a naturalist who founded XuXu at the site of an incredible seam of diamonds along a small river that empties unseen into one of the tributaries of the Amazon."

"Or the Amazon itself?" Grigsby looked back over his shoulder.

"He said nobody knows where. In Amazonia somewhere."

"Emilio Gonzalvo was real and he did found XuXu. Ferrua told you about our language, I assume."

"And about some experiments in government."

Grigsby laughed. "We've had some real beauties."

Rosa María said, "Gonzalvo said we should study the natural order if we were to understand ourselves. Since we were surrounded by a fabulous natural laboratory, that is exactly what we did."

"Gonzalvo was an unusual man for his time, because he was apparently untainted and unmoved by arguments of the church."

"An independent spirit," Hanna said.

"Yes, he was. He didn't want us to get distracted by religion, which he felt was the logical consequence of a creature able to consider its death in advance. Some animals survive by flying, some dig, some climb, others change colors; some animals discharge poison, some pull in their arms and legs, or simply attack. Only we humans attempt to escape by convincing ourselves that we're not animals at all, and we imagine afterlives for ourselves. Why *we humans* don't die like skunks and elephants and grasshoppers! *We're* made in God's image. *We're* eternal. *We* have souls! *We* go to heaven and hell! This is the logical equivalent of hiding in a thicket of the imagination or scurrying into a burrow of faith. It's entirely understandable, of course: all animals dodge death after their fashion. Why should we be any different?"

"But our turn still comes," Bodan said.

"Eh?"

"We still die."

Grigsby shrugged. "Unfortunately. We see by television, where peddling the conceit that we don't die if we donate enough money to Christian ministers has evolved into a highly profitable business in the United States . . ."

"Hustling the succor of medicine isn't a bad racket either," Hanna said.

"It'd have to be right up there," Bodan said.

"Gonzalvo knew he couldn't simply ban religion, but he believed it dulled the ability to ask intelligent questions. Gonzalvo believed that monotheism has been the source of more wars, butchery, grief, and pain than any other single human delusion—all piously and self-righteously proclaimed. In the name of hope, suffering. In the name of charity, profit. In the name of peace, war. In the name of truth, burned books and bounties on writers' heads. We XuXuians are confounded and in awe of ultimate questions too, but we leave those questions up to our theoretical physicists, who do the questing for intellectual entertainment for fun and not for profit or as a way to control people.

"Gonzalvo decreed that there should be precisely one hundred official gods in XuXu, each god spending no more than ten years on the list. We have a contest each year to see who can invent the most entertaining and useful deities, and the winners are added to the List of One Hundred, as the legal gods are called, with a grand party. XuXuians who are bored with the Friday night debates on philosophy and theoretical physics can create their own imaginative religions based on the permissible gods. We don't have professors in your sense of the word; our term might best be translated as 'one who has chosen to learn.' If you choose to learn in XuXu, we see that you have the best lab equipment and library possible."

Rosa María said, "We XuXuians set about to make our lives as creative, useful, and interesting as we possibly could —always aware of our capacity to destroy ourselves and everything about us if ever once we forgot what we are: cooperative predators; hairless big-brained apes. We have to deal with the plants and animals around us. We cannot ignore them. We must preserve them to preserve ourselves.

"Gonzalvo was well aware of the extractive nature of the human ape. He had been sent into the Amazon with the expressed noble purpose of mapping the rivers, but his backers were really interested in gold and gems, which is how he found our mother lode. Logic told Gonzalvo that certain resources were finite, and this fact has always been uppermost in our minds in XuXu. Over the years, and with the help of our Quayloos, we've done our best to conserve our diamonds. It has always been, and remains our goal still, to support ourselves in some nonextractive way, to achieve harmony."

"Who or what is a Quayloo?" Hanna said.

"Sorry," Grigsby said. "That's the reason we have to talk to you and Nicholas. Quayloo is XuXuian, and it may be simply translated as 'go-between.' The Quayloos have been our secret windows to a world of human predators that would surely devour us if we were discovered. There have been thirty-eight Quayloos over the years, including Emilio Gonzalvo, most of them artists, writers, scientists, or intellectuals, all of them sworn to secrecy. They work in pairs to market our diamonds and do our shopping for us, usually in Manaus, but in the case of scientific instruments, America and Europe."

"Hans was a Quayloo."

"Elongxa Quayloo," Rosa María said. "Lenny was Elluria Quayloo. Incidentally, the Quayloos have always kept their real identities secret from us, although we've deduced the identity of many and have secretly watched them unload their riverboats. We regard XuXu as a state of mind as much as a physical place. The Quayloos who have helped us we regard as XuXuian."

Bodan said, "So how did you come to deal with Senhor Kobayashi?"

"We've long known about television, of course, but the Quayloos always said no, they would not bring us television sets. Learn languages, they said. Read. But finally we just flat disagreed with the Quayloos. How were we supposed to market our creativity if we were prohibited from watching television? We just didn't agree that it would hurt us if we watched it with objectivity and detachment. Four years ago, we contacted a trader—it turned out to be Mr. Kobayashi—to provide us with television sets and antenna dishes. We didn't tell our Quayloos about the television sets. We bought them in secret."

Grigsby said, "It was a terrible error on our part not to tell Elongxa and Elluria Quayloo about our dealings with Kobayashi. How was Elongxa to know we were responsible, not Kobayashi? We wanted to buy television sets; he was willing to sell them. He can't be faulted for that."

"Boobie's right. It was our fault, not Senhor Kobayashi's; these particular sets weren't even bound for XuXu. He was taking them to Loucofilho."

Grigsby said, "That's just a fragment of the story, of course. As we're entirely without Quayloos now, it's important to us that you know the whole story. We have to go with our instincts and trust someone."

"We mustn't lose contact with the outside world," Rosa María said. "That would be very dangerous in the event we were simply blundered into by a prospector or got picked up on an aerial survey photograph. If that happens we'll need somebody who'll know how to help us. A famous artist and a respected scientist, a German and a citizen of the United Kingdom, Elongxa and Elluria were perfect. We knew they would do anything for us and in the end they did, which is why their death is so terribly sad."

Grigsby said, "Are you familiar with Charles Darwin's voyage on the *Beagle* in 1831?"

"Well, a bit," Bodan said. "Everybody knows about Darwin and the Galápagos."

"The Galápagos. But probably not much more than that, I bet. You might not know that one of the enduring mysteries of *On the Origin of Species* is precisely when and how Darwin got his wonderful insight into the forces of evolution. Do you know that Brazil was Darwin's first stop on that five-year voyage? You should read the Brazilian entries in his journal sometime; there's a particular entry about an evening spent at a ranch in the interior that has always charmed but slightly puzzled scholars, for there seemed to be no real reason for its inclusion. Why don't we have our picnic? Rosa María and I can tell you about Charles Darwin and XuXu and the origin of *On the Origin of Species*."

45

A PLEASANT GENEALOGY

✳

José María Quixote de la Balboa-Grigsby examined the Spam sandwich as though it were some strange object. Finally, he took a bite and chewed thoughtfully. He looked at it again. He took the last bite, swallowed with effort, and knocked the crumbs off his hand.

Still chewing, he began kneading the back of Rosa María's neck.

"*Mmmmm.* A man who knows how to knead a woman's neck," Rosa María said.

"Overall, I'd say we eat better in XuXu. Don't you think so, Rosa María?"

"I'd definitely say so," Rosa María said. She abandoned her half-finished sandwich and settled back against Grigsby.

"You were going to tell Nicholas and me about Charles Darwin," Hanna said. Grigsby said, "Captain Fitzroy of HMS *Beagle* had just returned to England after a long voyage charting the Pacific Ocean for the British navy and didn't want to go on another long expedition without a companion."

"He wanted someone to talk to," Hanna said.

"Fitzroy was lonely although he himself apparently wasn't much of a companion. Darwin later wrote that Fitzroy was given to maddening periods of sitting at his small table merely staring into space, saying nothing.

"The two Quayloos of that period, Elooxa and Eleena, met Fitzroy in Argentina, where they had gone to collect data on anthills that some XuXuians had read about. The *Beagle* was returning to England and had stopped for provisions. The British officers had been told there was gold in Argentina and advised Fitzroy to take a geologist with him on the next trip. However, Elooxa Quayloo had traveled with the explorer Alexander von Humboldt as a young man and Fitzroy was impressed with his stories. Elooxa said he and Eleena had spent twenty years in Amazonia developing a theory of natural history that they desperately wanted to communicate with a skilled naturalist in England."

Rosa María laughed and applauded. "Elooxa-mu! Elooxa-mu!"

Grigsby grinned. "Here is where Elooxa Quayloo made his famous lie, which Rosa María and I as schoolchildren learned as Elooxa-mu, which means 'Elooxa's Wonderful Lie That Was the Truth.' Elooxa was competing with gold for Fitzroy's interest, remember. In the seventeenth century two British clerics figured out the exact time of creation. James Ussher, archbishop of Armagh, calculated the year 4004 B.C. John Lightfoot, master of St. Catharine's Hall, University of Cambridge, calculated the time and day as 9 A.M., October 23. This time and date were noted in Anglican Bibles from 1701 well into the nineteenth century.

"Well, Elooxa told the pious Fitzroy that their remarkable theory of creation proved that Ussher's and Lightfoot's calculations of God's Perfect Plan were in fact true! We know virtually every detail of this episode because while the extroverted Elooxa did the talking, the more introverted Eleena, a brilliant Quayloo, memorized every word and gesture and later recorded it in his journal of the trip."

Rosa María said, "Elooxa Quayloo told Fitzroy that their remarkable theory was based on observations of the flora and fauna of Amazonia. But more data needed to be collected in a variety of locations. He assured Fitzroy this would forever close the mouths of skeptics of Christendom. Boobie once played Elooxa in a play, so he's got the scene down pat."

Grigsby said, "Elooxa told Fitzroy if only he and his scholar friends just had a *littt-tttle* help with the proof . . ."

Bodan said, "Just a little help."

"Boobie, do your impersonations of Elooxa and Fitzroy for them."

"What kind of help do you need? I'll help out any way possible. Name it and I will do my best to honor God's will." This was Grigsby's Fitzroy impersonation—serious, concerned, pious.

"A skilled naturalist with the ability to travel widely and collect the details necessary to demonstrate once and for all time the miracle of God's extraordinary creation." Here Grigsby was Elooxa, his voice concerned, a defender of the faith.

"A naturalist. I see." Grigsby's Fitzroy was grave, very serious.

"However, to silence the disbelievers forever, he should not be a cleric, or they'll say he twisted the evidence. We need to be scrupulously fair. All we need is someone with a logical mind and a passion for learning. God will take care of the rest."

"And Fitzroy agreed?" Bodan said.

Grigsby said, "When he got back to London, the captain made the appropriate inquiries. Two more experienced naturalists turned down the offer because they couldn't afford the expenses involved—the scientist traveling on the *Beagle* would have to pay his own living expenses for periods running to months at some stopovers. Finally Darwin, who was studying to be a minister, was recommended. Darwin's appeal was that while he was not yet a minister, he was studying to be one, which established his loyalties, but didn't violate the principle of a neutral observer—at least not from Fitzroy's viewpoint. There was one remaining obstacle, however." Grigsby closed his eyes and cupped his face in his hands and pretended to weep.

Rosa María said, "Fitzroy didn't like Darwin's nose, an astonishing footnote of history. Yes, it's true; read a Darwin biography. Because of his unattractive nose, Charles Darwin almost didn't get to take the trip on the HMS *Beagle,* and if that had been the case, today we would probably be referring to his chief intellectual competitor, Alfred Russel Wallace, as the great one, not Darwin."

"What?" Hanna looked incredulous.

"Fitzroy was initially inclined to turn Darwin down because of his nose, but since he found him personally charming, he took him on a tour of the *Beagle* anyway and history knows the rest. Darwin's warmth and obvious intelligence won the day against the handicap of his nose and Fitzroy invited him on the trip. Here was a man of science to take on the infidels."

Rosa María said, "Incidentally, Boobie should tell you that these stories about Charles Darwin are all memorized by schoolchildren in XuXu. On Darwin's birthday the children wear wooden noses carved to look like Charles Darwin's. My dad always had fun carving my nose every year. Nobody could carve a nose like he could. He always carved it out of Tupilipa wood; my Darwin nose was bright yellow with little red veins and smelled so good."

Grigsby grinned. "I always had a Tupilipa Darwin too, but my dad wasn't that great an artist, I don't think. My noses always looked more like a potato or something."

Rosa María got just a tad more comfortable, wiggling in against Grigsby's shoulder and arm. She said, "Elooxa was sick with a bronchial infection and so he and Eleena failed to meet Darwin when he was in Brazil from April 5, 1832, to July 5 of that year. Darwin landed at Montevideo, in what is now Uruguay, on July 26, and his journal entries that immediately follow collapse episodes from two successive years of exploring the east coast of South America below the Plata River. One trip he does include was an excursion from Maldonado on the north bank of the Plata, where he stayed ten weeks. On the third day of the trip, August 17, 1832, which Darwin does not date, but which we know about from Elooxa and Eleena's account, he met our Quayloos at the home of a certain Don Juan Fuentes together with certain unidentified 'guests.' You can read Darwin's journal, which is mostly filled with elaborate descriptions of animals and plant life, and check his curious inclusion of this night for yourself. He tells us that the women and men ate separately and that his host served one pile of roast beef, one pile of boiled beef, some pumpkin, and an earthenware jug of water. After supper, he says, they sang songs to the accompaniment of a guitar and they smoked, that is, they talked. It was there, after a supper of roast beef and pumpkin, that Elooxa and Eleena gave Darwin the outline of a theory of the evolution of species, the result of more than fifty years of thinking and rethinking since the idea first emerged by several thinkers almost simultaneously. The problem, of which the XuXuians were well aware, was that their theory lacked comparative evidence from outside their isolated world."

Bodan's mouth dropped. "What?"

"At the time experimental gardeners of XuXu were anticipating advances in genetics made by Gregor Mendel. Darwin doesn't give the details of his conversation in his journal because of *Darwin-arooo,* Darwin's Pledge. Remember hearing us say *ooo ooo* for Elongxa Quayloo? That comes from *Darwin-arooo* and is because Elongxa honored Darwin's sacred pledge, taken by all the naturalist Quayloos over these many years, never to reveal the existence of XuXu. Elongxa Quayloo kept our secret to the end. Boobie and I have a copy of a letter we'd like to show you. Now is the time, do you think, Boobie? Then I can answer the rest of their questions."

"I agree. I think they should read it now," Grigsby said.

Rosa María raised her small butt and slipped a piece of paper from the hip pocket of her cotton trousers. She gave the letter, in handwritten script, to Hanna, who read it. Hanna said "Shootie patoot!" and passed it on to Bodan.

> *Mar. 28, 1837*
> *Gt. Marlborough St.*
> *London*

Dear beloved XuXuians,

It has been some months since I returned from my long voyage on HMS Beagle, *and I apologize for not having written you sooner. I have been quite busy over the winter seeing to it that my collections of specimens will be properly cared for by the Brit. Museum, the Zoological Soc. of London, the Royal College of Surgeons, & et. cetera. They are so eager for the task, for which alas, I think the French might be better equipped in some cases. Nevertheless, they are honorable men & will do their best.*

I have recently spent much time discussing birds with John Gould, a taxidermist with the Zoological Soc., whose observations corroborate your own & the countless species & geological forma-

tions I saw on my long voyage of discovery. I started out as a young man with an interest in beetles, and now this. I can hardly believe it.

My burden & responsibility now is to report to my colleagues & the outside world, without revealing your identity, the details of your marvelous theory of the evolution of species. In my opinion you could not have arrived at such a clear & concise & accurate explanation of natural forces had you been suppressed by the burden of willful stupidity that follows obeisance to superstition, & which currently hampers scholars at both Oxford & Cambridge. Of course, I dare not utter a hint of my honest feelings in the public papers for fear the reaction would censor my report. I dare not be free even in my dreams, lest I cry out at night.

I will not detail here all the wonderful examples of flora & fauna & geologic formations that I found in Brazil, Argentina, Chile, the Galápagos, Tahiti, Australia, & New Zealand that corroborated the careful studies & conclusions you made independently in XuXu. I was astonished.

The years ahead will be a constant struggle against the church & its supporters whose interests, I am afraid, seem almost perniciously allied to willful ignorance. I pledge to you that I will honor your trust. I also pledge to you by all that's honorable among men that I will breathe not one word of your existence, lest you be devoured by predators you cannot handle. I will never forget the birds of the Galápagos Islands who were so tame, so unafraid of predators, that they could be simply snatched off a branch by hand or decapitated with a switch.

I regard XuXu as a cultural Galápagos in which your imaginations, alone of all that I have encountered or reported in the literature, are allowed to evolve free of superstition & with respect for open inquiry. Some splendid & unusual species evolved in the benign environment of the Galápagos precisely because they were isolated from predators. I urge you to stand by the principles of your founder Emilio Gonzalvo but prepare yourselves for the worst. We need only to remember the suffering of poor Copernicus, whose only crime was to point out what every intelligent star watcher of his day knew must surely be true, namely that the earth was not the center of the universe.

My only regret, other than that I did not grow up in XuXu, is that I cannot be resurrected, in the manner of the Hindus, in another 150 years, so that I can see what ideas you have come up with in the meantime. Biology plods tortoiselike, which culture cracks and pops overhead, thunder and lightning.

When two races of men meet, they act precisely like two species of animals—they fight, eat each other, bring diseases to each other, &c., but then comes the more deadly struggle, namely which have the best-fitted organization, or instincts (i.e., intellect in man), to gain the day. I shall have to tell our readers how our ancestor was an animal which breathed water, had a swim bladder, a great swimming tail, an imperfect skull, and undoubtedly was a hermaphrodite! Here is a pleasant genealogy for mankind.

I shall certainly send you a copy of the book when it is published. For now it is down to work to begin my end of our bargain. I am a slow & patient writer, but however long it takes to properly organize the evidence, ten, twenty, thirty years, I shall do it right. You may rest assured it shall eventually be handsomely published for all the world to share.

> *Best wishes always,*
> *Charles Darwin*

As if to underscore the gravity of the letter Grigsby rose solemnly and the foursome—Grigsby first, then Hanna, Rosa María, and Bodan—began the hike down the stream with the sun low over the top of the forest and cooling slightly.

"We regard Emilio Gonzalvo as the founding Quayloo. The only Quayloo who did not physically serve us on the river was Charles Darwin, but Darwin, in gathering evidence to support our theory and in making it available to the larger world in his famous volume, was a go-between in a far more important sense. The main lines of argument in that theory of evolution have stood the test of time, which has been and continues to be a source of great pride among

XuXuians. Gonzalvo and Darwin are our most famous Quayloos, but we regard almost all our go-betweens as heroic figures for their tireless, unrecognized hard work on our behalf. After all these years, the secret of our location is still intact."

After a while, Hanna said, "Which brings us to the question of just what the four of you are doing out of your hideaway."

Grigsby crossed the stream on a log, holding his arms out for balance. "We did our best to conserve our diamonds —we lived decade by decade knowing our economy depended on a finite resource. The Quayloos did everything possible to see to it we had what we needed to be self-sustaining, but as the years went by, things got more and more expensive. And then eventually, as we knew it would, the seam of diamonds began to thin. Our experimental farms are keeping us going right now, but we need hard currency or face a severe reduction in our standard of living. Rosa María?"

Rosa María said, "We have marketed fashion successfully, but when the owner of the *Barco* was murdered we discovered that we didn't have the money to buy a replacement riverboat for Elongxa and Elluria. We knew we were in trouble."

Grigsby said, "What happened was Elongxa and Elluria found Obatala's fish after a sloppy search by the army. They suspected they might be watched by the police, so they hid the fish in Belém and waited it out."

Bodan grinned. "Hans and Lenny found the fish!"

"They found that the best place in the world to fence the fish and get the most for it was right here in Amazonia. A fish that priceless is very difficult and dangerous to fence in the usual markets unless you're a professional. However, there are passionately religious men at Loucofilho who have struck gold worth millions of dollars and who would pay anything for the miracle fish. That's why Hans and Lenny agreed to take Kobayashi's boxes to Loucofilho, not for whatever reason they may have told you."

Bodan said, "They told me running cargo was more profitable than passengers and since they'd lost Padim's patronage they couldn't afford to turn down a run to Loucofilho. Smooth liars."

"But they knew it would be dangerous trying to sell it in Loucofilho by themselves. Going to Loucofilho via the Purus was dangerous—not only because of the rumors of Bocagrandes, but because of the increasing number of ambushes on isolated stretches of the river; they asked the XuXuian legislature if they might not have an escort for safety's sake. They said they had a customer who wanted to ship cargo to Loucofilho, which gave them a logical reason to go there.

"By a resolution of the XuXuian legislature facing severe budget problems, the four of us were given permission to break precedent: we would be the first party to officially set forth from XuXu and the first XuXuians ever to talk to a Quayloo. We agreed to meet Elongxa and Elluria at the Santarém docks."

"We talked while you two were on the ranch tour. They were opposed to us personally traveling on the *Barco* because they didn't want us mingling with outsiders. They did feel they needed a boat to travel with them for safety's sake, and they told us about the tactics currently popular with pirates; it turned out they were right. Also, we could hardly argue with them; you have to remember: until Santarém all XuXuians through the years had obeyed a code of honor by which they agreed never to directly address a Quayloo. When Elongxa and Elluria said they wanted us to remain off their stern on the way to Loucofilho, why, that's what we did."

"Santarém is where our problems began," Rosa María said.

Grigsby said, "We had good luck and bad luck in Santarém. The good luck began when the ranch owner invited you folks for a day trip to sample hamburgers; that gave us a chance to spend some time alone with Elongxa and Elluria to discuss the problem of selling the fish. Then came the bad luck."

Bodan said, "I take it this is where Mr. Murphy's law stepped in."

"I beg your pardon?"

"When things can go wrong, they will."

"Exactly. Elongxa and Elluria didn't tell us who was shipping a cargo to Loucofilho, only that they had a customer. Then, while you were still gone, we went out and had ourselves a good time with all those wonderful whiskeys and gins and vodkas and rums we found in Santarém bars. There's nothing like that in XuXu, believe me; we didn't handle it well."

Rosa María said, "Boobie's the only one of us who didn't spend half the night vomiting."

"But I made up for it with that headache. Ohhh, alcohol is terrible stuff!" Grigsby, grimacing, closed his eyes at the awful memory of his hangover. "Well, we were on our way back to our boat when we saw Kobayashi sitting there with you on the boat. We had led him to believe that we were a colony of environmental researchers from the University of São Paulo. He was clearly startled to hear us speak XuXuian. Elongxa and Elluria were shocked as well: there was no doubt that Kobayashi knew us personally."

"We were astonished to see Kobayashi with our go-betweens," Rosa María said.

"When it was obvious that the *Darwinia* was going under and we would have to board the *Barco Igaranha*, we decided to give Elongxa and Elluria an authentic XuXuian entrance, so we smoked a little marijuana and considered the possibilities. The more we smoked, the more we thought about the gold at Loucofilho—after all, we would be going there to help them sell Obatala's fish. The more we thought about the gold, the more we began dreaming up schemes to charm the miners out of a little extra donation to the XuXuian treasury coffers. We would be putting their treasure to impeccable use, after all."

"So that's how you got the idea of your Grigsby persona."

"I'm afraid so," he said.

"An entertaining way of conning the miners of Loucofilho."

José María Quixote de la Balboa-Grigsby sighed. His shoulders slumped and he stared at the deck. "Yes, that was the idea, typical XuXuian playfulness."

Hanna said, "You've told Nicholas and me that the Xu-Xuians don't mind untidiness and are more comfortable with the here and now. Tell us a little about the inevitable bumpy side. What goes wrong in XuXu?"

Rosa María laughed. "Well, just about everything if you worry about order. To be a XuXuian sometimes requires a great deal of patience, I'm afraid. Things have a tendency to go wrong or else just not get done. For example, we have some wonderful chefs but nobody wants to run the cash register. It's impossible to find a waiter in XuXu who doesn't want to sing to the customers and being XuXuian is no guarantee of musical talent, believe me. We can be too open-minded for our own good. Almost nobody has a license for anything because applications are never processed. Our supreme judge, a woman who plays first bassoon in our orchestra, finds it very difficult to come to a decision. When she is finally forced to decide a case in which a XuXuian must inevitably suffer, she can be heard playing melancholy songs on her bassoon in the middle of the night."

"Tell them about the cops, Rosa María."

"XuXuians are so open-minded nobody wants to enforce rules. So about a hundred years ago, we decided to do something about it. We instituted a draft so that all XuXuians must take a turn at being policemen, but they have a great deal of freedom in minor cases to invent their own punishment on the spot. For example, we have a general crime in XuXu called disrespect for the environment. A man caught dumping garbage in the woods, for example, might be sentenced to write a book-length essay on why fouling the forest is stupid and offensive, the cop to personally act as editor. The criminal must continue researching the reasons for the law and writing and rewriting and rewriting the essay until the cop is satisfied with its quality."

Grigsby said, "Nobody wants to do anything physical or mundane; status lies almost solely in science and the arts—that and one's prowess in bed. We XuXuians believe that sexiness depends on imagination and a sense of drama and so couples become erotic explorers. Each partner's body temperature remains the same, after all; sensuousness and sexiness lie in exercising creativity and imagination."

"In our opinion uncreative sex is illogical and boring, the same as endlessly rereading the same book," Rosa María said.

"I agree, certainly," Bodan said.

"We do have our fun in XuXu, but like I say, details can sometimes go wanting. For example, one of our biggest events of the year, rather like your World Series or the World Cup tournament is our annual XuXuian open chess championship. Two years ago one of the excited competitors showed up for his first game wearing no pants."

Grigsby laughed. "It was wonderful. He received a prolonged, standing ovation."

Rosa María shook her head. "You should talk, Boobie. You're as bad as he is, if not worse sometimes."

Grigsby looked mock offended. "I should let you slander me like that? It's a lie, I assure you, Hanna. A flat-out lie. What's wrong with you, woman?" He gave Rosa María a little hug.

"Boobie's really something. He dreams up all these grandiose and fanciful plans, but nothing ever comes of them. Your schemes always seem to get tripped up on an overlooked detail, don't they, Boobie?"

"Well, I wasn't elected President of XuXu for nothing."

Bodan said, "You're the President of XuXu?"

"Not now. I was. I'm proud to tell you I was drafted by acclaim and served one term."

Rosa María said, "Tell the whole truth, Boobie. Anybody who wants the office is disqualified so all candidates are drafted. Boobie's term was an honorable disaster; it was terrific fun but nothing got done."

"I'll be remembered as one of the great ones." Grigsby held his chin up.

"You were elected because you looked like a president ought to look, but if you had thought of yourself as a leader nobody would have voted for you."

Grigsby ran his fingers through his silver hair, pretending to be indignant. He turned his head slightly and regarded his wife out of the corner of his eyes, narrowing them slightly. "I was *famous* for the quality of my proclamations and declarations."

"And quantity! You loved your proclamations, Boobie, you have to admit. You popped out of bed every morning eager to write a new one."

"If I was only good for proclamations, why is it I was chosen to lead the first expedition outside XuXu?"

"Boobie, the XuXuian legislature never decides anything for practical reasons and you know it. You will remember it was specifically stipulated that you were not to set foot out of XuXu unless I went with you."

"Well, I may trip up on a detail now and then, but I've got sense enough to know that with Elongxa and Elluria dead, we don't have any choice but to get Obatala's fish to Loucofilho and negotiate the best deal possible for XuXu. There's nobody but us to do the job."

Rosa María said, "Yes, we do have to sell the fish. But now we've got a second problem. Tell them everything, Boobie."

Grigsby sighed. "Rosa María's right, I'm afraid. We do have a second problem. Unless we're allowed to exercise our imaginations in peace, XuXu will most certainly be consumed as Charles Darwin feared. If anything should happen to the four of us XuXuians, there has to be someone we can trust to maintain contact with the outside world."

"We urgently need two people who value inquiry and creativity to replace Elongxa and Elluria. It's dangerous for us to proceed without Quayloos." Rosa María looked at Hanna, then at Bodan.

"Us?" Hanna's mouth fell.

"What?" Bodan blinked.

Grigsby said, "Unless you say no, you're both Quayloos, because you've just been given the traditional briefing given all prospective go-betweens and we've never once been turned down yet. You can write your novels down here can't you, Nicholas? You don't have to live in the United States, do you? You have an agent to deal with your publishers. What do you have to go back to?"

"Bills and lawyers. My daughter could come down here to visit me, I suppose."

"Of course she could. And you can't go back to the United States, can you, Hanna?"

"I don't think I would want to try just yet. Is there any reason I couldn't set up a riverboat medical practice, turn a cabin into a combination examination room and operating room? I could bring medicine to the people who live in isolation out here."

Grigsby looked pleased. "There's no reason at all that we couldn't turn a riverboat into a medical clinic. That's the kind of imagination we XuXuians like to see. Done then: Quayloos the both of you."

46
A CEREMONY OF QUAYLOOS

＊

After the XuXuian briefing of the prospective Quayloos, the *Barco Igaranha* got under way again with Sanger Humpperman at the helm and with Hanna and Bodan sitting squat-legged on what was left of the aft cabin top, trying to comprehend the responsibilities of maintaining XuXu's secrecy while providing the tools necessary for the XuXuians to follow their imaginations.

Less than an hour later Humpperman pulled the *Barco* to the side of the river out of the main current, sent the anchor into the water, and killed the engine. Humpperman went below into the shattered hull of the forward cabin where his comrades waited, and a few minutes later he went to the aft cabin with a wooden nose resting on his forehead like sunglasses waiting for use—the nose held in place by an elastic band around his head.

"Well, if you two are ready, we all are," he said.

"Ready?" Hanna asked, glancing at the nose.

Humpperman looked surprised at her question but unaware that a wooden nose on his forehead was in any way unusual. "Why, to become our Quayloos! This is too serious a business not to have a XuXuian ceremony."

Bodan grinned. "I'm ready."

"Like getting married." Hanna accepted Humpperman's help in getting up.

Hanna and Nicholas followed Humpperman to the forward cabin where Grigsby, wearing his bemedaled uniform, his heavy sword tugging at his belt, waited with a large rolled scroll under one arm.

The XuXuians all knelt, saying, *"Ooo. Ooo. Ooo."*

Still kneeling, Grigsby unrolled the scroll. "As former

President of XuXu, carrying with it the lifetime power to issue proclamations and declarations, and as leader of this critical XuXuian expedition to sell Obatala's fish in Loucofilho, be it known:

"Hanna Doherty, inasmuch as your former husband died of AIDS, and you, in the act of slicing young squid for supper, noticed that the squid rings looked somewhat like the foreskins of newborns, you suddenly felt in hippie mood, longing for honorable days of imaginative protest.

"And as these hippie protest thoughts put you in a jousting mood, you set about to remind the public through jolly sport that a medical system geared to maximum profit with precious little public service was at least partly responsible for delays in AIDS funding and research; those of your colleagues who finally did apply for research grants routinely exaggerated the AIDS threat to heterosexuals in order to justify more money—popular reports of which unnecessarily frightened and confused men and women everywhere.

"There can be no denying that for these delaying and procrastinating physicians, foreskins are an entirely appropriate commemorative snack.

"And with regard to your second complaint, be it known that the primates of the world have had as much as fourteen million years to reject malfunctioning penises. Organic cocks function without a hitch on monkeys, chimpanzees, gorillas, and orangutans, as well as on hundreds of millions of **Homo sapiens** *in Southeast Asia, China, Japan, India, Africa, Australia, Europe, and South America—in fact, 85 percent of male babies born. The Semitic practice of circumcision originated for religious rather than biological or medical reasons; historically, it was adopted by Abraham as the external sign of his choice to renounce evil and to enter into God's Covenant, and the Muslims borrowed the practice from the Jews. Thus circumcision is culturally logical for Jews and Muslims but illogical for Gentiles, whose religion and philosophy make no such requirement. While circumci-*

sion is considered medically unnecessary in Western Europe, Great Britain, and Japan, it continues to be a common and routine surgery in the United States, performed on Gentile newborns for no logical reason other than a few extra bucks in the wallet of the doctor who removes the foreskin.

"Furthermore, as you yourself pointed out in your statements to reporters afterward, the doctors paid for the exotic at the cocktail hour. They expected something special and you didn't let them down. And as you also said, a farmer who earns his living picking cherries eats them openly and with pride; those whose appetite leads them to casually profit from the routine harvest of foreskins ought at least know what they taste like.

"So therefore:

"In view of your XuXuian-like protest in the name of your former husband—calling foreskins little black and white squids from Atlantis was the essence of the XuXuian imagination; we XuXuians have long identified with Atlantis, we being the lost colony long pursued by eaters and devourers from all over the world—I, Alom Pia, in accordance with the powers granted to me by XuXuian custom, do hereby name, declare, announce, and pronounce you, Dr. DeeDee Sarant, also known as Hanna Doherty, a Hero of XuXu, the first non-XuXuian other than Charles Darwin or a Quayloo ever to be awarded this honor, and you yourself shall be the go-between, Elooua Quayloo, our woman of questions.

"And to you, Nicholas Bodan, for being a faithful chronicler of the Barco's voyage so that the details may not be lost, I judge you a Scribe of XuXu, with full membership in the XuXuian Authors' League, and you shall be the go-between, Elanxa Quayloo, our man of imagination."

Having thus finished his declaration, Grigsby carefully rerolled the scroll and rose to his full height, joined by Humpperman and Lola Corona. He handed the scroll to a pleased Hanna, gave her a hug, and kissed her on the cheek.

"Alu, Seena, will you kindly do the honors of awarding the Charles Darwin noses, please."

The bearded Sanger Humpperman went behind Hanna and Lola Corona went behind Bodan. Hanna and Bodan each got a wooden nose on the forehead, Hanna's carved from yellow wood, Bodan's a crisp white.

Then, tears flowing, chin bobbing, Grigsby stood straight and tall and lowered his Charles Darwin nose over his own, and the others of the company did the same— Elooua and Elanxa Quayloo for the first time—and the Xu-Xuians, their shoulders jerking with sobs, embraced their new go-betweens.

On their last night before facing the lair of Bocagrandes, Grigsby anchored the *Barco Igaranha* at a point on the charts some ten to fifteen miles downstream from the great depths, and from the moment the sun disappeared beyond the forest on the far side of the Purus, the *Barco* was surrounded by banjomen catfish giving the travelers a final serenade.

Grigsby and his wife disappeared into the forward cabin, and Lola Corona and Sanger Humpperman in the aft, while the newest Quayloos, Elooua, with a bottle of XuXuian red wine in hand, and Elanxa, with a hunk of XuXuian smoked fish, took the aft cabin top.

The new Quayloos lowered the table flush to the floor and Hanna flopped a futon on the deck; in one motion, she tossed her raven hair to one side and squatted cross-legged. "This is the last bottle of XuXuian wine they brought aboard. Rosa María said they wanted to give it to us for a good-luck beginning."

"Sure, we can do some damage to that bottle. Be full-fledged Quayloos in no time." Bodan turned his head to one side. "Listen. Do you hear that?"

"No."

"Try again."

"A boat."

"Or boats," Bodan said. "Sounds like more than one to me."

"You're right. Boats."

"My God, they're coming right at us."

"Don't they see us?"

The lead boat bore straight down on the *Barco* and as it passed, seemingly yards off the *Barco*'s starboard rails— sending the riverboat rocking in its wake—Bodan and Hanna saw that it was a military vessel with deck guns, perhaps the one they had encountered earlier on the river.

Judging from its running lights and brightly lit deck, the second vessel was a passenger liner. As it grew closer, and larger, Bodan and Hanna heard the mellow *bee-bee boing-boing-boing bee-bee* patter of steel drums. The drums grew louder as the liner passed the *Barco*—huge and sleek, its engines at once deep, powerful, high-tech, and insistent— leaving an even larger wake than the gunboat. On a dance floor by a swimming pool, self-conscious, stiff-jointed passengers tried to act cool and loose.

"Oh, look, it's a love boat," Hanna said.

On a second ship—for that is what it in fact was, being about the same size as the first—a handsome man with a flamboyant smile and white teeth sang with a mellow Portuguese accent.

"Listen," Bodan said.

They could clearly hear the singer's lyrics on the third boat, which featured a singer with a guitar all duded up in a western outfit:

> *"And we 'tend mighty roundups*
> *Where, according to the Word,*
> *The angel cowboy of the Lord*
> *Will cut the human herd . . ."*

47
TO DIE WITH ONE'S BRAINS INTACT
✳

Hanna Doherty fell to sleep just before dawn but woke up a short while later, victim of a full bladder. She slipped from under Bodan's hairy leg, which was slung over her hip, and peered through the window of her compartment. She couldn't see anything because of a heavy fog that had settled over the water.

Bodan was awake. "Stay just the way you are, Hanna. I like you like that in the light. You might move your rump just a little to the left. A little more. That's it. Mmmm! Such a sweet, sweet ass."

Hanna wiggled it for him while he groaned in admiration, then she slipped back under the covers and under his leg. She still had to pee but the bed was nice and warm and the toilet was a hassle to get to. "It's foggy out there."

"Sanger and Lola set hand lines for a catfish breakfast. I wonder how they did?" Bodan's hand began roaming.

It didn't take much to flip Hanna's switch, but she couldn't get too excited on a full bladder. "Be right back," she said. She slipped into her robe and made a run to the toilet.

When she got back, pressure relieved, she succumbed to another round.

When they were finished, Bodan got up to take a shower, giving Hanna a chance to lie in the warm bed for a while looking out at the fog.

A few minutes later Rosa María rapped on the door with a breakfast of coffee, papaya, and slices of ham and cheese.

"Breakfast in bed is the least you and Nicholas deserve on your first day as Quayloos," she said. "Incidentally, Hanna, we XuXuians are aware that we are sojourners. We each have our turn and then our children take their turn and their children after that. We don't like this condition especially, but we try not to dwell on it. If there's a chance our turn is finished, we always want to go out celebrating how much life we could pack into our allotted turn; the only reason XuXuians mourn death is when the owner of a body wasted a chance to live. The XuXuian term for clarity at the surrendering of life, roughly translated, means 'to die with one's brains intact.' "

"Dress up, then, not down."

"We don't believe in mourning, besides which we don't have black anyway."

Hanna gave Rosa María a hug.

"Boobie's going the whole way, I think, one of the parody uniforms we made for him complete with sword. I say *we* made. Actually, Boobie both designed the uniform and did most of the sewing himself; most men in XuXu would be humiliated to be unable to design and sew their own clothes. It's the detail work that gets him down; he gets impatient and the result can be a little rough."

After Rosa María left, Hanna—deciding practical and colorful was the best bet—dressed in blue jeans, sneakers, and the Whitey Ford T-shirt Walter had given her when they were married—Walter being a Whitey Ford fan when he was a kid.

When Bodan got back and Hanna told him about the XuXuian custom of mourning, he chose sunglasses, jeans, a T-shirt with Leonard's Bar and Grill on the front and a naked woman with two kangaroos on the back.

When they were both ready, they made an appearance topside, where Humpperman and Lola were having a good time laughing about their attempt to catch a few catfish for breakfast. They had set out Lenny's hand lines baited with doughballs on treble hooks and in the morning—astonishingly—the bait was still there, there apparently being no fish remaining this stretch of the Purus save the starving Bocagrandes.

Bodan said, "Wait'll we turn on the engine and they know we're here. Then we'll have fun. We'll be like a bass plug plopped in front of those lunkers."

Lola wore skintight cotton trousers the tops of which came just above her pubic hair in front and showed off two neat dimples above her rump. She was barefoot and had both toenails and fingernails painted red to match her Cincinnati Reds baseball cap—this latter article having somehow miraculously found its way into the hands of the little XuXuian beauty. She wore her black hair in a long ponytail. Her white T-shirt—perhaps a trifle small—bared very delicate, delicious ribs and a tawny little belly. She carried two bad-ass bandoliers of ammunition slung over her shoulders and crisscrossed between her breasts. She wore a six-shooter on each hip with the wicked butts sticking forward. These were long-barreled beauties, engraved with tiny hearts and cupids.

Humpperman, who had one of the two 12-gauge shotguns that Weckert and Humphries had kept aboard the *Barco,* wore white sneakers, blue jeans, a cotton print shirt decorated with red and green and yellow parrots, and a wide-brimmed straw planter's hat.

"Well, what do you think?" he said, his hand at his beard.

"Smashing," Hanna said. "I like parrots."

This pleased Sanger, who proceeded to imitate a forest of parrots and tropical birds, all squawking and jabbering.

Rosa María had a green sweatband around her forehead and a translucent white blouse tied in a knot just beneath her breasts. She wore the same crisscrossed bandoliers of ammunition as Lola. She was also barefoot, her toenails and fingernails painted green to match her headband. She wore her brace of revolvers at a rakish angle on the hips of her skintight white jeans.

The mighty Grigsby emerged wearing an even more splendid uniform than the scarlet outfit in which he'd made his grand entrance on the river. This effort was perhaps more formal attire, a splendid blue with red trim and with buttons and epaulets of such gaudy excess as to make the first getup seem drab by comparison. He had a red-and-white feathered plume in the band of his broad-brimmed hat.

He tilted the brim at a stylish angle, looking from under it with steady pale blue eyes.

Grigsby's scabbard, an open-mouthed snake, yielded the handle of his mighty blade.

Here was a man to take on a Bocagrande.

A whiskered leviathan floated by, barely visible in the murk, whiskers looking like white ropes.

As the corpse was about to disappear into the fog, a larger Bocagrande rose soundless from the water and the dead fish was gone.

"Oh shit," Bodan said.

Grigsby said, "It eats a twelve-foot minnow, so what! Why, there's a woman in XuXu said to be able to swallow a . . ."

"Boobie!" Rosa María interrupted.

"Sorry. Anyway, is that all it can show us? So it eats a crumb." Grigsby looked solemn. "I won't have defeatist talk among my commanders. Besides, we'll be wearing Charles Darwin noses. What can happen to us? What can go wrong if we're wearing our Darwin noses?" He sucked air between his front teeth and adjusted his salt-and-pepper handlebars.

"By the way, Hanna, my colleagues and I have talked it over. You're the logical one to take the helm today. You've more than earned the reputation as a scrapper and we can't have a quitter in the bridge if we're to take on the depths. I feel my proper place is on the bow with my invincible blade."

This brought spirited applause from Sanger, Lola, and Rosa María.

"Elooua Quayloo!" Sanger said.

"Of course I'll pilot the boat. I'll run her straight and true with no apologies."

"It's done, then," Grigsby said. "Our new Quayloo, the woman of questions, will pilot us across the great depths."

48

WHEN YOU SWIM IN THESE WATERS

❋

Nicholas Bodan was on the bridge with Hanna Doherty as together they followed the charts carefully to see how close they were coming to the great depths. She took her time, getting a good feel for the boat although she had taken her turn at the helm before. There was no sense pushing the *Barco* now; she'd be getting plenty of action in a few minutes.

Curve by curve, they traced their progress to the great depths, marking all the checkpoints on the chart.

With two more curves before the lower end of the great depths, Hanna brought the *Barco* close to shore and throttled her down to an idle. "As near as Nicholas and I can figure out, the great depths should begin after the second bend coming up."

Grigsby drew his blade. "It's time, then."

Bodan went to the bow and started arranging his boxes of gasohol Molotov cocktails so he could get at them easily.

Lola spun the cylinders on one of her revolvers as Sanger slid loads of buckshot into his shotgun.

Bodan, pointing upstream, yelled, "Look! Look! Look!"

They turned in time to see a gullet open and a Bocagrande inhale a fallen brother and disappear into the water. These catfish, like the others, were far too small to threaten the *Barco*.

Hanna used the heel of one sneaker to knock out the shards of glass that remained around the edges of the windows of the bridge. She cleaned up the glass without hurry, tidying up the interior of the bridge.

She took a deep breath and flipped the toggle switch that started the anchor winch.

The brass handle that controlled the *Barco*'s engine felt cool in her hand.

She pushed it forward and they were off for the final curve. She turned on the fish finder. She rounded the bend and there, dead ahead, were the three luxury vessels and two Brazilian gunboats that had passed them in the night. They were anchored at the edge of what her charts said was the great depths of the Purus.

They had anchored the boats in a wide V—with the largest vessel at point—so that everybody had an unobstructed view of the river ahead. The gunboats were deployed in front of the point vessel, which was actually an oceangoing liner.

As she drew closer, Hanna could see a commotion on the deck of the liner where the crooner had held forth the previous night; videocameras and banks of reflectors were circled around someone or something.

Two Rancho Olivieres yellow-and-black air trucks hovered over the forest, cables dangling from their cabins.

She slowed the *Barco* even more.

"What do you think?" she said.

Grigsby said, "I suppose we better talk to them. They might not let us pass."

"Do you suppose they'll launch a small boat to meet us?"

A light began flashing on the deck of the gunboat, but the Morse code was gibberish to Hanna. A man frantically began waving flags.

She didn't understand that either.

A red flare shot up in front of the starboard gunboat.

"That means stop, I think." Hanna pulled even with the current and hit the anchor button, sending the anchor *ker-splash* into the water. The *Barco* drifted momentarily and came to a stop well starboard of the liner; she shut the *Barco* down.

While she waited, Hanna could hear the sound of the chain saws coming from the forest beneath the air trucks. One of the air trucks reeled in its cable and flew over the river, stopping directly above the gunboat in front of the *Barco.* A chair was lowered to the bow of the boat and a soldier got aboard. The airboat reeled him in and headed for the *Barco.*

Hanna waited, listening to the chain saws on shore. In a minute she heard footsteps on the roof.

The XuXuians and Bodan and Hanna gathered on the forward cabin top as a man opened the trapdoor above the bridge and came down the ladder. He was a lean and fit-looking Brazilian army officer in camouflage fatigues with a pistol on one hip and a clipboard in one hand. A tag on his chest identified as him as Captain Moraes.

Shaking his head, looking at the fractured and splintered deck and cabins, Moraes said, "How did this happen?"

"We were attacked by bandits a couple of nights ago," Bodan said.

"An ambush followed by a torch."

"That's what happened."

"How did you survive?"

"We saw them before they came upon us, so we had a chance to defend ourselves. Also we were traveling in tandem with another boat that rammed them."

"You should thank the Virgin. Who's in charge here? You?"

"He would be," Bodan said. He meant Grigsby.

Grigsby said, "Yes, I suppose that would be me, although the lady here is our chief pilot. The two gentlemen whose boat this was were killed by the bandits in the attack."

Moraes made a note on his clipboard. "Two men dead?"

"Four, actually. A priest and a river trader were also killed."

Moraes looked around at the shambles of the *Barco*'s deck. "I can believe that. And you did what with the bodies?"

"We buried them back by the river, although I'm not sure we could find the graves if we had to."

"I see." Moraes scribbled another note. "You're bound where? Loucofilho?"

"Yes."

"You're going to have to find another way of getting there. Passage over the great depths is momentarily prohibited. But you won't be allowed to return downstream until we get this business of bandits and dead bodies cleared up. Until I can send an officer over to take depositions, you'll have to anchor inside the arc formed by the larger vessels. After we're finished with our inquiry and depending on the results, you'll be free to return to Manaus if you wish."

"I see."

"I want all your passports and the ship's papers and licenses ready when my officer comes, do you understand?"

"We understand. Captain, can you tell us what's going on with the passenger vessels here?" Grigsby gestured to the resort liner off the *Barco*'s port rails.

Moraes looked mildly at the confusion of reflectors and cameras on the huge ship. "That's the American television evangelist Billy Gill."

"Really. *The* Billy Gill?" Hanna said.

Moraes looked at her. "He's broadcasting live right now. All over the world, he says." If Moraes had an opinion in the matter, he hid it well. He obviously had other things on his mind besides Billy Gill, or why the Brazilian army should be required to give him protection.

He put the clipboard under his arm and turned to the ladder that led to the trapdoor in the roof. "When I'm safely away, I want this boat out of here and inside the assigned area. Please do it quickly. If you attempt to proceed upriver, you will be fired upon and sunk. Do you understand?"

Grigsby nodded his head yes, he understood.

When Moraes disappeared through the trapdoor, Humpperman ran for the hold with Lola at his heels.

Hanna reeled the anchor in, wondering what they were up to. She piloted the *Barco* inside the protective V of the pleasure vessels. She anchored at a spot closest to the largest ship so she could watch some of the commotion around Billy Gill.

She heard electronic cheering from the aft cabin top. ". . . Pookie the Popper goes baseline and pokes it home as the Blazers put two more on the boards. The Lakers seem almost to be running out of gas here in the stretch. Steve . . ."

". . . word of Jesus, my friends, this is the word of the Lord, it's right here in the holy book . . ."

By the time Hanna had finished dropping anchor and shutting down the *Barco* and hustled back to the aft cabin, Bodan and the XuXuians were kicked back with the last of Humphries's supply of beer watching television. She grabbed one for herself and slipped onto the bench next to Bodan.

Sure enough, there he was: the Reverend Dr. Billy Gill, famous mustache and all, holding forth on the deck of the liner next to the *Barco.* Gill, a broad-shouldered man in his middle forties wearing a pale beige tropical, was a television regular, beaming the word from his electronic ministry in Dallas, Texas, and his rather curious face was familiar to any American who had ever waited in line at the grocery store with a magazine rack.

Gill's face was curious because of his full lips, which might have been sensuous on another man, but which, owing to a pronounced, pious overbite, looked somehow fishlike. He sought to detract attention from his unfortunate mouth by growing a handlebar mustache which—together with his sincere eyes—had become his evangelical trademark. These eyes, deep hypnotic pools of pale yellow, together with Gill's relentless, unsmiling sincerity and his repeated assurances that he was acting on the direct word of God, had a resoundingly profitable effect on his followers.

The Reverend Gill had thinning blond hair that was balding at the temples. He talked with his hands, chopping and gesturing to emphasize his famous not-to-be-questioned sincerity.

Behind him the yellow-brown Purus was tranquil for the moment, the buzz of chain saws on shore barely discernible.

". . . these special fish of God, suffering as did Jesus on the cross."

The camera cut to another Bocagrande rolling to the surface of the water. The legend *recorded earlier* was on the bottom of the picture.

"These peaceful creatures of the Lord, these calm and placid fish, want only to eat. They have been browsing in the bottom of these great depths that have been their home for millennia and now they are starving."

The camera cut back on Billy Gill, who periodically shouted a phrase or sentence for emphasis. He began his famous sincerity workup. To demonstrate sincerity, he leaned forward and bunched his lips until they turned pale. As a sign of resolve, he clenched his jaws and ground his teeth together. To demonstrate that he was capable of emotion, he crossed his arms over his chest and embraced himself. When he bunched his lips for sincerity, he often squinted his yellow eyes.

Now it was that he gave the viewers all these sincerity gestures at once: he bunched his lips; he clenched his teeth; he embraced himself; he squinted his eyes.

"My friends, Lord Jesus was not crucified without reason. He suffered on that cross for us and He died for *our* sins. So that *we* might have salvation. And make no mistake either, the Lord God did not without reason create these beautiful catfish that are, save for their size, *identical with a known, documented miracle fish! The Lord God did not draw attention to these starving fish without reason!* The Lord does nothing without reason. We're told the very name Bocagrande means 'Peaceful One.' We read in the Bible with sadness at Christ's being turned away, of His being scorned, of His being crucified—nailed to a cross—while people who should have known better did nothing, *just stood by and watched His suffering!*

"You ask, well, Billy Gill, just why is it that the Lord God in His benevolent wisdom chose this place for His lovely fish of love, here on the Purus River in the middle of the largest rain forest in the world? *He did it to give us a sign! It behooves us to pay attention!*

"You know, my friends, in the early days of Christianity there was such secrecy about the Lord Christ; He was spoken of as the Mysterious One. Such was His power that His name was never spoken; instead He was referred to as Ichthys, the Fish. That is how He is portrayed in early church art, as a fish. Today we are mocked by so-called rationalists and yet, sure enough, to restore our faith and bolster our spirit, He has chosen this great primal upwelling, these mysterious, inspiring depths, to give us a sign of hope, of baptism and rebirth.

"You could take your baby to the most secret and mysterious baptismal crypts beneath the oldest cathedrals in Europe and not find water as holy as this awesome upwelling for which science has no answer. No matter what your age or the condition of your spirit and soul, when you swim in these waters you swim as neophytes, as innocent little fishes, and *you will emerge born again.*

"Now I want you to think about something, friends. You, right there in your comfortable living rooms, *are put exactly in the position of those who stood by and watched the abuse and torture of our Lord Jesus Christ!* Nobody has to take this poor preacher's word for it. *The miracle is here for everybody to see! The sign is here for everybody to contemplate!*"

The tropical heat was getting to the animated Billy Gill, who mopped his forehead with his handkerchief, the handlebars of his mustache drooping from accumulated sweat.

"You know, just a few minutes ago a fishing boat arrived

loaded with the fishermen's catch for an entire week as their contribution to this cause of all Christians everywhere. On the way here bearing their valuable catch, the boat was ambushed by bandits and four impoverished, Jesus-loving fishermen were killed."

The camera cut to the *Barco Igaranha.*

"Hey, that's us," said Bodan.

"Pilgrims bearing food for Bocagrandes. On their way here they were ambushed by bandits and four of them were killed. And would you just look at their poor boat? It's afloat only by the grace of God. They are willing to go without food, *to sacrifice themselves so that these magnificent creatures of the Lord might eat and prosper."*

The camera panned the *Barco Igaranha,* closing in on the details of her hull, tattooed and laced by bullet holes, and of her shattered cabin tops, then cut back to Gill.

"Look at what those fishermen endured, my friends. Look at what they went through. It's time for us to give a little ourselves. The first thing we have to do is establish an airlift in here to see that these fish are properly fed. Right now, this very minute, we have men on shore clearing space for an airstrip. Only those of you who reach out now to open that purse or wallet and write that check will know that you honored Jesus, that you demonstrated your resolve to save His special fish.

"The choice is yours. You can watch these fish suffering and do nothing or you can make a small contribution. You don't have to give much, a hundred dollars, five hundred, a thousand, whatever you think you can spare. This is a Billy Gill people's project.

"While you get your checkbooks out to get this project of the Lord's off to a proper Christian start, Beatrice will sing us a little hymn. Do yourself a favor and reserve a place for yourself on God's list of special friends. Make that check payable to F-I-S-H, in care of the Reverend Billy Gill, Dallas, Texas. Beatrice?"

A beautiful blonde, microphone at her slender throat, stood before an electric organ and began playing.

"Thank you, Billy. It's a pleasure."

> *"On-ward, Christian sol-diers,*
> *March-ing as to war,*
> *With the cross of Jesus*
> *Going on before."*

Gill said, "Help us, friends. Help us spread word of this Miracle of God. Get your checkbook out. Write that check for an amount that maybe hurts a little. Know that you gave. Remember, this is Jesus' check, not mine. Write a check for Jesus now."

> *"On-ward, Christian sol-diers,*
> *March-ing as to . . ."*

Bodan punched the set off.

49

OF EMIGRATION VISAS AND

BLONDES WITHOUT LIMIT

❋

After shutting off Billy Gill's performance, the travelers sat down with iced tea to discuss what to do next. There were hours of daylight left and according to the charts the great depths were only thirty miles long, leaving them plenty of time for a crossing.

Bodan said, "The first thing they'll do is block the depths off with submarine nets to keep the Bocagrandes penned in. They'll have to. Having to blow up God's miracle fish with depth charges is bad PR."

"I'll bet they have submarine nets on the way right now," Hanna said.

"They have to do something," Bodan said.

"We came here to go to Loucofilho, not turn back like puppy dogs," Grigsby said.

Hanna said, "They're not going to blow us out of the water with the international media taking pictures. That's very bad PR. I say we crank her up and go for it."

"The element of surprise," said Humpperman.

"I agree," said Rosa María.

"And me," added Lola.

"Then let's go for it." Hanna started the engine and hit the anchor button at the same time.

A siren on the gunboat began blowing *whooop, whooop, whoop!*

Humpperman yelled, "Quick, quick, quick, Hanna!"

Hanna watched, her mouth dry, as the anchor light stayed red and stayed red and stayed red as the winch reeled the anchor up from the bottom. Then, green.

She gunned *Barco* hard to starboard. "Here we go." She put the *Barco* in full forward and the trashed riverboat shot out of the protective circle.

She wheeled the *Barco* to port and aimed square between the two gunboats, and she was suddenly free and running hard across the depths before the Brazilian sailors could respond.

Behind her she could hear the sirens going *whooop, whooop, whooop!* but the gunboats stayed in place.

"All right! Yes! Yes!" Bodan yelled. "They don't want to shoot us because of all those television cameras. Hoo hoo. Thank you, Billy Gill."

Grigsby, standing firmly on the bow, opened a small case and removed a trombonelike flute, which he gave a preemptory blow, a quivering, spooky vibrato. He then launched into the "Colonel Bogey" march, his heel hitting the deck with determination: *thump, thuump, thump, thuump.* One, two, one, two.

The little group aboard the *Barco* all whistled as loudly as they possibly could, lips puckered in determination.

305

Backed by his chorus of proud whistlers, Grigsby was magnificent. His leonine mane of silver hair blew proudly in the breeze. He stood tall, his weight on the heel of his right foot, as he set the determined beat with his left heel. His stomach was in. His shoulders were back. His elbows were high and his chin was up as he played his XuXuian instrument.

Hanna watched the digital numbers clicking off on the fathometer. Fifty meters deep, sixty, a hundred.

Their left heels rose and fell in step with Grigsby.

One hundred and fifty meters. Two hundred. Two hundred fifty.

Hanna saw the beginnings of what could be an enormous tail on the screen of the *Barco*'s fish finder. The thing moved. A great tail.

She turned hard to port, then headed into the current again. "We've got a friend right beneath us. A big one."

The whistling stopped.

About a quarter of a mile in front of the *Barco* a white fin cut through the water, then disappeared.

Grigsby put his instrument down.

"When he starts out of the water I'm going to take her hard one way or the other."

"We understand," Grigsby said. He drew his sword and pointed that wicked blade to the heavens.

Lola and Rosa María crossed their arms and drew their long-barreled pistols. The pistols looked as if they weighed half as much as Lola did, but she brandished them like Clint Eastwood.

Bodan, weighing a cocktail in his right hand, said, "Okay, big eater. Let's see your best stuff." He looked back up at Hanna. "Give 'em hell, Hanna."

It happened fast.

Before anyone could think.

Before them, a mouth. A chasm of desire.

Bodan spiraled a gasohol cocktail down that awesome gullet.

Humpperman and Grigsby blasted into the flames with buckshot.

Lola and Rosa María fired at will and with both hands, pistols bucking.

Hanna went starboard, bumped into something:

The corner of the Bocagrande's lip.

The bow was inside the fish's cavernous mouth.

"Oh shit!"

She yanked full reverse.

Bodan lit and threw. Another jar of gasohol sailed into the chasm spiraling like a football, fuse burning.

Ba-boom. Bodan's bombs exploded in wicked balls of orange flame, one on top of the next.

The stunned Bocagrande, its mouth wide, its innards on fire, shuddered and twisted and dove for deep water.

A whisker swept over the rails . . .

. . . knocking the defenders to the deck . . .

. . . and catching Bodan around his ankle like a giant whip, dragging him toward the rail.

Bodan clung momentarily to the rail . . .

. . . as Grigsby severed the whisker not a foot from Bodan's leg.

Hanna brought the *Barco* to full stop.

She waited, staying even with the current, a dangerous time. A half minute passed as everybody reloaded and Bodan got his bombs rearranged. "Fucking whisker had me around the ankle."

"Hang in there, Nicholas," Hanna said.

Humpperman said, "Good move backing out of the mouth like that." He had a notch cut in the bridge of his wooden nose to keep his glasses from slipping off.

"It didn't make any sense to keep going forward."

Grigsby, his mighty blade back in the scabbard and his shotgun reloaded, picked up the beat of "Colonel Bogey" as though he had never been interrupted.

Humpperman went back to his station on the bow and

everybody fell in with Grigsby once more, whistling, marching in place.

Hanna reached down and took the brass handle full in her palm and pushed it forward, and it felt wonderful. She leaned against it, squeezing so hard her knuckles turned white. The engine grumbled, then roared. Her hand vibrated with the surge of power. The *Barco* seemed almost to lift from the surface of the water as Hanna took it right roaring square and true straight at the waiting Bocagrandes.

Another mouth opened in front of the *Barco* . . .

"Get back," Hanna yelled, going for reverse . . .

. . . and closed . . .

. . . taking the little beauty Lola Corona . . .

. . . as the defenders scrambled back, firing their weapons.

The Bocagrande dove, leaving a gaping hole where the bow had been—exposing the storage area beneath the deck —but the bite was well above the waterline.

One of Lola's fancy pistols lay spinning on the deck.

The fish's bite, in addition to taking the rails and bow with both glass eyes and the deck above the prow, had sliced straight through the storage area for the passengers on the forward cabin top—in this case the belongings of the XuXuians.

There, in an open shoe box, was a six-inch-long ceramic fish that Weckert and Humphries had found aboard the *Barco.*

Humpperman was on his knees at the rail staring at the water where the Bocagrande had disappeared with his girl-friend in its innards. He got up, shaken, wiping his eyes with the back of his forearm; he picked up her revolver, embraced simultaneously by Grigsby and Rosa María.

With Obatala's fish in a shoe box at the feet of the defenders, Hanna piloted the *Barco* as close as she could to the shore and let the engine idle. "What's your pleasure, Presidente: do we push on or turn back?"

Nobody answered. They listened to the loping idle of

the engine. Lola Corona was dead, gone. It was hard for any of them to believe.

Humpperman wiped his eyes with the back of his arm. "She was everything to me."

"Shall we push on or turn back, what do you think, Sanger?"

"Boobie, please. Not now. It's all impossible foolishness. We must turn back."

"Sanger?"

"What do I have to go back to?"

Rosa María shook her husband by the shoulder. "Boobie, this isn't a joke. Lola's dead. It was a wonderful plan in theory, I know. It should have worked, but it didn't. Listen to me, Boobie, that's why you need me, to bring you back to reality once in a while."

A lock of Grigsby's silver hair fell down in front of his face. "So what am I supposed to do, Rosa María? Go back to XuXu and tell them that our high jinks resulted in Elongxa and Elluria's death?"

"Boobie, the mix-up at Santarém wasn't your fault. You had no way at all of knowing that Kobayashi was on board the *Barco.* He was on that stupid day trip when we talked to Elongxa and Elluria and they didn't mention his name. It was just bad luck, nothing more. There's no accounting for lousy luck."

"And do I also tell them back in XuXu that I had Obatala's fish in hand but was too timid to take it on to Loucofilho? Is that what I tell them? They trusted me, Rosa María. Some man of action I am."

"Boobie, they're XuXuians. They'll listen to reason, you know that. Under the circumstances it's not reasonable to continue. We have new Quayloos now. They'll help us find a way to sell the fish. Won't you, Hanna?"

"We'll find a way," Hanna said.

"Won't you, Nicholas?"

"I can find you people in San Francisco who know people who know people. It can be done, Presidente."

Grigsby twisted out of his wife's grasp and glared down at the fish in the shorn bow. "We need to buy a replacement for the *Barco*. We need medical equipment. We need this. We need that. What is there we don't need? When we get to Loucofilho I can still peddle promises of emigration visas and blondes without limit to the miners."

"Boobie, please." Rosa María grabbed for her husband, but Grigsby sidestepped her. "You must listen to me. You know how you get carried away. Be logical, Boobie. Don't let yourself be taken under by emotion. You can't casually cheat those miners. Be reasonable."

"Cheat them?" Grigsby raised an eyebrow. "Who says anything about cheating them? José María Quixote de la Balboa-Grigsby does not cheat people."

"Boobie, Boobie, what are you talking about? Of course you're cheating them."

"Not if I go to the United States and run for President and deliver on my end of the deal, I'm not. Not if I get my hands on the key to the American treasury."

"Boobie!"

"Just this century the Americans have elected a haberdasher president, a peanut farmer president, an actor president. They have professional basketball players and astronauts eyeing the presidency. Why not the man in the white boat in the White House? Isn't that what they're all waiting for? The man in the white boat."

"Boobie, darling, you're not thinking straight. The man on the white horse; we've been through that."

"Boat? Horse? What difference does it make? Everybody says I've got what it takes; I look good, don't I? Who's to match this presidential face and silver hair? Who? With the gold from Loucofilho, I'll mount an unstoppable campaign just like we planned and I'll ship XuXu all the foreign aid it can handle under the table. Nobody has to be the wiser."

"Boobie, none of this was anybody's fault. Not Elongxa's death, not Elluria's death, not Lola's. But it will be your fault if you insist we keep going and somebody else gets killed."

Grigsby looked back at the bow again. "We're not taking on water. There's no reason we can't go forward. I'll pilot the boat alone if necessary. The rest of you can walk back if you want; all you have to do is follow the water. It may be slow going, but eventually you'll get back to the gunboats and Billy Gill."

"Boobie, honey, it's not that simple. The proceeds from the fish belong to all XuXu, not just you. We're entrusted with the fish. We're responsible. What if you lose it to a Bocagrande? What do we do next? Our Quayloos both say they'll help us find a buyer somewhere."

"Sanger?"

"I say forward. Up theirs."

"Nicholas?"

Bodan took a deep breath. "Sure, forward."

"Hanna?"

"Downstream's no fun."

"Don't ask me, Boobie. Where you go I go. You know that."

Grigsby held his wife tightly and nodded at Hanna. "Shall we proceed, then?"

Hanna Doherty squeezed the cool brass handle and pushed it firmly forward and the *Barco* responded. Dry-mouthed, saying nothing, the defenders on the bow took their assigned places.

50

HOW BOCAGRANDES DINE

❋

As Hanna Doherty piloted the bowless *Barco Igaranha* into what the chart said was the heart of the great upwelling of the Purus, she took advantage of the riverboat's shallow draft and stayed about twenty yards offshore off the inside curve, figuring there couldn't be many Bocagrandes hanging out in the forest. An attack, if it came, would have to be mounted on the *Barco*'s starboard, or river, side.

She leaned against the brass handle as though she could somehow push it past its limit, powering the *Barco* through yellow-brown water and hot, wet air. She didn't have time to be considerate of the damage done to the *Barco*'s hull, the object was to get from point A to point B and safety, in the shortest time possible.

It was high noon and the *Barco* slid shadowless over the waters of her destiny.

Hanna piloted the boat around another bend and encountered the leading edge of what amounted to a great raft of debris—what must have been thousands if not tens of thousands of logs, heaps of branches, and boughs blissfully floating downstream. All this evidence of yet another wicked storm higher up the river.

"Brace yourselves," Hanna yelled.

"Take 'em on, Hanna," Bodan yelled back.

"Grab a rail, everybody," Grigsby said.

The hull hit the leading edge of the debris with a jolting *ka-whack* that buckled Hanna's knees, but she straightened up and kept her dead ahead. The hull struck logs with a *bam, ka-bump, ka-bump* racket that twisted her insides and momentarily thinned her blood. She held her breath. Branches *rippppppped* like knives at the waterline, but there was nothing she could do about that—a tidy hull was the least of her worries.

She gritted her teeth and stayed parallel to the shore with as much speed as she could get out of the *Barco* what with having to slam through the crap on the water.

"Ahead!" yelled Rosa María.

"I see it," Hanna said, it being the white back of a Bocagrande that rose from the water dead ahead. "I'll try to go around him." She turned the *Barco* starboard, although she didn't like it; the farther offshore they were, the more vulnerable they were. About two hundred yards out, still plowing through debris, seeing no more sign of Bocagrandes, she turned port again and headed upriver. "In a couple of minutes when we're around that thing, I'll go back toward shore."

"Spooky out here," Bodan said. He had his binoculars out looking back at the spot near the shore where the behemoth catfish had risen briefly from the water.

A mouth opened in the water in front of the *Barco*.

Hanna swung port.

The Bocagrande bit another chunk of the bow, consuming both Obatala's fish and Sanger Humpperman. Just like that, Humpperman was no more, his bones being shredded in the stomach of the catfish.

Hanna straightened the *Barco* out and looked back. The Bocagrande was gone.

The *Barco* took a hard jolt from aft.

Suddenly the engine raced, ran freely, the tachometer red-lined. Hanna yanked the brass handle back, wondering what went wrong. The engine was running, yet the boat drifted.

"I'll check it out," Bodan said. He ran aft and disappeared into the hold.

Hanna killed the *Barco*'s useless engine. "No sense drawing their attention with unnecessary racket."

She joined Rosa María and Grigsby to wait for Bodan's report. The *Barco* drifted peacefully, dangerously, along with the debris.

Bodan was back in a minute. "The damned thing chomped our screws like a bass hitting a spinner."

"What?" Hanna said.

"It bit off the underside of the fantail and the process managed to rip a yard-long hole in the hull. We're taking on water."

Grigsby closed his eyes. "Can it be fixed?"

"There's no replacing the screw even if we had an extra, and certainly no repairing the hull what with those things taking runs at us. There's a door behind the engine that has the aft sealed off, so we might not go under right off."

"We just drift, then, with no power and bloated with water," Grigsby said, his arm around Rosa María.

"That's what it looks like, Boobie."

"Maybe we can sneak ashore in one of the lifeboats," Hanna said. "It's not any larger than some of these islands of debris; we might blend right in."

"It looks like our only hope," Bodan said.

Grigsby nodded in agreement. "I agree."

Hanna looked at Rosa María.

"As I said before, where Boobie goes, I go."

"I think we should split up into both lifeboats," Hanna said. "Make 'em find two tidbits, not just one. If one boat gets eaten, the other might make it."

"Right again," Grigsby said.

Bodan said, "We'll need some food."

"Rosa María and I will get that," Hanna said.

"And mosquito repellent," Bodan added.

"Nicholas and I will get the boats ready."

Rosa María and Hanna ran to the galley. They were no sooner inside the forward cabin than the *Barco* took a hit that knocked both women off their feet. They got up without a word and were knocked down by another hit. Hanna grabbed a pillowcase off Weckert's bunk and Rosa María, seeing what she had in mind, did the same with Humphries's. They made it into the galley, where they grabbed can openers and spoons and started dumping tin cans into the pillowcases.

The *Barco* took a third and yet a fourth hit.

There was water at the feet of Rosa María and Hanna in the galley.

They ran back through the water in the cabin with their pillowcases of supplies. Hanna grabbed a plastic bottle of mosquito repellent left lying on Humphries's bunk.

When they were up on deck, Hanna looked down into the hold, which was filling with water. The boat listed sharply to port; she lost her balance and leaned against the cabin, flopping her pillowcase on the deck.

Then it was that she saw the extraordinary sight that had Bodan and Grigsby staring transfixed at the water. It took a full second for the sight to register. Bodan put his arm around Hanna and they held each other.

The *Barco* was surrounded by Bocagrandes, scores, if not hundreds, of them, acres of them, who had been drawn to the surface by the excitement of the attacks on the *Barco* and who had turned on one another in a frenzy. Jaws wide, they rose from the water like giant trained porpoises in a marine amusement park. When they dove, their whiplike white whiskers lashed the water with resounding pops and snaps. The Bocagrandes who attacked the *Barco* took only wood and metal; these Bocagrandes weren't interested in getting their mouths shredded by marine screws or consuming sections of hull or islands of logs and branches. They wanted meat. They wanted blood. The passengers on the *Barco*. Themselves. It didn't make any difference.

The *Barco Igaranha* was the vortex of the action—a binge of gluttonous leviathans rising from the water, eating and being eaten, engorging, diving as they ate and as great hunks and slabs of flesh were ripped from their pallid bodies. On the *Barco*'s port three Bocagrandes formed a daisy chain of passionate consumption. Dead ahead, a behemoth Bocagrande, having succeeded in stuffing a brother nearly as large as itself into its mouth, but incapable of actually swallowing the prize, shuddered in death throes as shimmering blind piranha—teeth chattering—popped, twisting, from its snow-white stomach.

The *Barco Igaranha*—the center of this fury of cannabilism—sank lower and lower into the water.

Bodan and Hanna both adjusted their Darwin noses and gave hugs to Grigsby and Rosa María.

"Good luck, José María Quixote de la Balboa-Grigsby," Hanna said gripping his thin body with all the strength she could muster, welling up with tears. "And to you too, Rosa María Sancho-Vargas. You're beautiful, both of you."

The *Barco* seemed to be sinking faster.

There was no lowering of lifeboats involved; the water was nearly level with the deck of the *Barco*. Bodan and Hanna Doherty boarded one boat, with Bodan at the oars. Grigsby and Rosa María took the second, with Grigsby rowing.

And so the two boats pushed off into the floating debris and feeding Bocagrandes, Bodan taking a downstream tack toward shore and Grigsby heading straight across the current.

"Bye-bye," Hanna called. "Goodbye, XuXuians! It was lovely meeting you."

"She was a beautiful boat, eh, Quayloos," Grigsby called.

"There was none lovelier."

"Bye-bye, Quayloos," Rosa María called.

"Good luck, Quayloos," said Grigsby. "We'll see you back in XuXu. We'll go birding and bake a wild hog and play chess and dance and I'll show you how to play the—"

Rosa Maria interrupted: "Boobie, you forgot to tell them how to . . ."

She didn't finish her sentence; an incredible Bocagrande with six-feet-long gashes and rips on its partly eaten body, scars of digestive combat, rose from the Purus and consumed Rosa María, her husband, and their boat.

The XuXuians were gone. Eaten.

"Oh shit." Bodan grabbed Hanna's hand.

"She was trying to tell him he forgot to tell us how to find XuXu."

"I know."

They watched the *Barco*'s final moments. Her hull had been tattooed by bullets and both cabins trashed, yet she was still beautiful, even serene in her final moments. She sank with a certain pride, sporting bullet holes like dueling scars. She rather yawned her way to oblivion as she slowly, very slowly succumbed to the water accumulating in her innards. Finally she slid bow first into the depths. Her stern bow followed and the water was covered with an upwelling of flotsam and jetsam including, clearly visible on the yellow-brown water, wet and disintegrating, Hans Weckert's watercolors of the beautiful fish of Amazonia.

Bodan pulled his oars in. "No sense drawing attention to ourselves, I wouldn't think. If we just drift along like we're washed down with the rest of this crap, we might have a chance."

A frenzied Bocagrande rose under their boat and dumped Hanna and Bodan into the water.

Hanna floated on her back. "Baptized in the abyss before I go."

"Float."

She floated, waiting. "Maybe we can find us a raft of branches."

"I got something better," Bodan said.

She turned her head to look and so he had. He'd found one end of the *Barco*'s roof, a perfect raft. She watched as Bodan pulled himself aboard the raft, but she was still ten yards away. She put her arms by her side and began sculling gently in the direction of the raft.

"Easy, Hanna, not too fast now. No quick movements."

She gained on the slab of roof, trying to will herself through the water without moving any part of her body, which is contrary to all laws of physics, but she attempted it nevertheless.

"Easy, Hanna."

"I want out of this water, dammit."

"Not too fast. You're gaining on it."

She made it at last; Bodan pulled her aboard.

The futon from the aft cabin top floated by and Bodan fished it out of the water. They flopped the futon on their raft, which was as stable as a Cadillac, and lay back together. They watched as the wounded and partly eaten Bocagrandes who had survived the frenzy of gluttony—having lost the fun and excitement of the crippled riverboat and having momentarily satisfied their appetites—disappeared into the darkness of the great depths where they had evolved.

51

THEY PASS A SURFACE FEEDER

✳

Hanna Doherty and Nicholas Bodan lay back on their futon hand in hand. She put half of Weckert's pillowcase over her face to protect it from the afternoon sun; Bodan used the other half.

"We're rather like delicious bugs floating along with wet wings," Bodan said from under his half of the pillowcase. "At their mercy. That's what you do with big-mouth bass, plop a dead-looking fake whatever out there on the water and up he comes, whap!"

"Now, now, back off on the imagination, Nicholas," she said from under her half. "They've just had a nice lunch, now they're going to take themselves a little nap. You know how it is. Your belly is full, so you sort of kick back in the bottom of the depths and have yourself a little snooze. Too much work to swim all the way back to the top."

"When I was a kid most fish bit early in the morning or late in the afternoon—bass, say. If you really wanted to catch anything you'd haul your butt out of the sack while it was still dark so you could be on the water at dawn. But the catfish back home on the Columbia were night feeders and bottom feeders. They'd eat almost any damned thing, the more rotten and smellier the better. We'd build a big bonfire on the riverbank and smoke dried willow roots."

"It's pitch-black all day long at the bottom of the great depths; that's why they're blind and albino. Tell me, Nicholas, what does smoking a willow root taste like?"

"Smoking willow roots was the reason I never took up cigarettes, to tell you the truth. But the great thing about smoking willow roots as a kid was their great shape. Fancy gentlemen paid a lot of money for cigars that were called blunts and crooks and so on. They've got nothing on a willow root smoker. Now, you take that same willow, why, in the springtime you cut yourself a length of new-growth branch and tap the bark with the handle of your knife just so and slip the bark off. Then you peel a little strip of wood off the stick and slide the bark back on. Then you cut yourself a mouthpiece and maybe a notch or two for a little scale and there it is, you've got yourself a helluva willow whistle. Course, where I grew up on the Columbia the willows are all gone now."

"What happened to them?"

"The dams took 'em under. They took under the willows and the salmon. In my opinion there's little in the world that's more sour or dead than water in a reservoir."

A triumphant pop of thunder over the distant forest heralded the arrival of the afternoon squall and the sky suddenly darkened. In minutes roiling banks of midnight black rolled past Bodan and Hanna. At first the lightning bolts were flashing spirits, then they turned downright ominous as the rain followed, dappling the water, then coming in a torrent—raindrops drilling the water. Bodan and Hanna turned on their sides with their hands over their ears to protect their faces from the sting.

A bolt of lightning hit an island of debris not fifty yards upstream and it was suddenly daylight, blue-white, followed by an exploding *crraaaaaaaakkkkkkkkkkk bbbbooooooommmmmmmmmm* directly overhead that sent them both screaming off the futon.

"Oh shit!" Hanna said.

"As I remember, the fishing was never worth a damn in a rainstorm," Bodan said. "Nobody I ever knew fished in the lightning. Better a little lightning than being eaten by a Bocagrande."

The lightning struck, dancing, twisting into darkness. Blue-white light.

Crraaaaaaaakkkkkkkkk bbbooooooommmmmmmm!

This one sent them both flying. They were suddenly in the heart of the storm, which was now directly above them, drilling islands of debris with twisting snakes of lightning, burst upon burst of snapping electricity.

Light.

Crraaaaaaaaaakkkkkkkkkk bbbooooooommmmmmmmm!

Great cracking arcs of lightning leaped and hopped from horizon to horizon.

Bodan and Hanna held on to each other as tightly as they could, the warm rain beating on them. There was an odd, sulfur smell to the air.

Then it was past; they'd made it. The lightning and thunder—grumbling, rumbling, and echoing into the darkness above Amazonia—moved across the water and continued over the forest on the far side of the river.

"So what now, Isaak Walton? Do catfish feed after a storm?" Hanna started taking her clothes off to wring the water out of them.

Bodan started undressing and squeezing too. "I don't think they paid any attention. They're still down there napping from their big feed. Woman, you've got the most beautiful butt on you, do you know that?"

"Thank you," she said. She treated him to a little wiggle and started spreading their clothes out to dry.

The tropical sun was low enough that they were comfortable; in fact it was lovely on the river, warm, but not hot. What with the humidity and all, it was like being in a mild sauna. There was nothing they could do except float and hope. They lay naked, entwined, dreamy dreamy, happy to be alive, their skin comforting, the sharing so grand that the rest of it—the loss of their friends and the possibility that they could yet be taken under—miraculously disappeared.

Their clothes were just about dry as the sun lowered

over the forest canopy. They dressed and smeared mosquito repellent on their hands and arms and faces, putrid-smelling stuff. They decided they should eat while they could still see what they were eating. They opened a can of tuna and one of tomatoes, which they ate with their fingers and washed down with yellow-brown water.

The futon was comfortable; their bellies were full; they lay back; they shared the warmth of their bodies and their goodwill and their hope. And the sunset too. The sunset was one of those zingers, with streaks of reds and oranges separated by deep blue.

Bodan's cheapie digital wristwatch said it was nine o'clock when they spotted the lights of the passenger vessels and the Brazilian gunboats. There was a large white moon out and they could see everything clearly. On the deck of the flagship, Billy Gill, under the glare of television lights, was offering, for contributions on behalf of Christ's fish, protection from the clutches of the devil.

"Look there, the old leechman's still at it," Hanna said.

"A surface feeder," Bodan said.

"I bet he doesn't care if it's night or day, surface or bottom. He just likes to feed."

The great raft of debris, both from the storm and from the sinking of the *Barco Igaranha,* was now strung out down the center of the river where the current was swiftest. In the middle of this debris, Bodan and Hanna floated on their padded Cadillac raft, Quayloos for Charlie Darwin's folks, going downstream to the Amazon again and to Belém from where they had started. The raft turned slowly one way and then the other, pushed by invisible eddies in the broad yellow river.

When they got to Belém, they decided, the first thing they were going to do was find themselves a great big tub of hot water. After they were clean and rested they could address the question of how they were supposed to find the unmarked, hidden, dilapidated little XuXuian dock along thousands of miles of shoreline in the waters of Amazonia.

The XuXuians were out there somewhere—in the white waters, the yellow waters, or the black waters.

With Nicholas Bodan's comforting arm around her shoulders, Hanna closed her eyes, remembering the terrible sight of the *Barco* slipping under the water. She saw Hans Weckert's beautiful watercolors spread out upon the water, the lovingly rendered images slowly disintegrating, the paper beginning nature's process of decay and return. She remembered Lenny Humphries, his eyes hopping with enthusiasm, telling his passengers about the many splendid varieties of catfish to be found in Amazonia.

Fighting back the tears, she slipped her Charles Darwin nose over her own and inhaled deeply as the empathetic Elanxa Quayloo, the man of imagination, understanding what she was feeling, pulled on his own Darwin nose and gave her a supportive hug.

Hanna Doherty thought the nose smelled of the forest. It smelled of Hans and Lenny and the sweet, sweet XuXuians. She remembered Grigsby's grand entrance. She remembered the XuXuian eulogy for Elongxa and Elluria Quayloo and Grigsby's trombonelike flute.

The XuXuians had named her Elooua Quayloo, woman of questions. Somebody had to carry the water. She inhaled again, breathing deeply through Charles Darwin's nose. Imagination! Inquiry! Such fragrance!

Aaahhhhhhhhhh!